THE INVISIBLE GUARDIAN

THE INVISIBLE GUARDIAN

A Novel

Dolores Redondo

Translated from the Spanish by Isabelle Kaufeler

ATRIA BOOKS

New York   London   Toronto   Sydney   New Delhi

ATRIA BOOKS
An Imprint of Simon & Schuster, Inc.
1230 Avenue of the Americas
New York, NY 10020

Copyright © 2013 by Dolores Redondo
English-language translation copyright © 2015 by Izzie Kaufeler
Originally published in 2013 in Spain by Ediciones Destino as *El guardián invisible*.

First Atria Books hardcover edition March 2016

ATRIA BOOKS and colophon are trademarks of Simon & Schuster, Inc.

For information about special discounts for bulk purchases,
please contact Simon & Schuster Special Sales at 1-866-506-1949
or business@simonandschuster.com.

The Simon & Schuster Speakers Bureau can bring authors to your live event. For more information or to book an event contact the Simon & Schuster Speakers Bureau at 1-866-248-3049 or visit our website at www.simonspeakers.com.

Design by Kyoko Watanabe

Manufactured in the United States of America

10 9 8 7 6 5 4 3 2 1

Library of Congress Cataloging-in-Publication Data is available.

ISBN 978-1-5011-0213-4
ISBN 978-1-5011-0215-8 (ebook)

For Eduardo, who asked me to write this book, and for Ricard Domingo, who saw it when it was invisible.

For Rubén and Esther, for making me cry with laughter.

Forgetting is an involuntary act. The more you want to leave something behind you, the more it follows you.

WILLIAM JONAS BARKLEY

This is no ordinary apple; it's a magic wishing apple.

WALT DISNEY'S *SNOW WHITE*

THE
INVISIBLE
GUARDIAN

AINHOA ELIZASU was the second victim of the *basajaun*, although the press was yet to coin that name for it. That came later, when it emerged that animal hairs, scraps of skin, and unidentifiable tracks had been found around the bodies, along with evidence of some kind of macabre purification rite. With their torn clothes, their private parts shaved, and their upturned hands, the bodies of those girls, almost still children, seemed to have been marked by a malign force, as old as the Earth.

Inspector Amaia Salazar always followed the same routine when she was called to a crime scene in the middle of the night. She would switch off the alarm clock so it wouldn't disturb James in the morning, pile up her clothes and, with her cell phone balanced on top of them, go very slowly downstairs to the kitchen. She would drink a cup of milky coffee while she dressed, leave a note for her husband, and get in the car. Then she would drive, her mind blank except for the white noise that always filled her head when she woke up before dawn.

These remnants of an interrupted night of insomnia stayed with her all the way to the crime scene, even though it was over an hour's drive from Pamplona. She took a curve in the road too sharply, and the squealing of the tires made her realize how distracted she was. After that she made herself pay attention to the highway as it wound its way upward, deep into the dense forest surrounding Elizondo.

Five minutes later, she pulled over next to a police sign, where she recognized Dr. Jorge San Martín's sports car and Judge Estébanez's off-roader. Amaia got out, walked around to the back of her car, and fished out a pair of Wellingtons. She sat on the edge of the trunk to pull them on, while Deputy Inspector Jonan Etxaide and Inspector Montes joined her.

"It's not looking good, chief, the victim's a young girl." Jonan consulted his notes. "Twelve or thirteen years old. When she didn't arrive home by eleven last night, her parents contacted the police."

"A bit early to report her missing," observed Amaia.

"True. It looks like she called her older brother on his phone at about ten past eight to tell him she'd missed the bus from Arizkun."

"And her brother waited until eleven before saying anything?"

"You know how it is, '*Aita* and *Ama* will kill me. Please don't tell them. I'm going to see if any of my friends' parents will give me a ride.' So he kept quiet and played on his PlayStation. At eleven, when he realized his sister still hadn't arrived home and his mother was starting to get hysterical, he told them Ainhoa had called. The parents went down to the station in Elizondo and insisted something must have happened to their daughter. She wasn't answering her cell phone and they'd already spoken to all her friends. A patrol found her. The officers spotted her shoes at the side of the road as they were coming around the bend." Jonan shone his flashlight toward the edge of the tarmac where a pair of black-patent high-heeled shoes glistened, perfectly aligned. Amaia leaned over to look at them.

"They look like they've been arranged like this. Has anyone touched them?" she asked. Jonan checked his notes again. The young deputy inspector's efficiency was a godsend in cases as difficult as this one was shaping up to be.

"No, that's how they found them, side by side and pointing toward the road."

"Tell the crime scene technicians to come and check the lining of the shoes when they've finished what they're doing. Whoever arranged them like that will have had to touch the inside as well as the outside."

Inspector Montes, who had stood silently staring at the ends of his Italian designer loafers until this point, looked up abruptly as if he had just awoken from a deep sleep.

"Salazar," he acknowledged her in a murmur, then walked off toward the edge of the road without waiting for her. Amaia frowned in bewilderment and turned back to Jonan.

"What's up with him?"

"I don't know, chief, but we came in the same car from Pamplona and he didn't open his mouth once. I think he might have had a drink or two."

Amaia thought so too. Inspector Montes had slipped into a downward spiral since his divorce, and not just in terms of his recent penchant for Italian shoes and colorful ties. He had been particularly distracted during the last few weeks, cold and inscrutable, absorbed in his own little world, almost reluctant to engage with the people around him.

"Where's the girl?"

"By the river. You have to go down that slope," said Jonan, pointing toward it apologetically, as if it were somehow his fault that the body was down there.

As Amaia made her way down the incline, worn out of the rock by the river over the millennia, she could see the floodlights and police tape that marked the area where the officers were working in the distance. Judge Estébanez stood to one side, talking in a low voice with the court clerk and shooting sideways glances to where the body lay. Two photographers from the forensics team were moving around it, raining down flashes from every angle, and a technician from the Navarra Institute of Forensic Medicine was kneeling beside it, apparently taking the temperature of the liver.

Amaia was pleased to see that everyone present was respecting the entry point that the first officers on the scene had established. Even so, as always, it seemed to her that there were just too many people. It was almost absurd. It may have had something to do with her Catholic upbringing, but whenever she had to deal with a corpse, she always felt a pressing need for that sense of intimacy and devotion she experienced in a cemetery. It seemed as though this was violated by the distant and impersonal professional presence of the people moving around the body. It was the sole subject of a murderer's work of art, but it lay there mute and silenced, its innate horror disregarded.

She went over slowly, observing the place someone had chosen for the death. A beach of rounded gray stones, no doubt carried there by the previous spring's floods, had formed beside the river, a dry strip about nine meters wide that extended as far as she could see in the gloomy predawn light. A deep wood, which got denser farther in, grew right up to the other bank of the river, which was only about four meters wide. Amaia waited for a few seconds while the technician from the forensics team finished taking photographs of the corpse, then she went over to stand at the girl's feet. As usual, she emptied her mind of all thoughts, looked at the body lying beside the river, and murmured a brief prayer. Only then did Amaia feel ready to look at the girl's body as the work of a murderer. A pretty brown color in life, Ainhoa Elizasu's eyes now stared into endless space, frozen in an expression of surprise. Her head was tilted back slightly, and it was just possible to make out part of the coarse string buried so deep in the flesh of her neck it had almost disappeared. Amaia leaned over the body to look at the ligature.

"It's not even knotted. The killer just pulled it tight until the girl stopped breathing," she said softly, almost to herself.

"It would take some strength to do that," observed Jonan from behind her. "Do you think we're looking for a man?"

"It seems likely, although the girl's not that tall, only five foot one or so, and she's very thin. It could have been a woman."

Dr. San Martín, who'd been chatting with the judge and the court clerk accompanying her until this point, bade them a rather flowery farewell and came over to the body.

"Inspector Salazar, it's always a pleasure to see you, even in such circumstances," he said jovially.

"The pleasure's all mine, Dr. San Martín. What do you make of this?"

The pathologist gave Jonan an appraising look, weighing his youth and likely knowledge, then took the notes offered to him by the technician and flicked through them quickly while leaning over the body. It was a look Amaia knew well. A few years earlier it was she who'd been the young deputy inspector in need of instruction in the mysteries of death, a pleasure that, as a distinguished professor, San Martín never let pass him by.

"Don't be shy, Etxaide. Come closer and perhaps you'll learn something."

Dr. San Martín put on a pair of gloves he'd pulled out of a leather Gladstone bag and gently palpated the girl's jaw, neck, and arms.

"What do you know about rigor mortis, Etxaide?"

Jonan sighed, then started to speak in a voice similar to the one he must have used when answering the teacher in his school days. "Rigor mortis is caused by a chemical change in the muscles. It is evident in the eyelids first and spreads through the chest, trunk, and extremities, achieving maximum stiffness after around twelve hours. The body starts relaxing again in reverse order about thirty-six hours later, when the muscles start to decompose due to the effects of lactic acid."

"Not bad. What else?" the doctor encouraged him.

"It's one of the principal indicators used to estimate the time of death."

"And do you think you can make an estimation based solely on the degree of rigor mortis?"

"Well . . ." Jonan hesitated.

"No," declared San Martín, "absolutely not. The degree of rigidity can vary according to the deceased's muscle tone, the temperature of the room or, as in this case, the environment, since extreme temperatures may give the semblance of rigor mortis, for example if a cadaver's been exposed to high temperatures, or when a body suffers a cadaveric spasm. Do you know what that is?"

"I think that's the term for when the extremities tense at the moment of death in such a way that it would be difficult to relieve them of any item they might have been holding at that precise instant."

"Correct, which is why forensic pathologists have to shoulder a great deal of responsibility. They shouldn't establish the time of death without keeping all these factors in mind and, of course, you can't forget hypostasis . . . you might know it as livor mortis. You must have seen those American TV series where the forensic pathologist kneels by the body and establishes the time of death in less than two minutes," he said, raising an eyebrow theatrically. "Well, take it from me, that's all lies. Analysis of the quantity of potassium present in the vitreous fluid represents a major step forward, but I'll be able to establish the time of death with any certainty only once the autopsy has been carried out. Now, based purely on what's in front of me, I can state: thirteen years of age, female. Taking into consideration the temperature of the liver, I would say she's been dead around two hours. Rigor mortis hasn't set in yet," he confirmed, palpating the girl's jaw again.

"That fits in more or less with the timing of her call home and her parents reporting her missing at the police station. Yes, two hours, if that."

Amaia waited for him to stand up and then took his place kneeling next to the girl. She didn't miss Jonan's look of relief at being released from the forensic pathologist's scrutiny. The girl's eyes stared blankly into infinity, and her mouth was half open in what looked like surprise, or perhaps a final attempt to inhale, giving her face an air of childlike amazement like a little girl on her birthday. All her clothing seemed to have been slit cleanly down the middle from her neck to her thighs and was pulled open to either side, like a half-unwrapped gift. The gentle breeze coming off the river moved the girl's bangs a little, and Amaia caught the scent of shampoo mixed with the more bitter aroma of tobacco. She wondered whether the girl had been a smoker.

"She smells of tobacco. Do you know whether she was carrying a bag?"

"Yes, she was. It hasn't turned up yet, but I've got officers combing the area as far as a kilometer downstream," said Inspector Montes, gesturing toward the river with his arm.

"Ask her friends where they were and who they were with."

"I'll do it first thing in the morning, chief," said Jonan, tapping his watch. "Her friends will be thirteen-year-old girls, they'll be asleep right now."

Amaia observed the girl's hands lying beside her body. They looked white and unblemished, and their palms were turned upward.

"Did you notice how her hands are positioned? They've been arranged like that."

"I agree," said Montes, who was still standing next to Jonan.

"Get them to photograph and preserve them as soon as possible. She may have tried to defend herself. Her nails and hands look fairly clean, but we might be in luck," she said, addressing the officer from forensics. Dr. San Martín bent over the girl again, opposite Amaia.

"We'll have to wait for the autopsy, but I'd suggest asphyxiation as the cause of death, and given the force with which the string's cut into her skin, I'd say it was very quick. The cuts on the body are superficial and were only intended to slash her clothes. They were made with a very sharp object, a knife, a cutter, or a scalpel. I'll confirm this for you later, but the girl was already dead by this point. There's barely any blood—"

"And what about her pubic area?" interrupted Montes.

"I think the killer used the same blade to shave off her pubic hair."

"Perhaps he wanted to take some away as a trophy, chief," suggested Jonan.

"No, I don't think so. Look at how it's been scattered at the sides of the body," observed Amaia, pointing out several small piles of fine hair. "It seems more likely he wanted to get rid of it to replace it with this." She gestured to a small, sticky golden cake that had been placed on the girl's hairless pubic mound.

"What a bastard. Why does someone do that sort of thing? As if it wasn't enough to kill a young girl without putting that there. What on earth could he have been thinking to do something like this?" exclaimed Jonan in disgust.

"Well, kid, it's your job to work out what that swine was thinking," said Montes, going over to San Martín.

"Was she raped?"

"I don't believe so, although I won't know for certain until I examine her more thoroughly. The staging is decidedly sexual . . . cutting her clothes, leaving her chest exposed to the air, shaving her pubic area . . . and, of course, the cake . . . It looks like some kind of cupcake, or—"

"It's a *txantxigorri*," Amaia interrupted him. "It's a local speciality made with a traditional recipe, although this one's smaller than normal. It's definitely a *txantxigorri*, though. Jonan, get them to bag it, and please," said Amaia, addressing the group, "don't mention this to anybody. It's classified information, at least for now."

They all nodded.

"We're finished here. She's all yours, San Martín. We'll see you at the institute."

Amaia got up and took one last look at the girl before climbing up the slope to her car.

2

INSPECTOR MONTES had chosen an eye-catching, and doubt-less very expensive, violet tie that morning, which stood out against his lilac shirt. The overall effect was elegant, but it did have an incongruous air of *Miami Vice* about it. The cops who joined them in the elevator must have thought the same thing, and Amaia didn't miss the disapproving looks they exchanged as they got out. She glanced at Montes since it was likely he'd noticed too, but he just continued checking the messages on his cell phone, enveloped in a cloud of Armani aftershave and apparently unaware of the effect he was having.

The meeting room door was closed, but before Amaia could even touch the handle, it was opened from inside by a uniformed officer, as if he'd been stationed there expressly to await their arrival. He stepped aside, giving them a clear view of a light, spacious confer-ence room and more people than Amaia was expecting. The com-missioner was at the head of the table with two empty spaces to his right. He waved them forward and began the introductions as they moved into the room.

"Inspector Salazar, Inspector Montes, you already know Inspec-tor Rodríguez from Forensics and Dr. San Martín. This is Deputy In-spector Aguirre from Narcotics, and Deputy Inspector Zabalza and Inspector Iriarte from the police station in Elizondo. They happened to be out of town when the body was found yesterday."

Amaia nodded a greeting to those she knew and shook hands with the others.

"Salazar, Montes, I've called you here because I've got a suspicion Ainhoa Elizasu's case is going to be trickier than expected," said the commissioner, taking his seat and gesturing to them to do the same. "Inspector Iriarte contacted us this morning to share some information that could be important when we see how the case you're working on develops."

Inspector Iriarte leaned forward, putting his enormous *aizkolari* woodsman's hands on the table.

"A month ago, on January fifth to be precise," he said, consulting a small black leather-bound notebook that was almost hidden by his hands, "a shepherd from Elizondo was taking his sheep to drink at the river when he found the body of Carla Huarte, a seventeen-year-old girl. She disappeared on New Year's Eve after going to the Cras Test nightclub in Elizondo with her boyfriend and a group of friends. She left with him at around four in the morning, and he returned alone about three-quarters of an hour later. He told a friend they'd gotten in a fight, and she'd become so angry she got out of the car and stormed off. The friend convinced him to go and look for her, and they went back an hour later but couldn't find any trace of her. They say they weren't too worried because there were a lot of courting couples and stoners around the area. Furthermore, the girl was very popular, so they assumed someone she knew had given her a ride. We found hair belonging to the girl and one of those silicon bra straps in the boyfriend's car."

Iriarte paused for breath and looked at Montes and Amaia before continuing.

"And here's the bit that might interest you. Carla's body turned up in an area about two kilometers from where Ainhoa Elizasu was found. She'd been strangled with packaging string and her clothes had been cut open from top to bottom."

Amaia looked at Montes in alarm.

"I remember reading about this case in the papers. Had her pubic area been shaved?" she asked.

Iriarte looked at Deputy Inspector Zabalza, who replied, "The truth is, there wasn't much of it left. Her whole pubic mound had been torn away by what looked like animal bites. The autopsy report mentions tooth marks from at least three different types of animals and hairs from a wild boar, a fox, and possibly a bear."

"A bear? Are you serious?" exclaimed Amaia incredulously.

"We're not one hundred percent sure. We sent molds of the tooth marks to the Institute for the Study of Pyrenean Plantigrades. Apparently, since bears walk on all fours with flat feet, they fall under their area of expertise. We haven't heard back from them yet, but—"

"What about the little cake?"

"There wasn't a little cake . . . well, maybe there was. That would explain the bites around the pubic area, since the animals would have been attracted by such a sweet, unfamiliar smell."

"Were there bite marks elsewhere on the body?"

"No, although there were some hoof and paw prints."

"What about pubic hair arranged around the body?" asked Amaia.

"We didn't find that either, but you should keep in mind that Carla Huarte's body was found submerged in the river from her ankles to her thighs and there had been torrential rain in the days following her disappearance. If there was anything, the rain would have washed it away."

"Didn't you remember this case when you examined the girl yesterday?" Amaia turned to the forensic scientist.

"Of course," confirmed San Martín, "but it's not that simple, they're only similarities. Do you have any idea how many bodies I see in the space of a year? There are common elements in many cases that are entirely unconnected. Anyway, yes, I did think of this case, but I needed to consult my notes from the autopsy before saying anything. In Carla's case, everything pointed to a sexual assault by her boyfriend. The girl had alcohol and all kinds of drugs in her system, several love bites on her neck, and a bite mark on her chest that matched the boyfriend's dental imprint. We also found suspicious fragments of skin under her nails that matched a deep scratch on his neck."

"Did you find traces of semen?"

"No."

"What did the boy have to say for himself? And what's his name, by the way?" asked Montes.

"He's called Miguel Ángel de Andrés. He told me he'd been drinking and had also taken cocaine and ecstasy, and I'm inclined to believe him." Aguirre smiled. "We arrested him on January sixth during the Reyes Magos Epiphany celebrations, and he was as high as a kite then too. He tested positive for four different drugs, including cocaine."

"So where's this little treasure now?" asked Amaia.

"He was refused bail and is on remand in the prison in Pamplona, awaiting trial for sexual assault and murder . . . He's got previous drug-related convictions," said Aguirre.

"I think this calls for a trip to the prison to question Miguel Ángel de Andrés again, don't you? Perhaps he wasn't lying when he said he didn't kill the girl."

"Could you give us a copy of Carla Huarte's autopsy report, Dr. San Martín?" asked Montes.

"Of course."

"What we're most interested in are the photos taken at the scene."

"I'll get them to you ASAP."

"And it's probably worth inspecting the girl's clothes again now that we know what to look for," added Amaia.

"Inspector Iriarte and Deputy Inspector Zabalza are leading the investigation at the station in Elizondo," intervened the commissioner. "That's where you're from originally, isn't it, Inspector Salazar?"

Amaia nodded.

"They'll give you all the help you need," said the commissioner. He got to his feet, bringing the meeting to an end.

3

THE BOY sitting opposite her was slightly hunched over as if he were carrying a heavy load on his shoulders, his hands were resting loosely on his knees, hundreds of tiny red capillaries showed through the skin of his face, and there were deep, dark circles under his eyes. Nothing like the photo Amaia remembered seeing in the papers a month earlier, in which he was posing defiantly next to his car. There was no trace of his former self-assurance or cockiness, and he looked visibly older. When Amaia and Jonan Etxaide entered the interview room, the boy was staring into space and had a hard time snapping out of it.

"Hello, Miguel Ángel."

He didn't answer. He sighed and looked at them in silence.

"I'm Inspector Salazar, and this"—she gestured to Jonan—"is Deputy Inspector Etxaide. We want to talk to you about Carla Huarte."

He lifted his head and, as if overwhelmed by immense fatigue, muttered, "I have nothing to say. Everything I have to tell you is in my statement . . . There's nothing to add, it's the truth, there's nothing to add, I didn't kill her and that's a fact, there's nothing to add, leave me in peace and talk to my lawyer."

He hung his head again and focused all his attention on his pale, dry hands.

"Right," said Amaia with a sigh. "I can see that we haven't got off to a good start. Let's try again. I don't think you killed Carla."

Miguel Ángel looked up, surprised this time.

"I think she was alive when you left the mountain, and I think that someone else approached her later and killed her."

"That's . . ." Miguel Ángel stammered. "That's what must have happened." Fat tears poured down his face as he started to tremble. "Yes, that's what must have happened, because I didn't kill her. Please believe me, I didn't kill her."

"I believe you," said Amaia, sliding a packet of tissues across the table toward him. "I believe you and I'm going to help you get out of here."

The boy clasped his hands together, as if praying. "Please, please," he muttered.

"But first you have to help me," she said, almost sweetly. He dried his tears but was still sniveling as he nodded. "Tell me about Carla. What was she like?"

"Carla was great, she was an amazing girl, really pretty, really outgoing, she had a lot of friends . . ."

"How did you meet?"

"At school. I'd already left, and I work . . . until all this happened I worked with my brother, tarring roofs. I was good at it, and it was money in my pocket; it's a shitty job but it pays well. She was still studying. She was repeating a year, though, and wanted to drop out, but her parents insisted and she gave in."

"You said she had a lot of friends. Do you know whether she was seeing anyone else? Any other boys?"

"No, no, nothing like that," he said, regaining some energy and frowning. "She was with me and no one else."

"How can you be so sure?"

"I am. Ask her girlfriends, she was crazy about me."

"Did you have sex?"

"Yes, and it was good," he said, smiling.

"When Carla's body was found, there were marks from your teeth on her chest."

"I already explained this at the time. That's how it was with Carla, she liked it like that and so did I. All right, we liked rough sex, so what? I never hit her or anything like that, they were just games."

"You say that she was the one who liked hard-core sex. However, in your statement," Jonan said, consulting his notes, "you said that she didn't want to have sex that night, and that this made you angry. Something doesn't add up here, wouldn't you agree?"

"It was because of the drugs. One moment she was like a motor-bike going full throttle and the next she was acting all paranoid and said she didn't want to . . . Of course I got angry, but I didn't force her and I didn't kill her. It had happened to us before."

"And when it happened before, did you make her get out of the car and leave her stranded on the mountainside?"

Miguel Ángel shot him a furious look and swallowed before answering.

"No, that was the first time, and I didn't make her get out of the car. She was the one who ran away and didn't want to get back in, even though I asked her to . . . Eventually I got fed up and left."

"She scratched your neck," said Amaia.

"I've already told you, she liked it that way; she'd leave my back in shreds sometimes. Our friends can tell you. They saw the bite marks on my shoulders in the summer when we were sunbathing, and they had a great laugh about it, calling her a she-wolf."

"When was the last time you'd had sex before that night?"

"Um, probably the day before. Whenever we saw each other, we ended up fucking. As I said, she was crazy about me."

Amaia sighed and got to her feet, signaling to the guard.

"Just one more thing. How did she like to keep her pubic area?"

"Her pubic area? You mean the hair around her pussy?"

"Yes, the hair around her pussy," said Amaia without blinking. "How did she keep it?"

"She shaved it, she just left a tiny bit," he said, barely hiding his smile.

"Why did she shave it?"

"I've already told you that we both liked that sort of thing. I loved it . . ."

As they made their way to the door, Miguel Ángel got to his feet. "Inspector," he said. The guard gestured at him to sit down.

Amaia turned toward the boy. "Tell me, why now and not before?"

The inspector looked at Jonan before replying, considering whether that cocky little shit deserved an explanation or not. She decided that he did.

"Because another girl has been found murdered, and the crime is a bit similar to what happened to Carla."

"Well, there you go! Don't you see? When will I get out of here?"

Amaia turned toward the exit before answering. "We'll keep you posted."

4

AMAIA WAS looking out the window as the room started to fill up behind her. As she heard the scraping of chairs and the murmur of conversations she put her hands against the glass that was pearly with microscopic drops of breath. The cold left no doubt that it was still winter outside, and Pamplona looked damp and gray on that February evening as the light fled rapidly toward darkness. The gesture filled her with nostalgia for a summer that was so distant it seemed to belong to another world, a universe of light and warmth where dead girls would never be found abandoned on a river's icy bank.

Jonan appeared at her side, offering her a cup of milky coffee. She thanked him with a smile and held it in both hands, hoping in vain that the warmth from the cup would transfer to her frozen fingers. She sat down and waited while Montes closed the door and the general murmur abated.

"Fermín?" said Amaia, inviting Inspector Montes to start things off.

"I've been to Elizondo to talk to the girls' parents and the shepherd who found Carla Huarte's body. Nothing from the parents. Carla's say that they didn't like their daughter's friends, that they went out a lot and got drunk, and they are convinced her boyfriend did it. One important detail: they didn't report her missing until the fourth of January, bearing in mind that the girl left the house on the thirty-first . . . Their explanation is that the girl turned eighteen on the first, and they thought she'd left home like she'd often threatened to do. It was only after they contacted her friends that they realized she hadn't been seen for days.

"Ainhoa Elizasu's parents are in complete shock and are here in Pamplona at the Institute of Forensic Medicine, waiting for the Institute to give them the body after the autopsy's taken place. The girl was wonderful, and they don't understand how someone could have done this to their daughter. The brother hasn't been much help either; he blames himself for not having said anything sooner. And her friends from Elizondo say that they were at one of their houses first and then they wandered around town. Ainhoa suddenly realized what time it was and had to run; nobody went with her to the bus stop because it was very close to where they were. They don't remember being approached by anyone suspicious, they didn't argue with anyone, and Ainhoa didn't have a boyfriend and she wasn't messing around with anyone. The most interesting thing was talking to the shepherd, José Miguel Arakama, who's a real character. He's sticking to his initial statement, but the most important thing is something he remembered days later, a detail he didn't think was important at the time because it didn't seem to be at all related to the discovery of the body—"

"Are you going to tell us, then?" interrupted Amaia impatiently.

"He was telling me that a lot of whores hang around that area and leave it in a real mess, with cigarette butts, empty cans, used condoms, and even underpants and bras lying around, when he happened to mention that one day one of them left a pair of brand-new red party shoes there."

"The description matches the ones that Carla Huarte was wearing on New Year's Eve, and they weren't found with the body," pointed out Jonan.

"And that's not all. He's sure that it was New Year's Day that he saw them. He was working that day and, although he didn't take the sheep down to drink there, he saw the shoes clearly. In his own words, 'It looked as if someone had left them like that deliberately, like when you go to bed or for a swim in the river,'" he said, reading from his notes.

"But didn't they find Carla's shoes when her body was discovered?" asked Amaia, looking at the report.

"Someone had taken them," clarified Jonan.

"It seems that the killer left the shoes behind on purpose to mark the area, so it wouldn't have been him," said Montes, who considered this idea for a moment and then continued, "Other than that, we know both girls were students at the high school in Lekaroz and, even if they knew one another by sight, which is fairly likely, they weren't close: different ages, different friends . . . Carla Huarte lived in the Antxaborda neighborhood. You must know it, Salazar"—Amaia nodded—"and Ainhoa lived in the neighboring town."

Montes bent over his notes, and Amaia noticed his hair was covered in an oily substance.

"What have you put in your hair, Montes?"

"It's brilliantine," he said, running his hand over the back of his neck. "They put it on at the barber's. Can we continue?"

"Of course."

"Right, well, there's not much more at the moment. What have you got?"

"We've been speaking to the boyfriend," Amaia replied, "and he's told us some very interesting things, like that his girlfriend liked rough sex with scratching and love bites and such. This has been confirmed by Carla's girlfriends, with whom she liked to share her sex life in explicit detail, 'explicit' being the operative word here. That would explain the scratches and the love bite on her chest. He's sticking to his earlier statements—the girl was really feeling the effects of the drugs she'd taken and she became paranoid. It's in line with the toxicology report. He also told us that Carla Huarte normally shaved her pubic hair, which would explain why there was no trace of it at the scene."

"Chief, we've got the photos of the crime scene where Carla Huarte was found."

Jonan spread them out on the table, and everyone leaned in around Amaia to see them. Carla's body had turned up in an area where the river tended to flood. Her red party dress and her underwear, which was also red, appeared to have been slashed from her chest down to her groin. The cord with which she'd been strangled wasn't visible in the photo due to the swelling of her neck. Something semitransparent was hanging from one of her legs. Amaia initially thought it was skin but then identified it as the remains of Carla's underpants.

"She's quite well preserved given that she spent five days out in the open," observed one of the technicians. "It must be due to the cold: it didn't get above forty-three degrees during the day that week, and the temperature dropped below freezing for several nights."

"Look at the position of her hands," said Jonan. "They're turned upward, like Ainhoa Elizasu's."

"'For New Year's Eve, Carla chose a short, red, strappy dress and a white jacket made of some kind of plush fabric, which hasn't been found,'" read Amaia. "'The murderer tore her clothing from the neckline to the hem, separating the underwear and the two parts of the dress so they lay to either side. An irregular-shaped piece of skin and flesh, about ten centimeters square, is missing from the pubic area.'"

"If the murderer left a *txantxigorri* on Carla's pubic mound, it would explain why the vermin only bit her there."

"And why didn't they bite Ainhoa?" asked Montes.

"There wasn't time," replied Dr. San Martín as he entered the room. "Sorry I'm late, Inspector," he said, taking a seat.

"And fuck the rest of us," murmured Montes.

"Animals come down to drink at first light. Unlike the first girl, she was there for barely a couple of hours. I've brought the autopsy report and a lot of news. The two girls died exactly the same way, strangled with a cord that was pulled tight with extraordinary force. Neither of them defended herself. Both girls' clothes were slashed with a very sharp object that produced superficial cuts on the skin of their chests and abdomens. Ainhoa's pubic hair was shaved off, probably using the same sharp object, and sprinkled around the body. A small, sweet cake was left on her pubic mound."

"A *txantxigorri*," commented Amaia. "It's a typical local delicacy,"

"No cake of any kind was found on Carla Huarte's body. However, as you suggested, Inspector, following careful examination of her clothing, we have found traces of sugar and flour similar to those used in the cake found on Ainhoa Elizasu's body."

"It's possible that the girl ate one for dessert and a few crumbs fell on her dress," said Jonan.

"She didn't eat any at home, at any rate. I checked," said Montes.

"It's not enough to link them," said Amaia, tossing her pen onto the table.

"I think we've got what you need, Inspector," said San Martín, exchanging a knowing look with his assistant.

"What are you waiting for, Dr. San Martín?" asked Amaia, getting to her feet.

"For me," answered the commissioner, entering the room. "Please don't bother getting up. Dr. San Martín, tell them what you told me."

The pathologist's assistant attached a comparative analysis graph with various colored lines and numerical scales to the whiteboard. San Martín stood up and spoke with the confidence of someone who is used to being believed without question.

"Our tests confirm that the cords used in the two crimes are identical, although this, in itself, is not conclusive. It's packaging string, which is commonly used on farms, in construction, in the wholesale business . . . It's made in Spain and sold in hardware stores and big DIY chain stores like Aki and Leroy Merlin." He paused theatrically, smiled, and continued, looking first at the commissioner and then at Amaia. "What is conclusive is the fact that the two pieces came consecutively from the same ball," he said, displaying two high-definition photographs of two pieces of string of the same size whose ends matched perfectly. Amaia sat down slowly without taking her eyes off the photos.

"We've got a serial killer," she whispered.

A ripple of suppressed excitement spread around the room. The growing murmur ceased immediately when the commissioner began to speak.

"Inspector Salazar, you told me you're from Elizondo, didn't you?"

"Yes, sir, my family all lives there."

"I think your knowledge of the area and certain aspects of the case, together with your training and experience, make you the ideal candidate to lead the investigation. Furthermore, your time in Quantico with the FBI could prove very useful to us right now. It seems we've got a serial killer on our hands, and you did in-depth work with the best in this field during your time there . . . methods, psychological profiling, background research . . . In any case, you're in charge, and you'll receive all the support you need, both here and in Elizondo."

The commissioner raised his hand in a farewell gesture and left the room.

"Congratulations, chief," said Jonan, grinning as he shook her hand.

"My felicitations, Inspector Salazar," said San Martín.

Amaia didn't miss Montes's expression of disgust as he watched her in silence while the other officers came over to congratulate her. She did her best to escape the slaps on the back.

"We'll leave for Elizondo first thing tomorrow. I want to attend Ainhoa Elizasu's funeral. As you already know, I have family there, so I'll definitely be staying. The rest of you," she said, turning to the team, "can drive up each day for the duration of the investigation. It's only fifty kilometers and the roads are good."

Montes came over before leaving. "I've just got one question," he said in a markedly scornful tone, "will I have to call you 'chief'?"

"Don't be ridiculous, Fermín, this is just temporary and . . ."

"Don't bother, chief. I heard the commissioner, and you'll have my full cooperation." He gave her a mock military salute and stalked out.

5

AMAIA WALKED slightly distractedly through the old town of Pamplona, making her way toward her house, an old restored building right in the middle of Calle Mercaderes. In the 1930s there had been an umbrella shop on the ground floor, and the old sign announcing *Izaguirre umbrellas—Hold quality and prestige in your hands* was still visible. James always said that the main reason he had chosen the house was for the space and light in the workshop, a perfect location to install his sculptor's studio, but she knew that the thing that had prompted her husband to buy the house in the middle of the bull-running course was the same desire that had brought him to Pamplona in the first place. Like thousands of North Americans, he felt an enormous passion for the San Fermín festival, for Hemingway, and for this city, a passion that seemed almost childish to her and that he revived each year when the festival arrived. Much to Amaia's relief, James didn't take part in the bull running, but every day he would stroll along the eight hundred and fifty meters of the course from Santo Domingo, learning by heart each curve, each stumbling block, each paving stone all the way to the square. She loved the way he would smile each year as the festival drew near, the way he would dig his white clothes out of a trunk and set out to buy a new neckerchief, even though he seemed to have hundreds already.

James had been in Pamplona for a couple of years when Amaia met him. He was living in a pretty apartment in the city center at the time and renting a studio to work in very near the town hall. When they decided to get married, James took her to see the house on Calle Mercaderes, and she thought it was magnificent, although too big and too expensive. This wasn't a problem for James, who was already starting to earn a certain prestige in the art world. Furthermore, he came from a wealthy family of state-of-the-art uniform manufacturers in the United States. They bought the house, James installed his studio in the old workshop, and they promised themselves to fill it with children as soon as Amaia became an inspector on the homicide team.

It was four years since she'd become an inspector, San Fermín came around each year, James became more famous in artistic circles, but the children didn't arrive. Amaia lifted her hand to her stomach in a subconscious gesture of protection and longing. She quickened her pace until she overtook a group of Romanian immigrants who were arguing in the street and smiled when she saw the light glowing in James's workshop between the slits in the shutters. She looked at her watch, it was almost half past ten and he was still working. She opened the front door, left her keys on the old table that acted as a sideboard, and went to the workshop, passing through what used to be the house's entrance hall, which still retained its original floor of large round stones and a trapdoor that led to a blind passage where wine or oil had been stored in the old days.

James was washing a piece of gray marble in a sink full of soapy water. He smiled when he saw her. "Give me a minute to get this great toad out of the water and I'll be with you."

He arranged the stone on a rack, covered it with a piece of linen, and dried his hands on the white cook's apron he normally wore when he was working.

"How are you, my love? Tired?"

He wrapped his arms around her, and she felt like there were butterflies in her stomach, as she always did when they embraced. She breathed in the scent of his chest through his sweater and waited a moment before replying.

"I'm not tired, but it's been a strange day."

He drew back enough to be able to see her face.

"Tell me about it."

"Well, we're still working on the case of the girl from my town. It turns out that her case is quite similar to another one from a month ago, also in Elizondo, and it's been established that the cases are related."

"Related in what way?"

"It looks like it's the same killer."

"Oh, God, that means there's an animal out there who kills young girls."

"They're almost still children, James. The thing is, the commissioner has put me in charge of the investigation."

"Congratulations, Inspector," he said, kissing her.

"It hasn't made everyone all that happy, Montes didn't take it very well. I think he got quite angry."

"Don't worry about him, you know Fermín. He's a good man but he's going through a difficult time right now. He'll get over it, he admires you."

"I'm not sure . . ."

"But I am, he admires you. Believe me. Are you hungry?"

"Have you made something?"

"Of course. Chef Westford has prepared the house special."

"I'm dying to taste it. What is it?" asked Amaia, smiling.

"What do you mean what is it? Beggars can't be choosers! Spaghetti with mushrooms and a bottle of Chivite rosé."

"You go and open it while I shower."

She kissed her husband and headed for the shower. She closed her eyes and let the water run down her face for a while, then rested her hands and her forehead against the tiles, which were cold in contrast, and let the jet of water stream down her neck and shoulders. The day's events had followed on from one another in quick succession, and she hadn't yet had the chance to consider the consequences the case might have for her career or for her immediate future.

A gust of cold air surrounded her as James got into the shower. She stayed where she was, enjoying the warmth of the water, which seemed to carry any coherent thought down the drain with it. James stood behind her and kissed her shoulders very slowly. Amaia tilted her head sideways, offering him her neck in a gesture that always made her think of the old Dracula films, in which his naïve and virginal victims surrendering themselves to the vampire would uncover their necks as far as the shoulder and half close their eyes in the hope of superhuman pleasures. James kissed her neck, pressing his body against hers, and turned her as he searched for her mouth. Contact with James's lips was enough, as always, to banish all other thoughts from her mind. She ran her hands sensuously over her husband's body, delighting in the feel of him, in the smooth firmness of his flesh, and let him kiss her sweetly.

"I love you," James groaned in her ear.

"I love you," she murmured. And she smiled at the certainty that this was true, that she loved him more than anything, more than anyone, and at how happy it made her to have him between her legs, inside her, and to make love with him. When they finished, this same smile would last for hours, as if a moment with him was enough to exorcise all the world's ills.

Deep down, Amaia thought that only he could really make her feel like a woman. In her daily professional life she let her feminine side take second place and concentrated solely on doing a good job, but outside work, her height and her slim, sinewy body, together with the rather sober clothes she usually chose, made her feel quite unfeminine when she was around other women, particularly the wives of James's colleagues, who were shorter and more petite, with their small, smooth hands that had never touched a dead body. She didn't normally wear jewelry except her wedding ring and small earrings that James told her were like a little girl's; her hair in its practical ponytail and the minimal makeup she wore combined to give her a serious and rather masculine appearance, which he loved and she cultivated. In addition, Amaia knew that the firmness of her voice and the confidence with which she spoke and moved were enough to intimidate those bitches when they made malicious comments about her delayed motherhood—a subject she found upsetting.

They chatted while they ate and then went to bed right away. She envied James's ability to disconnect from the day's troubles and close his eyes as soon as his head hit the pillow. It always took her a long time to relax enough to sleep; sometimes she read for hours before she managed it, and she would wake up at even the smallest noise during the night. The year she was promoted to inspector, she used to become so tense and nervous during the day that she would fall exhaustedly into a deep, amnesiac sleep, only to wake up two or three hours later with her back paralyzed by a painful spasm that would prevent her from dropping off again. The tension had decreased with time, but she still wasn't getting good-quality sleep.

She used to leave a small lamp on the landing switched on so that its slanting light would reach the bedroom and help her orient herself when she woke with a start from one of her frequent nightmares. Now she tried in vain to concentrate on the book she was holding. Eventually, exhausted and preoccupied, she let it slip to the floor. She didn't turn out the light, though, but stared at the ceiling, planning the coming day. Attending the funeral and burial of Ainhoa Elizasu. With crimes like these, the killer often knew his victims, and it was probable that he lived near them and saw them every day. These murderers demonstrated a remarkable audacity. Their self-confidence and morbid tastes would often lead them to collaborate with the investigation, taking part in the search for the missing victims and attending vigils, funerals, and burials, in some cases offering public displays of their sympathy and distress. For the moment she couldn't be sure of anything, not even the relatives had been ruled out as suspects. But as a starting point it wasn't bad. It would be useful to get a feel for the situation, to observe reactions, to listen to comments and people's opinions. And, of course, to see her sisters and her aunt . . . It hadn't been long since she'd last seen them, only a month ago on Christmas Eve, and Flora and Ros had ended up arguing. She sighed deeply.

"If you don't stop thinking out loud, you'll never get to sleep," said James drowsily.

"I'm sorry, darling, did I wake you up?"

"Don't worry." He smiled, sitting up beside her. "But do you want to tell me what's going on in your head?"

"You already know I'm going up to Elizondo tomorrow . . . I've been thinking about staying for a few days. I think it would be better to be there, to speak to the families and friends and get more of a general impression. What do you think?"

"It must be pretty cold up there."

"Yes, but I'm not talking about the weather."

"I am, though. I know you, you can never sleep if you've got cold feet, and that would be terrible for the investigation."

"James . . ."

"I could come with you to keep them warm for you if you want," he said, raising an eyebrow.

"Would you seriously come with me?"

"Of course I would. I'm well ahead of schedule with my work and it would be nice to see your sisters and your aunt."

"We'd stay at her house."

"Great."

"I'll be really busy and I won't have much free time, though."

"I'll play mus or poker with your aunt and her friends."

"They'll clean you out."

"I'm very rich."

They both laughed at this, and Amaia carried on talking about what they could do in Elizondo until she realized that James was asleep. She kissed him gently on the head and covered his shoulders with the duvet. When she got up to use the toilet, she noticed bloody marks on the paper as she wiped herself. She looked at herself in the mirror as the tears welled up in her eyes. With her long hair falling over her shoulders, she looked younger and more vulnerable, like the little girl she had once been.

"Not this time, either, darling, not this time either," she whispered, knowing that there would be no consolation. She took a painkiller and, shivering, got back into bed.

6

THE CEMETERY was full of neighbors who had taken time off work and even closed their shops in order to attend the burial. The rumor that Ainhoa might not be the first girl to die at the hands of this criminal was beginning to spread. During the funeral, which had taken place barely two hours earlier in the parish Church of Santiago, the priest had implied in his sermon that evil appeared to be stalking the valley, and during the prayer for the dead, around the open grave in the ground, the atmosphere was tense and ominous, as if an inescapable curse were hovering over the heads of those present. The silence was broken only by Ainhoa's brother who, supported by his cousins, doubled over with a harsh, convulsive groan that came from deep inside him and reduced him to heartrending sobs. His parents, standing nearby, seemed not to hear him. Holding one another for support, they wept silently without taking their eyes off the coffin that contained their daughter's body. Jonan recorded the entire service from his position leaning on top of an old vault. Standing behind the parents, Montes observed the group just opposite them, closest to the grave. Deputy Inspector Zabalza had stationed himself near the gate in an unmarked car and was taking photos of all the people who entered the cemetery, including those heading toward different graves and those who didn't actually go in but stayed outside, talking in huddles or standing by the railings.

Amaia saw her Aunt Engrasi, who was holding Ros's arm, and

wondered where her slacker of a brother-in-law could be—almost certainly still in bed. Freddy had never made an effort in his life. His father had died when he was only five and he had grown up anesthetized by the fuss made over him by a hysterical mother and a multitude of aging aunts who had spoiled him rotten. He hadn't even turned up for dinner last Christmas Eve. Ros hadn't eaten a bite while she watched the door with an ashen face and dialed Freddy's number time and again, only to be told it was unavailable. Although they had all tried to pretend it didn't matter, Flora had been unable to resist the opportunity to say exactly what she thought of that loser, and they had ended up arguing. Ros had left halfway through dinner, and Flora and a resigned Víctor had followed suit as soon as dessert was over. Since then things between them had been even worse than normal. Amaia waited until everyone had offered the parents their condolences before approaching the grave, which the cemetery workers had just closed with a gray marble cover that did not yet feature Ainhoa's name.

"Amaia."

She saw Víctor coming over, making his way through the parishioners who were flooding out of the cemetery after Ainhoa's parents. She had known Víctor since she was a young girl, when he had first started going out with Flora. Although it was now two years since they had separated, to Amaia Víctor was still her brother-in-law.

"Hello, Amaia, how are you?"

"Fine, given the circumstances."

"Oh, of course," he said, casting a troubled glance at the tomb. "Even so, I'm very happy to see you."

"Likewise. Did you come by yourself?"

"No, with your sister."

"I didn't see you."

"We saw you . . ."

"Where is Flora?"

"You know her . . . she's already gone, but don't take it the wrong way."

Aunt Engrasi and Ros were coming up the gravel path. Víctor exchanged a friendly greeting with them and left the cemetery, turning to wave when he reached the gate.

"I don't know how he puts up with her," remarked Ros.

"He doesn't anymore. Have you forgotten that they've separated?" said Amaia.

"What do you mean he doesn't anymore? She's like a dog in the manger. She neither eats nor lets others eat."

"That does describe Flora rather well," agreed Aunt Engrasi.

"I've got to go and see her. I'll let you know how it goes later."

~

Founded in 1865, Mantecadas Salazar was one of the oldest confectionary and patisserie companies in Navarra. Six generations of Salazars had run it, although it had been Flora, taking over from their parents, who had known how to make the necessary decisions to keep such a company going in the current market. The original sign engraved on the marble façade had been retained, but the wide wooden shutters had been replaced by huge frosted windows that prevented people seeing in. Making her way around the building, Amaia arrived at the door to the warehouse, which was always open when there was work under way. She gave it a rap with her knuckles. As she went in, she saw a group of workers chatting while they made up boxes of pastries. She recognized some of them, greeted them, and made her way to Flora's office, breathing in the sweet smell of sugared flour and melted butter that had been a part of her for so many years, as integral to her sense of identity as her DNA. Her parents had been the forerunners of the process of change, but Flora had steered it to completion with a steady hand. Amaia saw that she had replaced all the ovens except the wood-fired one and that the old marble counters on which her father had kneaded dough were now made of stainless steel. Some of the dispensers had been upgraded, and the different areas were separated by sparklingly clean windows. If it hadn't been for the powerful aroma of syrup, it would have reminded her more of an operating room than a pastry workshop. In contrast, Flora's office was a big surprise. The oak desk that dominated one corner was the only piece of furniture that looked at all businesslike. A large rustic kitchen with a fireplace and a wooden worktop acted as the reception area; a floral sofa and a modern espresso machine completed the ensemble, which was really very welcoming.

Flora was making coffee and arranging the cups and saucers as if she was receiving guests.

"I've been waiting for you," she said without turning around when she heard the door.

"This must be the only place you wait. You almost ran out of the cemetery."

"That's because I, Amaia, don't have time to waste. I have to work."

"So do the rest of us, Flora."

"No, not like the rest of you, sister dear, some more than others. I'm sure that Ros, or rather Rosaura, as she now wants to be called, has time to spare."

"I don't know what makes you say that," said Amaia, somewhere between surprised and upset by her older sister's dismissive tone.

"Well, I say it because our darling sister's got problems with that loser Freddy again. She's been spending hours on the phone recently trying to find out where he is, that is, when she's not wandering around with puffy red eyes from crying over that shit. I tried to tell her, but she just wouldn't listen . . . Until one day, two weeks ago, she stopped coming to work under the pretext of being ill, and I can tell you exactly what was wrong with her. She was in a temper with a capital t thanks to that PlayStation champion. He's no good for anything except spending the money Ros earns, playing his stupid computer games, and getting off his head on dope. To get back to the point, a week ago Queen Rosaura deigned to turn up here and hand in her resignation. What do you think of that?! She says she can no longer work with me, and she wants her final paycheck."

Amaia looked at her in silence.

"That's what your darling sister did. Instead of getting rid of that loser, she comes to me and asks for her final paycheck. Her final paycheck," she repeated indignantly. "She ought to reimburse me for having to put up with all her shit and her complaints, her martyr's face. She looks like she's got the weight of the world on her shoulders, but she's the one who chose to carry it in the first place. And do you know what I think? So much the better. I've got twenty other employees, and I don't have to hear sob stories from any of them. Let's see if she gets away with half of what she has here in her next job."

"Flora, you're her sister . . ." murmured Amaia, sipping her coffee.

"Yes, and in exchange for that honor I have to put up with all her ups and downs."

"No, Flora, but one would hope that as her sister you might be a bit more understanding."

"Do you think I haven't been understanding?" Flora asked, raising her head as she took offense.

"Perhaps a little patience wouldn't have done any harm."

"Well, that's the final straw." She huffed as she tidied the items on her desk.

Amaia tried again. "When she hadn't been to work for three weeks, did you go to see her? Did you ask her what was wrong?"

"No, no I didn't. What about you? Did you go and ask her what was wrong?"

"I didn't know anything was wrong, Flora, otherwise you can be sure I would have gone to see her. But answer me."

"No, I didn't ask her because I already knew what the answer would be: that that shit has made her into a complete mess. Why ask when we all know the answer?"

"We also knew the reason when it was you who was suffering, but both Ros and I stood by you."

"And now you can see that I didn't need you. I dealt with it how you should deal with these things, by cutting my losses."

"Not everyone is as strong as you are, Flora."

"Well, you ought to be. The women of this family always have been," she said, tearing a piece of paper loudly and tossing it at the wastepaper basket.

The resentment in Flora's words made it clear she saw her sisters as weaklings, handicapped, and half-baked, and looked down on them with an unsympathetic mixture of contempt and disdain.

While Flora washed the coffee cups, Amaia looked at some blown-up photos that were sticking out of an envelope on the table. They showed her older sister dressed as a pastry chef and smiling as she kneaded some sticky dough.

"Are these for your new book?"

"Yes." Her tone softened slightly. "They're the ideas for the front cover. They only sent them to me today."

"I understand the last one was a success."

"Yes, it worked out quite well, so the publishers want to continue along the same lines. You know, basic pastries that any housewife can make."

"Don't downplay it, Flora. Almost all my friends in Pamplona have a copy and they love it."

"If someone had told *Amatxi* that I'd become famous for teaching people how to make madeleines and doughnuts, she wouldn't have believed it."

"Times have changed . . . home baking's become exotic and trendy."

It was easy to see that Flora felt comfortable with the praise and the taste of her success. She smiled, looking at her sister as if trying to decide whether or not to share a secret with her.

"Don't tell anyone, but they've suggested I do a baking program for TV."

"Oh my God, Flora! That's amazing, congratulations."

"I haven't signed anything yet, but they've sent the contract to my lawyer so that he can go over it, and as soon as he gives me the go-ahead . . . I only hope all this fuss about the murders doesn't affect it. It's been a month since that girl was killed by her boyfriend, and now there's that other girl."

"I don't know quite how they would affect you and your work. The crimes have nothing at all to do with you."

"No, not in terms of doing my work, but I think my image and that of Mantecadas Salazar are inextricably linked with that of Elizondo, and you have to admit that a thing like this affects the town's image, tourism, and sales."

"Well, what a surprise, Flora. Here you are making much of your great humanity as usual. Don't forget we've got two murdered girls and two destroyed families. I don't think it's quite the right moment to think about how this might affect tourism."

"Someone has to think of it," Flora declared.

"That's what I'm here for, to catch the person or people who've done this and help Elizondo return to peace."

Flora stared at her skeptically. "If you're the best the Policía Foral can send us, God help us."

Unlike Rosaura, Amaia wasn't affected in the slightest by Flora's attempts to upset her.

She supposed that in the three years spent surrounded by men at the police academy, and the fact that she was the first woman to reach the rank of inspector in the Homicide Division, she'd experienced enough jokes and teasing along the way to leave her with a steely inner strength and cast-iron composure. She would almost have found Flora's spiteful comments funny if not for the fact that she was her sister, and Amaia was saddened to be reminded of how callous Flora was. Every gesture, every word that came out of her mouth was designed to wound and cause as much damage as possible. Amaia noticed the way Flora pursed her mouth slightly in a grimace of annoyance when she responded calmly to her provocations and the mocking tone her big sister used, as if she was talking to a stubborn, ill-mannered child. She was just about to answer when her phone rang.

"We've got the photos and the video from the cemetery, chief," said Jonan. Amaia looked at her watch.

"Great. I'll come now. I'll be there in about ten minutes. Gather everyone." She hung up and smiled at Flora. "I have to go. As you can see, in spite of my ineptitude, duty calls me too."

Flora looked as if she were about to say something, but in the end she thought better of it and remained silent.

"Why the long face?" Amaia smiled. "Don't be sad, I'll be back tomorrow. I want to ask you about something and have another of your delicious coffees."

As she was leaving the workshop, she almost collided with her brother-in-law, who was on his way in with an enormous bunch of red roses.

"Thank you, Víctor, but you shouldn't have gone to such trouble," exclaimed Amaia with a smile.

"Hello, Amaia, they're for Flora. It's our wedding anniversary today, twenty-two years," he said, smiling back at her. Amaia remained silent. Flora and Víctor had been separated for two years now, and although they hadn't divorced, Flora had stayed in their shared home and he had moved into the magnificent traditional farmhouse on the farm his family owned on the outskirts of town.

Víctor noticed her discomfort. "I know what you're thinking, but Flora and I are still married, on my part because I still love her and on her part because she says she doesn't believe in divorce. I don't mind what the reason is, but I've still got a chance, don't you think?"

Amaia put her hand over his hand that was holding the bunch of flowers.

"Of course you have, Víctor. Good luck."

He smiled. "When it comes to your sister, I always need luck."

1

LIKE THE police stations in Pamplona and Tudela, the new
Policía Foral station in Elizondo was of a modern design, in
contrast to the typical architecture of the town and the rest of the
valley. It was a truly unique building, characterized by its walls of
whitish stone and huge, thick plate-glass windows spread over two
rectangular stories, the second of which overhung the first, forming
a kind of inverted staircase effect and giving it a certain resemblance
to an aircraft carrier. A couple of patrol cars parked under the overhang, the surveillance cameras and the mirrored glass all underlined
the building's purpose. During Amaia's brief visit to the Elizondo
commissioner's office, he had reiterated the expressions of support
and assurances of collaboration that he had given her the day before,
along with the promise to provide every assistance she might need.
The high-definition photographs didn't reveal anything they might
have missed at the cemetery.

The funeral had been well attended, as they usually were in such
circumstances. Entire families, plenty of people Ainhoa had known
since her childhood, among whom Amaia recognized a few of her
own classmates and old friends from school. All the staff and the
head teacher were there, as well as a few local councillors and Ainhoa's friends and classmates, forming a chorus of tearful girls with
their arms around one another. And that was all—no delinquents, no
pedophiles, nobody with an outstanding arrest warrant, no solitary

man wrapped in a black raincoat, wolfishly licking his lips as the sun glinted off his canines. She tossed the mountain of photos onto the table with a look of disgust, thinking how often this job could be so frustrating and disheartening.

"Carla Huarte's parents didn't attend the funeral or the burial, and they weren't at the reception at Ainhoa's home afterward," remarked Montes.

"Is that strange?" asked Iriarte.

"Well, it's unexpected. The families knew each other, if only by sight, and keeping in mind that and the circumstances of the girls' deaths . . ."

"Perhaps it was to avoid fueling any gossip. Let's not forget that they've believed Miguel Ángel to be their daughter's killer all this time . . . It must be hard to accept that we don't have the killer and, furthermore, that he's going to be released from prison."

"You could be right," admitted Iriarte.

"Jonan, what can you tell me about Ainhoa's family?" asked Amaia.

"After the funeral, almost all the mourners went back to their home. The parents were very upset but quite calm, supporting one another. They held hands the whole time and didn't let go even for an instant. It was hardest for the boy; it was painful to see him, sitting on a chair all by himself, looking at the floor, receiving everyone's condolences without his parents even deigning to look at him. It was a shame."

"They blame the boy. Do we know whether he was really at home that night? Could he have gone to pick his sister up?" inquired Zabalza.

"He was at home. Two of his friends were with him the whole time, it looks like they had to do a project for school and then they got absorbed in playing on the PlayStation. One other boy joined them later, a neighbor who dropped in for a game. I've also spoken to Ainhoa's friends. They didn't stop crying or talking on their cell phones the entire time, a really bizarre combination. They all said the same thing. They spent the evening together in the square and wandering around town, and then they went to a bar on the ground floor of the building where one of them lives. They had a bit to drink, although not very much according to them. Some of them smoke, although Ainhoa didn't. Even so, it would explain why her skin and clothes smelled of tobacco. There was a little gang of boys drinking beer with them, but they all stayed where they were after Ainhoa left. It looks like she was the one with the earliest curfew."

"And much good it did her," commented Montes.

"Some parents think that making their daughters come home earlier keeps them safe from danger, when the most important thing is that they don't come home alone. By making them come home before the rest of the group, they're the ones putting them at risk."

"It's difficult being a parent," murmured Iriarte.

8

A S SHE walked home, Amaia was surprised by how quickly the light had faded that February afternoon, and she had a strange sense of being cheated. The early nights during winter made her uneasy. As if the darkness carried an ominous charge, the cold made her shiver beneath the leather of her jacket and yearn for the warmth of the quilted anorak James had tried so hard to persuade her to wear, which she had rejected because it made her look like the Michelin Man.

The warm atmosphere of Aunt Engrasi's house dispersed the unwelcome remnants of winter that clung to her. The scent of the wood in the hearth, the huge rugs that covered the wooden floor, and the incessant chatter from the television, which was permanently on even though nobody ever watched it, welcomed her back again. There were much more interesting things to do there than listen to the TV, and yet it was always on in the background like a poltergeist, ignored as an absurdity and tolerated out of habit. She had once asked her aunt why, and she had replied, "It's an echo of the world. Do you know what an echo is? It's the remnants of a voice you can still hear once it has died away."

Back in the present, James took her by the hand and led her over to the fire.

"You're frozen, my love."

She smiled, nuzzling her nose into his sweater and inhaling the scent of his skin. Ros and Aunt Engrasi came out of the kitchen carrying glasses, dishes, bread, and a tureen of soup.

"I hope you're hungry, Amaia, because your aunt's made enough food to feed an army."

Aunt Engrasi's footsteps may have been slightly slower than they were at Christmas, but her mind was as clear as ever. Amaia smiled tenderly as she noticed this detail, and her aunt snapped at her, "Don't look at me like that. I'm not slow, it's these damn shoes your sister gave me that are two sizes too big. If I pick my feet up I'm likely to go flying, so I have to walk as if I'm wearing a dirty diaper."

They chatted while they ate, with James telling jokes in his American accent and Aunt Engrasi sharing the local gossip, but Amaia couldn't help noticing the deep sadness that lay behind the smile with which Ros tried to follow the conversation and the way she tried to avoid eye contact with her sister.

While James and her aunt took the plates through to the kitchen, Amaia caught her sister's attention with just a few words.

"I was at the workshop today."

Ros looked at her as she sat down again, with an expression that revealed both her disappointment and relief at being found out.

"What did she tell you? Or rather, how did she tell you?"

"In her own way. As she does everything. She told me that they're going to publish her second book, that they've brought up the possibility of a television show, that she is the backbone of the family, a paragon of virtue, and the only person in the whole world who knows the meaning of the word 'responsibility.'" She recited the litany in an exaggerated singsong voice until she managed to make Ros smile.

"And she also told me that you don't work at the workshop anymore and that you have serious problems with your husband."

"Amaia . . . I'm sorry that you found out that way. Perhaps I should have told you sooner, but it's something that I'm working through bit by bit, something that I have to do by myself, that I should have done a long time ago. Anyway, I didn't want to worry you."

"Don't be silly. You know worrying is part of my job description and I'm good at my job. As for the rest, I agree with you. I don't know how you managed to work with her for so long."

"I suppose it was all there was. I didn't have any other options."

"What are you trying to say? We all have more than one option, Ros."

"We're not all like you, Amaia. I suppose it was what everyone expected, that we would continue to run the workshop."

"Are you trying to reproach me for something? Because if that's the case—"

"Don't take this the wrong way, but when you went, it was as if I didn't have any choice."

"That's not true. You have a choice now and you had a choice then."

"When *Aita* died, *Ama* started behaving very strangely—I suppose it was the first symptoms of Alzheimer's—and I suddenly found myself trapped between the responsibility Flora demanded of me, *Ama's* episodes, and Freddy . . . I suppose at that point Freddy seemed like an escape route."

"And what's changed now? Because there's something you mustn't forget: although Flora acts like the owner and boss of the workshop, it's as much yours as it is hers, and I gave up my share to you two on that condition. You're as capable of running the company as she is."

"That may be so, but it's more than just Flora and work at the moment. It's not only because of her, although she has played her part. I suddenly felt like I was drowning there, listening to her and her endless list of complaints every day. On top of the problems in my personal life, it was just unbearable. Having to go there every morning and listen to the same old story made me so anxious I felt physically ill and emotionally drained. But somehow I also felt as calm and clearheaded as ever. Determined, that's the word. And all of a sudden, as if the heavens had opened and sent me a sign, it all became clear: I wasn't going to go back, I didn't go back, and I won't go back, at least not for the time being."

Amaia brought her hands up to head height and began to clap slowly and rhythmically. "Well done, Ros, well done."

THE INVISIBLE GUARDIAN / 43

Ros smiled and gave a mock curtsey.

"And now what?"

"I'm working at an aluminum factory, keeping the accounts. I manage the payroll and organize the weekly schedule, arrange the meetings. Eight hours a day, Monday to Friday, and when I leave the office I forget all about it. It's nothing to get too excited about, but it's just what I need right now."

"And what about Freddy?"

"It's bad, really bad," she said, biting her lip and shaking her head.

"Is that why you're here, staying with Aunt Engrasi?" She didn't answer. "Why don't you tell him to leave? When all's said and done, it's your house."

"I've already told him, but he refuses to even consider moving out. Since I left, he spends all day going from the bed to the sofa and the sofa to the bed, drinking beer, playing on the PlayStation, and smoking joints," said Ros with disgust.

"That's what Flora called him, 'the PlayStation champion.' Where's he getting the money from? Surely you're not . . . ?"

"No, that's all stopped. His mother gives him money, and his friends keep him well supplied."

"I can pay him a visit, if you want. You know what Aunt Engrasi says, a man with plenty to eat and drink can go a long time without working," said Amaia, laughing.

"Yes," replied Ros with a smile, "she's absolutely right, but no. This is exactly what I wanted to avoid. Let me sort things out, I will sort them out, I promise."

"You're not going to go back to him, are you?" said Amaia, looking her in the eye.

"No, I'm not going back."

For a moment Amaia wasn't convinced. Then she realized her doubt must be showing on her face and was reminded of Flora and her lack of faith in other people. She made herself smile openly.

"I'm glad for you, Ros," she said with all the conviction she could muster.

"That part of my life is behind me now, and that's something that neither Flora nor Freddy can understand. Me changing jobs at this point is incomprehensible to Flora, but at thirty-five years of age, I don't want to spend the rest of my life working under my older sister's yoke. Putting up with the same reproaches every day, the same snide comments and malicious remarks, as she shares her poison with the whole world. And Freddy . . . I suppose it's not his fault. For a long time I thought that he was the answer to all my questions, that he'd have the magic formula, a kind of revelation that would give me a new way of living. So opposite to everyone else, so rebellious, a nonconformist, and most of all, so different from *Ama* and Flora, and with that ability to really irritate her." She smiled mischievously.

"That's true. The guy does have the ability to get on Flora's nerves, and I like him just for that," replied Amaia.

"Until I realized that Freddy isn't so different after all. That his rebellion and his refusal to accept the rules are nothing more than a cloak to hide a coward, a good-for-nothing capable of giving forth like Che against the evils of consumer society while spending the money that he wheedles out of his mother or me on getting stoned. I think it's the only thing on which I agree with Flora: he is the PlayStation champion. If he was paid money for it, he'd be one of the richest men in the country."

Amaia looked at her with tenderness.

"At a certain point, I found myself on a different path from the one we'd been on together. I knew I wanted a different way of life and that there had to be something more to life than spending every weekend drinking beer at Xanti's bar. That, and having children. Perhaps that's the real issue, because as soon as I decided to change, having a child suddenly became really important to me, an urgent need, my role in life. I'm not an idiot, Amaia, I didn't want to have a child only to bring it up in a cloud of smoke from all the joints, but even so, I stopped taking the pill and hoped, as if everything would just happen according to a plan drawn up by destiny."

Her face darkened, and her eyes seemed to lose their sparkle. "But it wasn't to be, Amaia. It looks like I can't have children either," she said in a whisper. "I got more and more desperate as the months passed without my getting pregnant. Freddy told me that perhaps it was for the best, that we were fine as we were. I didn't answer him, but the rest of the night while he was asleep, snoring at my side, a voice was thundering inside me saying, 'No, absolutely not, I am not fine like this.' And the voice kept thundering in my head while I got dressed to go to the workshop, while I dealt with the telephone orders, while I listened to Flora's tireless litany of reproaches. And that day, when I hung my white overall in my locker, I already knew I wouldn't go back. While Freddy was moving onto the next level of Resident Evil and I was warming the soup for supper, I also realized that my life with him was over. Just like that, without shouting or tears."

"You shouldn't be embarrassed, tears are necessary sometimes."

"That's true, but the time for tears had passed, my eyes had run dry from crying so much while he snored away beside me. From crying with shame, and understanding that I was ashamed of him, that I could never be proud of the man at my side. Something broke inside me, and what had, until that point, been pure desperation to save our relationship became a war cry from somewhere very deep inside me, and it condemned him. Most people are mistaken; they believe you can go from love to hate in a moment, that love suddenly breaks down, as if your heart had imploded. But that's not how it was for me. The love didn't suddenly break down, but I had a sudden realization that I had wasted myself in a relentless sanding-down process, scritch, scratch, scritch, scratch day after day. And that was the day when I realized that there was nothing left. It was more like suddenly seeing something that has been there all along. Making those decisions made me feel free for the first time in a long time, and that's made things straightforward for me, but neither our sister nor my husband were prepared to let me go that easily. You'd be surprised by how similar their arguments, their reproaches, their tricks were . . . because the two of them played tricks, you know, and they used the very same words." She smiled bitterly as she remembered them. "'Where are you going to go? Do you think you'll find something better?' And, finally, 'Who will love you?' They'd never believe it, but although their tricks were designed to undermine my conviction, they had just the opposite effect: I saw how small and cowardly they were, so inept, and anything seemed possible, easier without them dragging me down. I wasn't sure about everything, but at least I had an answer to the last question: *I am. I'm going to love myself and take care of myself.*"

"I'm proud of you," said Amaia, hugging her. "Don't forget you can count on me, I've always loved you."

"I know you have, and James, Aunt Engrasi, *Aita*, and even *Ama*, in her own way. The only one who didn't really value me was me."

"Then love yourself, Ros Salazar."

"There's been a change there, too: I prefer people to call me Rosaura."

"Flora told me, but why? It took you years to get everyone to call you Ros."

"If I have children one day, I don't want them to call me Ros, it's a stoner's name," she declared.

"You could say that about any name," said Amaia. "And tell me something, when are you planning to make me an aunt?"

"As soon as I find the perfect man."

"I should warn you that it's rumored he doesn't exist."

"You can talk, you've got one at home."

Amaia forced a smile. "We've tried too. And we can't, at the moment . . ."

"But have you seen a doctor?"

"Yes. At first I was afraid I had blocked tubes like Flora, but they told me everything appears to be in order. They recommended one of those fertility treatments."

"Oh, I'm sorry." Ros's voice trembled a bit. "Have you started yet?"

"We haven't been to the clinic; the very thought of having to undergo one of those painful treatments makes me feel ill. Do you remember how bad it was for Flora, and all for nothing?"

"Of course, but you shouldn't think like that. You said yourself that you don't have the same problem as her. Perhaps it will work for you . . ."

"It's not just that. I feel a sort of aversion to having to conceive a child that way. I know I'm being stupid, but I don't believe it should happen like that . . ."

James came in, carrying Amaia's cell phone.

"It's Deputy Inspector Zabalza," he said, covering the mouthpiece with his hand. Amaia took the phone.

"Inspector, a patrol has found a pair of girl's shoes left on the hard shoulder and positioned facing the highway. They let us know just now. I'll send a car over and meet you there."

"What about the body?" asked Amaia, lowering her voice and partially covering the phone.

"We haven't found it yet. The area's difficult to access, quite different from the previous cases: the vegetation's very thick, the river isn't visible from the road. If there's a girl down there, it's going to be a challenge to get to her. I keep asking myself why he's chosen a place like that. Perhaps he didn't want us to find her as easily as the others."

Amaia considered the idea.

"No. He wants us to find her, that's why he's left the shoes to indicate the location. But by choosing a place that isn't visible from the road he can guarantee that no one will disturb him until he's got everything in place to show his work to the world. Simply put, it avoids interruptions and hitches."

They were a pair of white patent Mustang court shoes with quite high heels. A police officer was taking photos of them from different angles under Jonan's direction. The camera flash made the plastic glimmer and shine, making them look even more strange and out of place, positioned there in the middle of nowhere. They almost seemed enchanted, like the shoes belonging to a princess in a fairy tale, or like the shocking and absurd work of a conceptual artist. Amaia imagined the effect of a long line of party shoes lined up in that remote wilderness. Zabalza's voice brought her back to reality.

"It's disturbing . . . the thing with the shoes, I mean. Why does he do it?"

"He marks his territory like a wild animal, like the predator he is, and he provokes us. He leaves them here to draw us in: 'Look what I've left you, Olentzero has been here and left you a little something.'"

"What a bastard!"

With a concerted effort, she managed to tear her gaze from the eerily enchanting shoes and turn toward the dense woodland. A metallic sound reverberated from the walkie-talkie in Zabalza's hand.

"Have they found her?"

"Not yet, but as I said, the river runs through the vegetation in a kind of natural canyon with steep walls around here."

The beams of light from powerful lanterns threw ghostly glimmers through the bare trees, which grew so close together that they produced the effect of an inverse dawn, as if the sun was emerging from the earth instead of in the sky. Amaia pulled on her boots while she considered the effect that the landscape had on her thoughts. Deputy Inspector Iriarte appeared from the thick vegetation with an agitated gasp.

"We've found her."

Amaia went down the slope behind Jonan and Deputy Inspector Zabalza. She noticed how the earth gave way beneath her feet, softened by the recent rain, which, in spite of all the thick foliage, had managed to penetrate deep into the ground, turning the fragments of leaves that coated the floor of the woods into a slimy and slippery carpet. The trees grew so close together that they were obliged to take a zigzag route down, but the branches did provide useful handholds. She could not help feeling a certain malicious satisfaction when she heard Montes's incoherent mutterings a few steps behind her as he came down in his expensive Italian shoes and leather jacket.

The woods stopped abruptly at the edge of a near-vertical rock face on either side of the river, which opened out, forming a narrow v like a natural funnel. They went down as far as a dark, low-lying area that the police officers were trying to illuminate with portable spotlights. The current and flow of the river were faster there, and there was less than a meter and a half of dry gravel between the steep walls and the riverbank on either side. Amaia looked at the girl's hands, which lay open at the sides of her despoiled body, stretched out in an ominous gesture of entreaty. The left one was almost touching the water, her long blond hair reached almost to her waist, and her green eyes were covered by a whitish steamlike film. Her beauty in death and the almost mystical scene that the monster had come up with achieved the intended effect. For a moment he had managed to draw Amaia into his fantasy, distracting her from protocol, and it was the princess's eyes that brought her back, those eyes crying out for justice from the bed of the River Baztán in spite of being clouded by the mist, which sometimes filled her dreams during her darkest nights. She took a couple of steps back to murmur a brief prayer and put on the gloves that Montes was holding out to her. Acutely sensitive to other people's distress, she looked at Iriarte, who had covered his mouth with his hands and brought them almost brusquely down to his sides when he felt he was being observed.

"I know her . . . I knew her, I know her family, she's Arbizu's daughter," he said, looking at Zabalza as if seeking confirmation. "I don't know her name, but she's Arbizu's daughter, there's no doubt about it."

"Her name is Anne, Anne Arbizu," confirmed Jonan, holding out a library card. "Her bag was a few meters upstream." He gestured to an area that was now dark again.

Amaia knelt down next to the girl, observing the frozen grimace on her face, almost a parody of a smile.

"Do you know how old she was?" she asked.

"Fifteen, I don't think she'd turned sixteen yet," replied Iriarte, coming over. He looked at the body and then started running. About ten meters downstream he doubled over and vomited. Nobody said anything, not then nor when he came back, wiping the front of his shirt with a tissue and murmuring his apologies.

Anne's skin had been very white, but not washed-out, almost transparent, plagued by freckles and red patches. It had been white, clean, and creamy, completely hairless. Covered as it was by droplets from the river's mist, it was like the marble of a statue on a tombstone. In contrast to Carla and Ainhoa, this girl had fought. At least two of her fingernails seemed to be torn down to the quick. There seemed to be no fragments of skin beneath the rest. No doubt she had taken longer to die than the others; the burst blood vessels that indicated death by asphyxiation and the suffering caused by oxygen deprivation were visible in spite of the clouding that covered her eyes. Furthermore, the killer had faithfully reproduced the details of the previous murders: the thin cord buried in her neck, the clothes torn and pulled open to the sides, the jeans pulled down to her knees, the shaved pubic area, and the fragrant, sticky cake placed on her pubic mound.

Jonan was taking photographs of the hair scattered on the ground near the girl's feet.

"It's all the same, chief. It's like looking at the other girls all over again."

"Fuck!" a restrained yell was heard from several meters downstream, together with the unmistakable thunder of a shot that bounced off the rock walls, producing a deafening echo that stunned them all for a moment. Then they drew their weapons and pointed them toward where the river narrowed.

"False alarm! It's nothing," shouted a voice from the direction of a flashlight that was moving toward them along the riverbank. A smiling uniformed officer came walking over with Montes, who was visibly upset as he looked at his gun.

"What happened, Fermín?" asked Amaia, alarmed.

"I'm sorry, it caught me by surprise. I was searching the riverbank and I suddenly saw the biggest fucking rat ever, the beast looked at me and . . . I'm sorry, I fired instinctively. Fuck! I can't stand rats, and then the officer told me it was a . . . I'm not sure what."

"A coypu," clarified the officer. "Coypus are a kind of mammal that originally came from South America. Some of them escaped from a French breeding farm in the Pyrenees a few years ago, and they happened to adapt well to the river. Although they've more or less stopped spreading, you still see one or two. But they're harmless, in fact, they're herbivorous swimmers, like beavers."

"I'm sorry," repeated Montes, "I didn't know. I'm musophobic, I can't stand the sight of anything that looks like a rat."

Amaia looked at him uncomfortably.

"I'll submit the weapons discharge form tomorrow," he muttered. He looked at his shoes in silence for a while, then moved aside and stood there without saying anything more.

Amaia almost felt sorry for him and for the fun the others would have at his expense over the next few days. She knelt by the body again and tried to empty her mind of everything other than the girl and her immediate surroundings.

The fact that the trees didn't grow all the way down to the river along that stretch meant that there was no scent of soil and lichen, which had been so powerful up in the woods. Down there, in the gorge that the river had carved in the rocks, only the mineral odors from the water competed with the sweet, fatty smell of the *txantx-igorri*. Its aroma of butter and sugar filled her nose, mixed with another more subtle scent that she recognized as that of recent death. She panted as she tried to contain her nausea, staring at the cake as if it were a repulsive insect and asking herself how it was possible for it to smell so strong.

Dr. San Martín knelt at her side. "Goodness, doesn't it smell good?"

Amaia looked at him aghast.

"That was a joke, Inspector Salazar."

She didn't reply but stood up to give him more room.

"But to tell the truth, it does smell very good and I haven't had supper."

Unseen by the pathologist, Amaia grimaced in disgust and turned to greet Judge Estébanez, who was making her way down between the rocks with enviable ease in spite of her skirt and heeled boots.

"I don't believe it," muttered Montes, who didn't seem to have recovered from the incident with the coypu yet. The judge gave a wave of general greeting, then went over to Dr. San Martín to listen to his observations. Ten minutes later, she had already gone.

It took them more than an hour and a real team effort to get the coffin containing Anne's body up from the gorge. The technicians had suggested putting her in a body bag and hoisting her up, but San Martín insisted that she should be in a coffin in order to perfectly preserve the body and avoid the multiple bumps and scratches it might receive if it were dragged up through the junglelike forest. At certain points, the narrowness of the gaps between the trees forced them to turn the coffin on its end and wait for fresh hands to take over. After several hairy moments, they managed to carry the coffin as far as the hearse that would transport Anne's body to the Navarra Institute of Forensic Medicine in Pamplona.

~

Each time Amaia had seen the body of a minor on the autopsy table, she had been overwhelmed by a sense of her own impotence and helplessness and that of the society she lived in. A society where the death of its children signified its inability to protect its own future. A society that had failed. Like she had. She took a deep breath and entered the autopsy room. Dr. San Martín was filling in the paperwork before the operation and greeted her as she made her way over to the steel table. Already stripped of all clothing, Anne Arbizu was laid out under the harsh light that would have revealed even the slightest imperfection on any other body, but in her case only underlined the unscathed whiteness of her skin, making her seem unreal, almost painted. Amaia thought of one of those marble Madonnas found in Italian museums.

"She looks like a doll," she murmured.

"I was saying the same thing to Sofía," the doctor agreed. The technician raised a hand in greeting. She would have made an excellent model for one of Wagner's Valkyries.

Deputy Inspector Zabalza had just come in.

"Are we waiting for anyone else, or can we get started?"

"Inspector Montes should have arrived by now . . ." said Amaia, consulting her watch. "You start, Doctor, he'll arrive any moment."

She dialed Montes's number but it went straight to voice mail; she supposed he must be driving. Under the harsh lights she could see some details she hadn't noticed before. There were several short, dark, quite thick hairs on the skin.

"Animal hairs?"

"Probably, we found more stuck to the clothes. We'll compare them with the ones that were found on Carla's body."

"How long do you reckon she's been dead?"

"Judging by the temperature of the liver, which I took when we were by the river, she might have been there two or three hours."

"That's not very long, not long enough for any animals to approach the body . . . the cake was intact, it almost seemed freshly baked, and you could smell it as well as I could. If there had been animals close enough to leave hairs on her, they would have eaten the cake like they did in Carla's case."

"I'd have to ask the forest rangers," commented Zabalza, "but I don't think it's somewhere the animals normally go to drink."

"An animal could get down there easily," Dr. San Martín observed.

"Yes, they could get down there, but the river forms a narrow pass at that point, which would make escape difficult, and animals always drink in the open where they can see as well as be seen."

"Well, in that case, how do you explain the hairs?"

"Perhaps they were on the murderer's clothes and were transferred during contact."

"That's a possibility. Who would wear clothes covered in animal hair?"

"A hunter, a forest ranger, a shepherd," said Jonan.

"A taxidermist," added Sofía, the technician who was assisting Dr. San Martín and who had remained silent until that point.

"Right, we'll have to track down anyone who matches that profile and was in the area, and also take into account that it must have been a strong man, a very strong man, in my opinion. If it weren't for the intimacy required by this sort of fantasy, I'd say there was more than one murderer. But one thing is certain, and that's that not just anybody would have been able to carry a body down that slope, and it's clear from the lack of scratches and grazes that he carried her down in his arms," said Amaia.

"Are we sure she was already dead when he took her down there?"

"I'm sure. No girl would go down to the river at night, even with someone she knew, and she certainly wouldn't leave her shoes behind. I think he approaches them, then kills them quickly before they suspect anything. Perhaps they know him and that's why they trust him, perhaps not and he has to kill them right away. He gets the string around their necks and they're dead before they know it. Then he takes them to the river, arranges them just as he imagined in his fantasy, and once he's completed his psychosexual rite he leaves us a sign in the form of the shoes and lets us see his work." Amaia suddenly fell silent and shook her head as if waking from a dream. They were all looking at her as if spellbound.

"Let's move on to the string," said San Martín.

The technician grasped the girl's head at the base of the cranium and lifted it high enough for Dr. San Martín to extract the string from the dark channel in which it had been buried. He paid special attention to the sections adhering to the sides, on which small whitish fragments of something that looked like plastic or glue could be seen.

"Look at this, Inspector, this is something new. Unlike the other cases, there are bits of skin attached to the string. You can see that by pulling so hard he inflicted a cut, or at least a graze, which took away some of the skin."

"Given the absence of fingerprints, I thought he must be using gloves," Zabalza chipped in.

"It would seem likely, but sometimes these killers can't resist the pleasure they get from feeling a life end under their own hands, a feeling that would be deadened by gloves. As a consequence, they sometimes end up taking them off, if only at the key moment. Even so, it's sometimes enough for us."

As Amaia had expected, Dr. San Martín agreed that Anne had defended herself. Perhaps she had seen something that her predecessors hadn't, something that had made her suspicious and was enough to prevent her from going to her death submissively. The symptoms of asphyxia were obvious, and it was clear that the killer had tried to use Anne to recreate his fantasy. He had succeeded up to a certain point, because at first glance that crime and all the paraphernalia the killer had used were identical to the previous ones. However,

Amaia had the inexplicable impression that the killer hadn't been at all pleased with the death, that this little girl with her angelic face, who could have been the monster's masterpiece, had been tougher and more aggressive than the others. And although the killer had made an effort to arrange her with the same care as he had the others, Anne's face didn't reflect surprise and vulnerability but rather the fight for her life that she had kept up to the last and a parody of a smile that was actually rather terrifying. Amaia observed some reddish marks that had appeared around her mouth and extended almost as far as her right ear.

"What are those red marks on her face?"

The technician took a sample, using a swab. "I'll let you know as soon as we know for certain, but I would say that it's"—she smelled the swab—"gloss."

"What's gloss?" asked Zabalza.

"It's like lipstick, Deputy Inspector, a greasy, shiny lipstick with a fruit flavor," explained Amaia.

In her time as a homicide inspector, she had attended more autopsies than she wanted to remember and considered that she had more than fulfilled her quota of "What I need to do to prove a woman can do this." With that in mind, she didn't stay to watch the rest. The brutality of the y-shaped incision performed on a corpse is unparalleled by any other surgical procedure. The process, which consisted of removing and weighing the organs and then replacing them in the cavities, was never pleasant, but when the body belonged to a child or a young girl, as in this case, it was unbearable. She knew that it had less to do with the technical, unvarying steps of the autopsy procedure than the inexplicable reasons that a child would be on that steel table, which ought to be forbidden as a matter of course. The incongruity of that diminutive body that barely filled the surface it had ended up on, the explosion of brilliant colors inside it and, most of all, the girl's small, pale face with tiny drops of water still trapped in her eyelashes acted like clamorous cries to which she could not help but respond.

9

BASED ON the amount of light, Amaia guessed it must be about seven in the morning. She woke Jonan, who was asleep under his anorak in the back of the car.

"Good morning, chief. How did it go?" he asked, rubbing his eyes.

"We're going back to Elizondo. Has Montes called you?"

"No, I thought he was at the autopsy with you."

"He didn't turn up and he's not answering his phone. I keep getting his voice mail," she said, visibly annoyed.

Deputy Inspector Zabalza, who had come down to Pamplona in the same car as them, climbed into the backseat and cleared his throat. "Well, Inspector, I'm not sure if I should get involved in this, but I don't want you to worry. When we left the ravine, Inspector Montes told me he'd have to go and change because he'd arranged to have dinner with someone."

"To have dinner?" She couldn't contain her surprise.

"Yes. He asked whether I was going to Pamplona with you for the autopsy, I said yes, and he told me that in that case he'd be less concerned, that he supposed that Deputy Inspector Etxaide would be going too, and that everything would be fine if that was the case."

"Everything would be fine? He was well aware that he should have been here," said Amaia furiously, although she immediately regretted making a fool of herself in front of her subordinates.

"I . . . I'm sorry. From the way he was talking I assumed that you'd agreed to it."

"Don't worry, I'll talk to him later."

She wasn't at all tired in spite of not sleeping. The faces of the three girls stared into the void from the surface of the table. Three very different faces but made equal in death. She carefully studied the enlargements of the pictures of Carla and Ainhoa she had requested.

Montes came in silently with two coffees, placed one in front of Amaia, and sat down a short distance away. She looked up from the photos for a moment and gave him a penetrating stare until he dropped his gaze. Another five officers from her team were also in the room. She took the photos and slid them toward the center of the table.

"Well, gentlemen, what do you see in these photos?"

They all leaned over the table expectantly.

"I'm going to give you a clue."

She added Anne's picture to the other two.

"This is Anne Arbizu, the girl who was found last night. Do you see the pinkish marks that extend from her mouth almost as far as her ear? Well, they're from lip gloss, a pink, greasy lip gloss that makes the lips look wet. Take another look at the photos."

"The other girls aren't wearing any," observed Iriarte.

"Exactly, the other girls aren't wearing any, and I want to know why. They were very pretty and trendy, they had high heels, handbags, cell phones, and perfume. Isn't it strange that they weren't wearing even a trace of makeup? Almost all girls their age start wearing it, at least mascara and lip gloss."

She looked at her colleagues, who were regarding her with confused expressions.

"I think that he removed Anne's makeup, which would explain the traces of lip gloss, and that he had to use makeup remover and a tissue or facial wipes to do it. I also think it highly likely that he did it by the river. There was next to no light down there, and even if he had a flashlight with him, it wasn't enough, because he didn't finish the job on Anne.

"Jonan and Montes, I want you to go back to the riverbank and look for the wipes. If he used them and didn't take them with him, we might be able to find them somewhere around there." She didn't miss the look on Montes's face as he glanced down at his shoes, a different style, brown this time, and clearly expensive. "Deputy Inspector Zabalza, please speak to Ainhoa's friends and find out whether she was wearing makeup the night she was killed. Don't bother her parents with this, especially since she was young and it's quite possible that even if she did wear makeup, her parents wouldn't have known . . . Lots of teenage girls put it on after they've left the house and take it off before they get back. As for Carla, I'm sure she would have been wearing more makeup than a clown wears face paint. She's got it on in all the photos we have of her alive and, furthermore, it was New Year's Eve. Even my Aunt Engrasi wears lipstick on New Year's Eve. Let's see if we can find anything by this afternoon. I want everyone back here at four."

SPRING 1989

There were some good days, almost always Sundays, the only day her parents didn't work. Her mother would bake crisp croissants and raisin bread at home, which would fill the whole house with a rich, sweet fragrance that lasted for hours. Her father would come slowly into the girls' bedroom, open the blinds on the windows facing the mountain, and go out without saying anything, leaving the sun to wake them with its caresses, unusually warm for winter mornings. Once awake, they would stay in bed, listening to their parents' light chatter in the kitchen, savoring the feeling of their clean bedding, the sun warming the bedclothes, its rays drawing capricious paths through the dust in the air. Sometimes, before breakfast, their mother would even put one of her old records on the record player, and the house would resonate with the voice of Machín or Nat King Cole and their boleros and cha-cha-chas. Then their father would put his arms around their mother's waist and they would dance together, their faces very close and their hands entwined, going around and around the whole living room, skirting the heavy hand-finished furniture and the rugs woven by someone in Baghdad. The little girls would get out of bed, barefoot and sleepy, and sit on the sofa to watch them dance while the adults smiled rather sheepishly, as if, instead of seeing them dance, their daughters had surprised them in a more intimate act.

Ros was always the first to clasp her father's legs to join in the dance; then Flora would attach herself to their mother. Amaia would smile from the sofa, amused by the clumsiness of the group of dancers singing boleros under their breath as they turned. She didn't dance, because she wanted to keep watching them, because she wanted that ritual to last a bit longer, and because she knew that if she got up and joined the group, the dance would end immediately as soon as she brushed against her mother, who would leave them with a ridiculous excuse, like she was tired already, she didn't feel like dancing anymore, or she had to go and check on the bread baking in the oven. Whenever that happened, her father would give her a desolate look and carry on dancing with the little girl awhile longer, trying to make up for the insult, until her mother came back into the living room five minutes later and turned off the record player, claiming that she had a headache.

10

AFTER A brief siesta, from which she woke disorientated and confused, Amaia felt worse than she had in the morning. She took a shower and read the note that James had left her, a bit annoyed that he wasn't at home. Although she would never tell him, she secretly preferred him to be nearby while she slept, as if his presence could soothe her. She would feel ridiculous if she ever had to put into words what waking up in an empty house did to her and her wish that he had been there while she was asleep. She didn't need him to lie down beside her, she didn't want him to hold her hand, but it wasn't enough for him to be there when she woke up. She needed his presence while she was asleep. If she had to work at night and sleep in the morning, she would often do it on the sofa if James wasn't at home. She didn't manage to sleep as deeply there as when she was in bed, but she preferred it, because she knew that if she got into bed it would be impossible. And it didn't make a difference if he went out once she had fallen asleep: although she might not hear the door, she would immediately notice his absence, as if there wasn't enough air, and on waking up she would know for certain that he was not in the house. *I want you to be at home while I sleep.* The thought was obviously and rationally absurd, which was why she couldn't say it, couldn't tell him that she woke up when he went out, that she felt his presence in the house as if she detected it with a sonar system, and that she secretly felt abandoned when she woke up and found he had left his place at her side to go out and buy bread.

Back at the police station and three coffees later, she wasn't feeling much better. Seated behind Iriarte's desk, she was heartened to observe the evidence of his domestic life. The blond children, the young wife, the calendars with pictures of the Virgin, the well-tended plants that grew near the windows . . . he even had saucers under the pots to collect the excess water.

"Have you got a moment, chief? Jonan said you wanted to see me."

"Come in, Montes, and don't call me 'chief.' Please take a seat."

He made himself comfortable in the chair opposite and looked at her, his mouth forming a slight pout.

"Montes, I was disappointed that you didn't attend the autopsy. I was concerned that I didn't know the reason why you weren't there, and it made me very angry that I had to find out from someone else that you weren't coming because you were going out for dinner. I think you could at least have saved me the embarrassment of spending the whole night asking after you, wasting my time on phone calls you didn't answer, only for Zabalza to tell me what was going on."

Montes looked at her impassively. She continued.

"Fermín, we're a team, I need absolutely everyone in place all the time. If you wanted to go I wouldn't have stopped you. I'm just saying that with what we've got on our plates, I think you could have at least called me or told Jonan or something, but you certainly can't disappear without giving any explanation. Right now, with another murdered girl, I need you at my side constantly. Well, anyway, I hope it was worth it." She smiled and looked at him in silence waiting for a response, but he continued to stare straight through her with an expression that had twisted from the childish pout to disdain. "Aren't you going to say anything, Fermín?"

"Montes," he said suddenly. "Inspector Montes to you. Don't forget that although you might be in charge of this investigation for the moment, you're speaking to an equal. I don't have to explain myself to Jonan, who's my subordinate, and I let Deputy Inspector Zabalza know. My responsibility stops there." His eyes half closed with indignation. "Of course you wouldn't have stopped me going out for dinner, that's not up to you, even if you have begun to think so lately. Inspector Montes had already been working on the homicide team for six years when you started at the academy, chief, and what's pissing you off is looking incompetent in front of Zabalza." He settled back in the seat and gave her a challenging look. Amaia looked at him with a feeling of sadness.

"The only one who looked incompetent is you, incompetent and a poor policeman. For God's sake! We'd just found the third body in a series, we still don't have anything, and you go off for dinner. I think you resent me because the commissioner assigned the case to me, but you have to understand that I had nothing to do with that decision, and what we ought to be worried about now is solving this case as soon as possible." She softened her tone and looked Montes in the eye, trying to gain his support. "I thought we were friends, Fermín. I would have been happy if it were you. I thought you respected me, I thought I'd have every possible help from you . . ."

"Well, keep thinking that," he muttered.

"Don't you have anything else to say to me?" He remained silent. "All right, Montes, have it your way, I'll see you at the meeting."

~

The girls' dead faces were there again, their eyes gazing into infinity and veiled by death, and, beside them, as if to emphasize the great loss they represented, were other photos, colorful and bright, showing Carla's mischievous smile as she posed by a car that undoubtedly belonged to her boyfriend, Ainhoa holding a week-old lamb in her arms, and Anne with her school theater group. A plastic bag contained various wipes that had almost certainly been used to remove the makeup from Anne's face, and there was another that held the ones that had been found at the scene of Ainhoa's death. No one had paid them any attention at the time because it had been assumed that they had blown down to the river from the esplanade up by the road where couples often met.

"You were right, chief. The wipes were there, they'd been dumped a few meters away, in a crack in the riverbank. They've got pink and black marks on them, from the mascara, I suppose. Her friends say she usually wore makeup, and I've also got the original lipstick, which was in her handbag. It'll help us confirm whether it's the same one. And these," he said, pointing to the other bag, "are the ones found where Ainhoa was killed. They're the same kind with the same stripy pattern, although these have got less makeup on them. Ainhoa's friends say she only used lip gloss."

Zabalza got to his feet. "We haven't been able to find anything where Carla was killed. Too much time has passed and we have to bear in mind that the body was partially submerged in the river. If the killer left the wipes nearby, it's likely they were washed away by the floodwater . . . We've confirmed with her family that she used to wear makeup pretty much every day, though."

Amaia stood up and started to walk around the room, moving behind her colleagues, who remained seated.

"Jonan, what do these girls tell us?"

The deputy inspector leaned forward and touched the edge of one of the photos with his index finger. "He removes their makeup, takes off their shoes, which are high heels, women's shoes in all three cases. He arranges their hair so it hangs to either side of their faces, he shaves off their pubic hair, he makes them into little girls again."

"Exactly," Amaia agreed vehemently. "It seems to this guy that they're growing up too fast."

"A pedophile who likes little girls?"

"No. No, if he were a pedophile he would choose little girls in the first place, and these are teenagers, more or less young women, at the stage when girls want to seem older than they are. It's nothing unusual, it's part of the adolescent growing-up process. But this killer doesn't like these changes."

"What's most likely is that he knew them when they were smaller and he doesn't like what he sees now, and that's why he wants to make them go back to how they were," said Zabalza.

"It's not enough to take off their shoes and makeup and shave off their pubic hair and leave their sexes like a little girl's," Amaia continued. "He slashes their clothes and exposes their bodies, which are not yet those of the women they wished they were, and instead of a body that symbolizes sex and the profanation of his concept of childhood, he gets rid of the body hair, which is a sign of maturity, and replaces it with a pastry, a soft little cake, which symbolizes past times, the traditions of the valley, the return to childhood, and perhaps some other values. He disapproves of how they dress, the fact that they wear makeup, their adult ways, and he punishes them by using them to represent his idea of purity. That's why he never violates them sexually; it's the last thing he'd want to do. He wants to preserve them from corruption, from sin . . . And the worst of all is that, if I'm right, if this is what torments our killer, we can be sure that he won't stop. More than a month passed between the murders of Carla and Ainhoa, and barely three days between the murders of Ainhoa and Anne; he feels provoked, confident, and like he has a lot of work to do. He's going to continue recruiting young girls to return to purity . . . Even the way he arranges their hands facing upward symbolizes surrender and innocence. Where have you seen hands and expressions like these before?" She looked at Iriarte and pointed at him with her finger.

"Inspector, can you bring me the calendars from your desk?"

Iriarte was back in barely two minutes. He put a calendar with a picture of the Immaculate Conception and another with a picture of Our Lady of Lourdes on the table. The virgins smiled, full of grace, as they held their open hands at either side of their bodies, generous and without any reserve, showing their palms, from which shone rays of sunlight.

"There you have it!" exclaimed Amaia. "Like virgins."

"This guy is completely crazy," said Zabalza, "and the worst thing is that if there's one thing we can be sure of, it's that he's not going to stop until we make him."

"Let's update his profile," said Amaia.

"Male, age between twenty-five and forty-five," said Iriarte.

"I think we can narrow it down a bit more. I'm inclined to think that he's older. This resentment he shows toward youth doesn't really match up with a young man. There's nothing impetuous about him, he's very organized, he takes everything he might need with him to the scene, and yet he doesn't kill them there."

"He must have some other place, but where could it be?" asked Montes.

"I don't think it can be a building, at least not a house. It's impossible that all the girls would agree to go to a house, and we have to remember that they didn't put up a fight, with the exception of Anne, who resisted at the end, at the moment he attacked her. There are two possibilities: either he stalks them and carries out surprise attacks somewhere he might be seen, which doesn't really fit his modus operandi, in my opinion, or he persuades them to go somewhere or, even better, takes them there himself, which implies that he has a car, a large car, because he has to transport the body afterward . . . I prefer the latter theory," said Amaia.

"And, bearing in mind what's going on, do you think girls would get into just anyone's car?" asked Jonan.

"They might not in Pamplona," explained Iriarte, "but in a small town it's normal. You're waiting for the bus and some neighbor or other stops and asks where you're heading; if it suits them they'll give you a ride. It's not at all unusual and would confirm the fact that it's someone from the town who's known them since they were little and who they trust enough to get into his car."

"Okay, a white man, age between thirty and forty-five, perhaps slightly older. It's likely he lives with his mother or elderly parents. It's possible he had a very strict upbringing, or entirely the opposite, that he ran wild as a child and he created his own moral code that he now applies to the world. It's also possible that he suffered abuse as a child or that he lost his childhood in some way. Perhaps his parents died. I want you to look for any man who has a history of harassment, indecent exposure, loitering . . . Ask the couples who hang out around there whether they know of or have heard about any incidents. Remember, these delinquents don't just appear, they come from somewhere. Look for men who lost their families as a result of violence, orphans, victims of abuse, loners. Question every man in the Baztán Valley with a history of abuse or harassment. I want everything added to Jonan's database and, while we haven't got anything else to go on, we'll continue questioning the families, friends, and closest acquaintances.

"Anne's funeral and burial are taking place on Monday. We'll carry out the same process we did for Ainhoa's, and at least we'll have some material to compare. Make a list of all the men who attended both funerals and match the profile. Montes, it would be interesting to speak to Carla's friends to find out whether anyone recorded the funeral or burial on a cell phone or took photos. It occurred to me when Jonan said that Ainhoa's friends didn't stop crying or talking on their phones. Teenagers don't go anywhere without their phones, so check it out," she said, leaving out the "please" on purpose. "Zabalza, I'd like to speak to someone from the Guardia Civil's Nature Protection Service or the forest rangers. Jonan, I want all the information you can find about bears in the valley, sightings . . . I know they've got a few GPS tagged, let's see what they can tell us. And I want to know immediately if anyone finds anything, no matter what time it is. This monster is out there and it's our job to catch him."

Iriarte came over as the other officers left.

"Inspector, go along to my office. You've got a phone call from the general commissioner in Pamplona."

Amaia picked up the phone.

"I'm afraid I can't give you any good news, Commissioner. The investigation's moving forward as fast as possible, although I'm afraid the killer is quicker than we are."

"It's all right, Inspector. I think I've put the investigation in the best possible hands. I received a phone call an hour ago from a friend, someone connected to the *Diario de Navarra*. Tomorrow they'll be publishing an interview with Miguel Ángel de Andrés, Carla Huarte's boyfriend who was in prison accused of her murder. As you know, he's been released. There's no need to tell you where that leaves us. In any case, that's not the problem: in the course of the interview, the journalist insinuates that there's a serial killer on the loose in the Baztán Valley, that Miguel Ángel de Andrés was freed after it was discovered that the murders of Carla and Ainhoa are linked and, on top of all this, the murder of the latest girl, Anne"—it sounded like he was reading from notes—"Urbizu, will be made public tomorrow."

"Arbizu," Amaia corrected him.

"I'll fax you a copy of the articles exactly as they're going to appear tomorrow. I warn you that you're not going to like them, they're revolting."

Zabalza came back with two printed sheets on which several sentences appeared to have been underlined.

"Miguel Ángel de Andrés, who spent a month in Pamplona prison accused of the murder of Carla Huarte, confirms that the officers are linking the case with the recent murders of young girls in the Baztán Valley. The killer slashes their clothes, and hairs of nonhuman origin have been found on the bodies. A terrible lord of the woods who kills within his domains. A bloodthirsty *basajaun*."

The article about Anne's murder was headlined, "Has the *Basajaun* Struck Again?"

11

T HE ENORMOUS Baztán forest, which before its transforma-
tion by man consisted of beech woods up in the mountains, oak
woodland on the low ground, and chestnut, ash, and hazel trees in
between, now seemed to be almost entirely covered in beech trees,
which reigned despotically over all the rest. Meadows and scrubland
comprising furze or gorse, heather, and ferns made up the carpet
on which generation after generation of Baztáneses walked, a truly
magical place comparable only to the forest at Irati but now stained
by the horror of murder.

The wood always gave Amaia a secret feeling of proud belonging,
although its immense size also gave her a sense of fear and vertigo.
She loved it, but hers was a reverent and chaste love based upon
silence and distance. When she was fifteen, she had briefly joined
a hiking group. Walking in their boisterous company hadn't been
as pleasant as she'd expected, and she quit after three outings. She
returned to the woodland paths only once she'd learned to drive,
attracted again by the forest's magnetic pull. She had been amazed
to discover that being alone on the mountain provoked in her a
terrifying anxiety, the sensation of being watched, of being in a forbidden place or of committing an act of sacrilege. Amaia had gone
back down to her car and returned home, excited and unnerved by
the experience, and conscious of her atavistic fear, which seemed
ridiculous and childish in Aunt Engrasi's living room.

But the investigation had to continue, and Amaia returned to the thick undergrowth of the Baztán forest. Winter's death throes were more noticeable in the forest than anywhere else. The rain that had been falling all night was taking a break now, leaving the air cold and heavy, weighed down by humidity that penetrated both her clothes and her bones, so that she shivered, in spite of the heavy blue anorak James had made her wear. Darkened by the excess water, the tree trunks shone like the skin of an ancient reptile in the tentative February sun. The trees that hadn't lost their leaves gleamed with a green worn by the winter, the gentle breeze revealing silvery reflections on the undersides of their leaves. The presence of the river could be detected farther down in the valley, flowing down through the woods and acting as a mute witness to the horror with which the killer had adorned its banks.

Zipping up his jacket, Jonan increased his pace until he reached her side.

"There they are," he said, pointing out the Land Rover with the forest rangers' emblem on it.

The two uniformed men watched them approach from some distance away, and Amaia guessed that they were making some kind of jokey remark because she saw them look away and laugh.

"Here we go, the typical yokel comments about girls," murmured Jonan.

"Easy, tiger, it's not a big deal," she muttered as they approached the men.

"Good afternoon. I'm Inspector Salazar from the Policía Foral's homicide team; this is Deputy Inspector Etxaide," she introduced them.

The two men were extremely thin and wiry, although one of them was almost a head taller than the other. Amaia noticed that the taller man stood up straighter on hearing her rank.

"I'm Alberto Flores, Inspector, and this is my colleague Javier Gorria. We're in charge of keeping watch over this area. It's a very big area, more than fifty square kilometers of woodland, but if we can help you in any way, you can be sure that we will."

Amaia looked at them in silence without replying. It was an intimidation tactic that almost never failed, and it worked this time too. The ranger who had stayed leaning against the Land Rover stood up and took a step forward.

"Ma'am. We'll do everything we can to help. The bear expert from Huesca arrived an hour ago, he's parked a bit farther down," he said, indicating a bend in the road. "If you'll come with us, we'll show you where they're working."

"Good, and you can call me 'Inspector.'"

The path became narrower as they went into the wood, opening out again in small clearings where the grass grew green and fine like a beautiful garden lawn. In other areas the wood formed a sheltered, sumptuous, and almost warm maze, an impression reinforced by the endless carpet of pine needles and leaves that stretched before them. The water hadn't penetrated as far into that level, scrubby area as it had done on the slopes, and great dry, springy patches of windblown leaves crowded around the bases of the trees as if forming natural beds for the forest-dwelling *lamias*. Amaia smiled as she remembered the legends Aunt Engrasi had told her as a child. In the middle of the forest it didn't seem so far-fetched to accept the existence of the magical creatures that shaped the past of the people of the region. All forests are powerful, some are frightening by dint of being deep or mysterious, others because they are dark and sinister. The Baztán forest is enchanting, with a serene, ancient beauty that effortlessly brings out people's most human side, the most childlike part of them, which believes in the fantastical fairies with their webbed ducks' feet that used to live in the forest. These fairies would sleep all day and come out at nightfall and comb their long blond hair. A *lamia* would give her golden comb to any man who was sufficiently seduced by her beauty to spend the night with her in spite of her ducklike feet, thus granting him his heart's desire.

Amaia felt the presence of such beings in that forest so tangibly that it seemed easy to believe in a druid culture, the power of trees over men, and to imagine a time when the communion between magical beings and humans was a religion throughout the valley.

"Here they are, the Ghostbusters," said Gorria, not without a hint of sarcasm.

The expert from Huesca and his assistant were wearing garish orange overalls and were each carrying a silver-colored briefcase similar to the ones used by forensics officers. When Amaia and Jonan reached them, they seemed absorbed in observing the trunk of a beech tree.

"It's a pleasure to meet you, Inspector," said the man, holding out his hand. "I'm Raúl González and this is Nadia Takchenko. If you're wondering why we're wearing these clothes, it's because of the poachers. Nothing appeals to those riffraff like the rumor that there's a bear in the area, and you'll see them popping out from all kinds of places, even under rocks, and that's no joke. The big macho Spaniard sets out to catch a bear, and he's so terrified that the bear might catch him first that he'll shoot at anything that moves . . . It wouldn't be the first time they've shot at us thinking we were bears, hence the orange overalls. You can see them two kilometers away. In the Russian forests everybody wears them."

"What have you got to tell me? *Habemus* bear or not?" asked Amaia.

"Dr. Takchenko and I believe it would be too precipitate to confirm or refute something like that at this stage, Inspector."

"But you can at least tell me whether you've come across any sign, any clue . . ."

"We could say yes, we've undoubtedly come across traces that indicate the presence of large animals, but nothing conclusive. In any case, we've only just arrived. We've barely had time to inspect the area and the light is almost gone," he said, looking at the sky.

"Tomorrow at dawn we will get down to work, is that how you say it?" asked Dr. Takchenko in strongly accented Spanish. "The sample you sent us is certainly from a plantigrade. It would be very interesting to have a second sample."

Amaia decided it was best not to mention that the sample had been found on a corpse.

"You'll have further samples tomorrow," said Jonan.

"You can't tell me anything else, then?" persisted Amaia.

"Look, Inspector, the first thing you ought to know is that bears aren't often sighted. There have been no reports of a bear coming down into the Baztán Valley since the year 1700, which is when the last recorded sightings occurred. There's even a register that lists the compensation paid to the hunters who killed one of the last bears in this valley. Since then, nothing. There's no official record that a bear has come down this low, although there have always been rumors among the people in the area. Don't misunderstand me, this is a marvelous place, but bears don't enjoy company, company of any kind, not even their own kind. And especially not human company. It would be quite rare for a man to come across one by chance; the bear would smell him from several kilometers away and head away from the human without their paths crossing . . ."

"And what if a bear had, by chance, come down as far as the valley, following the scent of a female, for example? My understanding is that they're capable of traveling hundreds of kilometers with that as a lure. And what if it was attracted by something special?"

"If you're referring to a corpse, it's quite unlikely. Bears don't eat carrion. If there's a shortage of prey, they gather lichen, fruit, honey, young shoots, almost anything rather than carrion."

"I wasn't talking about a corpse, more something like processed foods . . . I'm afraid I can't be more specific."

"Bears are strongly attracted to human food. In fact, the chance to sample processed food is what leads bears to approach populated areas to search for garbage cans instead of hunting, unable to resist the scent of it."

"In that case, could a bear feel so attracted by the scent of processed food that it would approach a corpse, if that corpse smelled of it?"

"Yes, if we assume that a bear had come down as far as the Baztán Valley, which is pretty unlikely."

"Unless they've confused a bear with a, how do you say it? With a sobaka again," laughed Dr. Takchenko. Dr. González looked toward the forest rangers, who were standing a few steps farther away.

"Dr. Takchenko is referring to the supposed discovery of a bear's body very near here in August 2008. Following an autopsy, it was found to be that of a large sobaka dog. The authorities made a big fuss over nothing."

"I remember the story, it was in the papers. But on this occasion, aren't you the ones who are confirming that we're dealing with bear hairs?"

"Of course the hairs you sent us belong to a bear, although . . . In any case, I can't tell you anything more at the moment. We'll be here for a few days. We'll inspect the places where the samples were found, and we'll set up cameras at strategic points to try and film it, if there is one around here."

They picked up their briefcases and went back up the path along which the others had come. Amaia moved forward a few meters, walking between the trees, trying to find the traces that had so interested the experts. She could almost sense the hostile presence of the forest rangers behind her.

"And what can you tell me, gentlemen? Have you noticed anything out of the ordinary in the area? Has anything caught your attention?" she asked, turning around so as not to miss their reactions.

The two men looked at one another before answering.

"Are you asking whether we've seen a bear?" asked the shorter one in an ironic tone.

Amaia looked at him as if she'd only just noticed his presence and was still deciding how to classify him. She went over to him until she was so close she could smell his aftershave. She saw that he was wearing an Osasuna T-shirt beneath his khaki uniform shirt.

"What I'm asking, Señor Gorria—it is Gorria, isn't it?—is whether you've noticed anything worth mentioning. An increase or decrease in the number of deer, wild boar, rabbits, hares, or foxes; attacks on livestock; unusual animals in the area; poachers, suspicious day-trippers; reports from hunters, shepherds, or drunks; UFO sightings or the presence of a T. rex . . . absolutely anything . . . And, of course, bears."

A red flush spread down the man's neck and up to his forehead like an infection. Amaia could almost see the small drops of sweat forming on the taut skin of his cheeks; even so, she remained at his side a few seconds longer. Then she took a step back without dropping her gaze and waited. Gorria turned to his colleague again, looking for support that was not forthcoming.

"Look at me, Gorria."

"We haven't seen anything out of the ordinary," Flores intervened. "The forest has its own heartbeat, and its natural equilibrium seems unchanged. I think it's highly unlikely that a bear would come so far down into the valley. I'm not an expert on plantigrades, but I agree with the Ghostbusters. I've been working in these woods for fifteen years and I've seen a lot of things, I can tell you, some of them quite rare, or even extraordinary, like the body of the dog that appeared in Orabidea that the guys from the Environment Agency thought was a bear. We never believed it." Gorria shook his head. "But, in their defense, I will say it must have been the biggest dog ever and it was very decomposed and swollen. The fireman who retrieved the body from the pothole where it was found had an upset stomach for a month afterward."

"You've heard the expert, there's a possibility that it might be a young male who's strayed from his usual path following the scent of a female . . ."

Flores pulled a leaf off a bush and started folding it symmetrically in half while he considered his reply.

"Not this low down. If we were talking about the Pyrenees, fine, because however clever those expert plantigrade specialists think they are, it's likely that there are more bears than they've counted. But not here, not so low down."

"And how would you explain the fact that hairs that undoubtedly belong to a bear have been found?"

"If it was the Environment Agency that carried out the initial analysis, they'll be dinosaur scales until they discover that it's a lizard skin, but I don't believe it. We haven't seen tracks, animal bodies, dens, feces, nothing, and I don't think the Ghostbusters are going to find anything we've missed. There's not a bear here, in spite of the hairs, no sirree. Perhaps something else, but not a bear," he said, carefully unfolding the leaf he'd been folding, to reveal a dark, wet grid of sap.

"Do you mean another kind of animal? A large animal?"

"Not exactly," he replied.

"He means a *basajaun*," said Gorria.

Amaia put her hands on her hips and turned to face Jonan.

"A *basajaun*. Now, why didn't we think of that before? Well, I can see that your job leaves you time to read the papers."

"And to watch TV," added Gorria.

"It's on the TV too?" Amaia looked at Jonan in dismay.

"Yes, *Lo que pasa en España* ran a segment on it yesterday, and it won't be long before we've got reporters turning up here," he answered.

"Fuck, this is just like a Kafka novel. A *basajaun*. And what? Have you seen one?"

"He has," said Gorria.

Amaia didn't miss the way Flores glared at his colleague as he shook his head.

"Let me get this clear, you're telling me that you've seen a *basajaun*?"

"I didn't say anything," muttered Flores.

"Damn it, Flores! There's nothing funny about it, lots of people know about it, it's in the incident report, someone will end up telling her about it. You'd be better off doing it yourself."

"Tell me," insisted Amaia.

Flores hesitated for a moment before starting to speak.

"It was two years ago. A poacher shot me by mistake. I was in the trees taking a piss and I guess the bastard thought I was a deer or something. He got me in the shoulder, and I was left lying on the ground unable to move for at least three hours. When I woke up, I saw a creature squatting down at my side, its face was almost totally covered in hair, but not like an animal's, more like a man whose beard starts right below his eyes, intelligent, sympathetic eyes, almost human, except the iris covered almost the whole eye; there was barely any white, like a dog's eyes. I fainted again. I woke up when I heard the voices of my colleagues who were looking for me. Then it looked me in the eyes one more time and raised a hand, as if it were waving goodbye, and it whistled so loudly that my colleagues heard it almost a kilometer away. I passed out again, and when I woke up I was in the hospital."

He had folded the leaf up again while he'd been talking, and now he cut it into tiny pieces with his thumbnail.

Jonan went and stood next to Amaia and looked at her before speaking. "It could have been a hallucination as a result of the shock from being shot, the loss of blood, and knowing that you were alone on the mountain. It must have been a terrible moment. Or perhaps the poacher who shot you felt remorse and stayed with you until your colleagues arrived."

"The poacher saw that he'd shot me, but according to his own statement, he thought I was dead and he ran away like a rat. They stopped him hours later for a Breathalyzer test, which was when he told them what had happened. Ironic, huh? I still have to be grateful to the bastard. If he hadn't confessed, they wouldn't have found me. As for hallucination as a result of shock of being shot, it's possible, but in the hospital they showed me an improvised bandage made of overlapping leaves and grasses arranged to form a kind of imperme-able dressing that prevented me from bleeding to death."

"Perhaps you put the leaves there yourself before you lost con-sciousness. There are known cases of people who after suffering an amputation while alone have put on a tourniquet, preserved the amputated limb, and called the emergency services before losing consciousness."

"Sure, I've read about that online, but tell me something: How did I manage to press hard enough to keep the wound closed while I was unconscious? Because that's what that creature did for me, and that was what saved my life."

Amaia didn't answer. She raised her hand and put it over her mouth as if holding back something she didn't want to say.

"I see I shouldn't have told you about it," said Flores, turning to-ward the path.

12

NIGHT HAD fallen when Amaia reached the entrance of the Church of Santiago. She pushed the big door, almost sure that it would be closed, and was a little surprised when it opened smoothly and silently. She smiled at the idea that they could still leave the church doors unlocked in her hometown. The altar was partially lit, and a group of fifty or so children were sitting in the front few pews. She dipped her fingers in the holy water stoup and shivered slightly as the icy drops touched her forehead.

"Have you come to collect a child?"

She turned toward a woman in her forties with a shawl around her shoulders.

"Excuse me?"

"Oh, sorry, I thought you'd come to collect one of the children." It was obvious the woman had recognized her. "We were giving the first Communion classes," she explained.

"This early? We're still in February."

"Well, Father Germán likes to do these things properly," she said, with an apologetic shrug. Amaia remembered his long-winded speech during the funeral about the evil that surrounds us and wondered how many other things the parish priest of Santiago liked to do properly. "In any case, I don't think we have that much time left, just March and April, and then the first group are due to make their first Communion on the first of May." She suddenly stopped.

"Sorry, I'm sure I'm delaying you, you must be here to speak to Father Germán, aren't you? He's in the sacristy. I'll go and let him know you're here."

"Oh, no, don't trouble yourself. The truth is that I've come to the church for personal reasons," she said, employing an almost apologetic tone for the last two words, which immediately gained her the sympathy of the catechist, who smiled at her and took a few steps back like a selfless servant withdrawing.

"Of course, may God be with you."

Amaia walked up the nave, avoiding the main altar and stopping in front of some of the carvings that occupied the side altars, thinking all the while about those young girls and their washed faces, devoid of makeup and life, that someone had taken it upon himself to present as beautiful works of macabre imagery, beautiful even in that state. She gazed up at the saints and the archangels and the mourning virgins, their tense, pale faces bereft of color, expressing purity and the ecstasy achieved through agony, a slow torture, desired and feared in equal measure, and accepted with an overwhelming submission and surrender.

"That's what you'll never achieve," whispered Amaia.

No, they weren't saints, they wouldn't surrender themselves in a submissive and selfless manner. He would have to snatch their lives from them and steal their souls.

Leaving the Church of Santiago, she walked slowly, taking advantage of the darkness and the intense cold that had left the streets empty in spite of the early hour. She crossed the church gardens and admired the beauty of the enormous trees that surrounded the building, their height competing with that of the church spires, conscious of the strange sensation that came over her in those almost deserted streets. The urban center of Elizondo was spread across the plain at the bottom of the valley, and its layout was heavily influenced by the course of the River Baztán. It had three main streets, which ran parallel to one another and constituted the town's historic center, where the grand buildings and other houses built in the typical local style still stood.

Calle Braulio Iriarte ran along the northern bank of the River Baztán and was linked to Calle Jaime Urrutia by two bridges. The latter was the old main street until the construction of Calle Santiago, and it ran along the southern bank of the river. Crammed with spacious town houses and the construction of the highway from Pamplona to France at the start of the twentieth century, Calle Santiago was the starting point of the area's urban expansion.

Amaia arrived at the main square feeling the wind between the folds of her scarf as she looked at the brightly lit esplanade, which no longer possessed half the charm it must have had in the previous century when it had mostly been used for playing *pelota*. She went over to the town hall, a noble building dating from the end of the eighteenth century, which had taken Juan de Arozamena, a famous local stonemason, two years to build. On its façade was the familiar checkered coat of arms with the inscription BAZTÁN VALLEY AND UNIVERSITY, and in front of the building, at the bottom left of the façade, was a stone known as a *botil harri*, which was used for the type of *pelota* known as *laxoa*, in which the players wore gloves.

She reached out and touched the stone almost ceremonially, feeling how the cold spread up through her hand. Amaia tried to imagine how the square would have been. The two teams of four *pelotaris* would have lined up facing each other, a little like a game of tennis with too many players and no net, each with a *laxoa*, or glove, instead of a racket to pass the ball among themselves. In the nineteenth century this game had fallen into decline. Even so, she remembered her father once telling them that one of his grandfathers had been a great fan of the game and ended up gaining a reputation as a glove maker thanks to the quality of the gloves he sewed himself, using leather that he also treated and tanned.

This was her hometown, the place in which she had lived for most of her life. It was a part of her, like a genetic trace, it was where she returned to in her dreams, when she wasn't dreaming about the dead bodies, assailants, killers, and suicides that mingled obscenely in her nightmares. But when her sleep was calm, she went back to those streets and squares, to those stones, to the place she had always wanted to leave. A place she didn't know if she loved or not. A place that no longer existed, because what she was starting to miss now was the Elizondo of her childhood. However, now that she had returned almost sure there would be signs of definite change, she found things were pretty much the same. Yes, perhaps there were more cars in the streets, more streetlights, flower beds, and little gardens that painted the face of the town like fresh makeup. But not so much that it prevented her from seeing that its essence hadn't changed, that everything was still the same underneath.

She wondered whether the Alimentación Adela grocery or Pedro Galarregui's shop on Calle Santiago were still open, or the stores like Belzunegui or Mari Carmen where her mother used to buy their clothes, the Baztánesa bakery, Virgilio's shoe shop, or Garmendia's junk shop on Calle Jaime Urrutia. And she knew that it wasn't even this Elizondo that she missed, but rather the older and more visceral one, the place that formed part of her being and that would die in her only with her last breath. The Elizondo of harvests ruined by plagues, of children dying in the whooping cough epidemic of 1440. The Elizondo whose people had changed their customs to adapt themselves to a land that was initially hostile, a people determined to stay in that place near the church that had been the origin of the town. The Elizondo of sailors recruited in the square to travel to Venezuela in the employ of the traders belonging to the Royal Gipuzkoan Company of Caracas. The Elizondo of Elizondarras who rebuilt the town after the River Baztán's terrible floods and the times when it burst its banks. In her mind, she recreated the image of the altar from one of the side chapels floating down the street along with the bodies of livestock. And of the residents lifting it over their heads, convinced that its presence in the middle of that quagmire could only be a heavenly sign, a sign that God hadn't abandoned them and that they should endure. Brave men and women, forged thus by necessity, interpreters of signs from nature, who always looked to the heavens hoping for pity from a sky that was more threatening than protective.

She turned back along Calle Santiago and went down as far as Plaza Javier Ziga, where she set off across the bridge and stopped in the middle. Leaning on the low wall, she murmured as she ran her fingers over the rough stone where its name, MUNIARTEA, was engraved. She stared into the blackness of the water that carried its mineral aroma down from the peaks. There was still a commemorative plaque in Calle Jaime Urrutia on the house that had belonged to the *serora*, the woman who had been responsible for looking after the church and the rectory, which marked the point reached by the floodwaters on June 2, 1913. That same river was now witness to a new horror, one that had nothing to do with the forces of nature but rather with the most absolute human depravity, which turned men into animals, predators who mingled with the righteous in order to be able to approach them, to be able to commit the most deplorable act, giving free rein to desire, anger, pride, and the insatiable appetite of the most disgusting gluttony.

A shudder ran down her back, and she snatched her hands from the cold stone and put them in her pockets with a shiver. She took one last look at the river and set off for home as it started to rain again.

13

AMAIA COULD hear James's and Jonan's voices mingling with the omnipresent murmur of the television as they chatted in Aunt Engrasi's little living room. It sounded like they were sitting separately from the six old ladies who were making a real din as they played poker at a hexagonal table covered with green baize that wouldn't be out of place in a casino. Her aunt had had it brought all the way from Bordeaux so that honor and a few euros could be gambled on it each afternoon. When they saw her in the doorway, the two men moved away from the gaming table and came over to her. James gave her a quick kiss as he took her hand and led her to the kitchen.

"Jonan's waiting for you, he needs to talk to you. I'll leave you alone."

The deputy inspector came forward and handed her a brown envelope.

"Chief, the report on the samples has arrived from Zaragoza. I thought you'd want to see it as soon as possible," he said, looking around Engrasi's enormous kitchen. "I thought places like this didn't exist anymore."

"You're right, they don't, believe me," she replied, pulling a sheet of paper out of the envelope, "This is . . . enlightening. Listen, Jonan, the hairs we found on the bodies come from wild boar, sheep, foxes and, although they're still waiting for confirmation on this, possibly a bear, although that's not conclusive. Furthermore, the epithelial fragments we found on the string are, wait for it, goatskin."

"Goatskin?"

"Yes, Jonan, yes, we've got Noah's fucking ark here. I'm almost surprised they haven't found elephant snot and whale sperm—"

"Any human traces?"

"Nothing human, no hair or fluids, nothing. What do you think our friends the forest rangers would say if they could see this?"

"They would say there's nothing human because it isn't a human. It's a *basajaun*."

"In my opinion, that guy's an idiot. As he himself explained, *basajauns* are supposed to be peaceful creatures, protectors of the life of the forest . . . He said that a *basajaun* saved his life, so you tell me how that fits in with our story so far."

Jonan looked at her, considering her comment.

"Just because the *basajaun* was there doesn't mean he killed the girls. It's more likely the opposite: as the protector of the forest, it's logical that he would feel responsible, insulted, and provoked by the presence of this predator."

Amaia looked at him in surprise. "Logical? . . . You're just having a laugh about all this, aren't you?"

Jonan smiled.

"You love all this crap about the *basajaun*, don't deny it."

"Only the bits that don't involve dead girls. But you know better than anybody that it's not crap, chief, and I speak with authority, since I'm an archaeologist and anthropologist as well as a police officer."

"That's rich. Okay, then, let's hear your explanation: Why do I know better than anybody?"

"Because you were born and grew up here. Surely you're not going to tell me you weren't brought up on these stories? They're not nonsense; they form part of the culture and history of the Basque Country and Navarra. And we mustn't forget that what is now considered mythology was originally a religion."

"Well, don't forget that in 1610 in this very valley, in the name of the most extreme forms of religion, dozens of women were persecuted and condemned and died on the fires of the auto-da-fé as a result of beliefs as ridiculous as this one, which have, fortunately, been left behind by evolution."

He shook his head, giving Amaia a glimpse of the knowledge hidden behind his deceptively modest title of deputy inspector.

"It's well known that religious fervor and fear fed by legends and ignorant peasants did a great deal of damage, but you can't deny that it constituted one of the most overwhelming belief systems in recent history, chief. A hundred years ago, one hundred and fifty at the most, it was unusual to find someone who claimed they didn't believe in witches, *sorgiñas*, *belagiles*, *basajauns*, the *tartalo* and, most important, in Mari, the goddess, genius, mother, guardian of the harvests and livestock, whose whims could make the sky thunder and cause hailstorms that left the town suffering the most awful famines. It reached a point where more people believed in witches than in the Holy Trinity, and this didn't escape the notice of the church, which saw how its faithful would leave after Mass only to continue observing the ancient rituals that had formed part of their families' lives since time immemorial. And the ones who waged all-out war on the old beliefs were the half-crazed obsessives like Pierre de Lancre, the inquisitor of Bayonne, who managed to reverse the balance of belief through their madness. What had always formed part of the people's beliefs suddenly became something damned, to be persecuted, the object of absurd denunciations which, in most cases, were made in the hope that those who collaborated with the Inquisition would be free of suspicion themselves. But before this madness, the old religion had been an integral part of the inhabitants of the Pyrenees for hundreds of years without causing the slightest problem. It even coexisted with Christianity without significant issues, until intolerance and madness made their appearance. I think that our society could do with reclaiming some of the old values."

Impressed by these words from the normally rather introverted deputy inspector, Amaia said, "Jonan, madness and intolerance always make their appearance in every society, and you seem like you've just been talking with my aunt Engrasi . . ."

"No, I haven't, but I'd love to. Your husband told me that she reads cards and that sort of thing."

"Yes . . . and that sort of thing. You stay away from my aunt," said Amaia with a smile. "Your head's buzzing as it is."

Jonan laughed without taking his eyes off the roast that was sitting next to the oven waiting for its final browning before dinner.

"Speaking of buzzing heads, do you have any idea where Montes is?"

The deputy inspector was about to reply when he was overcome by a fit of discretion and bit his lip and dropped his gaze. His expression did not escape Amaia's notice.

"Jonan, we're conducting the most important investigation of our lives here, there's a lot riding on this case. Reputation, honor and, most important, getting that rat off the streets and making sure he doesn't do what he's already done to those girls to anybody else. I appreciate your sense of solidarity, but Montes is a bit of a loose cannon and his behavior could seriously interfere with the investigation. I know how you feel, because I feel the same. I still don't know what to do about it, and of course I haven't reported him, but much as it hurts me, much as I respect Fermín Montes, I won't allow his irresponsible behavior to prejudice the work of so many professionals who are slogging their guts out, ruining their eyesight, and losing sleep over this. Now, Jonan, tell me: What do you know about Montes?"

"Well, chief, I agree with you, and you already know my loyalty lies with you. If I haven't said anything before it's because it seemed to me to be something of a personal nature . . ."

"I'll be the judge of that."

"At lunchtime today I saw him eating at the Antxitonea restaurant . . . with one of your sisters," he finished in a mumbled rush.

"With his sister?" she said in surprise.

"No, with *your* sister."

"My sister? My sister Rosaura?"

"No, the other one, with your sister Flora."

"With Flora? Did they see you?"

"No. You know it has a semicircular bar that runs from the entrance and goes back toward the entrance to the *pelota* court. I was by the window with Iriarte, but I saw them come in. I was going over to say hello, but then they went into the dining room and it didn't seem appropriate for me to follow them. When we left half an hour later, I saw through the window into the bar that they had ordered and were about to eat."

~

Jonan Etxaide had never let rain intimidate him. In fact, walking in a downpour without an umbrella was one of his favorite things and, in Pamplona, he would walk in the rain with his anorak hood pulled up whenever he could, the only one meandering slowly as everyone else hurriedly fled to the nearest cafés or lined up under buildings' treacherous eaves, which dripped huge drops, making them even wetter. He walked the streets of Elizondo admiring the smooth curtain of water that seemed to fall across the roads, producing a curious effect like a slanting wedding veil. Car headlights pierced the darkness, drawing watery ghosts in front of them, and the red of the traffic lights seemed to spill out as if it were a solid, forming a pool of red water at his feet. In contrast with the deserted sidewalks, there was a steady flow of traffic at that hour, as if everyone was in a rush to get somewhere, like lovers on their way to a tryst. Jonan walked along Calle Santiago to the square, fleeing the noise with rapid steps that slowed as soon as he drew near enough to make out the clean outlines of the buildings, which immediately transported him back to an earlier era.

He admired the façade of the town hall and the casino beside it, built at the start of the twentieth century, a meeting place for the wealthier residents. Many business and political decisions had been made behind those windows, probably more than in the town hall itself, in a time when social position and its exploitation had been even more important than they were now.

He went down Calle Jaime Urrutia, captivated by the rain and the evocative architecture of the beautiful houses. At number 27 there was a passageway, or *belena*, to Calle Santiago that provided a path between the houses and the fields, stables, and vegetable gardens, some of which had disappeared long ago as a result of the construction of the current road. Opposite the houses' *gorapes*, or porticoes beneath the houses, which were occupied by shops on one side of the square, was Elizondo's old mill, which had been converted into the electricity plant halfway through the twentieth century. The architecture of a town reveals as much about its inhabitants' lifestyles and preferences as a man's habits do about his future behavior, thought Jonan. Places can show character traits, like being from a good family and upbringing, and this one spoke of pride, valor, and endeavor, of honor and glory achieved not only by pure force but also by ingenuity and skill. It was not for nothing that the town's shield was a chessboard, which the inhabitants of Elizondo displayed with the pride of those who have earned their place in the world through honor and loyalty.

And in the middle of that place of honor and pride, an assassin dared to display his extraordinary, macabre work, like a despotic black king advancing implacably across the board and devouring white pawns. The same boastfulness, the same showiness and vanity as all the other serial killers who had come before him.

For Jonan, predicting, outlining, discerning the profile of a killer in the darkness had almost become an obsession, a kind of game of chess in which progressing to the next move was paramount. It was a case of a single move defining how the rest of the game would develop and which of the opponents would be defeated. He would have given anything to attend one of those courses Inspector Salazar had taken. But in the meantime he would have to content himself with being near her, working at her side and contributing to the investigation through his suggestions and ideas, which she seemed to hold in high regard.

14

ROSAURA SALAZAR was feeling the cold, a horrible chill that gripped her both inside and out, making her walk bolt upright and with her jaw so tightly clenched it gave her the strange sensation of biting down on rubber. She walked along the riverbank under her umbrella, trying to use the freezing temperature of the almost deserted streets to alleviate her pain, the pain she was carrying inside her, and which threatened to become a scream at any moment. Unable to contain the tears that were burning in her eyes, she let them fall, aware that her misery was not as intense and visceral as it would have been only a few months earlier. She felt angry with herself even so, and at the same time she was secretly relieved to realize that back then she had felt as if the pain might destroy her. But not now. Not anymore. The tears suddenly stopped, leaving her with the sensation of wearing a warm mask on her frozen face that was gradually cooling and hardening on her skin.

She was ready to go home, now that she knew those tears would not betray her bitterness. Dodging the puddles, she passed the *ikastola* and automatically dried the rest of her tears with the back of her hand when she saw a woman coming toward her. She sighed with relief when she saw that it was a stranger so she wouldn't have to stop and chat or even say hello. But then the woman stopped and looked her in the face. Slightly confused, Rosaura came to a halt. It was one of the girls who lived in the town whom she knew by sight. Although she couldn't remember her name. It might have been Maitane. The girl looked at her, giving her such an enchanting smile that, albeit timidly, Rosaura smiled back at her without really knowing why. The girl started laughing, just a soft hint of a laugh at first, then gradually louder, until her cackling filled the night. Rosaura wasn't smiling anymore; she swallowed and looked around to find the reason for the girl's laughter. And when she looked back at the girl, she saw that her mouth had twisted into a sneer as disdainful as her gaze as she continued laughing. Rosaura opened her mouth to say something, to ask, to . . . But it wasn't necessary, because she saw everything clearly, as if someone had removed the blindfold from her eyes. As the realization sank in, Rosaura was assailed by the waves of disdain, evil, and arrogance that seemed to radiate from the little witch. They surrounded her and made her feel sick, while the laughter ringing in her ears left her so ashamed she wanted to die. She felt faint and cold, and just as she came to the conclusion that this could only be a nightmare, the girl stopped laughing and continued walking, keeping her cruel eyes fixed on Rosaura until she had gone by. Rosaura walked another fifty meters without daring to look behind her, then she went over to the wall at the edge of the river and threw up.

15

THE MERRY gang had been meeting to play poker on winter afternoons for years. Engrasi was the youngest of the group at over seventy, and Josepa was the oldest at about eighty. Engrasi and three of the others were widows; only two of the women in the group still had their husbands. Anastasia's husband had turned out to be afraid of the winter cold in the Baztán Valley and refused to leave the house during those months, and Miren's would be doing the rounds of the bars drinking *txikitos* with his cronies.

When they got up from the gaming table and said goodbye until the next day, they would leave the room full of vibrant energy, like the tension in the air before a thunderstorm. Amaia liked the girls, really liked them, because they each had the air of assurance and enviable contentment of someone who is on her way home and has enjoyed the journey. She was aware that not all of them had had easy lives. They had experienced illnesses, the death of husbands, abortions, unruly children, family issues, and yet, in spite of all this, they had left all resentment and bitterness toward life behind them, and they arrived each day as cheerful as teenagers coming to dance outdoors at a *verbena* on a summer's evening, as wise as the Egyptian queens. If she was lucky enough to be an old lady one day, she would like to be like that, like they were, independent but at the same time deeply aware of their roots, energetic and vital, exuding a sense of triumph over life that you see in those elderly men and women who make the most of every day without thinking about death. Or perhaps thinking about it in terms of stealing another day or hour from it.

After gathering up their scarves and bags, demanding a rematch the following day, and distributing kisses, hugs, and appreciative comments about what a nice young man James was, they finally left, leaving the living room full of the black and white energy of a coven.

"Old witches," murmured Amaia with a grin.

She looked down at the envelope she was still holding, and her face fell. Goatskin, she thought. She looked up, met James's inquisitive gaze, and tried to smile without succeeding in the slightest.

"Amaia, the Lenox Clinic called, they want to know if we'll make it to the appointment this week or if we'll need to postpone it again."

"Oh, James, you know I can't think about that right now. I've got enough to worry about."

James's expression became one of annoyance. "Well, we'll have to tell them something in any case we can't keep postponing forever."

She noticed the irritation in his voice and turned toward him and took his hand. "It won't be forever, James, but I can't think about that right now, I really can't."

"You can't or you don't want to?" he asked, pulling his hand away in a gesture of rejection that he seemed to regret immediately. He looked at the envelope she was holding.

"I'm sorry. Can I help at all?"

She looked at the envelope and her husband again.

"Oh, no, it's just a puzzle we need to solve, but not now. Make me a cup of coffee and then come and sit with me and tell me what you've been up to all day."

"I'll tell you but without the coffee. I can see you're jittery enough without caffeine. I'll make you a herbal tea."

She sat down next to the fire in one of the winged armchairs that faced the hearth. She slipped the envelope down the side of the cushion while she listened to Aunt Engrasi, who was busy in the kitchen, chatting to James. She turned her gaze to the flames that were dancing as they licked at a log, and when James handed her the cup of steaming tea, she knew that she'd lost several minutes to the fire's hypnotic heat.

"It looks like you don't need me to relax," exclaimed James, pulling a face.

She turned to him with a smile.

"I always need you, to help me relax and for other things . . . It's the fire," she said, looking around, "and this house. I've always felt good here. I remember when I was little and I used to come and take refuge here when I'd argued with my mother, which happened often. I'd sit in front of the fire and stay there until my cheeks were burning or I fell asleep."

James put a hand on her head and stroked it very slowly down to her neck, pulled out the band that was holding her hair up and spread it out, opening it like a fan so it hung below her shoulders.

"I've always felt as if this were my true home. When I was eight I even used to pretend that Aunt Engrasi was my real mother."

"You never told me that."

"No, it's been a long time since I've thought about it—and, furthermore, it's a part of my past I don't like. And being here again seems to stir up all those feelings, like resurrecting old ghosts." She sighed. "I'm also very worried about this case . . ."

"You'll catch him, I'm sure of it."

"So am I. But I don't want to talk about the case now. I need a break. Tell me what you got up to while I was out."

"I went for a walk around town. I bought some of that delicious bread they sell in the bakery on Calle Santiago, the one that makes such good madeleines. Then I took your aunt to the supermarket on the edge of town, where we bought enough food to feed an army, then we ate some amazing black beans at a bar in Gartzain, and in the afternoon I kept your sister Ros company while she went to her house to collect some things. The car is packed with cardboard boxes full of clothes and papers, but I won't know what to do with them until Ros gets here. I don't know where she wants to put them."

"And where's Ros now?"

"Well, that's the bit you're not going to like. Freddy was home. He was slumped on the sofa surrounded by beer cans when we went in, and he looked like he hadn't showered for several days. His eyes were red and swollen, and he was snuffling away wrapped in a blanket and with used tissues scattered all around him. At first I thought he had the flu, but then I realized he'd been crying. The rest of the house was just as bad; it looked like a pigsty and, believe me, it smelled like one too. I waited by the door, and he didn't look too pleased when he saw me, but he said hello. Then your sister started gathering together clothes and papers . . . He was following her from room to room like a whipped dog. I heard them whispering and, when I'd already loaded up the car, Ros told me that she was going to stay for a while, that she needed to talk to him."

"You shouldn't have left her alone."

"I knew you were going to say that, but what could I do, Amaia? She insisted, and the truth is that his attitude didn't seem at all threatening, in fact, he seemed quite the opposite. He was depressed and sulky like a little boy."

"Like the badly brought up little boy he is," she commented. "But we can't trust him. In lots of cases violence occurs at the moment when the woman announces the end of the relationship. It's not easy breaking up with those lowlifes. They tend to resist with pleading, tears, and begging, because they know perfectly well that they're nothing without their women. And if all that doesn't work, they resort to violence, which is why you shouldn't leave a woman alone when she's going to break up with the sponger of the moment."

"If I'd seen a single sign of any cockiness, I wouldn't have left her, and in fact I did hesitate, but she assured me she'd be fine and she'd be home in time for dinner."

Amaia looked at her watch. In Aunt Engrasi's house, they ate supper at around eleven.

"Don't worry. If she's not here in half an hour, I'll go and get her, okay?"

She nodded, pursing her lips. They heard the sound of the door almost at the same time as they felt the wave of intense cold that arrived in the house along with Ros. They heard her moving things

around in the hall, suspected that she was taking longer than necessary to hang up her jacket, and when she finally came into the living
room she seemed drained, her face grim and ashen but serene, like
someone who has come to terms with pain. She greeted James, and
Amaia noticed a slight tremble in her cheek when her sister leaned
over to kiss her. Then Ros went over to the sideboard and picked up
a small packet wrapped in silk and sat down at the gaming table.

"Aunt Engrasi . . ." she whispered.

Engrasi came in from the kitchen, drying her hands on a piece of
paper towel and sat down opposite her.

It wasn't necessary to ask what they were doing or even to watch;
she had seen that deck of cards wrapped in its black silk thousands of
times. They were the cards her aunt used for the Tarot of Marseilles,
which she had seen her shuffle, deal, and cut, arranging them in
crosses or circles. She had even consulted them herself. But that had
been a long, long time ago.

SPRING 1989

She was eight years old. It was May, and she had just had her First
Communion. Her mother had been unusually attentive to her
in the days before the ceremony, showering her with affection to
which she was not accustomed. Rosario was a proud woman and
deeply preoccupied with presenting an image of the luxurious life-
style expected of people during that era, doubtless influenced by
the fact that she had always felt herself to be the outsider who had
come in and married the most sought after bachelor in Elizondo.
The business was doing well, but almost all the money was being
reinvested in improvements. Even so, when the moment had come,
each of the girls had had a new dress for her First Communion in
a style sufficiently different from the ones her sisters had worn that
no one could mistake it for a hand-me-down. She had been taken
to the hairdresser, where they styled the mane of blond hair that
hung almost to her waist, teasing it into pretty curls that seemed to

spring from beneath the tiara of little white flowers that crowned her head. She couldn't remember when she had ever felt so happy either before or after.

On the day after her First Communion, her mother made her sit on a bench in the kitchen, braided her hair, and cut it off. The little girl didn't know what was happening until she saw the thick braid on the table that her mother was trying to tie up and that she thought was some strange little animal. She remembered feeling violated when she touched her head and being blinded by her boiling tears.

"Don't be stupid," her mother spat at her, "it's almost summer and you'll be nice and cool, and when you're older you can make yourself an elegant hairpiece like the ladies in San Sebastián wear."

Even now she could remember her father's exact words when he came in, alerted by the sounds of her crying.

"For the love of God! What have you done to her?" He groaned, picking Amaia up and carrying her out of the kitchen as if they were fleeing from a fire. "What have you done, Rosario? Why do you do these things?" he whispered while he rocked the little girl in his arms and his tears wet her head. He settled her on the sofa as if she were made of glass and went back into the kitchen. She knew what would happen next, a litany of reproaches whispered by her father, her mother's contained shouts, which sounded like an animal struggling below the surface of the water and which would give way to his entreaties as he tried to convince, persuade, trick her mother into agreeing to take those little white pills that stopped her despising Amaia. She asked herself whether it was in any way her fault that she looked so little like her mother and so like her dead grandmother, her father's mother. Was that a reason for not loving your daughter? Her father would explain to her that her mother wasn't well, that she took pills so as not to behave that way toward her, but the little girl felt worse and worse.

She put on a jacket with a hood and fled into the blessed silence of the street. She ran through the deserted town, rubbing her eyes furiously in an attempt to control the seemingly endless flow of salty tears. She arrived at Aunt Engrasi's house and, as usual, didn't knock at the door. She climbed up onto a huge pot of coleus plants as tall as she was and took the key down from the door lintel. She didn't call out to her aunt, she didn't run through the house looking for her. Her tears stopped as soon as she saw the small bundle of black silk lying on the table. She sat down in front of it, opened it, and started to shuffle the cards as she had seen her aunt do hundreds of times.

Her hands moved clumsily, but her mind was clear and concentrated on the questions she would silently ask, so absorbed in the silky feeling of the cards and the smell of musk they gave off that she didn't even notice the presence of Engrasi, who watched her in amazement from the kitchen doorway. The little girl laid the cards out on the table using both hands, then she chose one, which she positioned in front of her, and continued choosing them one at a time until they formed a circle like the face of a clock. She looked at them for a long time, her eyes jumping from one to another, calculating, divining the significance of this unique combination that held the answer to her question.

Afraid of breaking the mystic concentration she was witnessing, Engrasi went over very slowly and asked softly, "What do they say?"

"What I want to know," replied Amaia without looking at her, as if she were hearing her voice through headphones.

"And what do you want to know, sweetheart?"

"If it will stop one day."

Amaia pointed to the card that took the place of the number twelve on the clock. It was the Wheel of Fortune.

"A big change is coming, I'll have better luck," she said.

Engrasi took a deep breath but remained silent.

Amaia drew a new card, which she placed in the middle of the circle, and smiled.

"You see," she said, pointing at it, "one day I'll leave this place and never come back."

"Amaia, you know you shouldn't read your own cards. I'm very surprised at you. When did you learn to do it?"

The girl didn't answer. She took another card and laid it across the other one. It was Death.

"It's my death, Aunt. Perhaps it means that I will only come back here when I'm dead so they can bury me here, with *Amatxi* Juanita."

"No, it's not your death, Amaia, but it is death that will make you come back."

"I don't understand. Who's going to die? What could happen to make me come back?"

"Pick another card and put it next to that one," ordered her aunt. "The Devil."

"Death and evil," the little girl whispered.

"That's a long way off, Amaia. Things become clearer little by little. It's still too early to be able to see that, and it's not for you to divine your own future. Leave it alone."

"Why shouldn't I, Aunt Engrasi? Because I think the future has already arrived," she said, uncovering her head in front of Engrasi's horrified gaze. It took her aunt a long time to console her, to get her to drink a little milk and eat some biscuits. However, she fell asleep as soon as she sat down in front of the fire that was burning in Engrasi's hearth, despite the fact it was May. Perhaps the fire had been lit to combat the glacial winter that hung over them both like a harbinger of death.

The cards remained on the table, proclaiming the horrors destined to befall that little girl whom Engrasi loved more than anybody else in the world and who had a natural gift for sensing evil. She only hoped that the loving God had also blessed her with the strength to stand up to it. She started to gather the cards and saw the Wheel of Fortune that represented Amaia's future, a waterwheel governed by two monkeys with neither judgment nor wisdom who turned the wheel as they saw fit and could send you tumbling head over heels with any one of those irrational turns. Amaia's birthday was barely a month away, the moment when her ruling planet would enter her sign, the moment when everything that had to happen would happen.

She sat down, suddenly tired, without taking her eyes off the child, who was sleeping by the fire, and her pale scalp, which was visible through the clumsy haircut.

16

ENGRASI UNWRAPPED the little bundle and handed the deck to Rosaura to shuffle.

"Do you want us to leave?" asked Amaia.

"No, no, stay. We'll only be about ten minutes, and we'll eat right afterward. It'll be a short consultation."

"Okay. I meant that you might need to say something of a personal nature, something that we shouldn't hear . . . you know, perhaps you might need some privacy."

"That won't be necessary. Rosaura reads the cards as well as I do; soon she'll be able to do it by herself. The truth is that she doesn't need me to interpret them, but, as you know, you shouldn't read the cards for yourself."

Amaia shrugged.

"I didn't know you knew how to read the cards, Ros."

"I haven't been doing it for long. Recently it's seemed like everything in my life is new, I haven't been doing anything for long . . ."

"I don't know why you're so surprised. All my nieces have the gift of reading the cards, even Flora could read them well, but you most of all . . . I've always told you, you'd be an extremely good tarot reader."

"Is that true?" asked James, interested.

"No, it's not true," said Amaia.

"Of course it is, sweetheart. Your wife is a natural receptor, the same as her sisters. They're all very perceptive, they only have to find a suitable vehicle to release their clairvoyance, and Amaia is the one in whom it's most developed . . . Just look at the job she's chosen, one where, in addition to method, tests and data, and intuition, the ability to see what's hidden plays an extremely important role."

"I'd call it common sense and a science known as criminology."

"Yes, and a sixth sense that comes into play when you're a good receptor. To have someone sitting in front of you and to say that she's suffering, she's lying, she's hiding something, she feels guilty, tormented, dirty, superior to other people, is as common for me in my consultations as it is for you in your interrogations. The difference is that people come willingly to me but not to you."

"That makes sense," commented James. "Perhaps you ended up becoming a police officer because you're a natural receptor like your aunt says."

"It's just as I say," declared Engrasi.

Ros handed the well-shuffled deck to her aunt, who began to draw cards from the upper part of the deck, arranging them in a circle forming the classic twelve-card spread known as the World, in which the card that takes the place of the twelve on a clock represents the person for whom they are dealt. Engrasi didn't say a single word but kept her gaze fixed on Ros, who was absorbed in looking at the cards.

"We could explore this one further," she said, touching one of them.

Her aunt, who had been waiting, smiled in satisfaction. "Of course," she said, gathering the cards and returning them to the rest of the deck. She gave them to Ros again, who shuffled them rapidly and put them on the table. Engrasi laid them out in the shape of a cross, the typical quick spread of six cards she used when she wanted answers to more concrete questions. When she had turned them all faceup, she gave a half smile, somewhere between confirmation and weariness, and, pointing with one of her fingers, declared, "There it is."

"Fuck," whispered Rosaura.

"Fuck indeed, little one, it's clearer than water."

James had been watching them with an enjoyment tinged with tension, like a little boy in the house of horrors at a traveling fair. While they had been laying out the cards, he had leaned over to Amaia to ask her in a low voice, "Why shouldn't you read the cards for yourself?"

"It's logical that you're not as objective when you're trying to understand things about yourself. Fears, desires, and prejudices can cloud your good judgment. They also say that it's unlucky and attracts evil."

"Well, that's also common in police investigations, which is why detectives should never investigate a case to which they are directly connected."

Amaia didn't reply; it wasn't worth arguing with James. She knew the fact that her aunt used tarot cards fascinated him. He had accepted it right from the start, classifying it as "something strange," a kind of family claim to fame, as if instead of reading the cards she had been a well-known folksinger or an old retired actress. Watching them deal out the cards in silence, she herself had had the feeling of being left out of something important that only they shared, and in a moment she felt as excluded as if they had made her leave the room. The frequent expressions of comprehension, a knowledge that was theirs alone and that was forbidden to her. Although it hadn't always been that way.

"That's all," said Rosaura.

Engrasi gathered up the deck, placed it in the middle of the silk handkerchief, wrapped it carefully, knotting the ends to form a tight little parcel, and put it back in its place behind the glass door.

"Now we'll eat," she announced.

"I'm starving," said James cheerfully.

"You're always starving." Amaia smiled. "God only knows where you put it all."

He busied himself setting the table and, when Amaia walked past carrying some plates, he leaned over to her and said, "Later, when we're alone, I'll tell you exactly where I put everything I eat."

"Shhh," she warned him, putting a finger to her lips and glancing toward the kitchen.

Engrasi came in carrying a bottle of wine, and they sat down to eat.

"This roast is really delicious, Aunt Engrasi," said Rosaura.

"I almost had to push Jonan out the door. He came to bring me a report and he could barely tear his eyes away from the food while we were talking . . . He even made a comment about people not eating like this anymore," added Amaia, pouring herself a glass of wine.

"The poor thing," said Engrasi. "Why didn't you invite him to stay? We've got roast to spare, and I like the look of that boy. He's a historian, isn't he?"

"He's an archaeologist and anthropologist," commented James.

"And a police officer," added Rosaura.

"Yes, and a very good one. He's still lacking experience and his perspective is always colored by his studies, but working with him is proving to be very interesting. Furthermore, his conduct is impeccable."

"Quite unlike Fermín Montes," said Aunt Engrasi casually.

"Fermín . . ." Amaia emptied all the air from her lungs in a great sigh.

"Is he causing you problems?"

"Well, he seems to be causing them at any rate . . . Everyone seems to be acting strangely recently, as if a solar storm had short-circuited their common sense, or something. I don't know if it's the winter starting to drag on too long, or this case . . . Everything's so . . ."

"It's complicated, huh?" said her aunt, looking at her with a worried expression.

"Well, everything's happened very quickly, two murders in not much more than two days . . . You know I can't reveal any information, but the results from the analyses are very confusing; there's even a theory that suggests there might be a bear in the valley."

"Yes, that's what the paper said," Rosaura agreed.

"I've got some experts checking it out, but the forest rangers don't think it's a bear."

"I don't believe it either," said Engrasi. "There haven't been bears in the valley for centuries."

"Hmm, but they do think there is something . . . something big."

"An animal?" asked Ros.

"A *basajaun*. One of them even said he'd seen one a few years ago. What do you say to that?"

Rosaura smiled. "Well, there are other people who claim to have seen them."

"Yes, back in the eighteenth century, but in 2012?" Amaia was doubtful.

"A *basajaun* . . . What's that? Some kind of forest spirit?" asked James, his interest piqued.

"No, no, *basajauns* are real creatures, hominids about two and a half meters tall, with broad shoulders, long hair on their heads, and thick hair all over their bodies," Ros explained. "They live in the woods and are an intrinsic part of them, acting as their protectors. According to the legends, they make sure the harmony of the forest remains intact. And although they're not often seen, they used to be friendly with humans. At night the *basajaun* would watch over the sheep from a distance while the shepherds were asleep, and if a wolf came near he would wake the shepherds with loud whistles that had specific meanings and were audible several kilometers away. They also used to let the shepherds know from up on the highest mountains when a storm was coming, so that they would have time to take the flock to safety in the nearby caves. And the shepherds would thank them by leaving some bread, cheese, nuts, or milk from the sheep themselves on a rock or at the entrance to the cave, since *basajauns* don't eat meat."

"This is fascinating," said James, "tell me more."

"There's also a kind of genie, like the ones in the stories of *One Thousand and One Nights*, powerful, capricious, and terrible, who is female and called Mari. She lives in the caves and on the cliffs, always at the top of the mountains. Mari appears much earlier than Christianity, she symbolizes Mother Nature and the power of the earth. She's the one who watches over the harvests and livestock in labor, and who grants fertility not just to the soil and the animals but also to families. She can take on any natural form—a rock, a branch, a tree. These are always slightly reminiscent of her favorite form, a woman: a beautiful and finely dressed woman, like a queen. That's how she appears, and you never know it's her until she's gone."

James was smiling, enchanted, and Ros continued.

"She has many homes. She flies about from Aia to Amboto, from Txindoki to here. She lives in places that seem like crags, cliffs, or caves from the outside, but inside, at the end of a secret passage, are her luxurious and majestic halls, full of treasure. If you want to ask her a favor, you have to go to the entrance to her cave and leave her an offering there. And if what you want is a child, there's a place with a rock in the shape of a woman, which Mari sometimes inhabits to watch over the road. You have to go there and put a pebble you've brought with you from your own front door on the rock. After leaving your offering, you have to go away without turning around, walking backward until you can no longer see the rock or the entrance to the cave. It's a lovely story."

"Yes, it is," murmured James dreamily.

"It's mythology," interjected Amaia skeptically.

"Don't forget that mythology is based on beliefs that have endured for centuries, sister."

"Only for gullible bumpkins."

"Amaia, I can't believe you're saying such things. Basque-Navarrese mythology is recorded in reputable documents and essays by people like Padre Barandiarán, who, as a trained anthropologist, was not exactly a gullible bumpkin. And some of those ancient customs are still practiced today. There's a church at Ujué, in the south of Navarra, where women who want to become mothers complete a pilgrimage bringing a stone from their homes. There they leave it on a great pile of pebbles and pray to the statue of the Virgin, and the fact of the matter is that there are documents to show that women were already making pilgrimages to that place before the hermitage was built and that back then they used to throw their stones into a natural grotto, a kind of well or very deep mine. The efficacy of the ritual is famous. Tell me, what's Catholic, or Christian, or logical about taking a piece of stone from your house and asking Our Lady to give you a child? It's highly likely that, faced with the impossibility of putting an end to customs so deeply rooted in the community, the Catholic Church decided it was best to put a hermitage there and make a pagan ritual Catholic, like they did with the St. John's Day solstices and Christmas."

"The fact that Barandiarán collected them only means that they were very widespread, not that they were true," objected Amaia.

"But Amaia, what's really important? That fact that something is true or that so many people believe in it?"

"They're folk stories, destined to disappear. Do you really think that anyone is going to give these admittedly charming stories any credence in this era of cell phones and the Internet?"

Engrasi coughed gently.

"I don't mean to offend you, Aunt Engrasi," said Amaia as if seeking forgiveness.

"Faith grows scarce in these technological times," her aunt replied. "And tell me what good is any of it for preventing a monster from killing little girls and tossing their bodies onto the riverbank. Believe me, Amaia, the world hasn't changed that much. It's still a place that can be dark, where malign spirits surround our hearts, where the sea swallows up whole boats without anybody being able to find a trace of them, and there are still women who pray for the gift of conception. While there's darkness there will be hope, and these beliefs will continue to have a value and form part of our lives. We trace a cross in the top of a loaf of bread or hang an *eguzkilore* over the doorway to protect a house from evil; some people hang up horseshoes, German farmers paint their barns red and paint stars on them. We ask Saint Anthony to look after our animals and we pray to Saint Blaise to rid us of a cold . . . It may seem stupid now, but at the start of the last century a flu epidemic decimated Europe, and it originated here. And last winter, faced by the alarm caused by the influenza A outbreak, the governments spent millions on useless vaccinations. We've always asked for protection and help when we were most at the mercy of the forces of nature, and until not long ago it seemed impossible to live without it, whether it came from Mari or the saints and Virgins that arrived with Christianity. But when dark times come upon us, the old ways still work. Like when there's a power cut and you heat the milk in a metal pan over the fire instead of using the microwave. Is it a hassle? Is it complicated? Perhaps, but it works."

Amaia remained silent for a moment, as if absorbing what she had just heard.

"I understand what you're trying to tell me, Aunt Engrasi, but even so, I find it very difficult to believe that someone would walk to a rock or a cave to ask a genie to let her have a child. I think that any woman with half a brain would find herself a good stud."

"And if that doesn't work?"

"A reproductive specialist," said James, looking pointedly at Amaia.

"And if that doesn't work?" asked Engrasi.

"I suppose that then it would be left to hope . . ." Amaia gave in.

Her aunt nodded, smiling.

"I'd like to visit that place," said James. "Is it near here? Could you take me?"

"Of course," replied Ros. "We can go tomorrow if it's not raining. What do you think, Aunt Engrasi?"

"You go, but you'll have to forgive me, I'm not up to excursions like that anymore. The place is near where that girl, Carla, was found. You ought to see it too, Amaia, even if only out of curiosity."

James looked at her, waiting for her response.

"Tomorrow is Anne Arbizu's funeral, and I also have to go and see Flora and . . ." She remembered something, pulled out her cell, and dialed Montes's number. The call was picked up by the voice mail service, which invited her to leave a message.

"Montes, give me a call. It's Salazar. Amaia," she added, remembering that her sisters were also Salazars.

Ros excused herself and went toward the stairs, and James kissed Aunt Engrasi and caught his wife around her waist.

"It's best we go to bed."

Her aunt didn't move.

"Wait for her upstairs, James. Amaia, stay, please, I want to tell you something. Switch that light off, it's blinding me, put a couple of shots of orujo in the coffee, and sit here, opposite me. And don't interrupt." She looked her niece in the eyes and began to speak. "The week I turned sixteen I saw a *basajaun* in the forest. I used to go and collect wood every day until nightfall. Times were hard, and I had to collect enough for the ovens in the workshop, for the fireplace at home, and to sell. Sometimes I had to carry so much that, frustrated by my lack of strength, I would throw down my load at the side of the path and lie down on the ground and cry out of sheer exhaustion. That day, after crying for a while, I lay silently among the bundles of wood, asking myself how I would manage to carry them down to the town.

"Then I heard it. At first I thought it was a deer, which are very stealthy, unlike wild boars, which always make a hell of a racket. I raised my head above the heap of wood and I saw it. At first I thought it was a man, the tallest man I'd seen in my life. His torso was naked and very hairy, and he had a very long mane of hair that covered his whole back. He was scraping away at some bark with a small stick, collecting the bits with long, dexterous fingers and putting them into his mouth as though they were a real delicacy. He suddenly turned and smelled the air like a rabbit would. I was absolutely certain he knew I was nearby. With time, when I thought about it calmly, I reached the conclusion that he knew my odor very well as something that already formed part of the woods because I spent most of my life there. I would go up onto the mountain in the mornings as soon as the fog cleared, and I would work until midday. I would stop for a while with my sisters to eat the hot food our mother would bring us for lunch, then she and my older sister would take away the bundles we'd gathered during the morning on a little donkey we used to own, and I would continue working for a couple more hours or until darkness began to fall. My odor must have formed part of that area of the forest as much as that of a little animal would. We even had a pretty established spot where we would go to the toilet when we needed to, to avoid leaving shit all over the forest while we were hunting for wood. So the *basajaun* smelled the air, recognized me, and went about his business as if it were nothing, although he did turn around a couple of times with an uncomfortable look on his face, as if he expected to find someone standing behind him. He stayed there a few minutes longer and then went slowly away, stopping every so often to scrape little bits of bark and lichen from the trees. I stood and loaded myself up with the bundles with a strength that came from who knows where, although I know it wasn't panic. I was shocked, yes, but more like someone who's witnessed a miracle and can't believe she was the one who was chosen than like a little girl who's seen a bogeyman in the woods. I only know that when I arrived home I was as pale as if I'd dipped my face in a plate of flour and my hair was plastered to my head with a cold, clammy sweat that gave your grandmother such a shock she put me to bed and made me drink infusions of *pasmo belarra* until my throat was as dry as the woven sole of an *esparto*.

"I didn't say anything at home, I think because I knew that what I had seen was too bizarre for my parents to acknowledge, although I was sure what it was. I knew it was a *basajaun*: like all the children in the Baztán Valley, I'd heard the stories hundreds of times about *basajauns* and other creatures, some of them magical, who'd lived in the forest since long before men built Elizondo. The following Sunday, during confession, I told our priest we had then, Don Serafín was his name, a savage Jesuit who was a force to be reckoned with. And I can assure you there wasn't much that was angelic about him. He called me a liar, a trickster, and an idiot, and if that weren't enough, he came out of the confessional and dealt me a blow with his fist that brought tears to my eyes. Afterward he read me a sermon about the dangers of making up such stories, forbade me from mentioning the subject, even to my family, and gave me a penance of Our Fathers, Hail Marys, Credos, and Confiteors that took me weeks to finish, so I never told anyone about it ever again.

"Whenever I went to the forest to gather wood, I would make so much noise that I would frighten off any creature within a two-kilometer radius, I would sing the Te Deum in Latin so loudly I was almost shouting, and I was always hoarse when I got home. I never saw the *basajaun* again, although there were many times when I thought I saw signs that he had been in a place. Of course, they could have been left by deer or bears, which were still around then, but I always knew that my singing was a sign to him, that just hearing it would make him move away, that he was aware of my presence, that he accepted it, and that he avoided it as I avoided his."

Amaia looked at Aunt Engrasi's face. When she'd finished speaking, she continued to look at her niece with those eyes that were once as intensely blue as Amaia's and that now seemed washed-out like faded sapphires, although the alert, wise, and lively mind behind them still shone through.

"Aunt Engrasi," she began, "it's not that I don't believe that that was exactly how you experienced it and how you remember it, and I don't mean to be rude, but you've always had a lively imagination. Don't get me wrong, you know I don't think there's anything wrong with that . . . but you have to understand that I'm in the middle of a murder investigation and I have to look at it as an investigator . . ."

"You have excellent judgment," observed Engrasi.

"Have you considered the possibility," Amaia continued, "that what you saw wasn't a *basajaun* but something else instead? You have to bear in mind that girls of your generation weren't influenced by television and the Internet like they are nowadays, and yet, around here, and in rural areas in general, there are loads of legends like this. Look at it from my point of view. A prepubescent adolescent, alone all day in the woods, exhausted and half dehydrated from physical exertion, crying until she's worn out, perhaps even until she fell asleep. You seem like the ideal candidate for an apparition of the Virgin Mary in medieval times or alien abduction in the seventies."

"I didn't dream it. I was as awake then as I am now, and I saw it as plainly as I see you. But don't worry, I was expecting this reaction when I decided to tell you about it."

Amaia looked at her tenderly, and Engrasi smiled at her in turn, showing the perfect array of her false teeth, which for some unknown reason always made the inspector smile and experience an intense wave of love for her. Still smiling, her aunt pointed at her with a bony white finger, covered in rings.

"Yes, madam, I knew, and that's why, because I know how that little head of yours works, I've got another witness for you."

Her niece looked at her suspiciously. "Who? One of your poker cronies from the merry gang?"

"Be quiet, unbeliever, and listen. Six years ago, on a winter's afternoon after Mass, I found Carlos Vallejo waiting for me on the doorstep."

"Carlos Vallejo, my old schoolteacher?" Although it had been years since she had last seen him, the image of Don Carlos Vallejo that came to mind was as fresh as if she'd just left his classroom. His perfectly cut colored suits, his math textbook under his arm, his ever-neat mustache, his thick, graying hair slicked back with brilliantine, and his strong smell of aftershave.

"Yes, young lady." Engrasi smiled as she noticed her interest. "He was wearing hunting clothes that were completely soaking wet and covered in mud, and he even still had his rifle with him in its leather case. I was particularly surprised because, as I've said, it was winter and night was falling early. It wasn't the right time of day to go hunting, his clothes were drenched even though it hadn't rained for the last few days and, most of all, because of his face, which was as pale as a wet sheet. I knew that he was very fond of hunting. He'd sometimes driven past me in his car on his way back from the mountain in the middle of the morning, but he never wore hunting clothes around town . . . In fact, you know what they've always called him."

"The Dandy," murmured Amaia.

"Yes, indeed, the Dandy . . . Well, the Dandy had mud on his trousers and boots, and when I gave him a cup of chamomile tea I saw that his hands were covered with scratches and his nails were blacker than a coal miner's. I waited until he was ready to speak, since that's normally best."

Amaia nodded.

"He was silent for a long time with his gaze lost in the bottom of the cup, then he took a long sip, looked me in the eyes, and told me with all the elegance and good manners on which he has always prided himself, 'Engrasi, I hope you can forgive me for turning up at your house in this state.' I knew he wanted to say 'your consultation room.' I nodded slowly, waiting for him to continue."

"'I suppose you'll be surprised by my coming to you, but I didn't know where else to go, and I thought that you might, perhaps . . .' I encouraged him to go on until he told me, "'This morning in the woods I saw a *basajaun*.'"

17

T HE WHITEBOARD at the police station was covered with a Venn diagram the center of which was occupied by the pictures of the three girls. Jonan was going through the forensic reports over and over again while Amaia took small sips from the cup she held in her hands, which were wrapped around it for warmth. She looked at the whiteboard in an almost hypnotic trance, as if by studying those faces and words she might gain insight, some hint from the souls that were missing from the girls' dead eyes.

"Inspector Salazar," Iriarte interrupted her. He smiled when he saw her jump, and Amaia thought what a nice guy he was, with his office adorned with a calendar with pictures of the Virgin and a photograph of his wife and two blond little boys who smiled openly at the camera and must have inherited their mother's hair, since Iriarte's was sparse, black, and very fine.

"We've got the toxicology report on Anne. Cannabis and alcohol." Amaia read through the notes aloud.

" 'Fifteen years of age, a member of the Vincentian Marian Youth School gifted and talented program. Basketball team and chess club, library card. Her room contained: a pink bedspread, Winnie the Pooh stuffed animals, gossip magazines, and Danielle Steel novels.' Something doesn't seem quite right to me," she said, looking up at Zabalza.

"I thought the same, so this morning we spoke to a couple of

Anne's friends, and they told us a very different story. Anne lived a double life to keep her parents blissfully ignorant. According to her friends, she smoked pot, drank, and even did stronger stuff sometimes. She spent hours in online chat rooms and would publish risqué photos of herself on the net. According to them, she loved to show off her tits on the webcam. I'm quoting here: 'She was a slut disguised as a little angel, she even had an affair with a married man.'"

"A married man? Who? This could be very important. What else did they say?"

"They don't know who it was, or they don't want to say. It looks like the thing had been going on for a few months, but she was going to leave him; she told them the guy was getting obsessive and that it wasn't any fun anymore," he said, reading from his notes.

"For the love of God, Iriarte, I think we've struck gold here. She wanted to put an end to things and he killed her, perhaps he had some kind of relationship with Carla and Ainhoa too . . ."

"He might have with Carla. Ainhoa was a virgin, she was only twelve."

"Perhaps he tried, and when he was rejected . . . All right, I know it's a bit far-fetched, but we can look into this. Do we at least know whether he's from Elizondo?"

"The girls say he almost certainly is, although he might also be from a neighboring town or village."

"We need to find this guy who likes young girls. Get a warrant for the girl's computer and any diaries or notes that might be in her house, search her school locker too. Call the girls' parents and ask permission to speak to all her friends who are still minors, visit them at home . . . And I want everyone in plainclothes, the last thing I need is to make the people who ought to be collaborating feel uncomfortable. And Inspector," she said, looking at Iriarte, "not a word about this to Anne's parents for now. It's obvious they knew nothing about their daughter's double life."

She looked at her watch.

"I want everyone at the church or the cemetery in three hours' time, exactly the same operation we carried out for Ainhoa's funeral.

As soon as you've finished there, I want you all to come back to the station. Jonan's got an excellent digital photography program with really high resolution, and as soon as the images are ready, I want you here to pool our resources. Jonan, look and see if you can get anything from Anne's computer; really dig, I don't care if it takes you all night."

"Yes, chief, whatever it takes."

"Oh, and how's it going with the Ghostbusters from Huerta?"

"I've got a meeting with them at six this evening when they come back down from the mountain. I hope they'll be able to tell me something then."

"I hope so, too. Are you meeting them here?"

"Well, I suggested it, but the Russian one seems to be allergic to police stations or something like that. She tried to explain it to me on the phone, but I didn't understand half of what she was saying. We're meeting at the hotel where they're staying. The Baztán," he said, checking his notes.

"I know the one you mean. I'll try to drop by," said Amaia, putting a memo on her smartphone.

Zabalza burst into the room holding a sheaf of fax paper, which he placed on the table.

"They're calling from Pamplona, Inspector. Several media outlets want to cover the funeral and burial, and they're advising us to make a statement."

"That's Montes's job," she said, looking around. "Does anyone know where the hell he is?"

"He called this morning to say he wasn't feeling well and that he'd meet us at the cemetery."

Amaia snorted. "Well, I suppose it's possible . . . Whoever sees him first, please tell him to go to Inspector Iriarte's office as a matter of urgency. Zabalza, arrange a meeting for me with Anne's parents, please, around four in the afternoon if possible."

It had started raining an hour earlier, and the sweet scent of the flowers together with the mourners' damp jackets made the air inside the church difficult to breathe. The sermon was an echo of the previous ones, and Amaia paid it scant attention. Perhaps there were more people there—the morbid, the curious, and the journalists, whom the priest had allowed to observe the service on the condition that they did not record inside the church. Once again there were the same scenes of grief, the same cries of distress . . . And something new, a special atmosphere of horror that seemed to veil the faces of all those attending the funeral, subtle but omnipresent. In addition to the family, there was a large group of young boys and girls in the first few rows, undoubtedly Anne's classmates from school. Some of the girls were hugging one another and crying silently; their faces reflected the lack of energy she had also noticed in Ainhoa's friends. They had lost the natural brilliance of youth and the air of constant playfulness born of the confidence that they will never die. Death should have seemed a thousand light-years away for them, part of an unimaginable old age, but it had taken on a real and palpable presence. They were afraid, struck by the kind of fear that leaves you motionless and wishing you were invisible so death can't find you, and left ashen faced and old before their time by its proximity. All eyes were on Anne's coffin, where it stood in front of the altar, reflecting the light of the tall candles burning either side of it, and surrounded by the white flowers of a virgin bride.

"Let's go," whispered Amaia to Jonan. "I want to get to the cemetery before people start arriving."

The cemetery in Elizondo was located on a slight slope in the Anzanborda neighborhood, although to call the three large houses visible from the cemetery gate a neighborhood was a bit excessive. The slope, which was barely noticeable from the entrance, became more pronounced as you moved farther in among the graves. Amaia guessed it had been planned like that to avoid the frequent rains pooling inside the graves. Many of the tombs were aboveground and were closed by deep-set doorways, although in the lower part of the cemetery there were others that were more humble and traditional, marked by round stone slabs anchored in the earth.

These tombs brought to mind other elevated tombs: the ones

she had seen in New Orleans two years earlier. She had been taking part in a police exchange at the FBI's academy in Quantico, Virginia, which included a seminar on criminal profiling. The conference had finished with a trip to New Orleans, where part of the course on identification and concealment in the field was delivered, since a lot of crimes had been covered up by Hurricane Katrina, and remains and evidence continued to appear years later. Amaia had been surprised that the city still showed signs of the disaster so long afterward and yet retained a decadent and gloomy majesty redolent of the withered luxury associated with death in some cultures. One of the officers present, Special Agent Dupree, encouraged her to follow the procession of one of those magnificent funerals at which a jazz band accompanies the funeral party to the Saint Louis Cemetery.

"All the tombs here are elevated to prevent the seasonal floods from disinterring the dead," explained Dupree. "It's not the first time we've been visited by evil. The last time it was known as Katrina, but it's come many times before under different names."

Amaia looked at him, perplexed.

"I suppose you're surprised to hear an FBI agent talking this way but, believe me, this is the curse of my city; the dead can't be buried underground because we're six feet below sea level, so the bodies are piled up in stone tombs that can hold several generations or entire families, and I think that's the reason the dead don't rest in New Orleans, because they don't receive a Christian burial. It's the only place in the United States where cemeteries aren't called cemeteries but cities of the dead, as if the deceased somehow live on here."

Amaia stared at him before speaking.

"In Basque, the word for cemetery is *hilherria*. Literally, 'the town of the dead.'"

He looked at her with a smile. "We've already got several things in common: our close relationship with the French, our bull-running festivals on July seventh, and what we call our cemeteries."

Amaia came back to the present. Perhaps it was the idea of avoiding floods that had inspired the townspeople of Elizondo to design their new cemetery like this. In accordance with tradition, the original cemetery had surrounded the church, which at that time was just next to the town hall in the main square until eventually it was transported brick by brick and rebuilt on the site it currently occupied. The same was done with the cemetery, which moved to the Camino de los Alduides up in Anzanborda. There was only one entry in the town archives, which referred to the relocation of the graveyard for "reasons of public health," but it was easy to assume that if a great flood had knocked down the church, washing the stones from one of its towers so far away they couldn't be recovered, it could also wash the surrounding tombs away.

A skull stood guard above the cemetery gates like the shield above a city wall, its empty eye sockets keeping watch over the visitors, indicating who ruled over the city of the dead. There was a lone cypress just to the right of the entrance, a weeping willow a little beyond it, and a beech tree at the far end. A stone cross stood majestically in the middle of the graveyard, with four paved paths diverging from its foot, dividing the cemetery into perfect quarters among which the graves were distributed. The Arbizu family tomb was right at the beginning of one of the paths. On top of the pantheon rested an angel with an expression of indolence and boredom. Indifferent to human sadness, he seemed to be watching the grave diggers who had used some iron bars to roll the stone aside. Amaia went and stood next to Jonan, who seemed absorbed by the base of the stone cross.

"I always thought you only found stone crosses at crossroads," she commented.

"Well, you're mistaken, chief. The origin of those stone crosses is as old as it is uncertain. In spite of their undeniable link to Christianity, the fact that they're found at crossroads seems instead to be linked to a system of superstitions and beliefs that are more concerned with the underworld than with life on earth."

"But wasn't it the church that put them there?"

"Not necessarily. It's more likely the church Christianized them to absorb a pagan custom that was difficult to eradicate. The place where two roads cross has been considered a place of uncertainty since the olden days. You have to decide which road to follow without knowing whom you might cross paths with or who might come along the other path. Imagine it's the middle of the night with no light available and no signs to indicate which road to choose. The fear became so great that on reaching a crossroads, people would stop and wait for a while on the path along which they had come, listening, sharpening their senses, trying to discern the malign presence of a lost soul. There was a deep-rooted belief that those who had died a violent death and those who had killed them didn't rest in peace but wandered the roads looking for the right place to go, either to be avenged or to find someone to help them carry their burden. And a meeting with one of these beings could make you ill or even mad."

"Okay, I understand what you mean about crossroads, but why here, in the cemetery?"

"Don't look at this place as it is now. Perhaps before the cemetery was moved here, this was a place of uncertainty, perhaps three or four roads met here. Two of them are obvious, the ones to Elizondo and Beartzun; perhaps another led down the hill to Etxaide but has completely disappeared now that we have highways. Perhaps there was some need to sanctify the place."

"Jonan, it's a graveyard, it's all hallowed ground."

"Maybe I'm referring to an event that took place before the existence of the cemetery . . . They also used to erect crosses in places where a horrific act—a violent death, a rape—had been committed to purify them, and also in places where witches would meet. There are a lot of them around here. The cross has the double function of sanctifying a place and warning you that you're on uncertain ground. Or it may be that it was put in the cemetery because of its layout. Four paths," he said, pointing out how the place had been arranged, "perfectly laid out so they meet in the middle of the cemetery, but also, beneath it, in the underworld, which might be swarming with murderers and their victims."

Amaia looked at the young deputy inspector with admiration. "But would they have buried murderers in a graveyard? I thought they excommunicated them and they had to be buried outside holy ground."

"Yes, if they were known to be murderers. But if there are murderers who go unpunished today, imagine what it must have been like in the fifteenth century. A serial killer would have been in heaven, in all probability his crimes would have been attributed to some illiterate half-wit or other. The crosses were erected just in case, more as a defense against the occult than as a result of what was known to have happened. There's another argument that loses force in this case, since this one is inside a graveyard, which is that people weren't allowed to bury aborted babies, stillborn babies, or children who had died before being baptized in holy ground until well into the twentieth century. This presented a serious problem for the families who wanted to give their souls some kind of protection but were prevented from doing so by the law. In many cases, if the mother died in childbirth along with the baby, the family would hide the child between her legs in order to bury them together. Since burials weren't recorded, the families would go out in the middle of the night and bury their little ones at the foot of a cross, then carve their initials or a little cross on the base. And that was what I was looking for, but there's nothing here."

"Well, I can give you an anthropology lesson on that, if you'll let me. In the Baztán Valley, children who died before they were baptized used to be buried near their own home."

Amaia leaned forward and, on looking toward the entrance, thought she saw someone among the bushes that formed the boundary of the cemetery. She stood up, sure she'd recognized certain familiar features.

"Who is it?" asked Jonan from behind her.

"Freddy, my brother-in-law."

His gaunt face was dominated by the deep bags surrounding his red-rimmed eyes. Amaia took a step toward the hedge, but the face disappeared among the foliage. And then it began to rain. The countless umbrellas and the mourners' desire to hide themselves beneath them made the attempt to film the funeral much more difficult. Amaia spotted Montes positioned near Anne's parents. He acknowledged her with a nod and looked as if he was about to say something, but she gestured him to keep quiet.

Anne Arbizu's parents were old enough to be her grandparents. Anne had come to them when it seemed that there was no longer any hope of adoption, and she had been the center of their lives since then. The mother, who had clearly taken something, stood upright and was almost holding another woman, who might have been her sister-in-law, upright. Amaia had known them since she was a little girl, although she wasn't certain what the relationship between them was. Anne's mother held her arm protectively around the woman while she stared into space, her gaze falling somewhere between her daughter's coffin and the open grave in the ground. Anne's father was really crying. A few steps in front of his wife, he leaned forward, relentlessly caressing the coffin as if he was afraid to break the only connection that linked him to his daughter and brusquely rejecting the hands that tried to help him or the umbrellas that tried in vain to shelter him from the rain that was wetting his face and mingling with his tears. When they started to lower the coffin and he lost contact with the damp wood, he collapsed like a tree that has been cut down at its base, lying unconscious among the puddles that had formed on the gravel path.

It was his gesture that touched her soul, the father's refusal to let go of the coffin that was the last physical link to his daughter. This show of such intense love was enough to sweep aside the walls which, as a homicide detective, she should have used to protect her personal feelings. And it was the father's hand, in that gesture which made her secretly envy other parents she saw, that broke the dike holding back her emotions, and an ocean of fear, anxiety, and unfulfilled desire to be a mother flooded through the deep breach it opened. Assailed by the wave of emotions, Amaia took a few steps back and headed toward the stone cross, trying to disguise her uneasiness. The hand. That was the link. Although she had spent years trying to become pregnant, she didn't feel that special fascination for small babies she had seen in her friends or even in her own sisters; she didn't find her eyes drawn to babies held in their mothers' arms. But she was aware of the privilege she was missing out on when she saw a mother walking next to her child and holding him or her by the hand. The protection and confidence embodied by this intimate gesture was greater than any other that could exist between two human beings. Each small hand nestled into a larger one symbolized for her the love, devotion, and trust that she imagined were at the heart of being a mother, a role she had yet to play, that she might never play, depriving her forever of the honor of holding a child by the hand. Being a mother would allow her, through another being, blood of her blood, to make up for the happy childhood she had never had, the absence of love she had always felt from a deeply unhappy woman. Her own mother.

18

WHEN THE burial was over, the rain and the mourners
seemed to evaporate, to be replaced by a dense fog that
extended throughout the valley along the River Baztán, spreading
through the streets and making them seem, if possible, even sadder.
Frozen stiff, Amaia waited opposite the workshop for some time
until she saw her sister arrive.

"Well, well, the lady inspector! What an honor!" Flora joked.
"Aren't you supposed to be out there looking for a murderer?"

Amaia smiled and wagged her finger at her. "That's what I'm
doing."

Flora stopped with the key in her hand, suddenly interested and
perhaps a bit alarmed. "Here in Elizondo?"

"Yes, here. In a case like this, the murderer is often someone close
to the victim. If only we had one case . . . but there are three already.
It's got to be someone from here or somewhere very nearby."

They went into the workshop and were welcomed by the familiar
aroma Amaia had been breathing since her childhood and that lived
on in her memory. If she closed her eyes, she could almost see her
father in his white trousers and vest rolling out the sheets of puff
pastry with an enormous steel rolling pin while her mother weighed
the ingredients in a measuring jug, her hands covered in flour and
giving off the smell of aniseed, which Amaia would always associate
with her. She looked at the kneading trough, and a shiver ran up her

back and an intense feeling of nausea turned her stomach. She was suddenly stunned by an overwhelming wave of dark memories, and the echoes of the past made her freeze up completely. She squeezed her eyes tight shut, trying to fight down the horror she felt on seeing it again.

"What are you thinking about?" asked Flora, surprised by her sister's expression.

"*Aita* and *Ama*, how hard they used to work here and how happy they seemed," she lied.

"It's true, they did work hard," said Flora while she washed her hands. "But there were two of them, and now I have to do much more, but on my own . . . Although you don't seem too worried about that, do you?"

"I know it's a lot of work, Flora, but you didn't listen to the second part: how happy they seemed doing it. There's no doubt that was the key to their success, as it is to yours."

"Oh, really? What would you know? Do you think I'm happy doing this?" she said, turning to her sister as she lowered the office blinds.

"Well, you're doing very well from where I'm standing! You've written books, you're going to have a television program, Mantecadas Salazar is mentioned in the media throughout Europe, and you're rich. You're not exactly the embodiment of failure."

Her sister's face seemed attentive, weighing Amaia's words and doubtless trying to find a double meaning in them.

"I don't think you would have been so successful if your heart wasn't in your work," Amaia continued. "You've got good reason to be very satisfied, and satisfaction and happiness aren't so very different."

"Yes," admitted her sister, raising her eyebrows, "perhaps now, but in order to get here . . ."

"Flora, we all have to make our own way."

"Really?" she said indignantly. "Well, I'd like to know what way you've had to make?"

"I can assure you that I haven't got to where I am now without making an effort," replied Amaia, maintaining the calm, low tone of voice that so annoyed her sister.

"Fine, but you chose to make your effort; mine was imposed on me. I had no help, everyone failed me, you moved away, Víctor was propping up the bar, and as for your sister . . ."

Amaia remained silent for a moment, assessing the reproach she had heard from both her sisters in the space of twenty-four hours.

"You could have chosen too, if this wasn't what you wanted."

"And who asked me what it was that I wanted?"

"Flora . . ."

"No, tell me, who asked me if I wanted to stay here rolling out puff pastry?"

"Flora, you could have chosen, just like everybody else, but you chose not to choose . . . Nobody asked me either. I made my decision and chose the path I wanted to take."

"Not giving a damn about anyone else."

"That's not true, Flora, nor was anybody hurt by it. Unlike you and Ros, I never liked the workshop, not even when I was little . . . I always ran off as soon as I could, and I only used to come here because I was made to, and you know that as well as I do. I didn't want to work here, I studied and *Aita* was fine with that."

"*Ama* wasn't really, but in any case, they were happy enough: they already had me and Ros to continue the family tradition."

"You had a choice."

Flora exploded. "You have no idea what responsibility is." She turned and pointed an accusatory finger.

"Oh, please . . ." begged Amaia, disgusted.

"No please or anything else . . . Neither you nor your sister nor that loser Víctor know what the word means . . ."

"I can see you've got it in for everyone." Amaia gave a tired smile and kept her voice level. "Flora, you don't know me anymore, I'm not that little nine-year-old girl who used to run off out of the workshop. I can assure you that in my job, every day—"

"Your job?" Flora interrupted her. "Who's talking about your job? Only you, little sister. I'm talking about the family, the fact that someone had to look after the business."

"For God's sake, you sound like Michael Corleone . . . The business, the family, the Mafia." Amaia pretended to seal her lips, and this irritated her sister even more.

Flora looked at her furiously and slammed the cloth she was holding onto the table before sitting down, making the lamp that lit the desk shake.

"Flora, you and Ros spent your whole lives here. The two of you started showing an interest in pastry making when you were little, you loved spending hours here. Ros already knew how to make doughnuts and madeleines by the age of three . . ."

"Your sister," Flora murmured dismissively, "didn't stay passionate about it for long, not after she saw that it was real work. Or do you think the business would have lasted long the way our parents were running it? I renovated this workshop from the foundations to the roof, I modernized it, I made it competitive. Do you have any idea what sort of standards you have to meet in order to sell in Europe? The only thing that hasn't changed is the name, Mantecadas Salazar, and the plaque from when our great-great-grandparents founded it."

"Don't you see that I'm right, Flora? Only you were capable of this vision of the future, because you adored this company."

Her last words had made an impression on Flora. She saw how the lines of her face, which had been fixed in an expression of intolerant disdain, rearranged themselves into an expression of self-satisfied pride. She looked around, sitting up straight in her chair.

"Yes," she admitted, "but it wasn't a question of adoring it or, as you say, that it made me happy. Someone had to do it and, as usual, it fell to me, since, moreover, I'm the only one with the capacity to make it work. It required my good sense and responsible nature, but it was still an obligation and a burden. It was necessary to maintain the family heritage, the business that they worked so hard to pass on to us. To maintain the good name and the tradition. With pride, with strength."

"You talk as if you've had to carry the weight of the world on your shoulders. What do you think would have happened if you'd decided to do something different?"

"I can tell you straight, this wouldn't exist."

"Perhaps Ros would have taken it on. She always liked the pastry business."

"The business side, no; she likes making cakes, which is something different. I don't want to imagine what this place would be like with Ros in charge. You don't know what you're saying . . . She can't even manage her own affairs, she's irresponsible, a little girl who thinks money grows on trees. If our parents hadn't left her the house, she wouldn't have anywhere to live. With that disgrace of a husband of hers, the worst kind of stoner and good-for-nothing, who takes her money and goes off messing about with little girls. Is that the Rosaura who's capable of taking this company forward? She doesn't have what it takes. Otherwise, tell me, where is she now? Why isn't she here showcasing her talents?"

"Perhaps if you hadn't been so hard on her . . ."

"Life is hard, sister," said Flora with the sneering tone of an insult.

"I think that Rosaura is a good person, and nobody is immune from making a mistake when choosing a husband."

It was as if Flora had been struck by lightning. Amaia sat watching her in silence and guessed she was thinking about Víctor.

"I wasn't referring to Víctor."

"Sure," Flora replied. And Amaia guessed that she was about to bring out the big guns.

"Flora . . ."

"Yes, the two of you are wonderful, full of good intentions, but tell me something, Little Miss Wonderful: Where were you when *Ama* got ill?"

Amaia shook her head in disgust. "Do you really want to go over all that again?"

"What's wrong, Little Miss Wonderful? Does it upset you to talk about how you abandoned your sick mother?"

"For fuck's sake, Flora, you're the one who's sick," protested Amaia. "I was twenty, I was studying in Pamplona, I came home every weekend. You and Ros were here, you were both working here and you were both married."

Flora stood up and walked toward her.

"That wasn't enough. You used to come on Friday and leave again on Sunday. Do you know how many days there are in a week? Seven days, and the seven nights that go with them." She held up a hand and two fingers in front of Amaia's face. "And do you know who spent each night at *Ama's* bedside? Me, not you, me." She thumped her chest violently. "I used to spoon food into her mouth, I used to bathe her, I used to put her to bed, I used to change her diapers and put her back to bed, I gave her water to drink, and she peed again and again. She would hit and insult me, she would curse me, me, the only one at her side, the only one who was always at her side. In the morning, Ros would arrive and take her out to walk in the park while I opened the workshop, having spent the whole night on my feet. And when she went home, it was the same again, day after day with no kind of support, because I couldn't count on Víctor either. Although, all things considered, she wasn't his mother. He looked after his mother when she fell ill and died, but he was luckier—she caught pneumonia and it carried her off within two months. I had to fight for three years. So, you two little angels, tell me where you were and then tell me I don't have the right to call you irresponsible."

Flora turned her back on Amaia and walked slowly over to her table, where she sat down again.

"I think you're being unfair. I know that Ros did extra night shifts in order to be with her in the mornings, and you were the one who insisted that *Ama* come and live with you after *Aita* died. You always got on well, there was always something special between you that she didn't have with Ros and certainly not with me. Furthermore, you were the older sisters, I was just a young girl and I wasn't living locally. I came as often as I could, and you know that both Ros and I agreed entirely that she should be admitted when she got worse. We gave you our full support when it was necessary to commit her, and we offered money to help pay for the center."

"Money, that's how you irresponsible people try and make everything better. I'll pay up and then the problem will go away. No, it wasn't a question of money; you know that *Aita* left more than enough money when he died. It was a question of doing one's duty, and committing her wasn't my idea, it was that damned doctor's," she said, her voice breaking.

"For God's sake, Flora, I'm amazed we're talking about this again. *Ama* was ill, she was no longer capable of taking care of herself, let alone the business. Dr. Salaberria suggested it because he knew how difficult it was for us. You know that the judge wasn't in the slightest doubt it was the right thing to do. I don't know why you torment yourself about it."

"That doctor got involved without anyone asking him to, and you two gave him free rein. I shouldn't have let you commit her. It wouldn't have ended like that if her pneumonia had been treated at home. I knew it, I knew that she was very delicate and that the hospital was a bad idea, but you didn't want to listen to me, and it all went wrong."

Amaia found herself wincing at her sister's hostility. Once upon a time she would have leaped in impulsively with a retort, joining Flora in her game of reproaches, explanations, and condemnations, but her work as a police officer had taught her a lot about self-possession, control, and judgment, which she had had to put into practice hundreds of times when faced by people so mean-spirited they made Flora seem like a pig-headed, childish schoolgirl in comparison. She lowered her voice and almost in a whisper said, "You know what I think, Flora? I think you're one of those women who make sacrifices and dedicate themselves to being the rock of a family without anyone asking them to, just to have a good arsenal of blame and reproach to attack everyone else with. You're like a millstone, dragging all those around you under until you're alone with your self-sacrifice and your reproaches that nobody wants to hear. That's what's happening to you. In the end, by trying to act all moral and take charge and boss people around, all you manage to do is push everyone away from you. Nobody asked you to be a heroine or a martyr."

Flora stared into the middle distance. She was leaning her elbows on her desk and had her hands in front of her mouth, as if silencing herself, a silence that would be only temporary, that would be maintained only until she found the right moment to fire her poison arrows, and then she would be unstoppable. When she spoke, her voice had recovered its control and her normal urgent tone.

"I suppose you've come here for something other than to tell me what you think of me, so if you've got something specific to ask me, ask me now, otherwise you'll have to leave. I don't have time to waste."

Amaia took a small cardboard box out of her bag, opened the lid, and looked at her sister before removing the contents.

"What I'm about to show you is police evidence that was found at the scene of a crime. I hope you understand that all details pertaining to it are secret. You can't mention it to anybody or discuss it with anybody, not even with the family."

Flora nodded. Her expression had changed to one of interest.

"All right, then, take a look at this and tell me what it looks like to you," she said, taking the bag containing the aromatic little cake that had been found on Anne's body out of the box.

"It's a *txantxigorri*. Was that found at one of the murder scenes?"

"Yes."

"At all of them?"

"I can't tell you that, Flora."

"Perhaps the killer was eating it."

"No, it looks more likely that it was left there to be discovered, the bit that's missing is the bit we sent to the laboratory. What can you tell me?"

"Can I touch it?"

Amaia held it out to her. Flora took it out of the bag, lifted it to her nose, and smelled it for several seconds. She squeezed it between her thumb and forefinger and scraped a tiny bit off with her nail.

"Is there any chance this has been contaminated or poisoned?"

"No, they ran tests at the laboratory and it's clean."

She put a crumb in her mouth and tasted it. "Well, they will already have told you what the ingredients are."

"Yes. Now I want you to tell me everything else."

"Top-quality ingredients, fresh, and combined in just the right proportions. Baked this same week, I'd say it's not more than four days old, and, based on the color and porousness, it was most likely baked in a traditional wood oven."

"Incredible," said Amaia, genuinely impressed. "How can you tell all that?"

Flora smiled. "Because I know how to do my job."

Amaia ignored the veiled insult.

"And who makes these other than Mantecadas Salazar?"

"Well, I suppose that anyone with the recipe could make them. It's not a secret, *Aita's* recipe for them is in my first book, and it's also a typical local dessert. I'd say there are probably about a dozen variations on the recipe in the valley . . . although not of this quality, not with such finely balanced proportions."

"I want you to make a list of all the workshops, patisseries, and shops around here that sell or make them."

"That won't be difficult. The only people who make them of this quality are me, Salinas de Tudela, Santa Marta de Vera, and perhaps a workshop in Logroño . . . well, to be honest, theirs aren't this good. I can give you a list of my clients, but here in Elizondo I know they sell them to tourists and visitors as well as to locals. I don't know if it will be of much use to you."

"Don't you worry about that, just make the list. When do you think you can have it ready?"

"Last thing before I leave. I've got a lot to do today already, and you know who I can thank for that."

"This evening will be fine." Amaia didn't want to fall for her provocation. She picked up the bag with the remains of the cake. "Thanks, Flora. Inspector Montes will come by and collect it.

Flora remained impassive.

"They told me that you two had met."

"Well, it's nice to know that you're well informed for a change. Yes, I know him, he's very pleasant. Inspector Montes came by to introduce himself just when it was time to close up, so he kept me company for a while, I showed him around the town, we had coffee. He proved to be charming, and we talked about all kinds of things, including you."

"Me?" she asked, surprised.

"Yes, you, little sister. Inspector Montes told me how you tricked them into assigning this case to you."

"He told you that?"

"Well, not quite in those words, he's a true gentleman and very warmhearted. You're lucky to work with such a professional. Perhaps you'll learn something," she said with a smile.

"Did Montes say that too?"

"Of course not, but it's easy to work it out. Yes indeed, a charming man."

"I was thinking exactly the same thing," said Amaia, getting up to put her cup in the dishwasher.

"Yes, all your colleagues seem very charming . . . I saw you with a very handsome man in the graveyard this morning."

Amaia smiled, amused by her sister's malice.

"Your heads were very close together and he seemed to be whispering something in your ear. I wonder what James would have to say if he'd seen it."

"I didn't see you, Flora."

"I didn't come in. I couldn't attend the funeral because I had a meeting with my publishers, but I walked up to the cemetery afterward. I arrived early and I saw you standing in front of a grave. You were leaning over the grave and he embraced you."

Amaia bit her lower lip and smiled while she shook her head.

"Flora, Jonan Etxaide is gay."

Flora was unable to disguise her surprise or her disgust.

"I only leaned over the grave of one of my primary school teachers, Irene Barno, do you remember her? I slipped and he caught me."

"How sweet. Do you visit her grave?" Flora mocked her.

"No, I only leaned over to stand up a plant pot that had been blown over by the wind, then I recognized her name."

Flora looked her in the eye. "You never go and visit *Ama*."

"No, Flora, I never visit *Ama*. But tell me, what use would that be now?"

Flora turned toward the window and whispered, "No use at all, now."

There was the loud noise of a motor in the courtyard, and a shadow crossed her face for a moment.

"That will be Víctor," she murmured.

They went to the back door of the workshop, where Flora's husband was parking a vintage motorbike.

"Oh, Víctor, it's amazing, where did you get it?" asked Amaia in greeting.

"I bought it at a junkyard in Soria, but I can assure you it didn't look like this when I brought it home."

Amaia walked around it to take a better look.

"I didn't know you were interested in this sort of thing, Víctor."

"It's quite a new hobby, I got interested in motorbikes a couple of years ago. I started off with a Bultaco Mercurio and a Montesa Impala 175 Sport, and since then I've restored four including this one, which is an Ossa 175 Sport . . . One of the ones I'm most proud of."

"I had no idea. You've done a fantastic job."

Flora huffed, making her disapproval clear, walked toward the door, and said, "Well, let me know when you've finished playing. I'll be inside . . . working." She shut the door with a bang and disappeared.

Víctor forced a smile.

"Flora doesn't like motorbikes, she thinks this hobby is a waste of time and money." He tried to justify it. "When I was still a bachelor, I had a Vespa and I even used to take her out for rides."

"That's right! I remember it, it was red and white! You used to come and pick her up just here, in the courtyard, and when you said goodbye she always used to tell you the same thing, to be careful and . . ." She cut herself off abruptly.

"And not to drink," finished Víctor. "As soon as we got married she persuaded me to sell it, and, as you see, I only listened to the first part."

"I didn't mean to upset you, Víctor . . ."

"Don't worry, Amaia. I'm an alcoholic, it's something I've found hard to admit, but it's part of me and I live with it. I'm like a diabetic, although instead of living without cake I've been left to live without your sister."

"How are you doing? My aunt said you're living at your parents' house . . ."

"I'm doing all right. Apart from the house, and with excellent judgment, my mother left me a monthly sum to live on. I go to Alcoholics Anonymous meetings in Irun, I restore motorbikes . . . I'm not complaining."

"And what about Flora?"

"Well"—he looked toward the workshop door with a smile—"you know her, she's the same as always."

"But . . ."

"We haven't divorced, Amaia. She won't even hear it mentioned, and neither will I, although for different reasons, I think."

She stared at Víctor, in his freshly ironed blue shirt, shaved, smelling slightly of cologne, and leaning against his motorbike . . . He reminded her of the boyfriend he had once been, and she was struck by the certainty that he still loved Flora, that he had never stopped loving her, in spite of everything. This certainty perplexed her, and she immediately felt a wave of affection for her brother-in-law.

"The truth is that I made things pretty difficult for her. You can't imagine what alcohol can make you do."

I would say you can't imagine what twenty years of living with the Wicked Witch of the West can do to you, thought Amaia. I'm sure that drowning his sorrows made it easier to put up with her.

"Why do you go to AA meetings in Irun? Aren't there any closer ones?"

"Yes, in the parish center, on Thursdays, I think, but I prefer to keep being the familiar drunk here."

SPRING 1989

It was undoubtedly the ugliest school satchel that had ever been seen, dark green with brown buckles, a kind that nobody had used for years. She didn't touch it, at least not that day. Fortunately, the term was just about to finish and she wouldn't have to use it until September. That's what she thought. But she didn't touch it that day. She remained silent as she looked at that horror sitting on a kitchen chair and, unconsciously, lifted a hand and ran it through her extremely short hair, which had taken her aunt a great deal of trouble to even out, as if she understood on a very basic level that the two offenses were connected. Her eyes filled with the tears of a little girl on her birthday, tears of pure disappointment. Her two sisters looked at her with eyes as wide as saucers, half hidden behind large mugs of steaming milk. Neither of them said anything, although Rosaura would sometimes cry silently when Rosario told Amaia off.

"What's wrong with you now?" asked her mother, becoming impatient.

There were many things she wanted to say. That it was a horrible present, that she had already known she wouldn't be getting the denim dungarees, but she hadn't been expecting anything like this. That some presents were really intended to degrade, to humiliate, to wound, and this was a lesson that a little girl shouldn't learn on her ninth birthday. Amaia realized this as she looked at the horrific object, unable to hold back her tears. She was coming to realize that that satchel was not the result of negligence or a last-minute rush to find a present, nor did it fulfill a need. She had a perfectly good canvas shoulder bag she used to carry her books. No. It had been planned and chosen with the utmost care to cause the desired effect. A resounding success.

"Don't you like it?" asked her mother.

She wanted to say so many things, things she knew deep down or could somehow foresee but that her child's mind was incapable of processing. She only muttered, "It's for a boy."

Rosario gave a condescending smile, which showed just how much she was enjoying it all. "Don't be stupid, that sort of thing can be for boys or girls."

Amaia didn't answer. She turned around very slowly and headed for the door.

"Where are you going?"

"I'm going to Aunt Engrasi's house."

"There'll be none of that," said her mother, suddenly irritated. "Who do you think you are? You're ungrateful for the present your parents give you and now you want to go and take your sob story to your aunt the *sorgiña*. Do you want her to tell you your future? Do you want to know when you're going to get some denim dungarees like your friends have? If you want to get out of here, go and help your father in the workshop."

Amaia continued walking toward the door without daring to look at her.

"Take your present to your room before you go."

Amaia continued walking without turning around. She picked up her pace and even heard her mother call a few more times before she reached the street.

The workshop welcomed her with the sweet smell of aniseed. Her father was carrying in bags of flour and leaving them beside the bin into which he would empty them afterward. He noticed her presence immediately and went over to her, wiping the flour off his apron before giving her a hug.

"What sort of face is that?"

"*Ama* gave me my present," she moaned, burying her face in her father's chest and muffling her words.

"Come on, there now, it's over now," he consoled her, stroking her shorn head where her beautiful hair used to be. "Come on," he said, pulling her away from him enough to be able to see her face, "stop crying and go and wash that little face of yours. I haven't given you my present yet."

Amaia washed her face in the sink next to the table without taking her eyes off her father, who was holding a sepia envelope with her name on it in his hand. It contained a new five-thousand-peseta note. The girl bit her lip and looked at her father.

"*Ama* will take it from me," she said anxiously, "and she'll yell at you," she added.

"I've already thought of that, which is why there's something else in the envelope."

Amaia peered into the bottom and saw that it held a key. She gave her father a questioning look. He took the envelope and emptied it into her hand.

"This is a key to the workshop. I thought you could keep your money here, and when you need a bit, you can get in using your key while *Ama*'s at home. I've already spoken to your aunt, and she'll buy you those trousers you want in Pamplona, but this money is for you, for you to buy what you want with it. Try to be discreet and don't spend it all at once or your mother will notice."

Amaia looked around, already savoring the freedom and privilege represented by the key. Her father threaded a piece of fine string through the hole in the key, tied a knot in the ends and burned them with a match so that they wouldn't unravel, then hung it around his daughter's neck.

"Don't let *Ama* see you with it, but if she does, say that it's for your aunt's house. Make sure you lock up carefully when you leave, and there won't be a problem. You can keep the envelope under these jars of flavoring essence; we haven't used them for anything in years."

During the following days, Amaia gathered the little treasures she had been buying with her money in her school satchel, almost all of them stationery items. A diary with an extremely handsome Pierrot sitting on a crescent moon on the cover, a floral-printed ballpoint pen with rose-scented ink, a canvas pencil case whose pockets and buckles looked like the top of a pair of trousers, and a heart-shaped marker pen with three different-colored ink cartridges.

19

A T FOUR that afternoon, Anne's father met them in a living room that was as clean as it was full of photos of her. In spite of the slight tremor in his hands as he served the coffee, he seemed calm and in control.

"You'll have to excuse my wife. She's taken a tranquilizer and is in bed, but if it's important . . ."

"Don't worry, sir, we only want to ask some simple questions. There's no need to disturb her unless you think it necessary," said Iriarte with a note of emotion in his voice that did not go unnoticed by Amaia. She remembered the way he had reacted when he recognized Anne at the river. Anne's father smiled in a way that Amaia had seen many times before: the smile of a defeated man.

"Are you feeling better? I saw you at the cemetery . . ."

"Yes, thank you, it was the tension. The doctor told me to take these tablets," he said, pointing out a little box, "and not to drink any coffee." He smiled again as he glanced at the steaming cups on the side table.

Amaia took a few seconds to look at the man carefully and assess his pain, then she asked, "What can you tell us about Anne, Señor Arbizu?"

"Only good things. I wanted to tell you that we didn't have Anne biologically." Amaia noted that he was avoiding saying the words "she wasn't our daughter."

"We've had nothing but happiness since the day we brought her home . . . She was beautiful, look." He took out a frame with a picture of a smiling blond-haired baby from beneath a cushion. Amaia guessed that he had been looking at it when they arrived and had felt compelled to cover it with the cushion in order to keep things tidy. She looked at the photo and showed it to Iriarte, who murmured, "Beautiful," and handed it back. Señor Arbizu covered it with the cushion again.

"She got very good grades, you can ask her teachers, she's . . . she was very bright, much more so than we are, and very good, she never gave us any problems. She didn't drink or smoke like other girls her age, she didn't have a boyfriend. She used to say that she didn't have time for any of that with her studies."

He stopped and looked down at his empty hands. He remained like that for a few seconds, like someone who's been mugged and doesn't understand what has become of the thing he was holding just a moment earlier.

"She was the daughter anyone would be proud to have," he murmured, almost to himself.

"Señor Arbizu," Amaia interrupted, and he looked at her as if he had just awoken from a prolonged daze, "would you let us see your daughter's bedroom?"

"Of course."

They walked together down the hallway, both walls of which were hung with more photos of Anne, photos of her first Communion, at school age three or four, dressed as a cowgirl age seven. Her father stopped in front of each photo to tell them a little anecdote. Her room seemed a bit of a mess thanks to Jonan and the team that had come to take her computer and diaries away. Amaia gave it a general once-over. Shades of pink and purple in an otherwise typical bedroom. Good-quality cream-colored furniture. A bedspread with a floral pattern that was repeated on the curtains, and bookshelves holding more stuffed animals than books. She went over and ran her eye over the titles. Mathematics, chess, and astronomy mixed with romance novels. She turned to Iriarte in surprise, who, understanding the unspoken question, answered, "It's all in the report, the list of titles too."

"I told you my Anne was very bright," her father commented awkwardly from the doorway with an expression on his face that Amaia knew was an attempt to contain his tears.

She took a last look inside the closet, which contained the kind of clothes a good Christian mother would buy for her teenage daughter. She closed the doors and followed Iriarte out of the room. The man accompanied them on their way to the front door.

"Señor Arbizu, is there any chance that Anne was hiding anything from you, that she had important secrets or friendships you might not have known about?"

Her father gave a categorical denial. "It's impossible. Anne used to tell us everything, we knew all her friends, we had a really good relationship."

Anne's mother approached them as they were going down the stairs. Amaia supposed she must have sat there waiting for them. She was wearing a brown man's dressing gown over a pair of blue men's pajamas.

"Amaia . . . Excuse me, Inspector, do you remember me? I knew your mother, she and my older sister used to be friends, perhaps you don't remember." She twisted her hands into one another with such anxiety while she spoke that Amaia couldn't take her eyes off them. They were like two wounded animals seeking a shelter they would not find.

"I remember you," she said, holding out her hand.

Suddenly, before any of them realized her intention, the woman knelt down in front of Amaia, and her hands, those painfully empty hands, caught hold of Amaia's with a force that seemed impossible in such a fragile woman. She raised her eyes and begged her, "Catch that monster who killed my princess, my marvelous little girl. He killed her and there can be no peace for him."

Her husband groaned. "Oh, for God's sake, darling, what are you doing?"

He ran down the stairs and tried to embrace his wife. Iriarte lifted her under the arms, but even then she didn't let go of Amaia's hands.

"I know it's a man, because I've often seen how men look at my Anne, like wolves, with lust and fierce hunger . . . A mother can see these things, she can see them clearly, and I saw how they lusted after her body, her face, her wonderful mouth. Have you seen her, Inspector? She was an angel. So perfect it seemed unreal."

Crying silently, her husband looked her in the eyes, and Amaia saw that Iriarte was swallowing and breathing slowly.

"I remember the day I became a mother, the day they gave her to me and I held her in my arms. I couldn't have children, the little creatures would die in my womb during the first weeks of pregnancy, the miscarriages would come on suddenly. Natural, they used to call them, as if there were anything natural about your children dying inside you. I had five miscarriages before I found Anne, and by then I had lost any hope of being a mother. I didn't want . . . I didn't want to go through all that again, and I couldn't even imagine holding a healthy baby in my arms. The day I took Anne home, I couldn't stop trembling. I was trembling so much my husband thought the little one would fall out of my arms, do you remember?" she said, looking at him. He nodded silently. "On the way, while we were in the car, I couldn't take my eyes off her perfect face, she was so beautiful, she seemed unreal.

"When we got in, I put her on my bed and stripped her completely. In the report it said that she was a healthy little girl, but I was sure she must have some defect, a blemish, a horrible mark, something to mar her perfection. I inspected her little body all over and I could only marvel at what I saw. It felt strange, it was like looking at a marble statue." Amaia remembered the girl's white body, which had reminded her of a Madonna, perfect in its whiteness. "I spent the following days looking at her in amazement. Whenever I took her in my arms, I would feel so grateful that I would burst into tears of pure anxiety and gratitude.

"And then, in the course of those magical days, I found I was pregnant again, and when I found out, do you know, I hardly cared? Because I was already a mother. I gave birth from the heart and carried my daughter in my arms, and perhaps because of that, because carrying a child was no longer the object of my existence, the pregnancy went well. We didn't tell anybody, we didn't tell anybody anymore. After so many disappointments we had learned to keep it a secret. But this time the pregnancy continued, I reached the fifth month; my belly was more than obvious and people started to talk. Anne was almost the same age as the child I was carrying inside me, six months old, and she was beautiful, with blond hair that already covered her head and curled around her face, big blue eyes with those long eyelashes, they lit up her face and she was still just perfect. I would take her out in her pram wearing a little blue dress that I've still got, and I felt so proud when people would lean over to look at her that I was almost beside myself with joy. One of my sisters-in-law came over to me and kissed me. 'Congratulations,' she said. 'You can see how things are, you only needed to relax to get pregnant, and now you're finally going to have a child that's your own flesh and blood.' I felt frozen. 'Children aren't made of flesh and blood, they're made of love,' I told her, almost trembling. 'Yes, yes, I understand you,' she replied. 'Taking in a child from the children's home is very generous and everything, but if you think like that,' she said, touching my stomach, 'you won't hold onto that one long.'

"I went home feeling sick and disgusted. I took my daughter in my arms and I held her against my chest while my anxiety and panic increased and a burning sensation spread through my stomach from the place where that witch had touched me. That very night I woke up bathed in sweat and terrified by the certainty that my child was falling apart inside me. I felt as if the fine moorings that had tied him to me were breaking, and as the pain increased I felt a fierce power destroying my insides, immobilizing me so that I was incapable of reaching out to my husband, who was asleep beside me, or of doing anything more than moaning mutely until the burning liquid started to flow out between my legs. The doctor showed me the baby, with a purplish fully formed face that was transparent in some places. He told me that he'd had to operate on me, that he'd had to perform a curettage because the placenta hadn't come out whole. And, without taking my eyes off my dead son's awful face, I told him that he should tie my tubes or remove my uterus, that I didn't care, that my stomach was not a cradle but my children's tomb. The doctor hesitated, he told me that perhaps I could still become a mother later on, but I told him that I was . . . that I was the mother of an angel and that I didn't want to be a mother to anybody else."

Amaia listened to the woman's agonized tale with great sadness, recognizing that the story was not unlike her own; her stomach was a tomb for unborn children. Anne's mother continued pouring out the confession that seemed to be burning her up inside.

"I didn't speak to my sister-in-law for fifteen years, and the bitch didn't even know why. Until the funeral today. She came over to me with tears pouring down her face and whispered to me, 'Forgive me.' It moved me so much that I embraced her and let her cry, but I didn't answer her, because I'll never forgive her. I'm no longer a mother, Inspector. Someone has stolen the rose that grew from my heart, like in the poem, and now I have a tomb in my stomach and another one in my chest. Catch him, stop him and, when you find him, shoot him. Do it, or if you won't do it, I will. I swear by all my dead children that I will dedicate my life to finding him, waiting for him, stalking him until I can put an end to him."

When they went out into the street, Amaia felt strange and disoriented, as if she had just landed after a long flight.

"Did you see the walls, chief?" asked Iriarte.

She nodded, remembering the photographs that made the place seem like a mausoleum.

"She seemed to be looking at us everywhere. I don't know how they're going to get over this, living in that house."

"They won't," she said sorrowfully.

She soon became aware of a woman coming toward them at top speed, crossing the road diagonally with the obvious intention of speaking to them. As she stopped in front of them, Amaia recognized her as Anne's aunt, the sister-in-law whom her mother had refused to acknowledge for years.

"Have you just been to see them?" she asked, panting from the effort of her quick pace.

Amaia didn't answer, sure that the reason for all that effort was not to know where they'd just been.

"I . . ." She hesitated. "I love my sister-in-law dearly; it's terrible what's happened to them. I'm going to their house right now to . . . well, to be with them. What else can I do? It's horrible, and yet . . ."

"Yes?"

"That girl, Anne, wasn't normal . . . I don't know if you understand me. She was pretty, very bright, but there was something strange about her, something evil."

"Something evil? And what was that?"

"She was . . . she was the evil. Anne was a *belagile*, as dark inside as she was white outside. Even as a child she seemed to look daggers at you, and it felt like she radiated evil. And witches don't rest in peace when they die, you'll see. This isn't the end of Anne."

She stated this with the same gravity and certainty as if she were speaking before an Inquisitorial tribunal, without a shadow of embarrassment or doubt about pronouncing a word usually found only in murder mysteries or horror films. And yet Amaia had the impression that she was extremely uneasy, worried, even. They saw her walk away with the assurance of someone who has completed a painful yet honorable task.

After a few uncomfortable seconds, Amaia and the inspector continued walking along Calle Akullegi. A moment later Iriarte's phone rang.

"Yes, she's with me, we're just heading back toward the station now. I'll tell her."

Amaia looked at him expectantly.

"Inspector, it's your brother-in-law, Alfredo . . . He's in Navarra Hospital in Pamplona, he's tried to kill himself. One of his friends found him hanging in the stairwell. Fortunately, it seems he arrived in time, but his condition is very serious."

Amaia checked the time on her watch. It was quarter past five. Ros would be about to arrive home from work.

"Go to the station, Inspector. I'll go home; I don't want my sister to find out from just anyone. Then I'll go to the hospital. I'll come back as soon as I can. You take charge of everything here in the meantime, and if—"

He interrupted her. "Inspector, that was the commissioner, he asked me to accompany you to Pamplona . . . It looks like your brother-in-law's attempted suicide is related to the case."

Amaia looked at him, disconcerted. "Related to the case? To what case? To the case of the *basajaun*?"

"Deputy Inspector Zabalza is waiting for us at the hospital, he'll tell you more. I know as much as you do. Once we've been to the hospital, the commissioner wants to see us at headquarters in Pamplona at eight."

20

IN THE old days, Calle Braulio Iriarte used to be called Calle del Sol because all the houses faced the sun and the sun warmed and lit the street until it set. With time, its name had changed in tribute to a local benefactor who, after going to the Americas and making his fortune by founding the Corona beer empire, returned to the town and financed the construction of a *pelota* court, a charitable home, and various other important works. But Amaia still thought that Calle del Sol was more fitting, basic and reminiscent of times past, when man lived in communion with nature, a time that had been wiped out by the powerful worship of mammon. Amaia was grateful for the gentle rays that warmed her face and shoulders in spite of the February cold and the other much more intense cold that was reappearing inside her like a badly buried corpse, a cold that had returned with Iriarte's words. Her head would not stop spinning with all the information inside it. She had bombarded the police officer with questions in a desperate attempt to get at the answer, while he prudently refused to air any new theories. In the end she had sunk into a resentful silence, limiting herself to walking at his side. On arriving at Engrasi's house, they saw Ros's red Ford Fiesta pulling up outside.

"Hi, Amaia," Ros greeted her, happy to see her.

"Come inside, Ros, I need to talk to you."

Ros's smile disappeared. "Don't scare me like that," she said as she opened the door and they went into the living room. Amaia stared at her.

"Sit down, Ros," said Amaia, guiding her to a chair.

Ros sat down at the table in the same seat she chose whenever they read the cards.

"Where's Aunt Engrasi?" asked Amaia, suddenly aware that she hadn't seen her.

"I don't know. Oh, God, has something happened to her? I thought she must have gone shopping at Eroski with James . . ."

"No, she's fine . . . Ros, it's Freddy."

"Freddy?" Ros repeated, as if she'd never heard the name before.

"He tried to kill himself by hanging himself in the stairwell at your house."

Ros remained calm, perhaps too calm. "Is he dead?" she wanted to know.

"No. Fortunately one of his friends arrived at the house just then and . . . Do you know if there was a key hidden near the front door?"

"Yes, we fought about it several times. I didn't like the fact that his friends could come into the house whenever they liked."

"I'm really sorry, Ros," murmured Amaia.

Ros bit her lower lip and remained silent, looking at a point in the middle distance somewhere to the right of her sister.

"Ros, I'm heading to Pamplona right now. They told us that he's in Navarra Hospital." She omitted mentioning Freddy's potential connection with the case. "Leave a note for Aunt Engrasi, and we'll call James on our way."

Ros didn't move from her seat. "Amaia, I'm not going."

Amaia, who had already taken several steps toward the door, stopped.

"What do you mean you're not going? Why?" she asked, genuinely surprised.

"I don't want to go, I can't go. I don't feel strong enough."

Amaia studied her for a few seconds and then nodded. "It's all right, I understand," she lied. "I'll call you and tell you what we find out."

"Yes, it would be better to call me."

When she got into the car, she looked at Iriarte, who was already at the wheel.

"I really don't understand anything at all," she said. He shook his head, unable to help her.

The hospital welcomed them with its characteristic smell of disinfectant and a freezing draft that blew through the entrance hall.

"They're doing building work on the bit at the back, where the old ER entrance was, that's where the draft's from," explained Iriarte.

"Where's the ICU?"

"This way," he pointed, "near the operating rooms. I'll take you."

They went along corridor after corridor, following a green line painted on the floor, until Deputy Inspector Zabalza appeared out of a small room that contained only a low table and half a dozen chairs that were slightly more comfortable than the ones arranged in lines in the corridors.

"Come in, we can talk in here, there's nobody else here."

Zabalza went out into the corridor, signaled to the nurse in charge, and finally went back in.

"They're going to let the doctor know you're here, he'll come right away."

He made as if to sit down, but on seeing that Amaia was still standing and looking at him impatiently, he took out his notebook and started to read his notes.

"Today at around one p.m., Alfredo met a friend, the one who found him later and dialed 112. The friend says that he didn't look at all well, as if he was very ill or in a lot of pain."

Amaia thought how dejected and unwell he had looked when she saw him at the cemetery that morning.

Zabalza continued: "He says that he was shocked by his appearance, that he spoke to him but Freddy barely murmured a few incomprehensible words and left. His friend was worried, so he went by his house after lunch. He knocked, and when Freddy didn't respond, he looked through the window and saw that the television was on. He kept knocking and, since there was no response, he went into the house using the key that, according to him, is kept under a flowerpot by the front door so that Freddy's friends can visit whenever they like. He says that all his friends know about the key. He went in, found Freddy hanging by his neck in the stairwell and, in spite of the terrible shock it gave him, he got a knife from the kitchen, went upstairs, and cut the rope. According to the friend, Freddy was still kicking. He dialed 112 and went in the ambulance with him. He's in a room on the main ward, if you want to speak to him."

Amaia sighed. "Anything else?"

"Yes. The friend says that he hadn't been in good shape for a few days. It might not be this, but he says that his wife"—he looked at Amaia awkwardly—"that your sister had left him."

"That's correct," she confirmed.

"Well, that might be the reason. He left a note."

Zabalza showed them an evidence bag, which contained a dirty scrap of paper; it was crumpled and damp.

"It's crumpled because he was clutching it in his hand. They took it off him in the ambulance. And I suppose the dampness must be from his snot and tears, but you can read it even so: 'I love you, Anne, I'll always love you.' "

Amaia looked at Iriarte and then at Zabalza again.

"Zabalza, my sister's name is Ros, Rosaura. And I think we all know who Anne is."

"Oh," said Zabalza, "I'm sorry, I . . ."

"Bring the friend here," said Iriarte, shooting him a reproachful look.

When Zabalza had left the room, Iriarte turned to Amaia. "Forgive him, he didn't know; they told me on the telephone. The note establishes a connection between Freddy and Anne, and that's the reason the commissioner wants to see us."

Zabalza returned a few minutes later, accompanied by a thin, dark, bony man in his early thirties. His slightly overlarge jeans and black fleece jacket made him look even thinner, as if he were lost inside his clothes. In spite of the tough time he must have had, there was a glow of satisfaction on his face, perhaps the result of all the attention he was receiving.

"This is Ángel Ostolaza. These are Inspectors Salazar and Iriarte."

Amaia shook hands with him, noting a slight tremor in his hand. He seemed ready to recount the whole experience complete with every last detail, so he was a bit disappointed when the inspector moved the questioning into an area that he hadn't rehearsed.

"Would you say you're a close friend of Freddy's?"

"We've known each other since we were children. We went to elementary school and then we were at high school together until he left, although we've always been part of the same gang."

"But are you close enough to tell each other things that are, shall we say, very private?"

"Well . . . I don't know, yes, I suppose so."

"Did you know Anne Arbizu?"

"Everyone knew her, Elizondo is a very small town," he said, as if that explained everything.

"And Anne didn't go unnoticed, if you know what I mean?" he added, smiling at the two men, perhaps looking for a masculine camaraderie he failed to find.

"Did Freddy have any kind of relationship with Anne Arbizu?"

There was no doubt that he realized that his response would mark a distinct change in the interview's direction.

"No. What are you saying? Of course not," he replied indignantly.

"Did he ever make any comment to you that suggested he found her attractive or desirable?"

"What are you trying to suggest? She was a young girl, a very attractive young girl . . . All right, perhaps we made the odd comment on a couple of occasions; you know what guys are like." He turned to Zabalza and Iriarte for support for a second time, but they ignored him once again. "Perhaps we said she was getting very pretty, and that she was well developed for her age, but I'm not even sure that comment came from Freddy. It's equally likely I said it and the others agreed."

"Who? Who said it?" asked Amaia harshly.

"I don't know, I swear I don't know."

"All right, we may need your help again. You can go."

He seemed surprised. He looked at his hands and suddenly seemed devastated, as if he didn't know what to do with them. In the end he opted to bury them deep in his pockets and left the room without another word.

The doctor was visibly disgusted when he came in. He ran his eye over the group and his disgust seemed to intensify. After a brief introduction, he gave his update, directing his words to Zabalza and Iriarte, completely ignoring Amaia.

"Señor Alfredo Belarrain has suffered serious damage to his spinal cord and a partial fracture of the trachea. Do you understand the seriousness of what I'm telling you?" He looked from one man to the other and added, "In other words, I don't know how he's still alive; he nearly succeeded. We're most concerned by the damage to the spinal cord. We think that, with time and suitable rehabilitation, he will recover some mobility, but I doubt he'll be able to walk again. Do you understand?"

"Do the lesions correspond with a suicide attempt?" asked Iriarte.

"In my opinion, yes, they do, the lesions undoubtedly indicate a self-inflicted hanging. Manual, as it were."

"Is there any possibility that someone 'helped' him?"

"He doesn't have any defensive wounds or scratches, there are no bruises to indicate that he was pushed or forced into it. He went to the top of the stairs, tied the cord, and jumped. The injuries correspond with self-inflicted hanging, and there are no marks beneath those left by the rope that suggest that he was strangled before being hanged. Is everything clear? In that case, if you don't have any further questions, I'll leave you with the case solved and get back to work."

Amaia looked at him closely, her head slightly on one side.

"Wait, Doctor . . ." She stepped forward so she was barely a few centimeters from the man and stopped, reading his name on his name badge, "Dr. . . . Martínez-Larrea, is that right?"

He stepped back, visibly intimidated.

"I'm Inspector Salazar, from the regional Policía Foral homicide team, and I'm in charge of an investigation in which Señor Belarrain plays an important role. Do you understand?"

"Yes, well . . ."

"It's vitally important that I be able to question him."

"Impossible," he stammered, raising his hands in a conciliatory gesture. Amaia took another step forward.

"No, I can see that although you're so bright you've managed to do our job for us, you don't understand a word. This man is the prime suspect in a series of crimes and I need to question him."

He stepped back a few paces until he was almost standing in the corridor.

"If he's a murderer, you needn't worry, he's not going anywhere. His back and trachea are broken, he's got a tube in his mouth that goes down into his lungs, and he's in an induced coma. Even if I could wake him, which I can't, he wouldn't be able to talk, write, or blink his eyes." He took another step into the corridor. "Come with me, señora," he said. "I'll let you see him, but only for two minutes and only through the glass."

She nodded and followed him.

The room where they had put Freddy contained a typical hospital bed, but other than that it could just as easily have been a laboratory, an airplane cockpit, or the set of a futuristic film. Freddy was barely visible among the tubes, cables, and padded bandages that encased his head like a helmet. There was a tube running out of his mouth, which seemed unusually large to Amaia and was stuck to his cheek with a piece of white surgical tape that emphasized how pale Freddy was in comparison. The only note of color was a hint of purple around his eyelids, which seemed swollen, and the pearlescent brilliance of a tear that had run down his face to his ear. The image of him from that morning, when she'd seen him among the bushes of the hedge at the entrance to the cemetery, kept coming back into Amaia's thoughts. She spent a few more moments looking at him, asking herself whether she felt any compassion for him, and decided that she did. She felt compassion for that destroyed life, but not even all the compassion in the world would hinder her in her search for the truth.

On her way out, she saw Freddy's mother, coming to replace her at the window. She was about to greet her when the woman turned on her.

"What are you doing here? The doctor told me that you wanted to question my son . . . Why don't you leave us in peace? Don't you think your sister's already done enough damage? Your sister broke his heart when she left him, and the poor thing couldn't take it, he lost his mind. And now you want to question him? Question him about what?"

Amaia didn't answer. She went out into the corridor and joined Zabalza and Iriarte, who were waiting for her. The glass door cut off the woman's shouts.

"What's up?"

"The doctor understands perfectly . . . That absolute imbecile has told Freddy's mother that he's a murder suspect."

21

THE COMMISSIONER received Amaia and Iriarte in his office and, although he invited them to take a seat, he himself remained standing.

"I'll cut to the chase," he announced. "Inspector Salazar, when I made the decision to put you in charge of this case, with the support of the chief of police in Elizondo, I didn't imagine it would take such a turn. You must be well aware that the fact that one of your family members is implicated in the case puts you in a compromising position, and we can't risk a mistake of that type interfering with future judicial action."

He stared at Amaia, who remained impassive, although a slight nervous tremor was evident in her knee, as if it were connected to a high-tension cable. The commissioner turned toward the window and remained silent for a minute, looking outside. He sighed loudly and asked, "In what way do you think this individual might be involved in the case?"

It wasn't clear to which of them he was directing his question. Amaia glanced at Iriarte, who gave her an encouraging look.

"We knew that Anne Arbizu was having a relationship with a married man, but in spite of going through her computer, diaries, and phone calls with a fine-tooth comb, we didn't know who it was, although we did know that the girl had put an end to the relationship very recently. I think that it was Freddy she was seeing. But he doesn't fit the profile of the killer we're looking for at all. Freddy is chaotic, unreliable, and disorganized, and I'm sure that whoever killed Anne is the same person who killed the other girls."

"What do you think, Iriarte?"

"I totally agree with Inspector Salazar."

"I don't like this situation, Inspector, but, nonetheless, I will give you forty-eight hours to check out his alibi, if he has one, and rule out Alfredo Belarrain as a suspect. However, if this man is in any way implicated in the death of Anne Arbizu, or of any of the other girls, I'll have to take you off the case and Inspector Iriarte will take command. I've already spoken to the commissioner in Elizondo, and he's in agreement. And now you'll have to excuse me, I'm in a hurry." He opened the door, turned, and said, "Forty-eight hours," before leaving.

Amaia exhaled slowly until her lungs were completely empty.

"Thank you, Iriarte," she said, looking him in the eyes.

He stood up, smiling. "Let's go, we've got work to do."

Night had already fallen when they got back. In Aunt Engrasi's living room, the girls of the merry poker gang had been replaced by a sort of family wake without a deceased. James, sitting by the fire, seemed more worried than Amaia had ever seen him. Her aunt was sitting on the sofa next to Ros, who, strangely, seemed the most calm of the three of them. Jonan Etxaide and Inspector Montes both occupied chairs at the gaming table. Her aunt stood up as soon as she saw her come in.

"How is he, sweetheart?" she asked, unsure whether to move toward Amaia or stay where she was.

Amaia pulled up a chair and sat down facing Ros, leaving only a few centimeters between them. She stared at her sister for several seconds and answered, "He's really bad. His trachea was destroyed by the rope that almost broke his neck. He's also suffered damage to his spinal cord and won't walk again."

Amaia kept her eyes fixed on Ros while she listened to the gasps of dismay from her aunt and James. Ros blinked quickly and her lips were momentarily compressed in an expression of distaste. And nothing more.

"Ros, why didn't you go to the hospital? Why didn't you go to see your husband who tried to kill himself when you broke up with him?"

Ros stared at her and started shaking her head, but she didn't say anything.

"You already knew," asserted Amaia.

Ros swallowed, and doing so seemed to cost her considerable effort.

"I knew he was seeing someone," she said at last.

"Did you know it was Anne?"

"No, but I knew he was seeing another woman. If you'd seen him . . . He was a textbook cheat. He was euphoric, he gave up smoking joints and he wasn't drinking, he would shower three times a day, and he even started wearing the aftershave I gave him three Christmases ago and had never used. I'm not stupid, and he gave me every possible clue. It was obvious that he was seeing someone."

"And you knew who it was."

"No, I didn't know, I swear. But I knew that it had come to an end the day I went home to collect my things and I found him crying like a little boy. He was very drunk. His eyes were a mess, his face was buried in a cushion, and he was crying so hard that I could barely understand him. He was the living image of desperation. I thought that perhaps his mother, or one of his aunts . . . Then he managed to calm down a bit, and he started to tell me that everything had gone wrong because of him, and now everything was over, that he had never loved anybody like that, that he was sure he couldn't stand it. What an idiot! I thought for a moment that he was talking about us, about our relationship, about our love. Then he said something like, 'I love her more than I've ever loved anybody in my life' . . . Do you understand? I wanted to kill him."

"Did he tell you who it was then?"

"No," murmured Ros.

"Have you been to your house today?"

"No." Her thin voice was barely audible.

"Where were you between one and two this afternoon?"

"What sort of question is that?" asked Ros, suddenly raising her voice.

"The sort of question I have to ask you," replied Amaia, without a flicker of emotion.

"Amaia, do you think . . ." She left the sentence unfinished.

"It's just routine, Ros. Answer the question."

"I left work at one on the dot, and I went and had lunch at a bar in Lekaroz that serves food, like I do every other day. Then I had a coffee with the manager, and I went back to work at two thirty and stayed there until five."

"I need to ask you another question now," said Amaia, softening her tone. "Please be honest, Ros. Did you know who your husband was seeing? I know what you've already told us, but perhaps someone told you, or at least insinuated something."

Ros remained silent and looked down at her hands, which were twisting a tissue tighter and tighter.

"For the love of God, Ros, tell me the truth or I won't be able to help you."

Ros started to cry silently, fat tears rolling down her face, which became something like a parody of a smile. Amaia felt as if the floor was giving way beneath her feet. She leaned forward and hugged her sister.

"Please tell me," she said with her mouth by her sister's ear. "They saw you arguing with a woman."

Ros pulled brusquely free of the embrace and went to sit by the fire.

"She was a *belagile*," she murmured, distressed.

It was the second time that day she had heard someone use that word to describe Anne, Amaia thought to herself.

"What were you talking about?"

"We didn't speak."

"What did she say to you?"

"Nothing."

"Nothing? Inspector Montes, repeat what you told Zabalza yesterday," she said, turning abruptly toward the inspector, who had remained silent and grim faced until that point. He stood up as if he was giving testimony before a judge, straightened his jacket, and ran a hand over his slicked-back hair.

"Yesterday, after nightfall, I was walking along the east side of the river when I saw Rosaura and another woman together, standing facing one another on the other side of the river, level with the *ikastola*. I couldn't hear what they were saying, but I heard the girl laughing, she laughed so loudly that I heard it clearly."

"That's all she did," said Ros, looking nervous. "Yesterday afternoon, after leaving my house, I felt a bit stunned and I went to walk along the riverbank for a while. Anne Arbizu was coming in the opposite direction to me. She was wearing a hood that partly covered her face, and as we were about to pass one another I noticed she was looking me in the eye. I knew her by sight, but we had never spoken. I thought she was going to ask me something, but instead she stopped in front of me, barely two steps away, and started to laugh, to mock me, without taking her eyes off me."

Amaia saw the others' expressions of surprise, but she continued the questioning.

"What did you say to her?"

"Nothing. Why? I understood everything immediately; there was nothing to say, she was laughing at me. I felt embarrassed and humiliated, and also intimidated . . . If you'd seen her eyes. I swear that I have never seen such evil in a look in my whole life, so much malice and knowledge, as if I were looking at an old woman full of wisdom and scorn."

Amaia sighed loudly.

"Ros, I want you to think about what you've just told me. I know you spoke to a woman, Inspector Montes witnessed it, but it couldn't have been Anne Arbizu, because by that time yesterday, when you were on your way back from your house, Anne had already been dead for twenty-one hours."

Ros trembled as if she'd been caught by a wind that was blowing her in different directions and lifted her hands in a gesture of confusion and distress.

"Who did you speak to, Ros? Who was that woman?"

"I've already told you, it was Anne Arbizu, it was that *belagile*, that demon."

"For the love of God! Stop lying or I can't help you!" exclaimed Amaia.

"It was Anne Arbizu!" Ros shouted furiously, getting up and standing in front of her.

Amaia remained silent for a minute, then looked at Iriarte and nodded her permission.

"Could it have been a woman who looked like Anne? You said you'd never spoken to her; could you have mistaken another girl for her? If she was wearing a hood, perhaps you couldn't see her face properly," he said.

"I don't know. Perhaps . . ." admitted Ros without conviction. He went over until he was standing in front of her.

"Rosaura Salazar, we have applied for a warrant for your home, your cell phones, and your computers, which also includes the boxes that you took away with you yesterday," said Iriarte in a neutral voice.

"You don't need it, you can look through whatever you like. I suppose it's the way things have to be. The stuff in the boxes is all mine, Amaia, there's nothing of his."

"I'd thought as much . . ."

"Wait, am I a suspect? Me?"

Amaia didn't answer. She looked at her aunt, who had one arm across her chest and the other hand over her mouth. She felt terrible about how much pain this must be causing her.

Iriarte stepped forward, aware of the tension that was increasing with every passing moment. "Your husband was having an affair with Anne Arbizu, she's dead, murdered, and he tried to kill himself. Right now, he's the main suspect, but you also found out about the affair yesterday, first from him and then from that woman who was mocking you in the middle of the street."

"Well, I certainly wasn't expecting this . . . Isn't there supposed to be a serial killer out there who murders little girls? Have you got another theory up your sleeve now? Because Freddy is an imbecile, a bum, a shit, and useless besides. But he doesn't go around killing little girls."

Deputy Inspector Zabalza looked at Amaia and then intervened.

"Rosaura, it's a routine part of the investigation. We search the house, and if we don't find anything strange, we verify your alibis and rule you out as suspects. It's nothing personal, it's how we work. You don't need to worry."

"Anything strange? Everything's been strange during the last few months. Everything." She sat back down in the armchair and closed her eyes, as if overwhelmed by an extraordinary exhaustion.

"Rosaura, we need you to make a statement," said Iriarte.

"I just have," she replied without opening her eyes.

"At the police station."

"I understand." She stood up abruptly, picked up her bag and jacket, which were hanging on the back of the sofa, and headed for the door, kissing her aunt on the way but without looking at her sister.

"Whenever you're ready," she told Iriarte.

"Thank you," he said before following her out.

Amaia put her hands on the mantel and felt her trousers become so hot from the fire that it seemed they might burst into flames at any moment. Montes's, Jonan's, and her cell phones bleeped in unison to announce the arrival of a text message. "The search warrant?" she asked without looking at her phone.

"Yes, chief."

She accompanied them out and shut the living room door behind her.

"Go and meet up with the officers from Elizondo. Montes, you and Deputy Inspector Etxaide can help them. I'll wait at the station until you've finished so as not to compromise the investigation."

"But, chief . . . I don't think . . ." protested Jonan.

"It's my sister's house, Jonan. Search it, look for any evidence of the relationship between Anne and Freddy, and if there is any, look for anything that suggests that my sister was aware of what was going on beforehand. Be meticulous: letters, books, text messages, emails, photos, personal items, sex toys . . . Ask their telephone company for their telephone records or, even better, find the bill. Question both Freddy's and Rosaura's friends, someone had to know about it."

"I've gone through all Anne's emails and I can assure you that there was nothing addressed to Freddy. And there's nothing in her call or text message records to indicate that she ever phoned him. Although her friends were sure she was seeing a married man, in Anne's own words, she was going to end the affair because the guy had become too obsessed with her. Do you think he took the end of the relationship badly enough to kill her?"

"I don't think so, Jonan, and what about the other murders? If there's one thing we all agree on, it's that they form a series, and Anne's isn't an imitation, it was conducted following the same pattern. For that reason, if Freddy had killed Anne, he would have to have killed the other two girls as well. He's stupid enough to have a relationship with a minor ten times cleverer than he is, but he doesn't fit the profile of such a methodical killer: the coldness, the control, and the arrangement of the scene according to a protocol from which he never deviates don't match Freddy's character at all. Serial killers have no regrets, and they don't kill themselves because of their victims. Search the house, then we'll see."

The door closed behind Jonan, and Amaia went back into the living room. James and her aunt looked at her in silence.

"Amaia . . ." James began.

"Please don't say anything, this is all very difficult for me. Please, I beg you. I've done as much as I can. Now you've seen what I have to do every day, now you've seen how shitty my job is."

She picked up her anorak and left the house. She walked toward the *trinquete* with firm steps, went a little way onto the bridge, stopped, turned back toward Calle Braulio Iriarte, and walked determinedly toward Calle Menditurri, toward the workshop.

22

S HE DREW close to the door and tried the lock, aware of her
heart pumping in her chest. Without thinking, she raised her
other hand to her neck, looking for the string from which the key
had hung for so long. A voice behind her made her jump.

"Amaia."

She spun around, drawing her gun automatically.

"God, James! What are you doing here?"

"Your aunt told me you would come here," he said, looking at the
workshop door in confusion.

"My aunt," she muttered, cursing the fact that she was so predict-
able. "I almost shot you," she whispered, slipping the Glock back into
its holster.

"I was . . . We were worried about you, your aunt and I . . ."

"Sure, let's get out of here," she said, looking at the door, appre-
hensive all of a sudden.

"Amaia . . ." James went over to her and put an arm around her
shoulders, holding her against him as they walked toward the bridge.
"I don't understand why you've suddenly started behaving as if we're
all against you. I understand your job, and I understand that you've
done what you had to do, and your aunt knows that too. Ros made a
mistake in not telling you about the girl, but I can understand that.
However great a police officer you are, you're also her little sister and
I think she felt a bit embarrassed. You have to try and understand it,

because your aunt and I understand, and we realize that you tried to make things easier by being the one to question her and doing it at home, not down at the station."

"Yes," she admitted, letting her muscles relax and moving closer to her husband. "Perhaps you're right."

"Amaia, there's something else. We've been married for five years, and in all that time I don't think we've spent forty-eight hours straight in Elizondo. I always thought you'd become a radical urbanite like so many other people who grow up in small towns do after they move away. A girl brought up in a rural area who goes off to live in the city, becomes a police officer, and leaves her roots behind a bit . . . but there's something else, isn't there?"

He stopped and tried to look her in the eyes, but she avoided his gaze. James didn't give in and, taking her by the shoulders, made her look at him.

"Amaia, what's going on? Is there something you're not telling me? I'm really worried. If there's something important that affects us, you have to tell me what it is."

She looked at him, angry at first, but when she saw the concern and sense of helplessness behind his demands for answers, she smiled at him sadly.

"They're ghosts, James, ghosts from the past. Your wife, who doesn't believe in magic, divination, *basajauns*, or genies, is haunted by ghosts. I've spent years trying to hide away in Pamplona. I have a badge and a pistol and I've avoided coming here for a long time because I knew that if I came back they would find me. It's everything, all this evil, this monster who kills little girls and leaves them by the river, little girls like me, James." His eyes widened in confusion. But she wasn't looking at him, she was looking past him at a point somewhere in the middle distance. "It was evil that made me come back, the ghosts have risen up from their graves, alerted by my presence, and now they've found me."

James embraced her, letting her bury her face in his chest in that intimate gesture that always comforted her.

"Little girls like you . . ." he murmured.

23

T HE PATROL car that had taken Amaia to the police station parked under the overhang formed by the second floor. The officer wished her a good night, but she lingered inside the vehicle for a couple of seconds while she pretended to look for her phone and waited for her sister and Inspector Iriarte, who were coming out of the station and getting into his car so he could drive her home, to move away. A fine rain started to fall the moment she went through the door. An officer who was clearly still completing his training was chatting on his cell phone, which he switched off and clumsily hid as soon as he saw her. She walked toward the elevator without stopping, pressed the button, and looked again at the officer at the reception desk. She retraced her steps.

"Can you show me your phone?"

"I'm sorry, Inspector, I . . ."

"Let me see it."

He handed her a silver-colored cell phone that glinted under the lights of the entrance hall. Amaia inspected it carefully.

"Is it new? It looks like a good one."

"Yeah, it's pretty good," he declared with the pride of ownership.

"It looks expensive, it's not one of those ones you can buy with supermarket loyalty points."

"No, you're right, it's a limited edition and cost eight hundred euros."

"I saw someone else with one."

"Well, that must have been very recent, because I've only had mine a week. It went on sale ten days ago and I was one of the first to buy one."

"Congratulations, officer," she said and ran to catch the elevator before its doors closed.

On the table was a computer, a cell phone, a month's worth of mail including bills, and some evidence bags containing what looked like hash. Jonan was checking a bill against the information on his computer screen.

"Good evening," Amaia greeted him.

"Hi, chief," he answered vaguely, without taking his eyes off the screen.

"What have we got?"

"There's nothing in the email, but the cell is full of calls and the most heartrending messages . . . although not to Anne's number."

"No, to Anne's other number," she clarified. Jonan turned around, surprised.

"I've just seen a cell phone identical to Anne Arbizu's, a very expensive and exclusive one that's only been on sale for ten days. The length of her phone contract. But it seems a bit strange that a girl like Anne didn't have a cell phone at all until ten days ago, just when she got fed up with Freddy's calls and messages. She was a very practical girl, so she got rid of her old phone . . . She couldn't just lose the SIM card, so she 'lost' the whole phone and asked her *aita* to buy her a contract phone with a new number."

"Fuck," murmured Jonan.

"Ask her parents. We'll know enough from checking the number against Freddy's bill. Have you found anything else?"

"Nothing, apart from the hash. There were only personal items in Rosaura's boxes. I'm going to go through the mail, but it's only bills and junk mail, nothing to suggest your sister could have known about his affair." Amaia sighed and turned toward the big windows onto the street. Beyond the path to the station, which was lit up by the yellow light of the streetlamps, there was nothing but darkness. "I can deal with this, Inspector, but it will take me quite some time yet. Go and have a rest, I'll let you know if I find anything."

She turned around and smiled as she zipped up her anorak.

"Good night, Jonan."

She asked the patrol car to drop her off at Bar Saioa, where she asked for black coffee, which the owner set in front of her without complaint despite the fact that he had already cleaned the coffee machine. It was boiling hot and she drank it in small sips, savoring the strength of the brew and pretending not to notice the interest she was arousing among the few regulars who were still there at that time of night, drinking gin and tonic out of cider glasses complete with ice cubes and ignoring the Siberian cold that threatened outside. When she went out into the street, the temperature seemed to have dropped by a further five degrees in one go. She put her hands in her pockets and crossed the street. As in the rest of the valley, most of the houses in Elizondo were adapted to its damp, rainy climate with a square or rectangular façade, three or four floors, and a slanting tiled roof with large eaves, which constituted the outer edge of the building and, for more experienced walkers like herself, some slight refuge from the rain. According to Barandiarán, it was this narrow space, into which the rain poured off the roof, that used to be used for the burial of aborted fetuses and stillborn babies. There was a belief that their small spirits, the *mairu*, guarded the house, protecting it from evil and at the same time remaining in the maternal home forever as eternal infants. She remembered that her aunt had once told her that when a house had been knocked down and they were digging around it, they had found bones belonging to more than ten babies that had been buried beneath the eaves like guards during the passage of the centuries.

Amaia walked along Calle Santiago, staying close to the doorways in an attempt to shelter from the wind, which was even stronger when she turned down Calle Javier Ciga, past the imposing town house after which the bridge was named. The river was pouring over the dam with a deafening roar that made her wonder how the locals whose windows overlooked that small waterfall could sleep.

The lights of the *trinquete* were off. The street was as deserted as a ghost town. Little by little, carried by the current of that other river that flowed inside her, she went down what used to be Calle del Sol toward Calle Txokoto, until she arrived at the door to the workshop again. She took a hand out of her jacket pocket and put it on the icy handle. She leaned forward until her forehead touched the rough wood of the door and started to cry silently.

24

S HE HAD died. She knew this with the same certainty with which she had known that she had been alive before. She had died. And just as she was aware of her death, she was aware of everything that was happening around her: the blood that was still flowing from her head, the heart that had stopped in the middle of a beat that would never be completed now.

The strange silence in which her body had been plunged, which seemed almost deafening from the inside, allowed her to hear other sounds from her surroundings. A drop falling onto a metal sheet again and again. A panting noise, the effort and determination with which someone pulled on her lifeless limbs. Rapid, irregular breathing. A murmur, perhaps a threat. But it didn't matter anymore, because everything had come to an end. Death is the end of fear, and knowing this almost made her happy, because she was a dead little girl in a white tomb, and somebody, who was panting with the effort, had started to bury her.

The earth was soft and fragrant, and it covered her cold limbs like a cool, soft sheet. She thought that earth was kind to dead people. But the person burying her wasn't. She was hurling fistfuls of dust over her hands, over her mouth, over her eyes and her nose, covering her, hiding the horror. The earth got into her mouth and became a thick, sticky paste; it stuck to her teeth and grew hard on her lips. It got into her nose, invading her nasal passages, and then, despite the fact she had thought she was dead, she inhaled that merciful earth and started to cough. The shovelfuls of earth that were falling on her face increased, as did the kind of contained cry of panic emitted by the pitiless monster who was burying her. The earth of her white tomb flooded her mouth, but she shouted desperately in spite of this, "I'm only a little girl, I'm only a little girl."

But her mouth was full of mud and the words didn't get past her teeth, which were stuck together by the paste.

"Amaia, Amaia." James shook her.

She looked at him, still terrified, as she found herself coming out of the dream as if she were in an elevator going up at top speed out of the abyss in which she was trapped, and she forgot the details almost immediately. When she looked at James and answered, she could remember only the sensation of fear and being unable to breathe. James stroked her head tenderly, running his hand through her hair.

"Good morning," murmured Amaia.

"Good morning, I've brought you coffee." He smiled.

Having a cup of coffee in bed was a habit that went back to her days as a student in Pamplona, when she had lived in a tiny apartment with no heating. She would get up to make coffee and take a cup back to bed to enjoy it under the covers, and only when she had warmed up and was feeling sufficiently awake did she get out from under the sheets to dress quickly. James never had breakfast in bed, but he had fed her habit by waking her with coffee every day.

"What time is it?" she asked, trying to reach her cell phone on the bedside table.

"Half past seven. Don't worry, you've got time."

"I want to see Ros before she goes to work."

James shook his head. "She's just set off."

"Fuck, it was important. I wanted to . . ."

"Perhaps it's better this way. She seemed calm to me, but I think it's better you leave it a few hours, give her time to calm down. You can see her tonight, and I'm sure that everything will be back to normal by then."

"You're right," admitted Amaia, "but you know what I'm like. I like to resolve things as soon as possible."

"Well, for now you can drink this coffee and resolve this husband of yours whom you keep abandoning."

She put the cup on the bedside table and pulled on James's hand until he was lying on top of her.

"Done!"

And she kissed him passionately. She loved his kisses, the way he drew close to her, looking into her eyes and knowing that they would make love as soon as he touched her. First he would search for her hands, take them in his, and guide them up to rest on his chest or his waist. Then his eyes would follow the route that his lips would take later, from her eyes to her mouth, and when he finally reached her lips, his kisses would lift her off the ground. When James kissed her, she felt the passion and contained strength of a Titan, but she also felt the tenderness and respect of a man kissing the woman he loves. She thought that no other man on earth could kiss like that. James's kisses followed a pattern of connection as old as the world, the connection that meant that lovers would always seek and find one another. James belonged to her and she belonged to him, and that was a plan that had been forged a long time before she had been even the shadow of a life. And his kisses were the foretaste of what sex would bring later. James made love to her in a delicious way; sex with him was a dance, a dance for two in which neither one of them was more important than the other. James would run his hands over her body, overcome with passion but without hurrying or stumbling, conquering every centimeter of her body with his capable hands and making her tremble with the feverish kisses that he planted on her skin. He would conquer and master territories that were his by right, but to which he always returned with the same reverence he had shown the first time. He let her be herself, he lifted her up alongside him without directing her or forcing her. And she felt that nothing else mattered. Just the two of them.

James watched her closely as they lay naked and exhausted. He was studying her face with the utmost tenderness, trying to find a clue to the source of her disquiet. She smiled at him and he smiled back at her with a look in which Amaia detected a note of preoccupation that was surprising in him since he was naturally confident, with that slightly childish character that is specific to North Americans outside their home country.

"Are you okay?"

"I'm great, how about you?"

"I'm okay, although I am a bit cold," she complained affectionately.

He sat up, reached for the duvet, which had fallen onto the floor, and covered Amaia, holding her against his chest. He let a few seconds pass as he enjoyed the feel of her breathing against his skin.

"Amaia, yesterday . . ."

"Don't worry, my love, it was nothing, just stress."

"No, my love. I've seen you overwhelmed by cases on other occasions, and this is different. Then there are the nightmares . . . You're having them too often. And there's what you told me yesterday when I found you in front of the workshop."

She sat up so she could look him in the eyes.

"James, I swear that you don't need to worry, nothing's going on. It's a difficult case, with Fermín and his attitude and those dead little girls. It's stress, nothing more, nothing I haven't faced before." She gave him a swift kiss on the lips and got out of bed.

"Amaia, there's something else. I called the Lenox Clinic yesterday to rearrange this week's appointment, and they told me you'd already canceled the treatment."

She looked at him without replying.

"You owe me an explanation. I thought we'd agreed to start the fertility treatment."

"See? This is what I mean. Do you really think I can think about that right now? I've just told you that I'm stressed, and you're not making things any better."

"I'm sorry, Amaia, but I'm not going to give in. This is something that's very important to me, something I thought was important to you too, and I think you ought to at least tell me whether you're planning to have the treatment or not."

"I don't know, James . . ."

"I think you know, otherwise why did you cancel it?"

She sat on the bed and started tracing invisible circles on the duvet with her finger. Without daring to look at him, she replied, "I can't give you an answer right now. I thought I was sure, but in the last few days my doubts have been increasing so much that I'm not sure I want a child that way."

"By 'that way,' do you mean using fertility technology or do you mean us?"

"James, don't do this to me, there's nothing wrong between us," she countered, alarmed.

"You're lying to me, Amaia, and you're hiding things from me. You cancel the treatment without discussing it with me, as if you were going to have the child alone, and you say nothing's happening between us."

Amaia got up and headed toward the bathroom.

"Now's not a good time, James, I have to go."

"My parents called yesterday, they send their best regards," he said as she closed the bathroom door.

Mr. and Mrs. Westford, James's parents, seemed to have undertaken a campaign to acquire a grandchild, or die in the attempt. She remembered her wedding day when her father-in-law had raised a toast to her in which he asked for grandchildren as soon as possible, and when the children didn't arrive after several years of marriage, her parents-in-law's previously open attitude toward her had turned into a kind of veiled reproach that she imagined would not be so veiled from James.

James remained stretched out on the bed, staring at the bathroom door and listening to the water running, asking himself what the hell was happening to them.

25

JAMES WESTFORD had been living in Pamplona for six months when he met Amaia. She was still a young trainee police officer then, and she had come to the gallery where he was going to exhibit to inform the owner that petty thieves were operating in the area. He remembered her wearing her uniform, standing next to her colleague, captivated by one of his sculptures. James had been bending over a box, fighting with the packaging that covered the other works he was going to exhibit. He stood up without taking his eyes off her and, without thinking, went over to her and gave her one of the flyers the gallery had prepared for the exhibition. Amaia took it without smiling and thanked him without paying him any further attention. He felt frustrated when he realized that she wasn't reading it, she didn't even glance at it, and when they left he saw her put it down on a table near the entrance. He saw her again the Saturday following the opening of the exhibition. She was wearing a black dress and her hair was loose and brushed back off her face. At first he hadn't been sure that it was the same girl, but then she had gone over to the same sculpture as before and, waving to him, had said, "I haven't been able to get the image of this out of my head since I saw it the other day."

"Then you've been feeling the same as me. I haven't been able to get the image of you out of my head since I saw you the other day."

She had looked at him and smiled.

"Well, you're very ingenious and talented with your hands. What else are you good at?"

When the gallery closed, they walked through the streets of Pamplona for hours, talking nonstop about their lives and their jobs. It was almost four in the morning when it started to rain. They tried to reach a nearby street, but the intensity of the rain obliged them to seek shelter under the eaves of the nearest house. Amaia shivered under her thin dress and, ever the gentleman, James offered her his jacket. As she wrapped it around her, she had inhaled the aroma it gave off as the rain grew heavier, forcing them to move back until they were pressed against the wall. He looked at her with a sheepish smile and, trembling with nerves, she moved close enough to brush against him.

"Can you hold me?" she asked, looking into his eyes.

He pulled her against his body and embraced her. Amaia suddenly began to laugh. He looked at her, surprised.

"What are you laughing at?"

"Oh, nothing. I was just thinking that it's taken a torrential rain shower for you to hug me. I wonder what will need to happen next for you to kiss me."

"Amaia, anything you want from me, you only have to ask for it."

"Then kiss me."

26

ON THE other side of the large windows of the new police station, the day looked like it might not fully dawn. The light was
very dim and, together with the fine rain that hadn't stopped falling
since the previous night, it contrived to obscure the fields and trees,
which were mostly bare thanks to the effects of a winter that seemed
never-ending.

Amaia looked out the window, holding a cup of coffee in her
hands, and wondered, once again, what to do about Montes. His
insubordination and defiance had reached unexpected levels. She
knew that he dropped by the station every so often and chatted with
Deputy Inspector Zabalza or with Iriarte, but he hadn't answered any
of her calls and she'd barely seen him. He had reluctantly attended
the confrontation with Ros and had then been present for the search,
but he hadn't come to the meeting that morning. She told herself
once again that she had to do something about the situation, but she
hated the idea of making a complaint against Fermín.

She didn't really understand what was going on in his head. They
had been colleagues for the past two years, and perhaps even friends
for the last year, when Fermín had told her that his wife had left
him for a younger man. She had listened in silence with downcast
eyes, resolved not to look him in the face since she knew that a man
like Montes was not sharing his disgrace; he was confessing it. As if
making an act of contrition, he had enumerated his faults and her

reasons for leaving him, for not loving him. She had listened without saying a word and, as if in absolution, she had handed him a tissue as she turned away so as not to see his tears, so incongruous for a man like him. She followed the details of his divorce and went for various glasses of wine and beer with him, tainted with venom toward his ex-wife. They had invited him to come over for lunch on Sundays and, in spite of his initial reticence, he had got along well with James. He had been a good police officer, perhaps a little old-fashioned, but gifted with good instincts and perception. And a good colleague, who had always been respectful and conciliatory when faced with the macho attitudes of other police officers. That was why she was so surprised by this sudden attack of jealousy typical of a dethroned alpha male. She turned toward the table and the bulletin board where the pictures of the girls were on display. She had more important things to worry about at the moment.

She had had a meeting first thing with the team that worked on crimes against minors, since two of the victims had not yet reached the legal age. She had immediately concluded that these were not typical crimes against minors and that their usual profiles of victims and aggressors were very different from the kind of murders she was now facing. What was most shocking about the *basajaun*'s criminal profile was the almost textbook nature of his behavior. Amaia remembered her time at the FBI criminal-profiling course. Among other things she had learned there, the psychosexual paraphernalia that lots of serial killers arrange around the corpse indicates their wish to personalize them in order to create a link between themselves and their victims that would not otherwise exist. There was logic in his actions and he showed no obvious signs of a mental disorder. The crimes were perfectly planned and premeditated, to the point where the killer was able to reproduce the same crime over and over again with different victims. He wasn't spontaneous, he didn't make sloppy mistakes like choosing a victim at random or being opportunistic. Killing them was only one step of the many he had to carry out to complete his tableau, his master plan, his psychosexual fantasy, which he was compelled to repeat over and over again without his thirst ever diminishing, without his needs being satisfied. He needed to personalize his victims to make them part of his world, to link himself to them and to make them belong to him beyond mere sexual possession.

His modus operandi revealed a lively intelligence, in the care he took to protect his identity, in allowing the necessary time to commit his crime, make his escape, and leave his signature, the unmistakable sign that identified him beyond the shadow of a doubt. He didn't target prostitutes or drug addicts, who were accustomed to going with just anyone. And although at first glance teenage girls might have appeared vulnerable, the fact was that girls nowadays knew how to take care of themselves pretty well. They knew the risks with regard to assault and rape and tended to move around in fairly closed groups of friends, so it was unlikely that a girl would have agreed to go with a stranger. There was the fact that Elizondo was a small town, and like in most small towns, the majority of people knew one another. Amaia was sure that the *basajaun* knew his victims, that he was very likely an adult male and so would have a vehicle available with which to transport them and make his escape in the middle of the night, probably the same vehicle he used to entrap them. The *basajaun* chose low-risk victims. In small towns, it was normal for locals to stop at the bus stop when they saw somebody waiting and offer a ride, at least as far as the next town. Carla had ended up alone on the mountain when she argued with her boyfriend, and Ainhoa had missed the bus to the neighboring town. If she was near the bus stop, and bearing in mind that she would be nervous and worried about her parents' reaction, the possibility that she got into a car belonging to someone she knew, someone middle-aged, someone she'd known all her life, became stronger.

She looked at the girls' faces one by one. Carla was smiling seductively, her lips were very red and her teeth were perfect. Ainhoa was looking timidly at the camera, as people who know they aren't photogenic tend to do, and the photograph certainly didn't do justice to the youngest victim's emerging beauty. And then there was Anne, who looked at the camera with the indifference of an empress and a smile that was arch and demure at the same time. Amaia looked carefully at her green eyes, and it wasn't hard to imagine them lit up with scorn and ill will while she laughed in Ros's face. Although that was impossible, since she was already dead when Ros saw her. A *belagile*. A witch. Not a fortune-teller or a healer. A dark and powerful woman with a terrible pact hanging over her soul. A servant of evil capable of twisting and contorting facts until they bent to her will. *Belagile*. It was years since she had heard that word. In modern Basque, the word *sorgin* or *sorgiña* was used; *belagile* was the old word, the true word, the one that refers to the servants of evil. The word brought to mind childhood memories of her *amatxi* Juanita telling them stories about witches. Legends that were now considered part of popular folklore, attractive to tourists, but that came from a time not so long ago when people believed in the existence of witches, servants of evil, and in their sinister powers of raising chaos and destruction and even causing the death of those who stood in their way.

She picked up the copy of José Miguel Barandiarán's *Witchcraft and Witches* again, which she had sent someone to borrow from the library as soon as it opened. The anthropologist asserted the popular belief, deep-rooted throughout the north of the country, and especially in the Basque Country and Navarra, that someone was undeniably a *belagile* if there wasn't a single mark or freckle on the whole of her body. The image of Anne's naked skin on the autopsy table had kept coming back to her, her mother's story about the day she took Anne home, the constant references to her marble-white skin. Surely it had been the strangeness of her skin that had alarmed the sister-in-law.

Amaia read the definition of a witch: "I use the term 'witchcraft' to refer to that manifestation of the popular spirit which considers certain people to be in possession of extraordinary talents, by virtue of their magical abilities or their communication with infernal powers." It would have sounded laughable if not for the fact that belief in the existence of witches and wizards had brought death, torture, and horrible suffering to hundreds of people accused of making pacts with the devil in the valleys of Navarra that surrounded Elizondo, for the most part women accused by Pierre de Lancre, the ferocious inquisitor of the diocese of Bayonne. A large part of Navarra had belonged to the diocese in the fifteenth century, and de Lancre was an insatiable persecutor of witches, convinced of their existence and their demoniacal power. He expressed these convictions in a book published at the time, in which he explained in great detail the infernal hierarchy and its corresponding hierarchy on earth, a work of complete fantasy and paranoia that described absurd practices and ridiculous signs of the presence of evil.

Amaia looked up until she saw Anne's eyes again.

"Were you a *belagile*, Anne Arbizu?" she asked aloud.

She thought she saw a shadow stretch out toward her from Anne's green eyes. A shiver ran down her back. She sighed and tossed the little book onto the table while she cursed the central heating in the brand-new police station, which was barely warming the building on that cold morning. The corridor was getting noisier. She looked at her watch and was surprised to realize that it was already midday. The police officers came into the room with a rumble of dragged chairs and a rustle of papers, carrying the damp on their clothes like a crystalline sheen.

Iriarte started to speak without preamble. "Well, I've checked the alibis. On New Year's Eve, Rosaura and Freddy went to his mother's house for dinner, along with his aunts and some friends of the family. At around two in the morning, they went to some of the bars in town; lots of people saw them over the course of the night and well into the morning, and they were together the entire time. On the day Ainhoa was killed, Freddy was at home all day with various friends who arrived as others left; he wasn't alone at any point. They played on the PlayStation, went to Bar Txokoto to pick up a few sandwiches, and watched a film. He didn't leave the house. His friends say he had a cold."

"Okay, that rules him out as a suspect," said Jonan.

"Only for the murders of Carla and Ainhoa, not for Anne. It seems he wasn't as sociable as usual during the last few days. Rosaura wasn't living at the house anymore, and his friends say that although

178 / DOLORES REDONDO

they went around several times, he sent them away with the explanation that he wasn't feeling very well. They all swear that they didn't know anything about Anne and they thought he was genuinely ill. He was complaining about his stomach, and the same day that Anne was killed he said something about going to the ER."

"Have you spoken to all of them? Ángel what's-his-name too? The one who found Freddy at home. He seems to be the one who was most worried about him. Perhaps he can tell us something."

"Ostolaza," supplied Zabalza, "Ángel Ostolaza."

"He's the one I'm missing. He has a job at a workshop in Bera, but his mother couldn't tell me what it is called, although she did have the telephone number. He comes home for lunch, so he'll come down to the station at around half past one."

"Have we got anything else?"

"You were right with regard to the girl's cell phone, chief. She changed phones two weeks ago. She told her father that she'd lost it and didn't want to keep the same number. We found Freddy's latest bill among the mail; with his wife no longer at home he didn't bother to hide or destroy it, and pretty much all the calls and texts to Anne's old number are on it. Anne's computer reflects a very intense social life, lots of followers but no intimate friends. She didn't trust anybody enough to tell them her secrets, although she did boast about her relationship with a married man. There's nothing more."

Jonan lingered for a few moments when the meeting had finished, leafing through the copy of *Witchcraft and Witches*. Amaia smiled when she noticed.

"Come on now, chief, don't tell me you're going to try to look at this case from a different perspective."

"I don't know what perspective to look at it from anymore, Jonan. I feel like I know more and more about this killer, and that we've done a good job, but everything's happened so fast I almost feel dizzy, and in any case, you shouldn't confuse logic and common sense with such savage thinking. I learned a lot about serial killers while I was in Quantico, and the first lesson is that however much we analyze their behavior, they're always a step ahead, turning up the pressure.

I don't believe in witches, but perhaps the killer does, or at least in a certain type of evil, specific to very young women, based on certain signs that he interprets in his own way in order to choose his victim. And this," she said, gesturing to the book, "is because of what various people have said to me about Anne and to give me something to think about."

~

Ángel Ostolaza gave her the impression once again that he was really enjoying his involvement in the investigation. She had seen it on other occasions, but it never ceased to surprise her that someone should feel secretly proud of finding himself implicated in a violent death.

"Let's see, Anne Arbizu was killed on the Monday, right? Well, Freddy called me that day to say that he was in agony with his stomach. It's not the first time it's happened to him, you know. A couple of years ago he had an ulcer, and it's happened to him several times since then, mostly after the weekend when he drinks too much and doesn't eat . . . Well, you know how these things go. He'd felt awful all day Sunday, and on Monday he had a pain he just couldn't get rid of. It would have been about half past three when he phoned. I was still at work so I told him to go to the walk-in center, but Freddy never goes anywhere by himself; either Ros or I used to go everywhere with him. So when I finished work I went to pick him up and I went to the ER with him."

"And what time was that?"

"Well, I get off at seven, so I'd guess about seven thirty."

"How long were you at the ER?"

"How long? Awhile, almost two hours. There were a lot of people with the flu and that sort of thing, and the poor guy was exhausted by the time they saw him. They took an X-ray and ran a few tests and eventually they injected him with some Tylenol. We left at eleven and, since Freddy wasn't in pain anymore and we were hungry, we went to the Saioa for a couple of steak sandwiches and some *patatas bravas*."

"Freddy ate *bravas* having just been to the ER with a stomach-ache?" asked Iriarte in surprise.

"It wasn't hurting him anymore, and what makes him feel the worst is not eating."

"Okay. What time did you leave the bar?"

"I don't know, but we stayed a good while, at least an hour. Then I took him home and we played a game on the PlayStation, but I didn't stay long because I have to get up early for work." Ángel looked down and stayed like that for a few moments, then he made a sort of wheezing noise and Iriarte realized he was crying. "What's going to happen now? He's definitely not going to be able to walk again, he doesn't deserve that, he's a good guy, you know? He doesn't deserve that." He covered his face with his hands and continued to cry. Iriarte went out into the corridor and returned a minute later with a cup of coffee, which he placed in front of the man. He looked at Amaia.

"If our friend Ángel is telling the truth, and I think he is," he concluded in a kindly voice, smiling at Ángel, who looked at him hopefully, "it will be very easy to prove it. I'll drop by the walk-in center. They have security cameras, and if they were there like he says they were, the footage will be his alibi. I'll send you an email. I'll send the report exonerating Freddy to the commissioner."

"Thank you," she said. "I'm off to meet with the bear experts."

27

FLORA SALAZAR made herself a cup of coffee and sat down behind the desk in her office before looking at the clock. Six on the dot. Her employees started to make their way toward the exit, saying goodbye to one another and waving to her through the glass of the door, which she had left half open after telling Ernesto that she needed him to stay an hour later. Ernesto Murúa had been working for Flora for ten years and acted as workshop manager and head pastry chef.

Flora heard the unmistakable sound of a truck stopping at the entrance to the warehouse, and a minute later Ernesto's skeptical face appeared at her office door.

"Flora, there's a truck here from Harinas Ustarroz. The driver says we've ordered a hundred fifty-kilo sacks of flour. I've told him it must be a mistake, but the guy's really insistent."

She picked up a ballpoint, took the cap off, and pretended to write something on her calendar.

"No, it's not a mistake, I placed that order. I knew they would bring it now and that's why I asked you to stay late today."

Ernesto looked at her in confusion. "But Flora, the warehouse is full, and I thought you were happy with Harinas Lasa's service and quality. We tried Ustarroz a year ago, remember, and we decided that their quality was inferior."

"Well, now I've decided to give them another try. I haven't been too happy with the quality of the flour recently; it's lumpy and the texture seems different, even the smell of it has changed. They made me a good offer, and it was all I needed to make up my mind."

"And what shall we do with the flour we already have?"

"I've arranged it with the guys from Ustarroz. They'll take away the stuff from the flour bin, and you can throw out the stuff from the kneading trough and the jars. I want you to replace all the flour in the workshop with new flour and get rid of what we had before. We can't use it because it's not good enough, so out it goes."

Ernesto nodded, not in the least convinced, and went to the entrance to show the driver where he should put the sacks he had delivered.

"Ernesto," she called him again. He came back. "Naturally I expect discretion in this matter. Admitting that our flour was bad is something that could really damage us. Not a word, and if one of the workers asks you, just say they made us a very good offer and nothing more. It's best to avoid the subject."

"Of course," replied Ernesto.

Flora stayed in her office for another fifteen minutes, which she spent washing her coffee cup and cleaning the coffee machine while a sinister thought took shape in her head. She checked the door was locked and walked toward the wall where she'd hung a painting by Javier Ciga, which she had bought two years earlier to decorate the office. She took it down with the utmost care and placed it on the sofa, revealing the steel safe hidden behind the painting. She turned the little silvery wheels with deft fingers, and the safe opened with a creak. Envelopes containing papers, a bundle of receipts for bills, and wallets and folders containing documents were piled up in an ordered heap from largest to smallest, beside which was a small velvet bag. She picked up the whole pile and took it out of the safe, revealing a large leather-bound journal that had been hidden against the back wall. As she picked it up, she had the impression that it was damp and weighed more than she remembered. She carried it to her table, sat down in front of it, looking at it with a mixture of excitement and urgency, and opened it. The cuttings hadn't been stuck in, but perhaps by dint of the length of time they had spent pressed between those pages, they had stayed exactly where she had placed them more than twenty years earlier. They had barely yellowed, although the ink had faded a bit and was now gray and worn, as if it had been washed many times. She turned the pages, taking care not to alter the chronological order in which they had been arranged, and reread the name that a voice had been repeating in her head ever since Amaia left the workshop. Teresa Klas.

Teresa had been the daughter of Serbian immigrants who had arrived in the valley at the start of the 1990s, fleeing justice in their own country according to some, although those were only rumors. They had immediately found work in the town, and when Teresa, who wasn't doing too well at school, was old enough to work, she got a job at the Berrueta farm, looking after the aged mother, who had significant mobility problems. What Teresa lacked in brains she made up for in beauty, and she knew it. Her long mane of blond hair and her body, which was well developed for her age, were the subject of much comment in the town. She had been working at the farm for three months when she was found dead behind some haystacks. Police interrogated all the men who worked there, but they didn't manage to arrest anybody. It was summer, there were a lot of outsiders around, and they reached the conclusion that the girl had gone out into the fields with a stranger and had been raped and murdered there. Teresa Klas, Teresa Klas. Teresa Klas. If Flora closed her eyes, she could almost see that little whore's face.

"Teresa," she murmured. "All these years later and you're still making my life difficult."

She closed the journal and returned it to its place at the back of the safe, hiding it behind the other documents. She put the little bag back in its place, unable to resist loosening the silk cord that held it closed. The dim light of the office was enough to bring out a glint in the red patent of the shoes. Overwhelmed by a strong sense of disquiet, she touched the smooth curve of the heel with her index finger. This was a new emotion for her, and more annoying than any other she had ever experienced. She locked the safe and rehung the picture, being careful to leave it exactly parallel to the floor. Then she picked up her bag and went out into the workshop to inspect the work. She waved to the truck driver and said goodbye to Ernesto.

When he was sure that Flora had gone, Ernesto went into the workshop, picked up a roll of five-kilo bags, and started to fill them with the old flour from the bin. He took a handful and raised it to his nose; it smelled the same as always. He took a pinch between his fingers and tasted it.

"The woman's mad," he murmured to himself.

"What was that?" asked the truck driver, thinking Ernesto had been speaking to him.

"I was saying to take a couple of bags of flour home with you if you want."

"Okay, thanks," said the man, surprised.

Ernesto filled ten five-kilo sacks, and when it looked like enough, he carried them to the trunk of his car, which was parked by the entrance. He put the rest in an industrial garbage bag, which he tied and took to the trash can. The driver had almost finished unloading the flour already.

"These are the last ones," he announced.

"In that case, don't put them in the workshop. Bring them here and I'll pour them into the kneading trough," said Ernesto.

SPRING 1989

They ate early in Rosario's house, as soon as Juan got back from the workshop, and the girls often had to finish their homework after supper. After they had eaten dinner, while the girls were clearing the table, Amaia turned to her father.

"I need to pop around to Estitxu's house. I didn't write my homework down properly and I don't know what page I need to study for tomorrow."

"Okay, go, but don't be long," answered her father, who was sitting on the sofa next to his wife.

The little girl sang softly to herself on her way to the workshop, smiling and fingering the key under her sweater. She checked both sides of the street to reassure herself that nobody could tell her mother that they'd seen her go in. She put the key into the keyhole and breathed a sigh of relief when the lock turned with a click that seemed to echo around the warehouse. She went into the darkness and locked the door behind her without forgetting to put the bolt across, and only then did she switch the light on. She looked around with the sense of urgency that always filled her when she came by herself; her heart was thumping so loudly that her inner ear was full of the loud beating of blood pumping through her veins. At the same time she savored the privilege of the secret she shared with her father and the responsibility represented by having a key. She went toward the jars without delay and bent down to get the manila envelope hidden behind them.

"What are you doing here?" her mother's voice thundered in the empty workshop.

All her muscles tensed as if she had received an electric shock. Her hand, which had managed to brush against the envelope, sprang back as if all her tendons had snapped at once. The impulse made her lose her balance and she found herself sitting on the floor. She felt fear, a logical and reasoned fear, while she thought about the fact that she had left her mother at home in a housecoat and slippers watching the television news and the certainty that she had been here, waiting in the dark, in spite of that fact. The flat, neutral tone of her mother's voice transmitted more hostility and threat than Amaia had ever known before.

"Aren't you going to answer me?"

Slowly, and without managing to get up from the floor, the girl turned until she met her mother's harsh gaze. She was wearing outdoor clothes, which she must have been wearing beneath her housecoat all along, and shoes with low heels instead of the slippers. Even at that point she felt a jolt of admiration for that proud woman who would never go out into the street in her housecoat or without smartening up.

Her voice sounded suffocated. "I only came to look for something." She knew immediately that her excuse was poor and incriminating.

Her mother remained exactly where she was, merely tilting her head back slightly before speaking in the same tone.

"There's nothing of yours here."

"There is."

"Is there? Let me see."

Amaia retreated until she felt a column against her back and, without taking her eyes off her mother, she used it to help her stand up. Rosario took two steps, swept the heavy bin aside as if it were empty, picked up the envelope with her daughter's name on it, and tipped the contents into her hand.

"Are you stealing from your own family?" she said, slamming the money onto the kneading table with such force that a coin escaped, fell to the floor, and rolled three or four meters to the workshop door, where it remained upright on its edge.

"No, *Ama*, it's mine," stammered Amaia, unable to take her eyes off the crumpled notes.

"Impossible, it's too much money. Where did you take it from?"

"It's from my birthday, *Ama*. I've saved it, I swear," she said, pressing her hands together.

"If it's yours, why don't you keep it at home? And why do you have a key to the workshop?"

"*Aita* . . . let me have it." As she spoke, something broke inside her and she realized that she was betraying her father.

Rosario remained silent for a few seconds, and when she spoke her tone was that of a priest reprimanding a sinner.

"Your father . . . Your father, always indulging you, always spoiling you. Until he manages to make you into a little whore. Of course it was him who gave you the money to buy all those pieces of junk you were hiding in your satchel . . ."

Amaia didn't answer.

"Don't worry," her mother continued, "I threw them all in the trash as soon as you left the house. Did you think you were deceiving me? I've known about this for days, but not about the key. I didn't know how you were getting in."

Without realizing what she was doing, Amaia raised her hand to her chest and clutched the key beneath the fabric of her sweater. Tears filled her eyes, which were still fixed on the mound of notes that her mother was folding and tucking into her skirt pocket. Then she smiled, looked at her daughter and, with feigned tenderness, said, "Don't cry, Amaia. I'm doing all this for your own good, because I love you."

"No," she whispered.

"What did you say?" Her mother was surprised.

"No, you don't love me."

"I don't love you?" Rosario's voice was acquiring a dark, threatening twist.

"No," said Amaia, speaking more loudly, "you don't love me. You hate me."

"I don't love you . . ." her mother repeated incredulously. Her anger was already obvious.

Amaia shook her head, still crying.

"I don't love you, you say . . ." moaned her mother before her hands shot out toward her daughter's neck, groping with blind fury. Amaia took a step back, and her mother's fingers caught the cord with the key hanging from it, and locked around it like grappling hooks, imprisoning it. The little girl tugged in confusion, twisting her neck and feeling the cord slip over her skin with a burning sensation. She felt a couple of strong yanks, and she was sure that the cord would break, but her neck muscles resisted the pulls, making her stumble like a puppet caught up in a tornado. She bumped against her mother's chest, and her mother hit her hard enough to knock her over. Amaia would have fallen were it not for the cord that held her up by the neck, digging even deeper into her skin.

She looked up, fixed her eyes on her mother's and, her courage renewed by the adrenaline coursing through her veins, spat, "No, you don't love me, you've never loved me." And with a powerful tug she broke free from Rosario's hands. Her mother's expression changed from one of surprise to one of absolute urgency as she ran through the workshop in a desperate search.

Amaia was overwhelmed by a panic she had never experienced before, and she knew, instinctively, that she needed to flee. She spun around, turning her back on her mother, and began to make her way toward the door in such frantic terror that she fell over and then everything started to look strange. Whenever she remembered that night she saw once again the tunnel into which the whole workshop had morphed; the corners became dark and the edges became rounded, bending reality until it became a wormhole full of cold and fog. At the end of the tunnel was the door, which seemed distant and radiant, as if a powerful light shone on the other side of it and the rays filtered around its edges and through the cracks in its frame, while everything grew darker around her and faded to black and white, as if she'd suddenly become color-blind.

Crazy with fear, she turned toward her mother in time to see the approach of the blow from the steel rolling pin her father used to roll out the puff pastry. In vain, she lifted a hand to protect herself, and she felt her fingers break before the side of the cylinder slammed into her head. After that, everything went dark.

~

Rosario leaned against the doorjamb in the small living room and looked hard at her husband, who was smiling, engrossed in the sports on the television. She didn't say anything, but her chest was heaving as she panted from the effort of running.

"Rosario," he said, surprised. "What's wrong?" he asked, getting to his feet. "Do you feel ill?"

"It's Amaia . . ." she answered. "Something's happened . . ."

With his pajamas on beneath his dressing gown, he ran through the streets that separated the house from the workshop. He felt his lungs burning and a stitch in his side that threatened to choke him, but he continued running, urged on by the throbbing pain deep inside him that told him something awful had happened. The certainty of what he already knew was sinking in, and it was only a strong desire not to accept it that pushed him to redouble his efforts, both in his running and in his desperate prayer: *please, no, please.*

Juan noticed from some way off that there were no lights on in the workshop, which he would have been able to see through the cracks in the blinds and the narrow vent near the roof, which was always open, summer and winter.

Rosario caught up with him at the door and took the key out of her pocket.

"But is Amaia here?"

"Yes."

"Then why is it dark?"

His wife didn't answer. She opened the door and they went inside; only when the door was closed again did she turn on the light. He couldn't see a thing for a couple of seconds. He blinked, forcing his eyes to adapt to the intense light while his gaze searched frenetically for his daughter.

"Where is she?"

Rosario didn't answer. She leaned against the door and cast a sideways glance. A parody of a smile appeared on her face.

"Amaia!" her father yelled frantically. "Amaia!"

He turned to look at his wife, and the expression on her face made him turn pale. He advanced toward her.

"Oh, my God, Rosario! What have you done to her?"

A step farther and he discovered the slippery pool of blood beneath his feet. He stared at it, as it was already starting to take on a darker shade and, horrified, looked up at his wife again.

"Where is the girl?" he asked in a small voice.

She didn't answer, but her eyes opened wider and she began to bite her lower lip as if enjoying a sublime pleasure. He advanced, crazed by anger, fear, and horror, took her by the shoulders, and shook her as if she had no bones. He leaned in close to his wife's face and shouted, "Where is my daughter?"

An expression of profound disdain shone in the woman's eyes, and her mouth became as thin as a knife blade. She stretched out a hand and pointed toward the kneading trough full of flour.

This was similar to a marble drinking trough, with enough capacity for four hundred kilos, and the sacks were emptied into it before the flour was used in the workshop. He looked where Rosario was pointing and noticed two large drops of blood that had sunk into the flour, almost like crumbly biscuits on the surface. He turned to look at his wife again, but she had turned to face the wall, determined not to meet his eyes. He moved forward, mesmerized by the blood, which he could smell, feeling all his senses become alert, listening, trying to discover what it was she knew that was escaping him. He noticed a small movement on the smooth, perfumed surface of the flour and gave a shout when he saw a small hand emerging from that snowy sea, convulsing with a violent tremor. He took the hand with his and pulled on his daughter's body, which emerged from the flour like a drowned woman from the waves. He placed her on the kneading table and, with the utmost care, began to remove the flour that blinded her eyes and blocked her mouth and nose, speaking to her all the while, aware of his tears falling onto his daughter's face drawing salty paths among those that were already visible on his little one's skin.

"Amaia, Amaia, my little girl . . ."

Amaia was trembling as if attached to an intermittent electric current, convulsing her fragile little body in rough jolts.

"Go and get the doctor," he ordered his wife.

She didn't move from where she stood; she had her thumb in her mouth and was sucking on it childishly.

"Rosario," Juan shouted, about to lose his temper.

"What?" she shouted, turning around angrily.

"Go and get the doctor right now."

"No."

"What?" He spun around, incredulous.

"I can't go," she replied calmly.

"What are you trying to say? You need to bring the doctor here right now, the girl's already in a very serious condition."

"I've already told you I can't," she murmured, smiling timidly. "Why don't you go and I'll stay here with her."

Juan picked up the child, who was still trembling, and went over to his wife.

"Look at me, Rosario. Go to the doctor's house right now and bring him here." He spoke to her as if she were a stubborn child. He opened the door of the workshop and pushed her outside. That was when he realized that his wife's clothes were covered in flour and there was blood on the fingers she had been licking.

"Rosario . . ."

She turned and started running up the street.

An hour later, the doctor was washing his hands in the sink and drying them on the towel Juan offered him.

"We've been very lucky, Juan, the girl is okay. The little finger and ring finger on her right hand are fractured, although what worries me most is the cut on her head. The flour acted as a natural compress, soaking up the blood and forming a scab that stopped the bleeding almost immediately. The convulsions are normal for someone who's suffered a serious head trauma—"

"It was my fault," Juan interrupted him. "I gave her a key so that she could get into the workshop whenever she wanted and, well . . . I didn't imagine that a little girl could hurt herself in here on her own . . ."

"Come on now, Juan," said the doctor, turning to face him in an attempt to see his expression. "There's something more. She had flour in her ears, her nose, her mouth . . . In fact, your daughter was completely covered in flour . . ."

"I suppose she slipped on some butter or oil, banged her head, and fell into the kneading trough."

"She could have fallen forward or backward, but she was completely covered in it, Juan."

Amaia's father looked at his hands as if they held the answer.

"Perhaps she fell in forward and turned over when it felt like she was drowning."

"Yes, perhaps," the doctor conceded. "Your daughter's not that tall, Juan. If she collided with the edge of one of the tables, it's unlikely that her weight would have tipped her into the kneading trough. It's more likely she would have crumpled to the floor. Furthermore," he added, looking down, "look where the pool of blood is."

Juan covered his face with his hands and started to cry.

"Manuel, I . . ."

"Who found her?"

"My wife," he groaned desolately.

The doctor sighed, letting the air out noisily.

"Is Rosario taking the medication I prescribed for her? You know perfectly well that she can't stop taking it for any reason."

"Yes . . . I don't know . . . What are you insinuating, Manuel?"

"Juan, you know we're friends, you know that I respect you. What I'm going to say to you is between you and me, I'm speaking to you as a friend, not a doctor. Get the child out of your house; keep her away from your wife. Patients with the kind of disorder she suffers from sometimes turn on someone close to them, making them the object of their anger. That someone, as you well know, is your daughter, and I think we both suspect that this isn't the first time it's happened. Amaia's presence changes her and makes her angry. If you keep her away, your wife will calm down, but most of all you have to do it for the little one, because the next time she might kill her. What happened today is very serious, very, very serious. As a doctor I ought to submit a report about what I've seen tonight, but as a doctor I also know that if Rosario takes her medication, she'll be fine, and I know what a report could do to your family. Now, as both a friend and a doctor, I have to ask you to get the little girl out of your house, because she's in serious danger. If you don't do as I ask, I'll be obliged to file that report. I beg you to understand."

Juan leaned against the table without taking his eyes off the pool of coagulating blood that was shining in the light like a dirty mirror.

"Is there no possibility that it could have been an accident? Perhaps Amaia hurt herself and Rosario didn't react very well when she saw the blood, perhaps she put her on top of the kneading trough while she came to find me." His own words suddenly seemed to him like a convincing argument. "She came to find me, doesn't that mean anything?"

"She wanted an accomplice. She went to tell you because she trusted you, because she knew that you would believe her, that you would make every effort to believe her and deny the truth, and in fact that's what you're doing, it's what you've been doing for all these years since Amaia was born, or do I have to remind you what happened. She's a sick woman, she's got a mental disorder that we can treat with medication. But if she carries on like this, you'll have to take more drastic measures."

"But . . ." he groaned.

"Juan, there's a recently washed steel rolling pin in the sink. In addition to the cut on the top of her head, Amaia's got an injury above her right ear. She has two fractured fingers, which are clearly a defensive injury from trying to stop the first blow like this." He raised his hand like an upturned umbrella. "She must have lost consciousness, and the second blow didn't cause a cut because it was flatter. There's no blood, but since her hair's so short even you can see that your daughter has a considerable bump and a more sunken area where she was hit. It's the second blow that worries me, the one she struck when Amaia was already unconscious. Her intention was to make sure she had really killed her."

Juan covered his face again and wept bitterly while his friend cleaned up the blood.

28

W E'VE GOT another dead girl, chief," announced Zabalza.

Amaia swallowed before replying. Zabalza had said "we've got another" as if they were trading cards in a collection. This was speeding up in a way that was rarely seen. If the crimes continued to occur at an increasing rate, the killer would go into a spin and it would be more likely he'd commit an error that might lead them to him, but the price paid in lives would be very high. It was already very high.

"Where?" she asked firmly.

"Well, that's where the difference lies: this one isn't by the river."

"Where, then?" she said, on the verge of losing patience.

"In an abandoned hut on a hill near Lekaroz."

Amaia stared at him, evaluating the importance of this new information.

"This is quite a big change in the modus operandi . . . Did he leave the shoes? How did they find her?"

"Well," said Zabalza slowly, as if considering the effect of his words, "that's the other strange thing. It looks like some children found her yesterday, but they didn't say anything. One of them mentioned it at home today, and the father went to the hut to see if it was true and then called the Guardia Civil. There was a patrol car in the area that responded, and they confirm that there's a body belonging to a young girl. They've put all the protocol for homicide and sexual crimes into action. It looks like it could be a girl whose disappearance was reported days ago—"

Amaia interrupted him. "Why didn't we know about any of this?"

"The mother reported her missing to the Guardia Civil barracks in Lekaroz, and you know how these things are."

"Well, how are relations with the Guardia Civil in the valley?"

"We have a good relationship with the *guardias*. They do their job, we do ours, and they collaborate wherever they can."

"And what about the commanders?"

"Well, that's a completely different story. There's always some problem or other with whose jurisdiction it is, a petty rivalry, information being withheld. You know the drill."

"So there might be more girls missing in the valley that we don't know about because their disappearances were reported to the Guardia Civil?"

"Lieutenant Padua is in charge of the investigation, he's waiting there to speak with you, and he says that there wasn't really a formal report, although the mother had been coming in daily for several days saying that something had happened to her daughter. However, there were witnesses who said that the girl had gone of her own accord."

~

Padua wasn't wearing a uniform, although he did get out of an official patrol car, accompanied by another *guardia*, who was in uniform. He introduced himself and his colleague while exchanging a firm handshake with Amaia and then went with her, walking at her side.

"She's called Johana Márquez. Fifteen years of age. She was originally from the Dominican Republic, but she's been living in Spain since she was four and moved to Lekaroz when she was eight after her mother got remarried to another Dominican. They've got another young daughter, age four. The girl had problems with her parents, to do with the hours she was keeping, and she ran away from home on a previous occasion two months ago; she was at a friend's house. It looked like the same thing this time. It seems she had a boyfriend and ran away with him; there were witnesses. Even so, the mother kept coming to the barracks every day to tell us that something bad had happened, that her daughter hadn't run away."

"Then it looks like she was right."

Padua didn't answer.

"Let's talk later," she suggested in the face of his silence.

"Sure."

The cabin turned out to be invisible from the road. It was only on approaching it cross-country that it could be seen half hidden by the trees, camouflaged by the numerous creepers that grew up over the façade and disguised it so it blended in with the tangled, wooded depths that surrounded it. Lieutenant Padua waved a greeting to the two *guardias* stationed to either side of the door. The interior was cool and dark, tinged with the unmistakable odor of a corpse that has started to decompose and by another sweeter, musky one, like perfumed mothballs. The aroma immediately made Amaia think of her grandmother Juanita's linen closet and the sets of folded sheets with their corners embroidered with the family initials, which were kept, perfectly aligned, in that wardrobe whose shelves were hung with little transparent bags containing balls of camphor that surprised anyone who dared open the doors with their sickening reek.

She waited a few seconds until her eyes became accustomed to the dark. The roof had begun to sag due to the weight of the previous year's snowfalls, but the wooden beams looked like they could hold it up for a few more winters to come. Blackened scraps of old fabric and cord hung from the crossbeams, and some of the creepers that grew up the front of the hut had made their way in through the hole in the roof and were entwined with hundreds of brightly colored, fruit-shaped air fresheners that hung from the rafters. Amaia was sure that unique combination was the source of the sickening perfume. The cabin consisted of a single rectangular room. It contained an old and unusually large table and an accompanying bench that seemed to have been upended on the floor beside it. In the center of the room was a strangely swollen two-seat sofa covered in damp and dark stains and positioned facing the blackened fireplace, which was full of scraps and trash that someone had tried unsuccessfully to burn. The top of a fairly clean foam-filled mattress was visible over the back of the sofa. The floor appeared to be covered by a fine layer of earth that was darker in the places where water had got in through the roof, forming puddles that had already dried up. Otherwise, it was clean and it seemed recently swept; the strokes of a broom that Amaia spotted leaning against the chimney were still visible. Not a trace of a body.

"Where . . . ?"

"Behind the sofa, Inspector." Padua pointed.

She shone the light of her flashlight toward the place he was pointing out to her.

"We need floodlights."

"They've already gone to get some, they're bringing them now."

The beam of her flashlight lit up silver-colored sneakers and earth-stained white socks. She took a couple of steps back while she waited for them to set up the floodlights and take the preliminary photos. She closed her eyes, said a brief prayer for the soul of this little girl, and began.

"I want everyone out of here until we've finished, just my team, the forensics officers, and Lieutenant Padua from the Guardia Civil," she said, meeting the gaze of all those present as if she were giving a presentation. Apart from one of the uniformed *guardias*, she was the only woman present, and her experience with the FBI had taught her the importance of using professional courtesy when taking charge of a case on which other police officers were already working. "They found the body and were kind enough to inform us. I want to know who's been in here and what they've touched, and that includes the children and the father of the boy who raised the alarm. Jonan, you're with me. I want photos of everything. Zabalza, give us a hand, we're going to move the mattress very carefully. Watch where you put your feet, everyone."

"Wow," exclaimed Jonan, "this is different."

The girl, an extremely thin teenager, had had tanned skin that now seemed rather swollen, and the swelling was a bright olive green. The clothes had been separated to either side of the body using rough, clumsy cuts, although some scraps had been used to cover her pubic area. A piece of cord hung from her bulky, purplish neck, its ends disappearing into the folds of the swollen skin. A bloodless hand rested on her stomach, holding a bunch of white flowers held together with a white ribbon. Her eyes were half open, and a film of whitish mucus was visible between her eyelashes. Dozens of small flowers at various stages of decay surrounded her head, arranged in her lusterless, wavy hair and forming a tiara that reached her shoulders and drew a silhouette around the body.

"Fuck," murmured Iriarte. "What is this?"

"She's Snow White," whispered Amaia, impressed.

Dr. San Martín, who had just arrived, walked around the sofa and stood next to Amaia.

He put on his gloves and gently touched the girl's jaw and arm.

"The state of the body indicates that she's been dead for several days, quite a while."

"Some of the flowers are more recent, a day old at the most," Amaia pointed out, gesturing to the bouquet the girl was holding against her stomach.

"Then I would say that whoever put the first flowers here has come back each day to add fresh ones. Some of these," he speculated, pointing to the drier ones, "have probably been here more than a week. Furthermore, someone has poured perfume onto the body."

"I'd already noticed that, as well as the air fresheners. I think"— Amaia stood up to look at Iriarte—"that the bottle might be somewhere in the pile of trash in the fireplace."

She had recognized the rather pompous, dark-colored little bottle as she came in. Ros had given her that same extremely expensive perfume two years earlier, which she had worn only a couple of times. James liked it, but she found the dizzying notes of sandalwood too sickly sweet. She knew she would never use it again. Iriarte raised his gloved hand, in which he held the ash-covered bottle.

"The body," continued San Martín, "completed the chromatic phase several days ago and has now entered the emphysematous stage. As you know, I'll be more precise following the autopsy, but I would say she's been dead for around a week." He touched the girl's skin, pinching the area between her fingers. "The skin hasn't started to disintegrate yet, and it still seems to be quite hydrated, but being in a cool, dark place such as this may have helped conserve it. However, the body has already started to swell from the gases generated during putrefaction, which is most noticeable here and here." He pointed to her green-tinged abdomen and her neck, which was so inflamed that the ends of the string hanging in the girl's dark hair were barely visible.

San Martín leaned over the body, looking at something that had caught his attention. Inside the girl's open mouth, larvae belonging to insects that had laid their eggs there were visible.

"Look at this, Inspector." Amaia covered her nose and mouth with the mask San Martín handed her and leaned over. "Look at her neck; do you see what I see?"

I can see two enormous, well-defined bruises, one on each side of the trachea."

"Yes, ma'am, and she's bound to have several more on her neck. We'll be able to see them once we can move her. In spite of what the cord is trying to tell us, this girl was strangled manually, and these two bruises correspond to where her killer's thumbs would have been. Take a photo of this," he said, turning to Jonan. "I hope to see you at the autopsy this time."

Jonan lowered the camera for a moment to look at Amaia, who continued talking without paying them any attention.

"Did he kill her here, Doctor?"

"I would say so, although it will be up to you to confirm that. But, in any case, if he didn't kill her here, he brought her here immediately, since the body wasn't moved after the two hours directly following the death. The cause of death was most probably strangulation, asphyxia. Date: it'll be necessary to analyze the larvae, but I would say a week ago. And location: certainly here. The body temperature has stabilized at that of the hut, and the livor mortis suggests she hasn't been moved since shortly after her death. Rigor mortis has almost completely disappeared, as one would expect at this stage, and it appears that signs of dehydration have been delayed by the obvious environmental humidity."

Amaia took a pair or tweezers and uncovered the girl's genitals. She moved aside slightly so that Jonan could take the photos.

"What can you tell me about the external lesions? I'd say she was raped."

"Everything would suggest that, yes, but at this stage of decomposition the genitals often appear quite swollen. I'll find out during the autopsy."

"Oh, no!" exclaimed Amaia.

"What's wrong? What have you seen?"

Amaia stood up as if she'd been struck by lightning. Going around the sofa, she caught hold of Iriarte's arm.

"Come on, help me."

"What do you want to do?"

"Move the sofa."

Taking an end each, they lifted it up, realizing that in spite of its appearance it was remarkably light. They moved it forward fifteen centimeters or so.

"Fuck!" exclaimed San Martín.

Judge Estébanez, who was just entering the cabin, came over cautiously.

"What's going on?"

Amaia stared at her. The judge had the impression that Amaia's look went right through her, penetrating through the walls of the hut, the forests, and the age-old rocks that made up the valley. Until she managed to speak.

"Her right arm is missing below the elbow. The cut's clean and there's no blood, so it was cut off when she was already dead. And we won't find it, it's been taken away."

The judge's expression became one of profound disgust.

SPRING 1989

Amaia lived with Aunt Engrasi from that day on, visiting her father in the workshop every day and going home to eat on Sundays. She remembered those meals as regular examinations. She would sit at the head of the table opposite her mother, the seat farthest away from her, and would eat in silence, responding in monosyllables to her father's feeble attempts to start a conversation. She would help her sisters clear the table afterward and, when everything was tidy, she would go to the living room, where her parents would be watching the three o'clock news. There she would say goodbye until the following week. She would lean over and kiss her father, and he would put a folded banknote in her hand. Then she would stand and look at her mother for a couple of minutes, waiting while she continued to watch the television without deigning even to look at her. Then her father would say, "Amaia, your aunt will be expecting you."

And she would leave the house in silence, with a shiver running down her spine. An enormous, triumphant smile would spread across her face as she gave thanks to the almighty God of children that her mother hadn't wanted to touch her, kiss her, or say goodbye to her that day either. She preferred it like that. She was constantly afraid that her mother might give some indication that could be interpreted as a desire for her to return home. She was terrified by just the idea of her mother looking at her face for more than two seconds, because when she did, while her father was searching for the wine in the cellar or leaning over the fireplace to stir up the fire, she felt so scared that her legs trembled and her mouth became as dry as if it were full of flour.

She was alone with her again on only two occasions. The first was a year after the attack, the following spring. Her hair had started growing back and had got a lot longer during the winter. It was the weekend when the clocks changed, but both she and her aunt had forgotten to change theirs, so she arrived at her parents' house an hour early.

"She knocked at the door, and when her mother opened it and stepped aside to let her in, she already knew her father wasn't at home. She went in as far as the middle of the living room and turned to look at her mother, who had stopped in the middle of the short hallway and was watching her from there. She couldn't see her face or the expression of her mouth because the hallway was dark compared to the sunny living room, but she could feel the hostility as if there were a pack of wolves in the hallway. She still had her jacket on, but she started to shiver as if she were being threatened by the cruelest Siberian winter instead of enjoying the warm spring weather. It must have been only a few seconds, but it felt like an eternity to her as she concentrated on the twitching noises and soft moans that came from somewhere where a little girl was crying. She could hear her clearly, although she couldn't see her while she kept a close watch on the threatening evil that was lying in wait in the hallway. The slightest movement, one step, and the girl who was crying began to shout like someone stricken by panic, with muffled howls that barely managed to make it out of her throat, failing to give voice to the madness that threatened her. They are the shouts from nightmares in which little girls scream themselves hoarse, but their screams turn into whispers as soon as they leave their throats. Another step. Another yell, or was it the same one. Either way, it seemed it would go on forever. Her mother reached the living room door, and Amaia could finally see her face. That was enough. In that same instant she realized that she was the little girl who was shouting muffled cries, and the certainty made her lose control of her bladder at the very moment that her father and sisters came through the door.

29

A MAIA MADE the journey to Pamplona in silence, immersed in an inner anxiety that had overwhelmed her since the moment she saw Johana's corpse. There were so many different elements to the crime that she found it difficult to even start establishing a preliminary profile, although she had been going over and over it in her head for the entire trip. The flowers in the girl's hair, the perfume, the bouquet resting on her stomach, the almost modest way the body's nudity had been covered up—all that contrasted with the obvious brutality of the blows to her face, the savage way in which the clothing had been almost torn into strips, the likely rape and the fury with which the killer had lost control, strangling his victim with his own hands. And then there was the matter of the trophy. Many serial killers took something that had belonged to their victims with them in order to be able to recreate the moment of death again and again in private, or at least until the fantasy ceased to be enough to satisfy their needs and they had to go in search of more. But it wasn't often that they took pieces of the body due to the difficulty involved in keeping them intact while at the same time having access to them whenever they wanted. They often chose hair or teeth, but not parts that might suffer a rapid deterioration. Taking a forearm and hand didn't fit with the profile of a sexual predator, and the almost exquisitely careful attention that had been paid to the corpse over several days didn't fit either.

It was lunchtime when they arrived at Pamplona. Their breath had condensed on the glass of the windows due to the cold outside, providing clear evidence of the suffocating heat inside the car, made even more uncomfortable by the presence of Lieutenant Padua. He had insisted on traveling with them but had not opened his mouth once during the journey. When the car finally stopped in front of the Navarra Institute of Forensic Medicine and they got out, a woman totally hidden beneath an umbrella emerged from a small group waiting at the entrance and moved forward a few steps in order to position herself in front of the stairs.

Amaia realized who she was as soon as she saw her: it wasn't the first time that a victim's relative had waited for her at the entrance to the morgue. There was no way they would be allowed to observe the autopsy; there was nothing they could do there. Even the popular belief that the family had to authorize the autopsy was false. Autopsies were carried out as part of judicial protocol under orders from the judge, and in cases where the identification of a body was necessary, this was done via CCTV and the family never entered the autopsy room . . . There was nothing for the family members to do there, but they still gathered at the entrance to the Institute as if called there and waited together, as if a nurse might come out at any moment and tell them that everything had gone smoothly and their loved one would recover in a few days.

When she started to get close to the woman, determined to avoid looking her in the eye, she noticed how pale her face was, the supplicant manner in which she held out a hand toward her while her other held that of a little girl, only three or four years old, whom the mother almost dragged along with her. Amaia sped up.

"Señora, señora, I beg you," said the woman, managing to brush Amaia's hand with her own rough, cold one. Then, as if she felt her behavior had crossed some line, she stepped back and clung to the little girl's hand again.

Amaia stopped short and shot a look at Jonan, who was trying to stand between them.

"Please, señora," begged the woman. Amaia looked at her, inviting her to speak. "I'm Johana's mother" was her sole introduction, as if she were assuming a sad title for which no explanation was necessary.

"I know who you are, and I'm very sorry about what's happened to your daughter."

"But it wasn't the *basajaun* who killed my daughter, was it?"

"I'm afraid I can't answer that question, it's still too soon to be certain. We're at a very early stage in the investigation, and the first thing we need to do is establish what happened."

The woman took another step forward. "But you must know, you know, you know that that murderer didn't kill my Johana."

"What makes you say that?"

The woman bit her lip and looked around, as if she might find the answer in the fat drops of rain that were falling.

"Did they . . . ? Did they abuse her?"

Amaia looked at the little girl, who seemed absorbed in contemplating the patrol cars parked at angles in the road.

"I've already told you that it's too early to tell, we can't be sure until we carry out the . . ." Suddenly, the thought of mentioning the autopsy seemed too brutal. The woman came so close that Amaia could smell her bitter breath and the scent of lavender water emanating from her damp clothing. She took Amaia's hand and squeezed it in a gesture that was both acknowledgment and desperation.

"Please, señora, at least tell me how long she's been dead."

Amaia placed her hand over the woman's. "I'll speak with you once the . . . once they've finished examining her. I give you my word."

She pulled free of the hand that was holding hers like an icy claw and moved forward toward the entrance.

"She's been dead for a week, hasn't she?" said the woman, her voice cracking with the effort. "Since the day she disappeared."

Amaia turned toward her.

"She's been dead for seven days. I know it," repeated the woman. Her voice broke completely and she started to cry, sobbing noisily.

Amaia went back to where she stood and looked around, weighing the effect Johana's mother's words had had on her colleagues.

"How do you know that?" Amaia whispered to her.

"Because the day my daughter died, I felt like something broke in here," said her mother, raising her hand to her chest.

The inspector realized that the little girl was clinging to her mother's legs and crying silently.

"Go home, señora, take the little girl away from here. I promise I'll come and speak with you as soon as I have anything to tell you."

The child was weeping, her expression one of infinite love, and the woman looked at her as if she had suddenly realized she was there and as if her existence was somehow miraculous.

"No," she answered firmly. "I'll wait here until they finish. I'll wait here so I can take my daughter away."

Amaia pushed the heavy door, but she was still able to hear the mother's prayer.

"Watch over my daughter, who is inside this building."

Fulfilling his promise to San Martín, Jonan had come into the autopsy room. Amaia was aware that it wasn't his first time, but as a rule he normally avoided this unpleasant experience, which he appeared to find very difficult. He stood in silence, leaning against the steel countertop, and his face gave no hint of any emotion, perhaps because he knew he was being observed by the others, who sometimes made jokes about him being a doctor—of archaeology and anthropology—and yet was squeamish about autopsies. However, Amaia didn't miss the fact that he had his hands behind his back, as if making clear his intention not to touch anything, either physically or emotionally. She had gone over to him before they went in to say that he could give an excuse and decline San Martín's invitation, that she could send him to talk to Johana's mother or to continue working on leads at the police station. But he had decided to stay.

"I have to go in, chief, because this crime is baffling me, and with what I know at the moment, I can't even begin to outline a profile."

"It won't be pleasant."

"It never is."

Normally when she arrived at an autopsy, the technicians had already removed the clothing, taken samples of nails and hair, and often washed the body. Amaia had asked San Martín to wait before doing any of this because she suspected that the way the clothes had been torn might provide some new information. Tying a single-use surgical gown behind her back, she went over to the table.

"Now then, ladies and gentlemen," said San Martín, "let's begin."

The technicians started to take samples of fibers, powder, and seeds that were attached to the different fabrics. Then they removed the plastic bag they had used to preserve the girl's hand, on which two nails were so broken they were hanging off, nails on which traces of skin and blood were evident.

"What does this body say to you? What story does it tell us?" Amaia got things going.

"It has elements in common with the other crimes. However, there are also a lot of differences," said Iriarte.

"For example?"

"The girl's age is similar, the way her clothes were arranged to the sides, the cord around her neck . . . And, perhaps in part, the way the scene was set up on previous occasions," observed Jonan.

"In what sense?"

"I already know for a start that the way the body was presented is different, but there is something virginal about how the flowers were arranged. Perhaps it's an evolution in the fantasy, or he wanted to distinguish this victim in some way."

"By the way, do we know what sort of flowers they are? It's February, I don't expect there are many flowers in the area."

"Yes, I sent a photo to a gardening forum and received a response right away. The little yellow ones are *Calendula officinalis*. They grow at the side of roads. And the white flowers are *Camellia japonica*, a variety of camellias that are only grown in gardens. It's very unlikely that they grow in the woods, although they're both in season as they flower early. I had a look online and found out that they were historically used as a symbol of purity in some cultures," explained a well-informed Jonan.

Amaia remained silent for a few moments considering the idea.

"I don't know, I'm not convinced," said Iriarte.

"What about the differences?"

"Her age aside, the girl doesn't fit the victim profile. Her style of dress was almost childish, jeans and a fleece, and although her clothes have been separated to either side, it looks like something that was done later. He tore her clothes in quite a clumsy way, for a start, some of them are in tatters; she's still wearing her shoes, which in this case are sneakers; the body seems seriously violated, but the pubic hair hasn't been shaved off. Her hands . . . her remaining hand is tense and shows signs of a fight, both in the nails that are half torn off and the half-moon marks on her palms, which tell us that she clenched her fists so tightly the nails broke the skin," said Iriarte, pointing to the wounds. "And of course there's still the matter of the amputation."

"What can you tell me about where she was found?"

"It's completely different. Instead of by the river, a natural, open setting that suggests purity, we found her in a covered, dirty, and abandoned place."

"Who might know about the existence of that hut?" Amaia asked Padua.

"Almost anyone from the area who goes up onto the hill. It's been used by hunters and hikers, and groups out for a picnic used it until the roof started caving in last year . . . In any case, judging by the remains of the trash, it doesn't seem long since it was used for something like that."

"What's the cause of death, Doctor?"

"She was strangled manually, as I already told you when giving my first impressions. This cord was added afterward, when the swelling was already established and, furthermore, this time it's a different kind of cord and it's been knotted."

"Perhaps he came back later to add the cord. Perhaps when they published the first information about the *basajaun*'s crimes . . ." Amaia suggested.

"Yes, it would appear we've got a copycat."

"Or rather an opportunist. A copycat kills imitating the scenario used by the previous killer; the opportunist is an upstart who isn't paying homage to the original killer but rather is trying to disguise his crime in order to have it attributed to the original killer."

The doctor leaned over the body again with a speculum and took a sample from inside the vagina.

"There's semen," he said, passing the swab to the technician, who proceeded to bag and label it. "There are tears to the interior walls of the vagina, and a hemorrhage that was interrupted by the girl's death. She probably died during the rape, since no blood is visible externally. Either that, or she was already dead when the rape occurred."

Amaia came in a bit closer. "What can you tell me about the amputation?"

"It took place postmortem, it didn't bleed, and it was performed with an extraordinarily sharp object."

"Yes, I can see how the bone was cut. The flesh looks a bit frayed higher up, though."

"Yes, I'd noticed that. I'm inclined to say that they're bites from an animal. We'll make a mold and let you know."

"And what about the cord, Doctor?"

"You can see it's different from the others just by looking at it, thicker and with a plastic coating. Clothesline. You'll find out for certain, but it doesn't seem likely that he's decided to change the kind of cord he uses at this stage."

The technicians removed the remains of the clothing, and the corpse lay exposed under the cold lights of the operating room. The bruises formed a purple map across the back and shoulders, on the thighs and calves, where the blood had accumulated due to its own weight after the heart had stopped. The inflammation had deformed the remains of the body on which the signs of puberty were barely visible. Once the earth had been washed from the face, the marks from various blows and the swelling from a punch that had knocked a tooth loose became clear. San Martín removed it with forceps while he gestured to Jonan to come closer. The aroma of the perfume was still very strong, even after washing the body, and when combined with the smell of serious decomposition, it really was repulsive.

Jonan, pale and upset, couldn't take his eyes off the girl's face, but he stayed strong. He kept his breathing steady, and from time to time he punctuated the deep silences with technical questions.

Amaia thought of the increasing popularity of forensic television series in which the most shocking thing was the fact that they resolved a case, or sometimes two, in the course of an hour, thanks to autopsies, identification, interrogations, and even DNA tests, tests that in the real world took at least a couple of weeks even when they were ordered as a matter of urgency, and took a month and a half when no one rushed them. They also had to contend with the fact that there wasn't a forensic laboratory in Navarra capable of carrying out DNA analyses, which had to be sent to Zaragoza, and the extremely high cost of certain tests, which made them almost out of the question. But what made her laugh most was the way the investigators on the shows would stand there, exchanging notes and reports across a body that would be giving off nauseating gases and smells even in the best-case scenario.

She had read that some judges and police officers considered jurors' skewed understanding of forensic techniques, often acquired from TV, to be harmful, since it encouraged them to ask for tests, analyses, and comparisons without any justification, although some scientists also argued that they could finally explain their discoveries without their work sounding like a foreign language. That was certainly the case for forensic entomologists. Ten years ago, their findings were mostly incomprehensible, while nowadays almost everybody knew that it was possible to establish the time and place of a death with great precision by establishing the age of larvae and other fauna found on the cadaver.

Amaia went over to the box in which they had put the remains of the clothes.

"Padua, we've got the remains of a pair of blue jeans, a pale pink Nike fleece, silver sneakers, and white socks here. Tell me, according to her mother's report, what was she wearing when she went missing?"

"Jeans and a pink sweater," murmured Padua.

"Doctor, would you say she could have died the same day she disappeared?"

"It's very likely."

"Could I use your office, Doctor?"

"Be my guest."

Amaia untied the knot at the back of the surgical gown and took one last look at the body, then went out toward the wash basins, saying, "Jonan, come out here and bring Johana's mother through."

In spite of the many occasions on which she had visited the Navarra Institute of Forensic Medicine, she had never been up to San Martín's office, since he seemed perfectly comfortable signing the reports in the small, cramped cubicle beside the autopsy room, which was intended for the use of the technicians. Amaia imagined she would find a room as unusual as its owner, but the luxury with which he had decorated it surprised her. There was no doubt that the office took up more space than he logically had a right to. The furniture was practical, the kind you would expect in the office of a senior scientist, and had simple, modern lines in contrast with the collection of bronze statues that were arranged with the utmost attention and carefully lit. An extraordinarily heavy-looking pietà measuring some seventy centimeters square stood on the large meeting table. Amaia wondered whether they moved it when the table had to be used for meetings.

At the other end of the table, Johana's little sister seemed enchanted by the large number of blank sheets of paper and box of colored pens Jonan had just set in front of her. Her mother sat in trancelike contemplation of the dead Christ in the arms of his mother.

Jonan went over to Amaia. "She's praying," he explained. "She asked me whether I thought the sculpture was consecrated."

"What's her name?"

"Inés, Inés Lorenzo. The little girl's called Gisela."

Amaia waited a minute longer, not wanting to interrupt the prayer, but the woman noticed her presence and turned toward her. Amaia invited her to sit down in one of the chairs and took the other herself. Jonan remained standing near the door, and Inspector Iriarte let Amaia take the lead, opting for one of the chairs at the meeting table, which he turned around so he was facing Amaia and could watch the woman from behind.

"Inés, I'm Inspector Salazar, and these are Deputy Inspector Etxaide, Inspector Iriarte, and Lieutenant Padua from the Guardia Civil. I think you've already met."

Padua picked up the seat behind the desk and moved it to one side. Amaia was grateful that he had decided not to sit behind the desk.

"Inés," began Amaia, "as you know, a Guardia Civil patrol found the body of your daughter today."

The woman stared at her, upright and attentive, as if she were holding her breath.

"During the autopsy, it was established that she'd been dead for several days. She was wearing the same clothes that are mentioned in the missing persons report you filed at the Guardia Civil barracks the day she disappeared."

"I knew it," she muttered, looking at Padua with an expression that wasn't as reproachful as might have been expected. Amaia was afraid she was going to start crying. Instead, she looked at Amaia again and asked, "Did he rape her?"

"Everything would suggest that she suffered a sexual assault."

Inés pursed her lips in a gesture of private self-control.

"It was him," she declared.

"Who do you think it was?" inquired Amaia.

Inés turned to look at the little girl, who had knelt up on the chair and was half lying on the table as she drew, partly hidden by the sculpture. Her mother looked at Amaia.

"I don't think it, I *know* it. My husband, my husband has killed my child."

"Why do you think that? Did he tell you so?"

"He didn't need to tell me, I know. I've known it the whole time but I didn't want to believe it.

"I was a widow when Johana was born. I came to Spain with nothing and I met him here. We got married and he brought my daughter up as if she were his own . . . But everything changed a while ago. Johana rejected him. I thought she was just being a teenager, if you know what I mean? Johana became pretty, as you've seen, and her father started telling me that I needed to keep her on a shorter leash because everyone knows girls get silly at that age and all that nonsense about boys starts, and I . . . Well, Johana was always a very good girl, she never gave me any kind of trouble, she was doing well at school and her teachers were pleased with her, they always told me so, you can ask them if you like."

"There's no need," Amaia assured her.

"She wasn't one of those teenage girls who become antisocial. She helped at home, looked after her little sister, but he was always on her case, what hours she kept, her comings and goings. She complained, and I . . . I let it be, because I thought he really was worried about her, although sometimes I felt things were going too far and that he wanted to control her. I did used to tell him so from time to time, and he would say to me, 'If you let her run wild, she'll go with boys and come back to you pregnant.' I was afraid. But other times I saw how he looked at her, and I didn't like it, no, I didn't like it one bit. But I didn't say anything, except for one time. Johana was wearing a short skirt and she bent down to play with her little sister. I saw how he was looking at her, and it made me sick, and I called him out for it, and do you know what he said? He said, 'That's the way men look at your daughter if she goes around flaunting herself.' Because she wasn't his daughter anymore; she was before, but now he talked to me about 'your' daughter. And all I did was send her to change her clothes."

Amaia looked at Padua before asking, "All right . . . Your husband was very worried about Johana, perhaps too worried, but why do you think he had anything to do with her death?"

"You didn't see him, Inspector, he was obsessed. He even put one of those tracking devices on her phone in order to know where she was every moment of the day. And as soon as she disappeared, I told him, 'Look for her with the tracker,' and he replied, 'I got rid of that service. I ended the contract, it's not necessary anymore. Your daughter went because she's a waste of space, you encouraged her, and she won't come back. She doesn't want to be found and that's the best thing for everyone.' That's what he told me."

Amaia opened the folder offered to her by Lieutenant Padua, who seemed resolved to remain silent for the most part.

"Let's see, Johana disappeared on a Saturday, and you filed the missing persons report the following day, Sunday. However, you called the barracks to say that Johana had returned home on Wednesday while you were at work to collect her things, her ID card, clothes, and some money, and to say that she had gone away with a boy. Is that correct?"

"Yes, I called because he told me to. When I arrived home, he told me she had come and had gone again and that she had taken her things with her. Why wouldn't I believe him? Johana had gone to stay at a friend's house twice before when he'd yelled at her. But I always knew that she was going to come back and I would say as much to him, 'She'll come back.' And do you know why? Because she didn't take her little mouse. A little cuddly toy she's had since she was tiny; she still keeps it on her bed. And I knew that if my daughter went back to my house one day she would take her Toothy, which was what she called him, with her. So I went into her room, saw that he was missing, and my heart fell. I believed him."

"What changed to make you go back to the barracks the next day to ask them to keep looking for her?"

"Her clothes. I don't know if you know what teenage girls are like when it comes to clothes, but I knew her very well, and when I saw which clothes were missing, I knew my daughter hadn't been there. She left her favorite jeans behind, and some of her outfits were only half missing. I don't know if you understand me; she had a specific T-shirt she would wear with a certain skirt or pair of trousers, and she had only taken one half of the outfit, summer clothes that you can't wear at the moment, a sweater that was too small for her . . . Even her newest clothes were still there, things that she had nagged me for like crazy until I bought them for her only a week ago."

"Where's your husband now?"

"When the Guardia Civil came around this morning to tell us that they'd found her body, he turned white as a sheet and was so ill he could hardly stand up. He had to go to bed, but I think he's ill because he knows what he's done, and he knows that they're going to go after him. They will, won't they?"

Amaia stood up.

"Stay here, I'll arrange a car to take you home." The woman started to protest, but Amaia interrupted her. "Your daughter's body will remain here for the moment, and now I need your help, I need you to go home. I want to put an end to this so that Johana and those who love her can be at peace, but you'll have to do what I ask of you."

Inés looked up until she met Amaia's eyes.

"I'll do as you say." And she started to cry.

They could see Inés from the office across the hallway, doubled over and pressing an already damp white handkerchief she had taken out of her bag against her face, and the little girl standing a couple of steps away from her mother, looking at her in desolation without daring to touch her.

"What's the husband's name?"

Padua, who had remained silent until that point, cleared his throat to strengthen his voice, which despite this came out huskily and too quietly. "Jasón, Jasón Medina," he said, literally collapsing into a chair.

"Did you notice that she didn't say his name a single time?"

Padua seemed to think about that.

"How do you want to take this forward? I want to question Jasón Medina. You tell me whether I should do it at the barracks or the police station."

Lieutenant Padua sat up a bit straighter and turned to look at a point on the wall before answering.

"The correct thing would be for it to happen at the barracks, after all, it's our case and we found the body, and if you rule it out as being a crime committed by the *basajaun* . . . I'll call right now and tell them to arrest him and take him to the barracks. I'll be sure to make your cooperation known in any case."

Padua got up, recovering his composure as he did so, rifled through his jacket until he pulled out a cell phone, dialed, and left the office, excusing himself awkwardly.

"I'll be sure to make your cooperation known in any case," Jonan imitated him. "He'll look like an idiot."

"What do you three think?" Amaia asked.

"He's an imitator, like I said before. He doesn't match my idea of the *basajaun*, although the fact that the husband isn't the girl's father is something we'll have to keep in mind. Lots of sexual assaults are perpetrated by the partner of the victim's mother. The fact that he no longer refers to Johana as his daughter helps him to distance himself and to see her as just another woman and not as a member of his family. And it's still strange that he lied about the girl being at home on Wednesday."

"Perhaps he did it to calm the mother down," suggested Jonan.

"Or perhaps because he had raped and killed her and he knew that the girl wouldn't come home, so his obsession immediately stopped and he even went as far as canceling the phone-tracking service."

Amaia frowned, unconvinced, as she looked from one to the other.

"I don't know. I'm almost certain the father had something to do with this, but there are details that just don't add up. Of course he's not the *basajaun*; the killer in this case is a bungling copycat who read the papers and decided to disguise his crime with all the details he remembered. On the one hand, there's the marked sexual element in the early aggression, which led him to hit her in a rage, tear her clothes off her, rape her, strangle her . . . And at the same time there's a beauty verging on adoration in this crime. It leaves me with two such opposing profiles that I would even hazard a guess that there are two killers who, on the other hand, are so different in their modi operandi and in the representation of their fantasy that it would be impossible for them to bring themselves to collaborate on the same crime. It's like a kind of cruel, bestial, bloody Mr. Hyde and a methodical, scrupulous, and remorseful Dr. Jekyll who had no qualms

about taking the girl's forearm but still wanted to preserve the body so much that he poured perfume on it, perhaps to prolong the sensation of life, perhaps to extend his own fantasy."

Padua burst into the small office, his phone in his hand.

"Jasón Medina has fled. A patrol just went to his house to bring him to the barracks and they found the house empty; he left so fast he even forgot to close the door. The drawers and closets are in a mess, as if he'd gathered the essentials for his escape, and the car's missing."

"Take his wife back as soon as you can, get them to see if there's any money missing and whether he's taken his passport. It's possible he'll try to leave the country. Don't leave her alone, station someone at the house. And send out an arrest warrant for Jasón Medina."

"I know how to do my job," said Padua coldly.

30

THE RAIN, which had not let up all day, became even heavier as they neared Elizondo. The evening light had fled rapidly toward the west, which was typical of winter evenings. Nonetheless, it still put Amaia in a bad mood every day due to her sense of being cheated and the disappointment that accompanied it. A thick fog was coming down off the hillsides, slow and heavy, moving across the ground meter by meter and reinforcing the impression of a boat in the middle of the sea, which had been her first thought on seeing the new police station.

Amaia uploaded the photos she had taken in the hut that morning onto the computer and painstakingly observed the images for the next hour. The place that Johana's killer had chosen was a message in itself, a message so different from the one sent by the other crimes that it had to hold some information. Why had he chosen that particular place? Padua had said that hunters and day-trippers often visited it, but it wasn't hunting season and the hikers didn't make their first appearance until the spring. Whoever took Johana there must have known this and must have been very certain that he wouldn't be interrupted while he carried out his crime. She went back to a photo that had been taken just at the point where the dirt track began and from which the hut was invisible. She picked up the phone and dialed Lieutenant Padua's number.

"Inspector Salazar, I was just about to call you. We accompanied Inés to the bank and she discovered that, according to the cashier, her husband had cleared out their account. It looks like he did it as soon as she left the house. His passport is also missing, and we've sent a warning out to the stations and airports."

"Good, but I'm calling you about something else . . ."

"Yes?"

"What did Jasón Medina do for a living?"

"He's a car mechanic. He works at a garage in the town . . . his job is basically to change people's oil and tires . . . We've asked for a warrant to search the garage as well . . ."

The police station was silent. After the tense day in Pamplona, Amaia had sent Jonan and Iriarte to get something to eat as soon as they arrived back in Elizondo.

"I don't think I'll be able to eat anything," Jonan had said.

"Go anyway; you'd be surprised what a squid sandwich and a beer can do for you."

Holding a cup of coffee so hot she could take only small sips, she studied the photos of the crime scene, sure that there was something more to them. All she could hear behind her was the rustling of pages coming from Zabalza's desk.

"Have you been here all day, Deputy Inspector?"

Zabalza stiffened, as if he suddenly felt uncomfortable.

"I was here all morning, but I went out for a while this afternoon."

"I suppose there's no news."

"Nothing major. Freddy is still stable in spite of the seriousness of his condition, and there's no news from the forensics laboratory. The bear experts called, they said something about having a meeting with you that you didn't attend, and I explained that you weren't available today. They left some telephone numbers and their address. They're staying at the Hotel Baztán, about five kilometers or so from here."

"I know where it is."

"Right, I always forget you're from here."

Amaia thought that she had never felt more of an outsider than in that moment.

"I'll call them later . . ."

She thought for a moment about whether to ask after Montes, and finally made up her mind.

"Zabalza, do you know whether Inspector Montes has been in at all today?"

"He came in first thing this afternoon. Since the warrant for the flour samples from the workshops had just arrived, he came with me to one of them at Bera and then we went to five other workshops around the valley. When we finished, we came back and sent the samples to the laboratory in line with procedure."

Zabalza seemed a bit nervous as he explained his actions, almost as if he was being examined. Amaia remembered the incident at the hospital and decided that perhaps Deputy Inspector Zabalza was the kind of person who took everything as a personal criticism.

" . . . Inspector?"

"Sorry, I didn't catch that."

"I was saying that I hope everything's okay, that you agree with the steps we've taken."

"Oh, yes, everything's okay, very good. Now we just have to wait for the results."

Zabalza didn't answer. He continued checking data at his desk, while observing Amaia when she bent over the computer again. He didn't like her. He'd heard of her, the star inspector who had spent time with the FBI in the United States, and now that he'd met her he thought she was an arrogant bitch who seemed to expect everyone to kowtow whenever she walked past. He felt uncomfortable because he knew deep down that he had put his foot in it with the thing about her sister, but since she had been around, even Iriarte seemed to give greater importance to things like that, which weren't that significant in the grand scheme of things. And now this fixation with Montes, an old-school guy whom he did like, in part, he supposed, because he had enough guts to face up to the star inspector. And as for him, he felt frustrated at times by this investigation that wasn't going anywhere and by having to put up with the bursts of brilliance from Inspector Salazar who, in his opinion, had made mistakes the whole way through. He wondered how long it would take the general commissioner to assign the case to one of the good detectives instead of continuing to encourage that show-off American crime series investigator.

His cell phone vibrated in his pocket, indicating that he had a new message. He recognized the number before he opened it; although he had deleted the name months ago, the messages kept coming and he kept opening them. There, covered in droplets of sweat, was a male torso he recognized instantly, plunging him into an ecstasy of desire and making him run his tongue involuntarily over his lips. He immediately became aware of where he was and bashfully hid the phone with his hands and looked behind him as if afraid that someone might be standing there. He hid the photo, but he didn't delete it. He knew all too well what would happen next. His mood would get worse and worse over the next few days as his sense of guilt increased. He wanted to stay with Marisa. They'd been together eight months, and he loved her, she was pretty, kind, they got on well together, but . . . the presence of that photo would torture him for the whole week, just because he wasn't able to gather the courage to delete it. He would try, as he had done with the previous ones, but he knew that that night, when he was on his own after Marisa went home, he would take one last look at those photos, and not only would he fail to delete them, he would have to make a serious effort not to dial Santy's number, not to ask him to come over, to conquer the intense desire running through his body.

They had met at a gym a year ago. Santy had been in a two-year relationship with a girl at that point, and Zabalza had been single. They arranged to go out running together, to go for a drink, Zabalza had even introduced him to a couple of girls with whom he'd had a bit of fun a few times. Then one morning the previous summer after their run, Santy had taken a shower at his house, which was closer to the route they ran, and when he'd got out of the shower, damp and naked, they had looked each other in the eye for a moment and fallen into bed together. They had met at his house every morning for a week, and every morning desire had conquered his confusion and his firm decision that it wouldn't happen again.

A week later, he went back to work, and things got serious with Marisa. He told Santy they wouldn't be seeing each other anymore and asked him not to call. They had both kept their word, but Santy employed this kind of passive resistance in which he didn't call him but sent him photos of his naked body that drove him so crazy he couldn't think of anything but the man and having sex with him. Those images would come to mind at any moment, causing him indescribable anxiety, especially when sex with Marisa became an endless marathon of feline mewling that turned him off completely and made him think of his passionate, vertiginous, febrile encounters with Santy. He felt irritable and impatient, like someone waiting for something to happen, for a wave or a gale to blow everything away, to put a definite end to his confusion, bringing a new dawn in which he could erase the last eight months.

Asking himself how much longer he could stand the pressure, he looked over at the inspector again. She was working at her computer, going over the photos they had already looked at a hundred times, and he hated everything about her.

Amaia again looked at the photos taken inside the hut. An antique wooden broom stood in a corner by the chimney, partially concealing a small mound of trash. She went back to one of the previous photos and enlarged the image again and again until she was sure of what she was looking at. She dialed the number for Johana's home and waited until she heard Inés's mournful voice.

"Good evening, Inés, it's Inspector Salazar."

She listened for two or three minutes to the details of what had taken place at the house, the missing money, documents, and more. She waited patiently while the woman went on, her tone bordering on triumph at having her suspicions confirmed. When the torrent of information ceased, Amaia continued.

"I knew about that, Lieutenant Padua called me half an hour ago . . . But there's something you can still help me with. Your husband is a car mechanic, is that right?"

"Yes."

"Has he always worked as a mechanic?"

"He did in the Dominican Republic, but he didn't find work in his own profession right away when he arrived here, and he worked for a livestock farmer for a year."

"What did his job involve?"

"He was a shepherd, he had to take the sheep into the mountains; sometimes he spent several days up there."

"I want you to look in the fridge, in the kitchen cupboards, in the pantry, anywhere you use to store food. Look and tell me if anything's missing."

The telephone must have been a cordless one because Amaia could hear the woman's agitated breathing and her hurried steps.

"Holy Mother of God! He's taken all the food, Inspector!"

Amaia cut the call short as politely as she could and called Padua.

"He won't try to leave the country, at least not by the usual routes. He's taken provisions for several weeks. He's up in the mountains, there's no doubt about it, he knows the herders' routes like the back of his hand. If he leaves the country, he'll do it via the Pyrenean border, and thanks to his knowledge of the area he'll be able to cross the valley and get into the mountains without being seen. And he knew the hut, there were sheep feces at the crime scene. They'd been swept up, but they were in a pile by the fireplace. I'd get in touch with his former boss. Inés told me he's a farmer from Arizkun. Speak to him, he could be very helpful in terms of the paths and the refuges. Of course, the guys from the Nature Protection Service will know the paths."

Amaia was aware of Padua's humiliation at the other end of the line in spite of his silence, and she suddenly felt furious. He wasn't going to congratulate her, it hadn't exactly been a job well done, but she herself was balancing on a tightrope in the midst of an investigation that had ground to a halt and had no suspect.

"Lieutenant, police officer to police officer, this remains between you and me."

Padua muttered his hurried thanks and hung up.

31

I'M A little girl," she whispered. "I'm just a little girl. Why don't you love me?"

The child wept as the earth covered her face. But the monster showed no pity.

She could hear the sound of the river nearby. Its mineral aroma filled her nose and its cold stones pressed into her back as she lay next to the riverbed. The killer leaned over her to brush her hair to either side, perfect golden locks that almost hid her naked chest. And she looked for his eyes, desperate to find pity. The killer's face stopped close to hers, so close that she could smell his age-old scent of the forest, the river, the rock. She looked into his eyes and discovered that there were only dark pools, black and bottomless, where his soul ought to be, and she wanted to shout, she wanted to release the horror that was gripping her body and driving her crazy. But her mouth couldn't open, the howls growing inside her couldn't climb up and out through her throat, because she was dead. She knew that that was what the death of murder victims was like, endlessly trying to give voice to the horror inside . . . Forever. He saw her anxiety, he saw the pain, he saw the condemnation, and he started to laugh until his laugh filled everything.

Then he leaned over her again and whispered: "Don't be afraid of *Ama*, little bitch. I'm not going to eat you."

The phone vibrated on the wooden bedside table, making a noise like an electric saw. Amaia sat up in bed, confused and shocked, almost sure she had shouted out, and pushing away the locks of sweaty hair that had stuck to her forehead and neck, she looked at the thing that was moving around the table propelled by the vibration as if it were a gigantic evil beetle.

She waited a few seconds while she tried to calm herself down. Even so, she felt her pulse beating like a drum inside her head when she held the phone to her ear.

"Inspector Salazar?"

Iriarte's voice brought her back to reality with all the speed of a magic spell.

"Yes, what is it?"

"Did I wake you up? I'm sorry."

"Don't worry, it doesn't matter," she answered. I almost owe you a favor, she thought.

"It's something I remembered. When you saw the body, you said something that's been going around and around in my head ever since. You said, 'She's Snow White,' do you remember? It's sinister, but I also had that impression, and your comment only strengthened my feeling that I'd seen this before, somewhere else in a different context. I finally remembered when and where. Last summer I went to a hotel on the coast at Tarragona with my wife and children, you know, one of those ones with a huge swimming pool and an activities club for the kids. One morning we noticed that the children were particularly on edge, somewhere between upset and excited. They were going from one side of the garden to the other, collecting sticks, small stones, and flowers, and acting extremely strangely. I followed them and saw that at least a dozen of the smallest ones had gathered in a corner of the garden and formed a huddle. I went over, and in the middle of the huddle I saw that they had arranged a sort of chapel of rest for a dead sparrow. It was lying on a mound of tissues surrounded by round pebbles and shells from the beach, and they had put flowers all around the little bird, forming a garland around it. I was moved. I congratulated them on their work and warned them about the diseases a dead bird might carry and that they should wash their hands. I almost had to drag them away from there afterward. I managed to put the thought of that little bird out of their heads by playing with them, but I saw groups of children going to the corner where the sparrow lay over the course of several days. I told one of the managers about it and he removed it, despite the complaints and disgust on the part of the kids, even though the poor creature was completely riddled with worms by that point."

"Do you think it was the boy who found her?"

"His father said that the boy had been up on the hill with some friends. It seems likely to me that the children found the body, but earlier than the day they mentioned it. I think they discovered it and decided to prepare a chapel of rest, the flowers . . . it was probably them who covered her up. Furthermore, I noticed that the prints that appeared on the perfume bottle were really quite small. We assumed they belonged to a woman, but they could also be a child's. I'm almost sure it was them."

"Snow White and her little dwarves."

~

Eight-year-old Mikel knew that he was in serious trouble. He sat on the visitor's chair in Iriarte's office swinging his feet backward and forward in an attempt to calm himself while his parents looked at him with encouraging smiles, which, far from reassuring him, made him even more aware of his parents' concern. They were trying to hide it, but their behavior gave it away. His mother had straightened his clothes and brushed his hair at least three times, and each time she had looked him in the eyes with that worried expression she had when she wasn't at all sure about what was happening. His father had been more direct. "Don't worry, nothing bad's going to happen to you. They'll ask you a few questions, you just tell them the truth as clearly as possible."

The truth. If he told the truth clearly, something bad was bound to happen to him. Now that he had seen his friends arrive through the half-open door, filing down the corridor accompanied by their parents, and had exchanged some truly desperate glances with them, he knew that there was no escape. Jon Sorondo, Pablo Odriozola, and Markel Martínez. Markel was ten and might stand firm, but Jon was a ninny, he'd tell them everything as soon as they asked. He looked at his parents again, sighed, and turned to Iriarte.

"It was us."

It took them a good half hour to calm the parents down and convince them that there was no need for a lawyer, although they could call one if they wanted. Their sons were not being accused of any crime, but it was vital for them to speak to the children. In the end they agreed, and Amaia decided to move everyone to the meeting room.

"Well, boys," Iriarte began, "does anyone want to tell me what happened?"

The children looked at one another, then at their parents, and finally remained silent.

"All right, would you prefer it if I asked you questions?"

They nodded.

"Do you normally go to that hut often?"

"Yes," they answered all at once, like a timid class of frightened students.

"Who found her?"

"Mikel and me," answered Markel in a whisper, which was not entirely devoid of pride.

"This is very important. Do you remember what day it was when you found her?"

"It was Sunday," answered Mikel. "It was my grandma's birthday."

"So you found the girl, told the others, and you went back each day to see her."

"To take care of her," clarified Mikel. His mother covered her mouth, horrified.

"But she was dead, for God's sake!" exclaimed his father.

A feeling of confusion and revulsion rippled through the adults, who started murmuring. Iriarte tried to calm them down.

"Children have a different way of seeing things, and death makes them very curious. So, you went back to take care of her," he said, addressing the boys, "and you took good care of her. But was it you who arranged the flowers?"

Silence.

"Where did you get so many? There are hardly any flowers in the countryside at the moment . . ."

"From my grandma's garden," admitted Pablo.

"That's true," added his mother. "My mother called me to tell me about it, she told me that the boy went there every afternoon to pick the flowers from one of the bushes. She asked me if he was taking them for me, and I told her no. I assumed they were for some girl or other."

"And so they were," said Iriarte.

His mother looked shocked as she considered that thought.

"Did you take her perfume, too?"

"I took it from my mother," answered Jon, almost whispering.

"Jon!" exclaimed his mother. "How—"

"It was one you didn't use. It was sitting there full and unopened in the bathroom cabinet . . ."

His mother lifted a hand to her forehead as she realized he had taken her most expensive perfume, the one she used least, the one she kept for special occasions.

"Fuck! Did you take the Boucheron?" She suddenly looked more angry that he'd taken a five-hundred-euro bottle of perfume than that he'd poured it over a corpse.

"It was for the smell, she was smelling worse and worse . . ."

"Was that why you hung up the air fresheners?"

The four of them nodded. "We spent all our pocket money on them," said Markel.

"Did you touch the body at all?"

He noticed that the question made the parents uncomfortable. They shifted in their seats and took deep breaths while shooting him reproachful looks.

"She wasn't covered up," said one of the boys, justifying their action.

"She was naked," said Mikel. A titter spread among the boys but was rapidly cut off by the horrified expressions of their parents.

"So you covered her, you wrapped her up, did you?"

"Yes, with her clothes . . . they were torn," said Jon.

"And with the mattress" admitted Pablo.

"Did you notice whether the girl was missing anything? Think carefully before you answer."

They looked at each other again, nodding, and Mikel spoke.

"We tried to move her arm so that it would hold the bouquet, but we saw that she didn't have a hand, so we left it where it was because seeing the wound scared us."

Amaia was amazed at how the infantile mind worked. They were afraid of a wound and yet they were impervious to the horror of discovering a desecrated body. They were scared by a clean, albeit brutal, cut, but they had spent all their free time the previous week keeping a vigil over a body that was decomposing further every minute without experiencing any fear at all, or perhaps the fear was overwhelmed by curiosity and the herd mentality that children sometimes display and that always surprised her when she came across it.

Amaia intervened. "The whole hut is very clean. Was it you who cleaned it?"

"Yes."

"You swept the floor, hung up air fresheners, and tried to burn the trash . . ."

"But it gave off a lot of smoke and we were afraid someone might see it and come and then . . ."

"Did you see anything that looked like blood, or dried chocolate milk?"

"No."

"There was nothing poured over the body?"

They shook their heads.

"You went every day, right? Did you notice whether anyone other than you had been there during those days?"

Mikel shrugged.

Amaia made her way to the door. "Thank you for your help," she said, addressing the parents. "And you boys should know that if you find a body, you should call the police immediately. That girl has a family who were missing her. Furthermore, her death wasn't natural, and the delay in telling the police could mean that her murderer, the person who killed her, might escape. Do you understand how important what I'm telling you is?"

They nodded.

"What's going to happen to the girl now?" Mikel wanted to know.

Iriarte smiled as he thought of his own children. Snow White's little dwarves. They were in a police station, they had just been interrogated, their embarrassed parents were torn between horror and disbelief, and they were worrying about their dead princess.

"We'll give her back to her mother, they'll bury her . . . They'll put flowers on her grave . . ."

They looked at one another and nodded in satisfaction.

"Perhaps you'll be able to visit her grave in the cemetery."

They smiled enthusiastically, and their parents gave him a last scandalized look at such a suggestion before pulling their little ones toward the door.

Amaia sat down facing the bulletin board, to which they had added the photos of Johana, and marveled again at how adaptable a child's mind was. Iriarte came in with Zabalza and smiled openly as he placed a cup of milky coffee in front of her.

"Snow White." He laughed. "I'm sorry for the poor kids, their parents will be taking them straight to the psychologist. And there'll be no more trips to go exploring up on the hill."

"Well, what would you do if they were your children?"

"I suppose I'd try not to be too hard on them. Once upon a time I might have given you a different answer, but I've got kids now, Inspector, and I can assure you that I've learned a lot over the last few years. We've all gone out exploring like that, especially those of us who've grown up in rural areas. Having come from around here, you must have gone down to the river to explore too."

"Yes, a degree of childish curiosity seems perfectly normal, but we're talking about a body here. You'd expect that to send kids running and screaming."

"Perhaps for the majority, but not all once the initial shock had passed. The fear factor in children has much more to do with imaginary terror than real horrors. That's why they are victims in so many cases, because they're incapable of distinguishing between real and imaginary risks. I expect it gave them a good shock when they saw her, but then curiosity and their morbid fascination grew, children are incredibly morbid. I know it's not really comparable, but we found a dead cat when I was seven years old. We buried it in a mound of gravel on a building site, we made a cross for it out of some sticks, we laid flowers and even prayed for it, but a week later my brother's friends dug it up and then buried it again, just to see what state it was in."

"Yes, that sounds more like childish curiosity to me, but it was just a cat. They must have been horrified faced with a human body. It's in our nature to instinctively reject the idea of identifying ourselves with death when it appears in its human form."

"That's true of adults, yes, but children are different. It's not the first time something similar's happened. A few years ago the body of a girl who'd disappeared from home several days earlier was found at some gardens near Tudela. She'd died of an overdose, and some young boys found the body. Instead of reporting it, they covered her with plastic bags and pieces of timber. When the police did find her, there was a lot of confusion and uncertainty over what had happened to her. The overdose was revealed by the autopsy, and the police quickly traced the boys from all the fingerprints they'd left at the scene, but their actions had still altered the investigators' first impressions."

"Incredible."

"But true."

Jonan knocked as he entered the room. "Inspector, Lieutenant Padua just called. They've arrested Jasón Medina at Gorramendi. He was in a hut on the mountainside not far from Erratzu. They also found the car hidden among trees about twelve kilometers away from there. There was a sports bag containing girls' clothing, Johana's passport, and a cuddly mouse in the trunk. They're holding him at the barracks in Lekaroz. Padua said he'll wait for you to arrive before he starts the interrogation."

"How kind of him!" joked Iriarte.

"Don't you believe it, he owes me a favor," she said, picking up her bag.

The facilities at the Guardia Civil barracks were old-fashioned compared to the new police station, but Amaia noticed that, in spite of this, they had a modern CCTV system with the latest cameras. A uniformed *guardia* greeted them at the door and directed them to an office to the right of the entrance. Another *guardia* led them down a narrow, poorly lit passage to a group of dilapidated doors that showed signs of more than one change of locks. The room was spacious and well heated. There was an alcove by the door containing an image of the Our Lady of the Pillar and an ear of dried corn and various chairs and tables to either side. A handcuffed man of about forty-five was sitting in front of one of them. He was thin, short, and dark skinned, which made his pallor and the redness that had developed beneath his eyes and mouth stand out.

His cuffed hands loosely held a tissue that he didn't seem inclined to use, in spite of the tears and snot that were running down his face to his chin, where they dripped onto the dark surface of the table. Beside him sat a young legal aid lawyer, who Amaia calculated must be under thirty. She was putting some papers in order while listening intently to the instructions someone was giving her by phone and looking at her client with visible disgust.

Padua came up behind them.

"He hasn't stopped crying and shouting since the guys from the Nature Protection Service found him. He confessed as soon as he saw the officers. They told me that he didn't shut up at all during the journey, and he hasn't done anything except sob since we sat him here. In reality we've had to take his statement because he hasn't stopped repeating that it was him and he wanted to confess since he arrived. He must be exhausted from all that wailing."

They went over to the table. A *guardia* switched on a tape recorder and, following the greetings, introductions, and the statement of date and time, they took their seats.

"First of all, I have to say that this is very irregular. I don't understand how they took his statement without my being present," complained the lawyer.

"Your client hasn't stopped shouting out his confession since the moment he was arrested, and he insisted on making a statement as soon as he got through the door."

"Even so, I could invalidate it . . ."

"We haven't interrogated him yet, señora. Why don't we wait and see what he has to say?"

The lawyer pursed her lips and pushed her chair a few centimeters back from the table.

"Señor Jasón Medina," Padua began. It seemed as though the mention of his name brought the man out of the trance he had been in. He sat up straighter in the chair and stared at the sheets of paper Padua was holding. "According to your statement, on Saturday the fourth, you asked your stepdaughter, Johana Márquez, to go with you to wash the car, but instead of going to the gas station where you usually did this, you drove up the hill. When you reached a little-frequented area, you asked her to kiss you. When she refused, you got angry and hit her. Johana threatened to tell her mother and even to go to the police. You got angrier still and became very agitated, so you hit her again and, in your own words, she fainted." Jasón nodded. "You started the car and drove for a while longer, but on seeing her unconscious, as if she were asleep, you thought you could have sex with her without her resisting. You found a secluded place on a forest road, stopped the car, tipped the passenger seat back, and climbed on top of Johana with the intention of having sex with her. But then she woke up and started to shout, is that correct?"

Jasón Medina nodded continuously, giving the impression he was bobbing up and down, and the mixture of snot and tears continued to drip from his nose.

"According to your own words, you hit her again and again. The more Johana screamed, the more aroused you became. You hit her again, but she kept on defending herself, so you had to hit her harder. In spite of this, she didn't stop shouting or hitting you as hard as she could. You grabbed her by the neck and squeezed until she became still. When you saw that you had killed her, you decided that you had to find a place to abandon the body. You knew the hut on the mountain because you had been there several times when you were working as a shepherd. You drove along the path until you were nearby, then you carried the body to the hut and left it there. But before you left, you remembered what you had read about the *basajaun* in the papers over the last few days, and you decided that you could make the crime look similar. You tore Johana's clothes in the way you remembered reading about, and you were so aroused that you raped her body."

Jasón closed his eyes for a moment, and Amaia thought he might be feeling guilty, but he was obviously reliving the moment of her death, which had been burned into his memory in full detail. He shifted in his seat, catching the attention of his lawyer, who moved away in disgust when she saw the bulge of an imminent erection forming in his trousers.

"For the love of God!" she exclaimed.

Padua continued as if he hadn't noticed.

"But you didn't have string or cord to arrange it how you remembered, so you went home before your wife returned, showered, took a piece of leftover clothesline, and went back to the hut to position it around your stepdaughter's neck. Then you returned home. When your wife insisted on reporting the disappearance, you took some of Johana's clothes and personal items, put them in the trunk of your car, told your wife that Johana had been home to collect her things, and persuaded her to retract the report . . . Señor Medina, do you agree that this is what you said?"

Jasón looked down and nodded.

"I need to hear you say it for the record, señor."

The man leaned forward as if he were about to kiss the tape recorder and said clearly, "Yes, señor, that's exactly what happened and God knows it." His voice was smooth and slightly high-pitched, with a trace of false servility that made his lawyer blink.

"I don't believe it," she whispered.

"Do you confirm your statement, Señor Medina?"

Jasón leaned forward again. "Yes."

"Do you agree with everything I've read or do you want to add or remove anything?"

Another parody of reverence. "I agree with all of it."

"Right. Señor Medina, now, although everything is quite clear, we'd like to ask you some questions."

The lawyer sat up slightly straighter, as if she understood that she would finally have some work to do.

"I've already introduced Inspector Salazar from the Policía Foral, who wants to question you."

"I object," spat the lawyer. "You've already made my client's life difficult enough with this statement, he's already confessed. Don't think I don't know who you are," she addressed Amaia, "or what you're trying to do?"

"What do you think I'm trying to do?" asked Amaia patiently.

"Charge my client with the crimes committed by the *basajaun*."

Amaia laughed, shaking her head.

"Don't worry. I'll tell you right now that the modus operandi doesn't match. We knew from the very beginning that this wasn't the *basajaun*, and with the information your client provided in his statement regarding the cord he used, we can almost rule him out."

"Almost?"

"There's one element of the crime that caught our attention. Whether or not your client can give us a plausible explanation will determine how this investigation moves forward."

The lawyer bit her bottom lip.

"Look, let's make a deal: I'll ask, and your client only answers if you authorize him to . . ."

The lawyer looked anxiously at the little pool of liquid that had spread across the surface of the table and nodded. Padua made as if to get up and give Amaia his seat facing Medina, but she stopped him, stood up, walked around the table, and stopped just to the man's left, leaning over a little to speak to him and standing so close that she was almost touching his clothing.

"Señor Medina, you said that you hit Johana a number of times and that you raped her. Are you sure you didn't do anything else to her?"

The man shifted uncomfortably.

"To what are you referring?" asked the lawyer.

"The corpse presented with a complete amputation of the right hand and forearm," she said, placing blown-up pictures on the table showing the full crudity of the wound.

The lawyer frowned and leaned forward to whisper something in her client's ear. He shook his head.

Amaia waited impatiently for a few seconds.

"Listen, after what you said in your statement, the amputation of an arm will be secondary. Did you do it so we wouldn't be able to identify the corpse using the fingerprints?"

"No."

"Look at the photos," Amaia insisted.

Jasón looked briefly at the photos, then looked away, disgusted.

"For God's sake! No, I didn't do it. When I went back to put the cord in place, she was already like that. I thought it had been an animal."

"How long did it take you to go home and then back to the hut? Think about it carefully."

Jasón started to cry, great sobs that came from deep down inside, racking his whole body.

"We'll have to leave it there. Señor Medina needs to rest," suggested the lawyer.

Amaia lost patience. "Señor Medina will rest when I say he can."

She gave the table a hard thump, spraying drops from the little pool in all directions, and leaned forward until her face was right next to the man's. His weeping stopped immediately.

"Answer me," she ordered in a firm voice.

"An hour and a half at the most. I was in a rush because my wife was due home from work."

"And when you arrived at the hut, the arm was no longer there?"

"No, I swear I thought . . ."

"Was there any blood?"

"What?"

"Was there any blood around the wound?"

"Perhaps a small amount, a very small amount, a tiny puddle, barely a mark . . ."

Amaia looked at Padua.

"The kids?" he suggested.

". . . on the plastic bag," murmured Jasón.

"What plastic bag?"

"The blood was on a white plastic bag," he mumbled.

Amaia stood up, nauseated by the man's fetid smell.

"Think hard about this. Did you see anyone near the hut when you returned?"

"I didn't see anybody, but . . ."

"Yes?"

"I thought there was someone else nearby, but I was very nervous at the time. I even thought someone was watching me. I thought it was Johana . . ."

"Johana?"

"Her spirit, you know what I mean, her ghost."

"Did you drive past any cars on the road leading to the hut or see any vehicles parked nearby?"

"No, but when I was about to leave I heard a motorbike, one of those mountain ones. They make a lot of noise. I thought it was one of the guys from the Nature Protection Service, they use those when they go up into the mountains. I couldn't get out of there fast enough."

ANOTHER SPRING

Things were very different the next time. Many years had passed. She was already living in Pamplona, although she went back to Elizondo on the weekends. Her mother, sickly and disabled, was confined to a hospital bed with complex pneumonia while the Alzheimer's devoured her. She had barely babbled a word or two of limited vo-

238 / DOLORES REDONDO

cabulary for months and then only to demand the most basic things. She had been in the University Hospital for a week at the request of her lead doctor and against Flora's will. She had resisted her mother's admission with all her strength, although she had had to give in when Rosario's breathing became so labored that she needed oxygen to keep her alive and had to travel in an ambulance. Even so, glorying in her perpetually essential role, she used every excuse in the book to avoid leaving her mother's bedside, although she never missed a chance to criticize her sisters for not visiting Rosario more often.

Amaia came into the room and, after listening to ten minutes of recriminations from Flora, sent her to the cafeteria, promising to stay and watch their mother. When the door closed behind her sister, Amaia turned to look at the old woman who was dozing as she half sat up in the hospital bed in an attempt to ease her labored breathing. She was aware of her fear—it was the first time that she had been alone with her since she'd been a child. She walked on tiptoe past the end of the bed to the chair next to the window, praying that her mother wouldn't wake up and ask for anything. She wasn't sure what she might feel if she had to touch her.

She sat down in the chair and leaned slowly backward to pick up one of Flora's magazines from the windowsill, as carefully as if she were handling an explosive. She glanced at her mother again and couldn't suppress a yelp. Her heart was threatening to burst out of her chest. Her mother was looking at her, leaning up on her left side with a twisted smile and eyes shining with lucidity and malice.

"Don't be afraid of your *ama*, little bitch. I'm not going to eat you."

She lay back down, closed her eyes, and her breathing immediately began to sound watery and noisy again. Amaia had curled up in a ball and saw that she had crushed her sister's magazine without realizing it. She stayed like that for a few seconds, her heartbeat out of control and her logic insisting that she had imagined it, that fatigue and her memories had played a bad joke on her. She got up without taking her eyes off her mother's face, which seemed as vacuous and lethargic as it had during the previous months. The old woman whispered something. A string of spittle lay on her cheek, her eyes remained closed. A muffled murmur, an incomprehensible word. The oxygen tube had become unhooked from behind one of her ears and was hanging at an angle, making a soft hissing noise. She seemed to be dreaming, she was babbling, asking for water perhaps? Her voice was so weak it was inaudible. She went over to the bed and listened.

"Naaa waaaaaa."

Amaia leaned over her in an attempt to hear her words.

Rosario opened her eyes, her penetrating, cruel eyes that showed just how much she was enjoying this. She smiled.

"No, I won't eat you, although I would if I could get up."

Amaia stumbled to the door without taking her eyes off her mother, who continued to watch her with those malignant eyes, laughing in satisfaction at the fear she was provoking in her daughter, stentorian cackles that seemed beyond someone with such grave respiratory problems. Amaia closed the door behind her and didn't go in again until Flora came back.

"What are you doing here?" spat Flora when she saw her. "You should be inside."

"I was looking to see whether you were coming. I need to go now."

Flora looked at her watch and raised her eyebrows in that expression of recrimination Amaia had seen so many times.

"What about *Ama*?"

"She's asleep . . ."

And so she was, fast asleep when they went back in.

32

W HEN SHE got home, there was a note from James on the table telling her that they'd gone out for lunch and that he'd spend part of the day visiting the forest at Irati with Aunt Engrasi. They'd left food for her in the fridge and hoped to see her that evening. A quick "I love you" next to his name made her feel lonely and distanced from the world in which people went out for lunch and on day trips while she interrogated despicable men who raped their own daughters. She went upstairs, listening to the sound of her own breathing and the astonishing silence in that house where, while her aunt was at home, the television was never switched off. She took off her clothes and tossed them into the laundry basket, set the water in the shower running until it became warm, and looked at her reflection in the mirror. She was getting thin. She'd skipped a few meals in the last few days and had been more or less living on milky coffee. She ran her hand over her stomach and prodded it gently, then she rested her hands in the small of her back and bent backward, sticking out her stomach. She smiled until she met her own eyes in the mirror.

James was starting to get serious about the subject of fertility treatments. She knew how much he wanted a child, and she wasn't unaware of the pressure he had to put up with during each phone call from his parents, but just thinking of the terrible physical and mental test it represented made her feel as if something was shriveling up inside her. James, on the other hand, seemed to have found a panacea: for days he bombarded her with information, videos, and pamphlets from the clinic, showing smiling parents with their children in their arms. What they didn't show were the multiple humiliating tests, the constant analyses, the inflammation caused by the hormones, or the sudden mood swings due to the cocktails of pills you had to take. She had agreed, overwhelmed by the intense emotion of the moment, but now she thought she had been too hasty to give in. The words of Anne's mother echoed in her head: "I gave birth from the heart and carried my daughter in my arms."

She got into the shower and let the warm water run down her back, turning her skin red until the pleasure was almost painful. She leaned her head against the tiles and felt better on realizing that her bad mood was mostly due to the fact that James wasn't at home. She was tired and she would have felt better after a nap, but if James wasn't there when she woke up she would feel so bad that she would regret having slept. She turned off the water and stayed in the shower a few seconds longer while she waited for the final drops to run off her skin. Then she got out and wrapped herself in an enormous terry cloth bathrobe James had given her. She sat on the bed to dry her hair a bit and suddenly felt so tired that the idea of a siesta that she had previously discarded now seemed like a good idea. It would just be for a few minutes, she probably wouldn't manage to fall asleep.

The Glock 19 is a marvelous pistol with a spring-loaded firing pin; it's lightweight, as its casing is made of plastic: 595 grams when empty, 850 when loaded. It has no external safety catches, hammers, or other mechanisms that need to be released before the weapon is ready to fire. A good pistol for a police officer who has to go out on the streets, although there are those who are against the police carrying weapons without a safety, and even experts who claim that the noise produced by a weapon being cocked is more intimidating than just pointing a weapon at someone. Amaia wasn't a fan of guns, but she liked the Glock: it wasn't too heavy, it was fairly discreet, and it was very easy to maintain. Even so, she had to dismantle and grease it every so often, and she always chose to do so when she was completely alone in the house. She took it apart, arranging the pieces on a towel, cleaned the barrel, and put it back together again.

But while she manipulated it, she looked at her hands, too small to hold a gun. She realized that the hands she could see weren't hers but were those of a little girl. She took a step back to get a full view of the scene. Sitting on the bed was a little girl who was her, holding a big black gun with a pale hand while using the other to caress her head, which was barely covered by the blond hair that was starting to grow back and through which the whitish scar was still visible. She was crying. Amaia felt an infinite sympathy for the little girl that was her, and the vision of the child broken by pain opened a chasm inside her that she hadn't felt for many years. The girl was saying something, but Amaia couldn't hear it. She leaned forward and saw that the girl didn't have a neck; she had a deep dark empty stripe where it should have been. Amaia listened carefully, trying to identify the sounds mixed in with the weeping.

The child, a nine-year-old Amaia, was crying thick, black tears like motor oil, which fell, shining and crystalline like liquid jet, forming a puddle at her feet where the bed had been before. Amaia went closer still and recognized in the movement of her lips the urgent litany of a prayer that the child was repeating with neither expression nor pause: *Ourfatherwhoartinheavenhallowedbethynamethykingdomcome . . .*

The little girl raised the weapon using both hands, turned it toward herself, and lifted the barrel until it was resting against her ear. Then she let her right arm fall limply into her lap, and Amaia saw that her hand was missing as far as the forearm. She shouted as loudly as she could, aware all the while that it was a dream and certain that, in spite of this, that evil would be irreparable.

"Don't do it!" she shouted, but the black tears the girl had wept filled her mouth and muffled her words. She summoned up all her strength as she fought to wake up from the nightmare before it all came to an end. "Don't do it!"

Her cry broke free of the dream, and there was an instant when she felt herself flying out of that hell, conscious that she really had shouted, that it was her own voice that had woken her, and that the little girl had been left behind. She turned her head to look at her again and saw the girl lift her stump of an arm as she said, "I can't let *Ama* eat me all up."

She opened her eyes and saw a dark figure leaning over her face. "Amaia."

The voice seemed to drag her back through the years, back to its owner, but her logic kicked in, reminding her that this was impossible and driving away the remains of the nightmare. She blinked, trying to sweep away the vestiges of sleep that blinded her eyes like sand, making them heavy and useless.

An extremely cold hand brushed her forehead, and feeling that corpselike touch was enough to force her to open her eyes. Beside the bed, a woman was leaning over her and observing her with an expression somewhere between curiosity and amusement. She had a straight nose and high cheekbones, and her hair was tucked behind her ears in two perfect waves.

"*Ama!*" she shouted, suffocated by fear as she pulled awkwardly on the duvet and leaned back until she found herself sitting on the pillow.

"Amaia, Amaia, wake up, you're dreaming, wake up!"

A click that seemed to come from inside her head flooded the room with light from the bedside lamp.

"Amaia, are you all right?"

Visibly pale, Ros was looking at her with a perplexed expression without daring to touch her. Amaia felt terribly thirsty, and a fine layer of sweat had formed under the bathrobe she was still wearing.

"I'm all right, it was a nightmare," she said, panting and looking around the room as if trying to make entirely sure of where she was.

"You were shouting," her sister said, alarmed.

"Was I?"

"You were shouting a lot and I couldn't wake you up," said Ros, as if explaining it would make it make sense.

Amaia looked at her. "I'm sorry," she said, feeling exhausted and under the spotlight.

"And you scared me to death when I tried to wake you up."

"Yes," admitted Amaia. "I didn't recognize you when I opened my eyes."

"Well, I don't doubt that: you pointed your gun at me."

"What?"

Ros gestured toward the bed, and Amaia realized that she was still holding her pistol in her hand. The vision of the little girl raising the weapon to her head suddenly became so vivid and ominous that she dropped the weapon as if it were hot and covered it with a cushion before turning to her sister.

"Oh, Ros, I'm truly sorry. I must have fallen asleep after cleaning it, but it's not loaded . . ."

Her sister didn't seem entirely convinced.

"I'm sorry," she apologized again. "The last few days have been very intense, only today I interrogated the guy who killed his own stepdaughter, and I suppose that . . . Well, between that and the *basajaun* investigation, it's normal to be stressed."

"And I haven't helped," added Ros miserably, her lips forming a pout that reminded Amaia of the little girl she had once been. She felt a wave of affection for her sister.

"Well, I suppose we all end up doing the best we can, don't we?" she said with a sheepish smile.

Ros sat down on the bed.

"I'm sorry, Amaia, I know I should have told you. I just want you to know that it wasn't that I was trying to hide anything from you, I didn't think of that. I was just feeling quite ashamed about everything that was happening to me."

Amaia reached out her hand until she found her sister's.

"That's exactly what James told me."

"You see? Your husband's even perfect in that respect. Tell me, am I likely to share my marital problems with you when you have a husband like that?"

"I've never judged you, Ros."

"I know. And I'm sorry." Ros leaned toward her sister, who hugged her tightly.

"I'm sorry, too, Ros. I swear that it was one of the most difficult things I've had to do in my life, but I didn't have any other choice," she said, stroking her sister's hair.

When they finally pulled away from the embrace, they were smiling openly at one another, in a way that is reserved for sisters who've shared many such looks over the years. Making her peace with Ros made Amaia feel good in a way that she had forgotten over the last few days and that she normally experienced only on returning home, having a shower, and embracing James. Secretly, it had worried her, leading her to wonder whether she had succumbed to what murder investigators fear most: that the horror she faced on a daily basis had broken free of the dark place where it ought to remain locked away and had taken over her life, gradually making her into one of those police officers with no private life, left desolate and isolated in the knowledge that they are responsible for letting the evil break through the barriers and wash everything away. She felt as though a threat as dense and ominous as a curse had been hanging over her for the last few days, as though the old charms weren't strong enough to exorcise the evil she had to confront, which stuck to her body like a damp sweat.

She roused herself from her thoughts and realized that Ros had been watching her carefully.

"Perhaps you ought to be honest with me now."

"Oh, do you mean . . . Ros, you know I can't, that's part of the investigation."

"I don't mean the investigation, but what makes you cry out during your dreams. James told me that you have nightmares almost every time you fall asleep."

"For God's sake, James! It's true, but they're just nightmares, nothing more, and it's perfectly normal when you consider what my job entails. They come and go, when I'm very involved in a case I have more, when we finish a case they go again. You know I've slept with the light on for years."

"Well you had it switched off today," said Ros, looking at the bedside lamp.

"I dropped off. It was still light when I sat down to clean the gun, and I fell asleep without realizing it. But it doesn't usually happen. I leave it on precisely to avoid what happened today, because what I suffer from aren't exactly nightmares. What happens is that I enter a light sleep in which I'm constantly alert, and during the night I experience loads of semi-awakenings that make me jump a bit. I reorient myself and I go back to sleep . . . That's why it's important that there's a light on, so that when I open my eyes I can see where I am and calm down right away."

Ros shook her head as she looked at Amaia's expression.

"Are you listening to yourself? What you've described is a state of constant alertness. Nobody can live like that. If you want to talk yourself into believing that crap about the light, then that's fine by me, but you know what happened today isn't normal. You almost shot me, Amaia."

Her sister's words seemed to echo those spoken by James two days earlier outside the workshop door.

"And nightmares can be normal, but only up to a certain point. It's not normal that they cause you so much suffering, that you wake up with a jerk, incapable of telling whether you're asleep or awake. I saw you, Amaia, and you were terrified."

Amaia looked at her sister and remembered the feminine profile that had leaned over her face as she was waking up.

"Let me help you."

Amaia nodded.

They went downstairs in silence, aware of the strange atmosphere in the house in their aunt's absence. The furniture, the plants, the innumerable decorative objects seemed dull without her presence, as if her belongings became faded and less tangible in their mistress's absence, blurring the boundaries that anchored them in the here and now. Ros went to the sideboard and took out the little bundle of black silk containing the cards, put them in the center of the table, and went to the living room. A second later, Amaia heard the sound of commercials coming from the television. She smiled.

"Why do you do that?" she asked.

"To hear better," was her sister's reply.

"You know that's nonsense."

"And yet it's true."

She sat down and very carefully untied the knot that held the smooth fabric closed, picked up the deck of cards, removed the band holding it together, and set it down in front of her.

"You already know what to do. Shuffle the cards while you think about your question."

Amaia touched the deck of cards, which was strangely cold, and her mind filled with memories of the other times: the smooth feel of the cards as they slid through her fingers, the strange perfume they gave off as she moved them in her hands, and the peaceful communion achieved when she reached the exact moment when the channel opened and the question she was formulating in her mind was flowing in both directions, the instinctive way she would choose the cards and the ceremonial manner in which she would turn them over, knowing well before she did so what would be on the other side, and the mystery that was resolved in an instant when the route to follow appeared in her mind establishing relationships between the cards. Interpreting tarot cards was as simple and as complicated as interpreting a map of an unknown place, like plotting a journey from your house to a specific point. If you were clear about the destination, if you were capable of not getting distracted en route, like a mystical Little Red Riding Hood, the answers were revealed before you in a clear path, which, as is often the case, was not the only way of getting there. Sometimes answers are not the solution to an enigma, Engrasi had told her once when they were alone; sometimes the answers only generate more questions, more doubts.

"Why?" Amaia had asked her. "If I ask a question and I receive an answer, that ought to be the solution."

"It ought to be, if you knew what question to ask at a given moment."

She remembered Aunt Engrasi's teachings. "The question. There must always be a question, otherwise what's the point of carrying out a consultation? Opening the channel to allow the answers to arrive mixed with the cries of millions of souls, clamoring, howling, and lying. You have to direct the consultation, you have to plot the route on the map without leaving it, without letting the wolf seduce you by convincing you to go and pick flowers, because if you do that he will arrive at your destination before you do, and what you'll find on arrival will no longer be the place you were aiming for. You'll end up talking to a monster in disguise who passes himself off as your dear old granny and who has only one intention, to devour you. And he will, he will eat your soul if you leave the path." The warnings she had heard so many times in her childhood echoed inside her in Aunt Engrasi's clear voice.

"The cards are a door and, like a door, you shouldn't just open it for the sake of it, nor leave it open afterward. A door, Amaia. Doors don't do any harm, but what comes through them may. Remember that you must shut it when you finish your consultation, that what you need to know will be revealed to you, and that what remains dark belongs to the darkness."

The door opened up a world to her that had always been there, and in a few months she proved to be an expert traveler, learning to plot authoritative routes on the map of the unknown, directing the consultation, and closing the door with the care prompted by Engrasi's vigilant gaze. The answers were clear, concise, and as easy to understand as a lullaby whispered in her ear. But there was a moment, when she was eighteen and studying in Pamplona, when curiosity kept her tied to the deck of cards for hours. She would ask about the boy she liked again and again, about her grades, about what her rivals were thinking. And the answers that arrived started to become confused, muddled, contradictory. Sometimes, bewildered in her attempts to discern a reply, she would spend the whole night shuffling and dealing dark cards that didn't reveal anything and left her with the strange sensation in her heart of being deprived of something that belonged to her by right. She tried again and again, and without realizing it she began to leave the door open. She never gathered up the deck of cards, which was often on her bed, and she would get drawn into long sessions over and over again with the sole intention of trying to see. And she saw.

One morning, when she should have been leaving the house to go to the department, she got drawn into one of those rapid, direction-less consultations that ended up absorbing her for hours. But that morning the journey to nowhere brought her an answer without a question. When she was ready to deal the cards, an ominous charge ran through the smooth cardboard on which they were printed and shook her arm as if she'd been given an electric shock. One by one she turned them over and plotted the map of the desolation in her soul. When she reached the last one, she touched it gently with the tip of her index finger without turning it over, and all the cold in the universe gathered around her while she exhaled a wordless moan and, desolate, understood that the wolf had seduced her. He had de-ceived her into leaving the path, the damned son of a bitch had gone on ahead, had arrived before her, and she had spent days talking to evil poorly disguised as a dear old granny. The phone rang just once before she picked it up, and Engrasi told her what she already knew: that her father had died while she'd been off gathering flowers. She never dealt out the cards again.

The question.

The question had been thundering in her head for days muddled with others: Where is he? Why does he do it? But, most important, who is he? Who is the *basajaun*?

She set the deck of cards on the table and Ros arranged them in a line.

"Choose three cards," she requested.

Amaia touched them one by one with the tip of her finger. Ros separated them from the rest and turned them over, arranging them in a row.

"You're looking for someone, and he's a man. He's not young but he's not old either, and he's nearby. Choose three cards."

Amaia chose another three cards, which Ros arranged to the right of the first ones.

"This man is fulfilling an obligation. He has a job to do and he's committed to doing it, because what he does gives sense to his life and assuages his fury."

"It assuages his fury? A crime assuages a greater fury?"

"Choose three cards."

She turned them over next to the others.

"It assuages an ancient fury and an even greater fear."

"Tell me about his past."

"He was subjugated, enslaved, but now he's free, although a yoke hangs over him. He's always been fighting an internal war to dominate his fury, and now he thinks he has succeeded."

"He thinks he has? What does he think?"

"He thinks he's in the right, he thinks that reason is helping him, he thinks that what he's doing is a good thing. He's got a good opinion of himself, he sees himself as triumphant and victorious over evil, but it's only an act. Choose three cards."

She arranged them slowly.

"Sometimes he breaks down and his worst side surfaces . . ."

" . . . and then he kills."

"No. When he kills, he isn't at his worst. I know it doesn't make much sense, but when he kills he's the guardian of purity."

"What made you say that?" asked Amaia brusquely.

"What did I say?" asked Ros, as if returning from a dream.

"The guardian of purity, one who conserves nature, the guardian of the forest, the *basajaun*. Bloody arrogant bastard. What does he think he's preserving by killing little girls? I hate him."

"Well, that's not how he feels about you. He doesn't hate you, he doesn't fear you, he does your job."

Amaia went to point to one of the cards and, in doing so, she pushed another one out of the deck. The card slipped out unprompted and turned over, showing its face.

"That's a different matter. You've opened a different door."

Amaia looked at the card, reluctant, recognizing the presence of the wolf.

"What the hell . . . ?"

"Ask a question," ordered Ros firmly.

The sound of the door made them turn to look at James and Aunt Engrasi, who came in laden with various bags. They were chatting between fits of laughter, which was suddenly cut short when Engrasi noticed the cards. She approached the table with a firm step, assessed what was happening, and urged Ros on with a gesture.

"Ask the question," Ros repeated.

Amaia looked at the card, remembering the formula. "What is it that I ought to know?"

"Three."

Amaia gave them to her.

"What you ought to know is that there's another, let's call it an element, in the game." She turned another card over. "Infinitely more dangerous." She turned the last one over. "And he's your enemy, he's coming for you and for . . ." she stuttered, "for your family, and he's already arrived on the scene, and he will continue trying to attract your attention until you join his game."

"But what does he want from me, from my family?"

"Give me one."

She turned the card over, and the fleshless skeleton's empty eye sockets looked up at them from the table.

"Oh, Amaia, he wants your bones."

She remained silent for a few seconds. Then she gathered up the cards, wrapped them in the cloth, and looked up.

"Door closed, sister, there's very scary stuff outside."

Amaia looked at her aunt, who had turned alarmingly pale.

"Aunt Engrasi, perhaps you could . . ."

"Yes, but not today. And not with that pack . . . I have to think about it," she said as she went into the kitchen.

33

THE HOTEL Baztán was about five kilometers along the high-way from Elizondo and looked like any other mountain hotel built with the aim of catering to school groups, hikers, families, and friends. The façade formed a semicircle covered in balconies that overlooked a small drive, which acted as a parking area, where the yellow plastic chairs and tables looked incongruous. These were no doubt intended for summer evenings, but the hotel management made them available year-round, giving the place a colorful, tropical air more like a Mexican beachfront hotel than a mountain establish-ment. It was still early in spite of the fact that it had grown dark hours ago, and this was evident from the number of cars outside and locals crammed into the restaurant with its enormous windows.

Amaia parked next to a mobile home with a French number plate and headed for the entrance. Behind the reception desk, a teenager with her coarse hair tied back in a ponytail was playing an online game.

"Good evening. Could you let some of your guests, Señor Raúl González and Señora Nadia Takchenko, know that I'm here?"

"I'll be right with you," replied the girl in that fastidious tone that teenagers often use. She paused the game, and when she looked up she had transformed into a helpful receptionist.

"Yes, how can I help you?"

"I'm supposed to be meeting two of your guests. Could you give me their room number? Raúl González and Nadia Takchenko."

"Ah, yes, the scientists from Huesca," said the girl, smiling.

Amaia would have preferred them to be more discreet. The news that some experts were looking for bears in the valley could start rumors that, if unfortunately spread by the press, could complicate the progress of the investigation even further.

"They're in the restaurant. They asked me to send anyone who came to see them there."

Amaia went through the internal door that linked the reception area with the dining room and walked into the bar. A large group of students in hiking gear filled almost all the tables, laughing as they shared various portions of ham, *patatas bravas*, and meatballs. She saw a woman waving to her from the back of the bar, and it took her a few seconds to realize that it was Dr. Takchenko. Smiling, she went over to the woman, whom she hadn't recognized. Dr. Takchenko had brushed out her long hair and was wearing caramel-colored trousers and a beige blazer over a stylish shirt and even had high-heeled boots on. Amaia felt ridiculous when she realized that deep down she had expected to see her in the terrible orange overalls. The scientist smiled as she shook her hand.

"I'm glad to see you, Inspector Salazar," she said in her awful accent. "Raúl is ordering at the bar. We decided to leave this evening, but we're going to eat something first. I hope you'll join us, *da*?"

"Well, I'm afraid not, but we can chat for a while if you don't mind."

Dr. González came back carrying three beers, which he put on the table.

"Inspector, I'd begun to think we'd have to send you the report by mail."

"I'm sorry I couldn't meet with you before, because the truth is I'm very interested in your findings, but, as Deputy Inspector Zabalza will have explained, I've been busy."

"I'm afraid we can't be conclusive. We haven't found any dens or excrement, although we did find traces that might indicate the passage of a large plantigrade: places where lichen and bark have been scratched away and hairs from a male that match the ones you sent us."

"But?"

"It may be that a bear has been in the area. The hairs could have been there for some time; in fact, they look rather old, although this could also be due to the bear shedding its coat. I already told you that it's bit early for a bear to have woken from hibernation. Of course there is recent data suggesting that certain females haven't hibernated this year, probably due to global warming and the scarcity of food, which means they weren't ready to hibernate at the right time."

"And how do you know they belong to the same animal?"

"The same way we know they come from a male, by carrying out an analysis."

"A DNA analysis?"

"Of course."

"And you already have the results?"

"We've had them since yesterday."

"How is that possible? I still haven't received the results of the samples I sent off when I sent you those bear hairs . . ."

"It's because we sent them to Huesca, to our own laboratory."

Amaia was astonished. "Are you telling me that your laboratory, in a center for environmental studies, has sufficiently advanced technology to complete a DNA analysis within three days?"

"In twenty-four hours if we're in a rush. Dr. Takchenko usually does them, but since she's here, a student who normally works with us did them."

"Let's see, can you, for example, perform a DNA analysis of a mineral, animal, or human sample and establish whether or not it's identical to another?"

"Of course, that's exactly what we do. Ours is a system of comparison and elimination. We don't have the kind of database a forensic laboratory uses, but we can establish comparisons with absolute certainty. A hair from a male bear and another hair from a male bear have many alleles in common, even if they are not from the same animal."

Amaia studied Dr. Takchenko's face in silence.

"If I sent you samples of different brands of a substance, like common flour, could you establish for certain whether any of them was the flour used to make a specific loaf of bread?"

"Yes, probably. I'm sure that each manufacturer has a different method of milling and blending; furthermore, there may be combinations of grain from different sources. We could be more certain if we carried out a chromatographic analysis."

Amaia bit her lip pensively while a waiter placed a dish of calamari on the table along with some meatballs whose sauce was still bubbling in the little earthenware pot.

"It's a combination of techniques based on the principle of differential retention, whose objective is to separate the different components of a mixture, allowing the identification of the aforementioned components and the determination of their respective quantities," explained Dr. González.

"You're leaving tonight, is that correct?"

Dr. Takchenko smiled. "I know what you're thinking, and I'd be delighted to help you. In case you're at all unsure, back in my country I used to work in a forensic laboratory. If you give me the samples now, I'll have the results tomorrow."

Amaia's head was whirling at high speed as she assessed the advance that having those results in twenty-four hours would represent. Of course, the results wouldn't be of any value in court, but if they could discard some of the samples, it would speed up the investigation. They'd have to wait for confirmation from the official laboratory if they obtained any positive results, but the investigation would be relaunched if it had a certain direction in which to head.

She got up and dialed a number on her phone.

"Jonan, come to the Hotel Baztán with a sample from each of the flours that you guys collected from the workshops, and bring your bag with you. We're going to Huesca."

She hung up and looked at the scientists and the food laid out on the table with a grin, deciding that she'd recovered her appetite.

Twenty minutes later, a smiling Jonan joined them at the table.

"Well, you'd better tell us where we're going," he sighed.

"To the Bear Observatory of the Pyrenees, in the region of Sobrarbe, which was once an ancient kingdom in the north of Huesca. It's probably best to put Aínsa into your GPS, though."

"Aínsa, that rings a bell, it's a medieval town, isn't it? One of those ones that still have original buildings and cobbled streets."

"Yes, Aínsa was very important in medieval times, mostly due to its strategic location, a privileged position between the Ordesa y Monte Perdido National Park, the Sierra y Cañones de Guara Nature Reserve, and the Posets-Maladeta Nature Reserve. Having control of Aínsa must have represented a serious advantage back then."

"And are there bears in that area?"

"I'm afraid bears are much more complicated than most people think."

"Complicated bears," said Amaia, smiling at Jonan. "We have to do a profile of them all the same, so brace yourself."

"Well, don't think it's so absurd. We can only partially discern the mentality of a bear, that is, if we can assume he has one in the first place. From the moment we admit that bears have character, a way of being that differs from one individual to the next, we can start to understand the difficulty observing an individual entails, Dr. González explained.

"Dr. Takchenko and I," he said, looking at his companion, "travel to Central Europe, the Carpathians, Hungary, lost populations between the Balkans and the Urals and, of course, throughout the Pyrenees. Aínsa isn't exactly famous for its bear sightings, but it does have a great network of wildlife observation centers, in particular for birds, and it provided us with a perfect place for the laboratory and allows the company that funds it to make an income from the endangered species centers, guided tours, and donations from the many tourists and visitors who come to Aínsa throughout the year."

"So you don't just study bears?"

"No, not at all. We do work involving a great variety and number of species, reflecting the variety of habitats in this region. Given the good conservation status of the majority of the habitats, these valleys are one of the last refuges for a fair number of species. There are lots of diurnal birds of prey, golden eagles, red kites, peregrine falcons, goshawks, sparrow hawks, and nocturnal ones like long-eared owls, little owls, and barn owls . . . It's common to see large carrion birds, such as bearded vultures and buzzards, and a multitude of smaller birds. But Dr. Takchenko and I mainly concentrate on large mammals—wild boar, deer, foxes—although smaller mammals, such as bats, shrews, rabbits, squirrels, marmots, and dormice, are more abundant . . . We're busy year-round, although most of our sleepless nights are connected with the migration of large bears all around Europe, and we respond to any requests, like yours, where the presence of a bear is suggested."

"And what conclusion have you reached? Is it possible that there's a bear in the area? Or do you agree with the forest rangers that it's a *basajaun*?" asked Jonan.

Dr. González looked at him, perplexed, but Dr. Takchenko smiled.

"I know what this . . . this *basajauno*, is."

"*Basajaun*," corrected Jonan.

"Yes," she exclaimed, turning to her companion. "It's the same as the Home Grandizo, Bigfoot, the Giant, and the Sasquatch. They say that there's a giant, a Home Grandizo, in a place called the Val d'Onsera. They say he walks about accompanied by an enormous bear. And in my country there's also a legend about a huge, strong, not very evolved man who lives in the forests to protect nature's equilibrium. Is that the same as a *basajaun*?"

"Practically the same, except certain magical qualities are attributed to the *basajaun*, he's a mystical mythological creature."

"I thought that was just the name the press had given the criminal . . . because he kills in the forest," said Dr. González.

"Oh, that's not right at all," exclaimed Dr. Takchenko. "A *basajaun* doesn't kill. His role is to be a caretaker and preserve purity."

Amaia stared at her as she remembered her sister's words. The guardian of purity.

"And the forest rangers think the killer you're looking for is a *basajaun*?" asked Dr. González, surprised.

"Well, it would appear that they believe in the existence of the *basajaun,*" explained Jonan, "and they suggest that he could be the creature we've mistaken for a bear, but of course he wouldn't have anything to do with the murders, and his presence would only be due to the forces of nature summoning him to curb the predator's activity and restore the harmony of the forest once more."

"It's a lovely story," admitted Dr. González.

"But it's only a story," said Amaia, standing up and putting an end to the conversation.

She went out into the parking area, wrapping herself up in her anorak and deciding to travel in Jonan's car and leave hers there. She took out her phone to call James and let him know she was going to Huesca. There were no streetlamps outside, but the area was partially lit by the white light from the restaurant windows and warmer light from the windows of the rustic dining room on the other side. While she was waiting for James to answer, she noticed the two diners who were sitting closest to the window. Flora, dressed in a tight-fitting black blouse, was leaning forward with a surprisingly coquettish and studied expression. Her curiosity piqued, Amaia walked among the cars, searching for the angle that would afford her a better view of the scene. James finally answered and she briefly explained the idea she'd had and that she would call him when she was setting off to come back. Just as she was saying goodbye to him, her sister moved away from the window and leaned forward to hold her companion's hand. Inspector Montes smiled as he said something to Flora that made her older sister laugh, throwing her head back in a clearly seductive manner and looking outside. Shocked, Amaia turned quickly and tried to hide, dropping her cell phone, which disappeared under a car, before deciding that there was no way that Flora could have seen her standing in that ill-lit parking area from inside.

She recovered her phone while Jonan and the scientists were leaving the restaurant. She let Jonan drive without paying attention to what he was saying and sighed when they started to leave the hotel behind them, relieved and rather confused by how she had reacted.

34

ENGRASI OPENED the packaging containing a new Tarot of Marseilles deck. She took the cards out of their box and began a contact ritual, praying as she slowly shuffled them. She knew she was facing something different, although not something new, an old enemy she had already glimpsed once before a long time ago, the day on which Amaia had dealt the cards when she was young. And today, while Ros was trying to help her sister, that old threat had returned to poke its dirty, drooling nose into her little girl's life like an unpleasant memory.

Engrasi had felt close to Amaia ever since she was a child. Just like Amaia, she had loathed that place where she'd happened to be born, denying how important the ancient customs, traditions, and history were, and had done everything she could to get away from there until she had succeeded. She had studied, pushing herself to the maximum to obtain the grants that would let her go farther and farther from home, first to Madrid and finally to Paris. She studied psychology at the Sorbonne. A new world opened before her in a revolutionary Paris filled with ideas and dreams of freedom, making her feel like she'd finally joined the party and more alienated than ever from the dark valley where the sky was made of lead and the river thundered in the middle of the night. There was love in the Paris air and, together with the Seine flowing in majestic silence, it seduced her once and for all and confirmed what she already knew: she would never return to Elizondo.

She met Jean Martin during the final year of her studies. An esteemed Belgian psychologist, he was a visiting professor at the university and twenty-five years her senior. They courted in secret during that academic year and married in a small parish church on the outskirts of Paris as soon as she graduated. The wedding was attended by Jean's three sisters with their husbands and children and a hundred friends. Not a single one of Engrasi's relatives were there. She told her in-laws that her family was small and bogged down in work and that her parents were too old to travel. She told Jean the truth.

She didn't want to see them, she didn't want to speak to them or to have to ask after the neighbors and old acquaintances. She didn't want the influence of her hometown to reach her there, because she sensed that it would bring the energy of the water and the mountain, that tugging somewhere deep inside felt by anyone who was born in Elizondo. Jean had smiled while he listened to her, as if she were a child recounting a bad dream, and he had consoled her accordingly, gently reprimanding her.

"Engrasi, you're an adult woman. If you don't want them to come, they won't come." And he had continued reading his book as if the conversation were about nothing more important than choosing between a lemon tart and a chocolate one.

Life couldn't have been more generous to her. She lived in the most beautiful city in the world, in a university environment. Her mind was stimulated and her heart was full of that absurd security born of wanting for nothing, except children, who didn't arrive during the five years the dream lasted . . . right up until the day Jean died of a heart attack while walking in the gardens in front of his office in Paris.

She had no memories of those days. She assumed she had spent them in shock, although she remembered that she had appeared serene and in control of herself, with the self-control born of incredulity in the face of events. Week after week passed between sleeping pills and tearful visits from her sisters-in-law, who insisted on protecting her from the rest of the world, as if that were possible, as if her heart weren't buried in a Paris cemetery, as cold and dead as Jean's. Until one night she woke up sobbing and covered in sweat, and realized why she didn't weep during the day. She got out of bed and walked disconsolately around the enormous apartment, looking for a trace of Jean's presence. Although his glasses were there, his book still open at the page he had marked, his slippers were there, and his cramped handwriting filled the boxes on the calendar in the kitchen, she could no longer find him, and this realization left her desolate and made the apartment feel freezing. She could no longer bear to live in Paris.

She returned to Elizondo. Jean had left her enough money that she never had to worry again. She bought a house in that place she thought she didn't love, and she hadn't left the Baztán Valley since.

35

THE WIND was blowing hard in Aínsa. Jonan had not stopped talking for a single moment of the three hours it had taken them to get there, but Amaia's taciturn silence seemed to infect him for the last few kilometers, during which he first grew quiet and then turned on the radio and sang along with the choruses of the latest hits. The streets of Aínsa were deserted. Even the warm orange light of the streetlamps didn't manage to diminish the freezing impression of the medieval town, swept as it was by the nocturnal cold, and gusts of Siberian wind caused frost to form on the car windows. Jonan followed the bear experts' four-by-four as the car's tires jolted over the centuries-old cobbled streets until they arrived at a wide square that opened up in front of the entrance to what appeared to be a fortress. The scientists stopped their car next to the wall, and Jonan parked beside them. The cold hurt Amaia's forehead like an invisible hand driving a nail into it. She pulled up the hood of her anorak in an attempt to cover her head as they followed the scientists into the fortress. Apart from the lack of wind, it was not much better inside. They led Amaia and Jonan along narrow gray stone corridors until they arrived in a more open space in which stood a number of gigantic aviaries containing enormous sleeping birds that Amaia was unable to identify in the shadows.

"This is the rehabilitation area for birds that are brought to us injured, with gunshot wounds, after being hit by vehicles, following accidental collisions with high-tension cables, wind turbines . . ."

They set off down a different narrow corridor and went up a flight of about ten stairs where Dr. Takchenko stopped in front of a fairly average looking white door, which was, however, adorned with a number of security locks. The laboratory consisted of three light, ordered, and very spacious rooms, so modern that Amaia thought that if she'd been led there blindfolded she would never have guessed where she was. Nobody would have expected to find such a well-appointed laboratory in the heart of a medieval fortress.

The scientists hung their anoraks on some hooks and Dr. Takchenko put on a strange fitted laboratory coat that opened into a full pleated skirt and buttoned at the side.

"My mother was a dentist in Russia," she explained. "Her lab coats and a healthy set of teeth were all she left me when she died."

They went to the far end of the laboratory, where various machines stood grouped on a stainless steel workbench. Amaia recognized the DNA amplifier because she had seen them before. Similar to a futuristic yogurt maker, its cheap plastic appearance belied the ingenuity of one of the most sophisticated analytical machines around. A box beside the machine contained Eppendorf tubes, which looked a bit like small, hollow plastic bullets, in which the material for genetic analysis was placed.

"This is the DNA amplifier you were talking about. It normally takes between three and eight hours to carry out the analysis, and then you have to carry out an electrophoresis using agar gel in order to see the results; that would take us at least another two hours. And what we have here," continued Dr. Takchenko, "is the HPLC, the machine we'll be using to break down the different types of flour from the samples, because the DNA amplifier will be of use only if the flour is mixed with some kind of biological material."

She took some delicate plastic syringes, similar to those that used to be used to administer insulin, from a shelf.

"These are the syringes we'll use to transfer the samples once we've dissolved them in liquid; one injection per sample, and we'll have the results in little more than an hour. We don't need to do an electrophoresis like we would with the DNA amplifier, but we will have to use a processor with software that analyzes the peaks that appear in the samples. Each peak corresponds to a specific substance, so we can find hydrocarbons, minerals, residue from the water, wheat, biological substances that we will then have to identify using another analysis, and so on . . . Because of this, the most complicated part of the process is programming the software with the specific patterns we're looking for. The more different substances we find, the easier it will be to establish the origin of each type of flour. The whole process will take us four or five hours."

Amaia was fascinated. "I don't know what surprises me more, the fact that you have such a laboratory here or that a genius like you has dedicated herself to searching for bear traces," she said with a smile.

"We're very fortunate to have Dr. Takchenko working with us," agreed Dr. González. "She did exactly this kind of work for years in her own country, but she sent us her CV two years ago and decided to join us. We feel very lucky."

Dr. Takchenko smiled.

"Why don't you make some coffee for our guests, Dr. González?"

"Of course," he said, smiling. "Dr. Takchenko can't stand compliments. I'll be a little while, I have to go over to the other side of the building," he apologized.

"Go with him please, Jonan. I think one of us being present is enough."

"Dr. González is very pleasant," said Amaia when the men had left the room.

"I think so," replied Dr. Takchenko in her strong accent, "a really lovely man."

Amaia raised an eyebrow. "Do you like him?"

"Oh, naturally I hope so. He's my husband. It's best that I should like him, isn't it?"

"But you call him doctor and he calls you . . ."

"Doctor, yes." She shrugged and smiled. "What can I say? I take my work seriously and he finds it amusing."

"For God's sake, I really need to work on my powers of observation, I had no idea."

The scientist worked at the computer for at least an hour, entering the patterns for the analysis. She dissolved the samples that Jonan had brought from Elizondo and some crumbs from the *txantxigorri* found on Anne's body with the utmost care. She injected the samples into the machine one by one with an expert hand.

"You might want to pull up a chair, this will take some time."

Amaia pulled a wheeled stool over and sat down behind her.

"I know from your husband that you don't like compliments or praise, but I really must thank you. The results of this analysis could kick-start an investigation that has more or less ground to a halt."

"It's nothing, believe me. I'm delighted to do this."

"At two in the morning?" Amaia laughed.

"It's a pleasure to help you. What's happening in the Baztán Valley is terrifying. If I can do anything that might help you, then I'm delighted to do it."

Amaia maintained a rather awkward silence while the machine gave off a gentle hum.

"You don't think there's a bear, do you?"

Dr. Takchenko stopped what she was doing and turned right around on her chair to face Amaia.

"No, I don't . . . and yet there is . . . something."

"What sort of something? Because the hairs we found at the scene of the crime match all kinds of different animals, they've even found kidskin there."

"What if all the hair belonged to the same creature?"

"Creature? What are you trying to tell me? That there really is a *basajaun*?"

"I'm not trying to tell you anything, Inspector," she said, holding out her hands, "just that perhaps you need to be a bit more open-minded."

"It's strange to hear that from a scientist."

"Don't be so surprised. I'm a scientist, but I'm also very bright." She smiled and turned back to her work without saying anything more.

The hours passed slowly, watching Dr. Takchenko's precise movements and listening to the incessant chatter of Jonan and Dr. González in the background as they stood talking on the other side of the room. From time to time, Dr. Takchenko would lean toward the screen, observe the graphs that kept appearing there, and then return to her perusal of what looked like a thick technical manual, which hardly looked gripping but kept her entirely absorbed.

Finally, at four in the morning, Dr. Takchenko sat down in front of the computer again, and a few minutes later the printer spat out a sheet of paper. She took it and sighed deeply as she handed it to Amaia.

"I'm sorry, Inspector, there aren't any matches."

Amaia studied the paper for a long moment. She didn't need to be an expert to spot the difference between the peaks and valleys printed on the sheet and the ones that represented the sample from the *txantxigorri*. Silently, without taking her eyes off the printed sheet, she contemplated the consequences of those results.

"I've been extremely careful, Inspector," said Dr. Takchenko, visibly anxious.

"Oh, I'm sorry, this has nothing to do with you, you've stayed up all night to help me. But I was almost certain I'd find some kind of match."

"I'm sorry."

"Yes," she whispered, "I'm sorry too."

~

She drove back to Elizondo in silence without even putting music on the radio, letting Jonan sleep for the whole journey. She felt grumpy and frustrated, and for the first time since she had begun investigating the case she was starting to have doubts about whether they would ever solve it. The flour had not led them anywhere, and if the suspect had not bought the *txantxigorris* locally, where did that leave them? Flora had told her that they were definitely baked in a stone oven, but that wasn't much help either. Almost all the restaurants and rotisseries from Pamplona to Zugarramurdi had one, and that was without counting those that were still found at bakeries and the older farmhouses, albeit sometimes unused.

The highway from Jaca was new and in good condition, so she thought they would be in Elizondo in about three hours. The loneliness of the early morning wasn't doing much to lift her spirits. She looked over at the relaxed expression on Jonan's face as he slept with his head on his balled-up anorak. She almost wished he was awake so she would not feel so alone. What was she doing driving along the highway from Jaca at six thirty in the morning? Why wasn't she at home, in bed with her husband? Perhaps Fermín Montes was right and this case was too big for her.

Thinking of Fermín reminded her of what she had seen through the restaurant window, which she had repressed for a few hours until she had almost forgotten it. Montes and Flora. There was something about that partnership that struck her as jarring. She asked herself whether deep down it might be a kind of familial instinct, a strange kind of loyalty that made her maintain the link with Víctor. Jonan had already told her that he had seen the two of them together. She thought about the conversation she had had with Flora at the workshop and remembered that she had already made it clear that she found Montes charming. At the time she had thought it was one of those malicious comments so typical of her sister, but what she had seen at the hotel left no room for doubt: her sister was pulling out all the stops for Montes, and he seemed happy. But Víctor, with his freshly ironed shirt and his bunch of roses, had also seemed happy. She pursed her lips and shook her head without realizing it. The same old shit, the same old shit, the same old shit.

The sun had risen by the time they arrived in Elizondo. She parked opposite the Casa Galarza in Calle Santiago and woke Jonan. The café smelled of coffee and warm croissants. She carried their cups to the table herself while she waited for Jonan to finish in the bathroom. When he came back, his hair was wet and he looked much more alert.

"You can go and sleep for a couple of hours," she said, sipping her coffee.

"That's all right, I managed to have a bit of a snooze at least. You're the one who ought to be tired."

The idea of sleeping alone again did not appeal to Amaia at all. Besides, she felt as though staying awake would somehow prevent things from getting worse.

"I'm going back to the station, I need to go over the data. I guess we ought to be getting the results from the other girls' computers today too," she said, suppressing a yawn.

Strong gusts of damp wind were blowing up the street when they left the café, and some large, dense clouds drifted high above their heads. Amaia looked up and was surprised to see a falcon in flight, hovering motionless a hundred or so meters above the ground, displaying its disdain and majesty, watching her from the sky as if studying her soul. Seeing the stillness of that hunter, hovering impassively on the wind, made her feel like a fragile leaf in comparison, whirling wherever the capricious breeze blew her, and left her very uneasy.

"Are you all right, chief?"

She looked at Jonan, surprised to realize that she had stopped in the middle of the street.

"Let's go back to the station," she said, getting into the car.

Explaining the hunch that had taken her to Huesca was fairly pointless given the results. In spite of that, Iriarte agreed that it had been a good idea.

"An idea that doesn't get us anywhere," she declared. "What have you got?"

"Deputy Inspector Zabalza and I have been focusing on the girls' computers. At first glance there was nothing to suggest that they were members of the same social media forums or had friends in common. Ainhoa Elizasu's was untouched, but Carla's younger sister inherited hers following her death and has deleted almost everything. Even so, the hard drive still has the browser history and record of sites she visited. The only thing we know for certain is that all three visited blogs related to fashion and style, but they weren't even the same ones. They were quite active in social forums, in particular on Tuenti, but the groups are quite closed. There's no sign of stalkers, pedophiles, or cybercriminals of any description."

"Anything else?"

"Not much. The laboratory in Zaragoza called. It looks like the skin that was stuck to the cord, which turned out to be from a goat, has the remains of an unidentified substance encrusted on it. They're going to analyze it further, but I have nothing more to tell you, for now."

Amaia sighed deeply.

"A substance encrusted on goatskin," she repeated.

Iriarte opened his hands in a gesture of annoyance.

"It's fine, Inspector. I want you to visit all the workshops on the list and question the owners about any current or former employees who know how to make *txantxigorris*. It doesn't matter if those employees haven't worked there for a few years, we'll go and visit those people one by one. He had to learn to make them that well somewhere. I want you to talk to the girls' friends again, check again in case any of them have remembered anything, like someone who was watching them too closely, someone who offered them a ride, anyone pleasant who approached them under any pretext. I also want you to talk to their classmates and schoolteachers again.

"I also want to know whether anyone seemed friendlier than normal toward the girls. I noticed that at least two teachers taught all three girls at different stages. I've underlined their names. Zabalza, check them out: anything that's put them on our radar previously, but also any rumors. A small scandal is often hushed up out of solidarity."

She looked at the men in front of her. They wore worried frowns and looked at her expectantly as they listened carefully to her instructions.

"Guys, we're part of the team that has to chase down perhaps the most complex murderer of the last few years. I know that it's a big effort for all of us, but now is the time to make that effort. There has to be something that's escaped us, a detail, a little clue. In this type of crime, where the criminal develops such an intimate relationship with the victim, and I don't mean a sexual relationship but rather all the paraphernalia and effort put into setting up the crime scene before, during, and after the death, it's almost impossible that he hasn't left anything behind. He kills them, he takes their bodies to the riverbank, sometimes to places that are difficult to reach, and then he prepares them, he arranges them, like actresses in his production. Too much work, too much effort, an excessively close relationship with the bodies. We know what his work is like, but if we don't get anything in the next few days, the case might stagnate. What with the fears of the local population and the increase in patrols through- out the valley, it's quite unlikely he'll try anything until things have calmed down. There's no doubt that the pace seems to have picked up, the amount of time between the crimes has been getting shorter, but I don't feel like we're going to find ourselves facing a nutcase going into a spin. I think he simply saw an opportunity and acted. He's not stupid. If he thinks he's running a risk, he'll stop and go back to his normal life. Therefore, our only chance lies in carrying out an impeccable investigation and leaving no stone unturned."

They all nodded.

"We'll get him," said Zabalza.

"We'll get him," repeated the others.

Encouraging the officers working on the investigation was one of the steps they had taught her in Quantico. Mixing your demands with encouragement was fundamental when an investigation was dragging on without positive results and spirits were starting to flag. She looked at her reflection drawn on the window of the now empty meeting room like a ghost, and asked herself who out of the whole team was most demoralized. To whom had she really directed those words—to her men or to herself? She turned to the door and bolted it, then picked up her phone just as it started ringing.

James kept her on the phone for five minutes during which he questioned her about whether she had slept, whether she had eaten breakfast, and whether she was okay. She lied, telling him that since Jonan had driven, she had slept for the whole journey. Her impa- tience to hang up must have been evident to James, who dragged a promise out of her that she would be home for supper before he finally put the phone down, more worried than ever, leaving her conscience burdened by the fact that she had behaved badly toward the person who loved her most in the world.

She looked in her phone's address book. Aloisius Dupree. She glanced at her watch to work out what time it would be in Louisiana. It was half past nine in Elizondo, which made it half past two in New Orleans. With a bit of luck, and if Special Agent Dupree had kept the same habits, he wouldn't have gone to bed yet. She pressed the call button and waited. Agent Dupree's hoarse voice traveled down the line to her before the second ring, bringing with it all the southern charm typical of Louisiana.

"*Mon Dieu!* To what do I owe this unexpected pleasure, Inspector Salazar?"

"Hello, Aloisius," she replied, smiling with surprise at being so pleased to hear his voice.

"Hello, Amaia. Everything going well?"

"Well no, *mon ami*, nothing's going well at all."

"I'm listening."

She spoke nonstop for almost half an hour, trying to summarize everything without forgetting anything, suggesting and discarding theories as she went along. When she finished, the silence at the other end of the line seemed so absolute that she was afraid the call had been cut off. Then she heard Aloisius breathe.

"Inspector Salazar, you are undoubtedly the best investigator I've ever met, and I know a lot of them, and what makes you so good is not the flawless application of police techniques, we spoke about that a lot when you were here, if you remember? What makes you an exceptional investigator, the reason your boss put you in charge of this investigation, is that you possess the pure instincts of a tracker, and that, *mon amie*, is what distinguishes exceptional detectives from normal police officers. You've given me a mountain of information, you've produced a suspect profile worthy of any FBI agent, and you've moved forward with the investigation step by step. But I haven't heard you tell me what you feel in your gut, Inspector, what your instinct tells you. What do you feel about him? Is he nearby? Is he sick? Is he afraid? Where does he live? How does he dress? What does he eat? Does he believe in God? Does he have a healthy digestive system? Does he have sex often? And, most important, how did all this begin? If you stopped to think about it, you could answer all those questions and many more, but first you have to answer the most important one: What the hell is blocking the course of the investigation? And don't you tell me it's that jealous police officer, because you're above all that, Inspector Salazar."

"I know," she said in a small voice.

"Remember what you learned at Quantico: if you get stuck, reset and start again. Sometimes it's the only way to unblock a brain, be it human or cybernetic. Reset, Inspector. Switch off and on again, and start from the beginning."

When she went out into the corridor, she caught sight of the leather jacket belonging to Inspector Montes, who was heading toward the elevator. She lingered for a few moments, and when she heard the unmistakable hiss of the elevator doors closing, she went into Deputy Inspector Zabalza's office.

"Has Inspector Montes been up here?"

"Yes, he's just left. Do you want me to try and catch up with him?" he asked, standing.

"No, that won't be necessary. Can you tell me what you were talking about?"

Zabalza shrugged. "Nothing in particular: the case, the news, I filled him in on the meeting, and not much else . . . Well, we discussed yesterday's match between Barcelona and Real Madrid . . ."

She stared at him and noticed his discomfort.

"Have I done something wrong? Montes is part of the team, isn't he?"

Amaia looked at him in silence. The voice of Special Agent Aloisius Dupree resounded in her head.

"No, don't worry, everything's fine . . ."

As she was going down in the elevator, where the traces of Montes's aftershave lingered, she wondered to what degree her statement was a lie: yes they needed to worry, because nothing was fine.

36

THE FINE rain that had been falling for hours had left the valley so sodden that it seemed impossible that it would ever dry out again. Every surface was damp and shiny, and a hesitant sun filtered through the clouds, raising scraps of mist from the crowns of the leafless trees. Agent Dupree's question was still stuck in her head: What was blocking the course of the investigation? As always, she was overwhelmed by the brilliance of his prodigious mind. He was one of the FBI's top analysts despite his outlandish methods. In barely thirty minutes of telephone conversation, Aloisius Dupree had dissected the case, and Amaia herself and, with the skill of a surgeon, had indicated the problem with the same certainty with which he might stick a pin in a map. Here. And what was certain was that she had known it too, had known it before she dialed Dupree's number, had known it before he answered from the banks of the Mississippi. Yes, Special Agent Dupree, there was something blocking the course of the investigation, but she was not sure she wanted to look at the point marked by the pin.

She got in her car and closed the door, but she did not start the engine. It was cold inside, and the windows, clouded by microscopic drops of rain, contributed to its damp and melancholic air.

"The thing that's blocking the course of the investigation," Amaia whispered to herself.

An immense fury grew inside her, coming up from deep within

like a burning mouthful of fire, accompanied by a fear beyond all logic, which urged her to flee immediately, to escape from all that, to go somewhere, somewhere where she could feel safe, where danger did not grip her as it did now. Evil no longer lay in wait for her; it stalked her with its hostile presence, wrapping itself around her body like fog, breathing down her neck, and mocking the terror it provoked in her. She was aware of its watchful, silent, inevitable presence in the same way that people are aware of illness and death. The alarms were wailing inside her, begging her to flee, to make herself safe, and she wanted to, but she didn't know where to go. She rested her head against the steering wheel and stayed there for several minutes, feeling the fear and the rage take over her body. A rapping on the window made her jump. She was about to wind it down when she realized that she had not turned the engine on yet. She opened the door and a young female uniformed officer leaned down to speak to her.

"Are you all right, Inspector?"

"Yes, perfectly all right, it's just fatigue. You know how it is."

The young woman nodded as if she knew what Amaia was talking about and added, "Perhaps you shouldn't drive if you're very tired. Do you want me to find someone to take you home?"

"That won't be necessary," she said, trying to appear more alert. "Thank you."

She started the engine and headed out of the parking area under the police officer's watchful gaze. She drove around Elizondo for a good while. Down Calle Santiago and then along Calle Francisco Joaquín Iriarte to the market, along Calle Giltxaurdi as far as Menditurri, back onto Calle Santiago, along Calle Alduides to the cemetery. She stopped the car at the entrance and, still sitting inside it, watched a couple of horses from the neighboring estate who had come to the edge of the field and were poking their imposing heads into the road.

As always, the grilled iron gate seemed closed between its stone gateposts, although while she was there a man came out of the graveyard carrying an open umbrella in one hand, in spite of the fact that it was no longer raining, and a firmly wrapped parcel in the other. She thought about that custom typical of men who lived in the country or by the coast of never carrying bags, instead making neat bundles of whatever they needed to carry, whether clothes, tools, or a snack. They would roll it up into a compact bundle, then wrap it in a cloth or their own work clothes, and tie it with string, making it impossible to tell what was being carried inside. The man set off down the road toward Elizondo, and she looked at the cemetery gate again, which hadn't been fully closed after all. She got out of the car, went over to the fence, and shut it while taking a quick look into the town of the dead. She got back into her car and turned the ignition.

Whatever she was looking for, it wasn't there.

A mixture of annoyance, sadness, and anger was bubbling inside her, making her heart beat so hard she felt like she was suffocating. She wound down the windows and drove like that, sighing in confusion and splattering the inside of the car with the drops of water that had been clinging to its exterior. The sound of her telephone, lying on the front passenger seat, interrupted a dark train of thought. She looked at it in irritation and slowed down a bit before picking it up. It was James. "For fuck's sake, are you never going to give me a minute's peace?" she said without answering the call. She turned the ringtone to silent, now furious with him, and threw the phone onto the backseat. She felt so angry with James she could have hit him. Why did the whole world think they were so clever? Why did they all think they knew what she needed? Her aunt, Ros, James, Dupree, and that policewoman guarding the gate.

"Go fuck yourselves," she muttered. "Go to hell the lot of you, and leave me in peace."

She drove to the mountain. The winding road made her pay attention to her driving, so that little by little her nerves began to relax. She remembered how, years before, when she was studying and the pressure of her tests and exams drove her to the point where she couldn't remember a single word, she had got into the habit of driving around the suburbs of Pamplona. Sometimes she would head for Javier, or Eunate, and when she got back her nerves would have disappeared and she would be able to settle down to study again.

She recognized the area where she had met up with the forest rangers. She turned onto the forest trail and drove for a couple more kilometers, avoiding the puddles that had formed from the previous days' rain and remained on that clayey ground like ponds. She stopped the car in an area free of mud, got out, and slammed the door behind her when she heard her phone vibrate again.

She walked along the trail for a few meters, but the flat soles of her shoes stuck to the fine layer of mud, making each step difficult. She rubbed the soles on the grass and, feeling more and more angry, entered the dense forest as if summoned by a mystical call. The rain from earlier in the day had not penetrated the canopy, and beneath the crowns of the trees the ground was clean and dry, as if it had been swept recently by the mountain's *lamias*, those fairies of the forest and the river who wore gold and silver combs in their hair, who slept buried under the ground during the day and came out only at nightfall to try to seduce travelers. They rewarded the men who lay with them and punished the ones who tried to steal their combs, causing them to suffer horrible deformities.

On entering the vault formed by the tree branches, she felt the way she did when she entered a cathedral, the same sense of peace, and she was aware of the presence of God. She lifted her eyes in awe as she felt the rage abandon her body like a fierce hemorrhage that left her both free of evil but also without strength. She began to cry. The first tears welled up, trickling down her face, then loud sobs from the depths of her soul further weakened her body and made her lose her balance. She threw her arms around a tree like a crazed druid, like her forefathers may have done, and cried against its trunk, wetting it with her tears. Exhausted, she slid down until she was sitting on the ground, never letting go of the tree. Her weeping subsided and she stayed there, desolate. She felt like a house on a cliff left open to the mercy of a storm, and now an unholy rage was sweeping through her, blowing everything away, destroying all sense of order. The anger was all that was left, growing in the dark corners of her soul, filling the spaces that desolation had left empty. The anger had no object, no name, it was blind and deaf, and she felt it taking possession of her like a fire fanned by the wind.

The whistle was so loud that it instantly blocked out everything else. She turned briskly, searching for the source of the sound and moving her hand to her pistol. It had sounded forceful, like a train guard's. She listened carefully. Nothing. She heard the whistle again clearly, this time behind her. A long note followed by a shorter one. She stood up and peered carefully among the trees, sure she had noticed a presence. She couldn't see anybody.

Another short whistle, like a call for attention, sounded behind her back. She turned, surprised, and had time to catch sight of a tall, dark silhouette among the trees that hid itself behind a large oak. She went to draw her pistol but thought better of it because deep down she felt that there was no threat. She stayed still, looking at the place where it had disappeared, perhaps twenty meters from where she stood. She saw some low-hanging branches rustle about three meters to the right of the large oak, and the upright figure with its long brown and gray pelt appeared from behind them, walking slowly, as if executing an ancient dance among the trees, avoiding looking in her direction but letting itself be seen clearly enough to leave no room for doubt. Then it went back behind the oak and disappeared. For a while she was so quiet that she could hardly hear her own breathing.

Her visitor's departure had left her with a sense of peace that she did not think possible, a profound calm and the feeling that she had observed something marvelous, which manifested itself in a smile that spread across her cheeks and was still shining on her face when she looked at herself in the car's rearview mirror out of habit. She closed the flap of her holster, which she had opened instinctively but from which she had not drawn the Glock. She thought about the bizarre sensation that had enveloped her on observing him and how her initial fear had immediately turned into a deep sigh, a childish and boundless happiness that moved her in the same way that Christmas morning did.

Amaia sat in the car and checked her phone. Six missed calls, all from James. She looked for Dr. Takchenko's number in the phone's contacts and dialed. The phone started to sound a dial tone but it immediately cut off. She started the engine and drove carefully until she was off the track. She looked for a safe place, stopped the car on a clear corner, and again dialed.

Dr. Takchenko's strong accent greeted her on the other end of the line. "Where have you got to, Inspector? I can't hear you well at all."

"Dr. Takchenko, you told me you'd left some strategically positioned cameras in the woods, is that right?"

"Yes, that's right."

"I've just been to a place near to where we first met, do you remember it?"

"Yes, we've got one of the cameras there . . ."

"Dr. Takchenko . . . I think I saw . . . a bear."

"Do you?"

"I think so, yes."

"Inspector, I'm not doubting you, but if you really had seen a bear, you would be sure. Believe me, there'd be no doubt about it."

Amaia remained silent.

"Or perhaps you don't know what you saw."

"Yes, I do know," whispered Amaia.

"All right, Inspector," it sounded like *Inspectorr.* "I'll have a look at the footage and I'll call you if I see your bear."

"Thank you."

"Not at all."

She hung up and dialed James's number. When he answered, she simply said, "I'm on my way home, darling."

37

T HE ETERNAL blare of the television and the smell of fish soup
and warm bread filled the house, but the normality stopped
there. As an investigator, she did not miss the fact that things had
changed in her surroundings. She could almost feel the conversations about her that had taken place in the house, as if a haze of neg-
ative energy was still floating in the air like a bank of storm clouds
when she came in. She sat down opposite the fireplace and accepted
the herbal tea that James offered her while they waited for supper.
She took a sip, aware as she did so that she was making it easy for
them to continue their close scrutiny of her, which had begun the
moment she walked through the door. There was no doubt they were
worried, and yet she could not help feeling as though her privacy had
been violated, nor could she block out the voice inside her that kept
demanding, "Why don't you just leave me in peace?" The blind fury
that had overwhelmed her in the forest returned in a flash, fueled
by the grim glances her family shot at her, their conciliatory words
and muted, studied expressions. Didn't they realize that all they were
doing was annoying her? Why couldn't they behave normally and
leave her in peace? A peace like the one she had found in the forest.
That powerful whistle that still echoed inside her and the memory
of what she had seen managed to calm her again. She relived the
instant when she saw it emerge from the lower branches of the tree.
The quiet way it turned without looking at her, letting itself be seen.

The stories that her catechism teacher had told them about Marian apparitions to Bernadette or the shepherds at Fatima came to mind. She had always asked herself how it was possible that the children had not fled the apparition in terror. How were they so sure that it was the Virgin? Why were they not afraid? She thought of her own hand searching for her weapon and the fact that it had immediately seemed unnecessary. The sensation of profound peace and immense happiness had warmed her heart, dispersing any shadow of doubt, any trace of anxiety, any pain.

She didn't dare put a name to it, even in a secret thought. The part of her that was a police officer, a twenty-first-century woman, an urbanite, refused to even consider it, because there was no doubt it was a bear. It had to be a bear. And yet . . .

"Why are you laughing?" James asked, looking at her.

"What?" she said, surprised.

"You were laughing to yourself," he said, visibly satisfied.

"Oh . . . Well, it's one of those things I'm not allowed to talk about," she apologized, astonished by the effect that just remembering it had on her.

"Okay," he said, smiling. "In any case, I haven't seen you this happy for days."

Dinner passed peacefully. Her aunt told them something about one of her friends who was going traveling in Egypt, and James filled her in on their day spent visiting the winter market in a nearby town that seemed to have the best vegetables in the whole valley. Ros barely said anything, just giving Amaia some long, worried looks that succeeded in putting her in a bad mood again. As soon as they finished eating, Amaia apologized for being so tired and went upstairs.

"Amaia," her aunt stopped her. "I know you need to sleep, but first I think we ought to have a conversation about what is happening to you."

Amaia paused halfway up the stairs and turned slowly, mustering her patience but unable to avoid an expression of weariness. "I appreciate your concern, Aunt Engrasi, but nothing's happening to me," she said, addressing James and her sister, too, who had gone to stand behind Engrasi like a Greek chorus at the bottom of the stairs. "I haven't slept for two nights, and I'm under so much pressure . . ."

"I know, Amaia, I'm well aware of that, but rest isn't always achieved through sleep."

"Aunt . . ."

"Do you remember what you asked me yesterday when your sister dealt the cards for you? Well, the time is now. I'll deal the cards for you and we'll talk about the evil that's tormenting you."

"Please, Aunt," she said, giving James a sidelong glance.

"That's exactly why, Amaia. Don't you think it's time your husband knew about this?"

"Knew about what?" interjected James. "What should I know?"

Engrasi looked at Amaia as if asking her permission.

"For the love of God!" exclaimed Amaia, dropping down so she was sitting on the stairs. "Show a little mercy. I'm exhausted, I swear I just can't take any more today. Let's wait until tomorrow. Tomorrow, I give you my word, I've taken the day off, we'll talk tomorrow, but today I can't even think clearly anymore."

James seemed satisfied with the prospect of spending a day with her and, although it was obvious that he was intrigued, in the end he took her side.

"Perfect, tomorrow is Sunday. We thought we'd go to the mountain in the morning and afterward your aunt will cook roast lamb and your sister Flora will come and eat with us."

The prospect of sitting down to eat with her older sister was not in the least appealing, but faced with that or continuing the conversation, she gave in.

"Great," she said, standing up and going quickly up the stairs before they had time to say anything more.

⁓

Special Agent Aloisius Dupree took the bag that Antoine had brought out from the back room of his crowded shop and was now holding out to him. The tourists who came for the carnival loved that sort of place, full of knickknacks to do with the old religion and toned-down voodoo for visitors to New Orleans who wanted to take home amulets and necklaces to show their friends. Aloisius had gone straight to Antoine Meire and handed him the list of ingredients he needed, along with two fifty-dollar bills. It was expensive, but he knew that Nana would not accept the mediocre products anyone else might provide. He stopped beneath the balconies of an old inn on Saint Charles Street and watched one of the numerous Mardi Gras processions that traveled through the streets of the French Quarter, attracting crowds of noisy and sweaty locals in its wake. The sixty-five-degree heat, a little warm for February, and the damp from the Mississippi, which enveloped the regulars and made the doorframes swell, left the air thick and heavy, encouraging the consumption of beer among those devotees of the carnival who didn't need much encouragement.

When most of the group had passed, he crossed the street and went into one of the alleyways between the houses where the wood creaked from the heat and had not been touched by the paint provided by the local authorities to whitewash the façades. The marks that showed how high the water had risen during the time when they were visited by the evil curse that was Katrina were still visible. He climbed up a spiral staircase that creaked like an old person's bones and entered a dark passage lit by the feeble light from a Tiffany lamp that sat on the sill of a tiny window at the end of the hallway. It looked authentic and probably was. Inhaling the aroma of eucalyptus and sweat that filled the passage, he went straight to the last door. He knocked using his knuckles. A whispered voice from inside asked who was there.

"*Je suis Aloisius.*"

An old lady who barely came up to his chest opened the door and threw herself into his arms.

"*Mon cher petit Aloisius.* What brings you here to visit your old nana?"

"Oh, Nana, you never miss a thing. How are you so clever?" he said, laughing.

"*Parce que je suis très vieille.* That's the way life goes, *mon cher*, now I'm finally wise. I'm too old to go out and enjoy Mardi Gras," she complained as he smiled. "What have you brought me?" she asked, looking at the plain brown bag he was carrying, "Surely not a present?"

"It is, sort of, Nana, but not for you," he said, handing her the bag.

"*Mon cher enfant,* believe me when I say I hope I never need someone to give me that sort of present."

She peered inside the bag. "I see you've been to Antoine Meire's shop."

"*Oui.*"

"*Il est le meilleur,*" she said with approval as she smelled some dried, whitish roots that looked like the bones of a human hand in the dim light of the apartment.

"*J'aide une amie, une femme qui est perdue et doit trouver sa voie.*"

"A lost woman? *Comment perdue?*"

"Lost in her own abyss," he answered.

Nana arranged the more than thirty ingredients, carefully wrapped in little manila envelopes, small boxes like those used to store minerals, and tiny bottles full of pungent substances that were illegal in all fifty states, on the oak table that took up almost the entire room.

"*C'est bien,*" she said, "but you'll have to help me move the furniture so there's enough space, and you'll have to draw the pentagrams on the floor. Your poor nana is very clever, but that doesn't mean she doesn't have arthritis."

38

THE LAMP on the bedside table gave off an excessively bright
white light. Amaia spent twenty minutes going around the
house checking all the others for a lower-wattage bulb. She discovered two things: that Engrasi had replaced all the lightbulbs with
those horrible energy-saving ones with their fluorescent light and
that the lamps in her room were the only ones in the whole house
with a narrow screw fixture. James watched her from the bed without
saying anything; he knew the ritual by heart, and he knew that his
wife would not settle down until she found a way of feeling comfortable. She sat on the bed, visibly annoyed, glaring at the lamp as if it
were a repulsive insect. Eventually she took a purple pashmina from
the chair, partially covered the lampshade, and looked at James.

"That's still too bright," he complained.

"You're right," she admitted.

She picked up the lamp by its base and put it on the floor between
the wall and the bedside table, took one of the cardboard folders she
kept on the dressing table, and opened it like a folding screen a few
centimeters from the lamp, leaving it so that it was almost buried in
the corner. She turned to James, checking that the light level was now
much lower. She sighed and stretched out beside him, and he leaned
up on one elbow and started to stroke her forehead and hair.

"Tell me what you were doing in Huesca."

"Wasting time. I was almost sure that there would be some kind of match between some objects that appeared at the crime scenes. Those scientists agreed to run some tests for us that were otherwise going to take ages to come back to us from our laboratory. If we'd got the results I was hoping for, we would have had a much more concrete area to focus on. We could have questioned the vendors, who are all in towns with small populations, and the shop owners would remember who had bought . . . well, those things we need clues about. But we didn't discover anything, and this opens a whole world of possibilities: he bought them somewhere else, from another province, or, more likely, he made them himself or a member of his family did. It would have to be someone he is close to, someone he can ask to make them for him."

"I don't know. I can't see a serial killer taking an interest in artisanal methods . . ."

"I can see this one doing it. We think what he's really looking for is a return to tradition, and there's no denying that this is traditional. In any case, other killers have shown a predilection for making bombs, artisanal weapons, poisons . . . It makes them think that there's some sense to what they're doing."

"So what now?"

"I don't know, James. Freddy's been ruled out as a suspect, Carla's boyfriend's been ruled out as a suspect, Johana's stepfather had nothing to do with the other crimes, he's just an upstart. We didn't find anything when we questioned the girls' male relatives and friends, there are no registered pedophiles in the area, and the men with histories of sexual assault either have an alibi or are in prison. The only thing we can do is what no crime investigator likes doing."

"Wait," he said.

"Wait until that bastard acts again, wait for him to make a mistake, get nervous, or give us something more out of vanity, something that leads us directly to him."

James leaned over and kissed her, drew back to look into her eyes, and kissed her again. Amaia felt the impulse to reject him, but with his second kiss she felt her tension vanish. She lifted her hand to James's neck and slipped under his body, longing to feel his weight. She searched for the edge of his T-shirt and pulled it upward, revealing her lover's chest as he uncovered hers. She loved the way he tensed on top of her. Like a Greek athlete, with a perfect physique and a warmth that drove her crazy. She ran her hands urgently down his back to his behind, pausing on his taut buttocks and sliding a hand down to his thighs to enjoy his full strength while he busied himself kissing her neck and breasts. He liked his sex slow, smooth, certain, confident, and elegant, yet there were times when desire would overcome her so quickly, impetuous and intense, that she herself was surprised at the state of anxiety and desperation she reached in just a few seconds, clouding her reason and making her feel like an animal, capable of anything. She felt an urge to speak while they were making love, to tell him how much she wanted him, how much she loved him, and how happy sex with him made her. She would be so overwhelmed with passion that she couldn't put it into words. She knew what she needed to say, she could guess what should not be spoken, because when they loved one another in this warm and liquid way, when their mouths couldn't keep up, when their hands were not sufficient, when their words were hoarse and faltering, a whirlpool of feelings, passions, and instincts was unleashed inside her. It swept away her common sense and her capacity for reason to an extent that scared her but at the same time drew her in, like an abyss that hid all that should not be said, the most torturous desires, passionate jealousy, savage instincts, desperation, and the inhuman pain that she was fleetingly aware of before climaxing, that pain which was either the crown of God or the gates of hell. A path leading either to eternal life or toward the cruel discovery that nothing would come afterward, which her mind mercifully erased a moment after orgasm, when sleepiness wrapped her in a warm spider's web and submerged her in a deep dream in which she could hear Dupree's voice whispering.

She opened her eyes and was instantly calmed by the familiar outlines of the bedroom, bathed in the milky light given off by the half-hidden lamp in the corner. A hundred shades of gray to paint the nocturnal world to which she kept returning in her dream. She changed position and closed her eyes again, determined to sleep. Drowsiness immediately pulled her into a tranquil wakefulness in which she was half aware of herself, of her beloved James breathing at her side, of the rich aroma of his body, of the warmth of the flannel sheets, a warmth that drew her toward deep sleep.

And toward the presence. She felt her so close and so malignant that her heart thumped in her chest in a convulsion that was almost audible. She already knew she was there before opening her eyes, standing beside the bed. She had been observing Amaia with her twisted smile and her cold eyes, secretly amused at the prospect of terrifying her, like she used to do when Amaia was little and like she continued to do, since, after all, she lived in her daughter's fear. Amaia knew it, but she couldn't avoid the panic that weighed her down like a millstone, immobilizing her, transforming her into a trembling little girl who fought against herself not to open her eyes. *Don't open them. Don't open them.*

But she opened them, and she knew before doing so whose face would be leaning over her, drawing near like a feeding vampire, feeding not on blood but on breath. If she didn't open her eyes, the figure would get so close that she would breathe in Amaia's breath, she would open her mocking mouth and eat her up.

She opened her eyes, saw her, and yelled.

Her shouts mixed with James's, who was calling her from far away, and with the sound of bare feet running in the hallway.

Amaia leaped out of bed crazy with fear, a small part of her aware that her mother was no longer there. She stumbled into her trousers and sweater, picked up her pistol, and went downstairs, possessed by the urgent need to put an end to the fear once and for all. She didn't need to switch the light on because she knew exactly where to look. She felt around for the carved wooden box belonging to a game of tic-tac-toe that was exactly where it had always been. With agile fingers she rummaged through the thousand trinkets that had ended up inside it. Her fingertips brushed the cord and she pulled it out of the box with a jerk, spilling part of its contents, which fell onto the floor, clattering in the darkness.

"Amaia!" shouted James. She turned toward the stairs, where her aunt had just turned on the light. They were looking at her in terror, clearly wondering what on earth was going on. She didn't respond, but moved past them, made her way to the door, and went outside. She broke into a run, lifting the cord and the key she clutched in her fist to her face, and she realized that the nylon was still as smooth as when her father tied the key onto it for her on the day she turned nine.

The door to the workshop was barely lit. The old streetlight on the corner of the street gave off an orange, almost Christmassy, light that barely tinged the pavement. She fumbled at the lock with her index finger and inserted the key. The smell of flour and butter enveloped her, suddenly transporting her to a night from her childhood. She closed the door and reached up above her head in search of the light switch. It wasn't there, it wasn't there anymore.

It took her a few seconds to realize that she no longer needed to stretch to reach it. She turned on the light and started to tremble as soon as she could see. Her saliva became thick against her palate, like an enormous ball of bread crumbs, impossible to break up, difficult to swallow. She walked toward the storage jars, which were still all grouped together in the same corner. She looked at them, startled, as her breathing sped up at the fear of what was going to happen, what was coming next.

"What are you doing here?"

The question sounded perfectly clearly in her head.

Tears filled her eyes, blinding her for a moment. Her retinas were burning. She was gripped by an intense cold that made her tremble even more. She turned slowly and walked toward the kneading table. The terror made her shiver, but she stretched out her trembling fingers until she touched the clean surface of its metal bulk while her mother's voice thundered powerfully in her head. A steel rolling pin lay in the sink, and a drip from the tap splashed into the bottom of the basin with a rhythmic patter. The terror grew, blocking out everything.

"You don't love me," she whispered.

And she knew that she had to flee, because it was the night of her death. She turned toward the door and tried to reach it. She took a step, another, another, and it happened again, just like she knew it would happen. There was no point in fleeing because it was inevitable that she would die that night. But the little girl resisted, the little girl didn't want to die. And although she raised her hand as she turned to look at her mother in a vain attempt to protect herself from the mortal blow, she collapsed to the floor from the impact, terrified, feeling as if her heart was almost exploding from pure panic just a moment before stopping. She lay stretched out and broken. And although she felt the second blow, it didn't hurt anymore. There was nothing after that. The dense tunnel of fog that had formed around her dispersed, clearing her vision as if someone had washed her eyes.

Her mother was still there, leaning against the table, watching her. Amaia heard the short, rhythmic pants from her chest as she caught her breath. She heard her sigh deeply, almost in relief. She heard her turn on the tap, wash the rolling pin. She heard her come closer and kneel down beside her without taking her eyes off her. Amaia saw her leaning over her own face, studying her features—her dead eyes, her mouth frozen in a shout that would have been a prayer. Her mother's mouth was contracted in an expression of curiosity that didn't reach her frozen eyes, which remained unmoved. She came so close she almost brushed against her, as if, feeling remorse for her crime, she was about to kiss her. The mother's kiss that never arrived. She opened her mouth and licked the blood that was flowing slowly from the wound and running down Amaia's face. She smiled as she got up and didn't stop smiling as she picked the little girl up in her arms and buried her in the kneading trough.

"Amaia," the voice was calling.

Aunt Engrasi, Ros, and James were looking at her from the workshop door. He tried to move toward her, but her aunt stopped him, catching him by the sleeve.

"Amaia," she called her niece again, softly but firmly.

Kneeling on the floor, Amaia looked toward the old kneading

trough with an expression on her face that was almost a childish pout.

"Amaia Salazar," Engrasi said again.

Amaia jumped, as if the call had caught her by surprise. Her hand moved to her waist, and she pulled out her gun and aimed it toward the void.

"Amaia, look at me," ordered Engrasi.

Amaia's gaze remained blank, and she swallowed repeatedly, trembling as though she were out in the rain without any clothes on.

"Amaia."

"No," she murmured. Then she shouted, "No!"

"Amaia, look at me," ordered her aunt, as if talking to a child. Amaia looked at her, frowning. "What's happening, Amaia?"

"Don't let this happen, Aunt Engrasi." Her voice had dropped an octave.

"It's not happening, Amaia."

"Yes, it is."

"No, Amaia. This happened when you were a little girl, but you're a woman now."

"Don't let her eat me."

"Nobody can hurt you, Amaia."

"Don't let this happen."

"Look at me, Amaia. This will never happen again. You're a woman, you're a police officer, and you have a pistol. Nobody will hurt you."

The mention of the weapon made her look at her hands, and she seemed surprised to find the pistol there. She was aware of James and Ros's presence, that they were watching her from the entrance, pale and silent. She lowered the weapon very slowly.

James didn't let go of her hand on the way back home, nor when he sat down beside her to contemplate her in silence while Ros and her aunt made chamomile tea in the kitchen.

Amaia remained silent, listening to her aunt's distant whispering and assessing the tense expression on the face of her husband, who was smiling with the preoccupied air that parents have when they look at their injured children in the hospital. But it didn't matter. She felt secretly selfish and satisfied, because, along with the incredible fatigue assailing her, she felt renewed, like Lazarus rising from the dead.

Ros placed the cups on a low table near the sofa and concentrated on lighting the fire in the hearth. Her aunt came back into the living room, sat down opposite them, and uncovered the mugs, allowing the sickly smell of the chamomile to rise in a steaming cloud.

James stared at Engrasi. She nodded her head as if weighing the situation, and sighed.

"Well, I think the moment has now come for you to tell me what I ought to know."

"I don't know where to start," said Engrasi, pulling her dressing gown around her.

"Start by explaining what happened tonight and what I saw in the workshop."

"What you saw was a terrifying episode of post-traumatic stress."

"Post-traumatic stress? That's the paranoia suffered by some soldiers after returning from the front line, isn't it?"

"Precisely, but it's not only soldiers who suffer from it. It can occur in anyone who's suffered a one-time or continuous episode in which he genuinely felt he was about to die a violent death."

"And that's what happened to Amaia."

"Yes, it is."

"But why? Because of something that happened to her at work?"

"No. Fortunately, she's never felt that exposed to danger while at work."

James looked at Amaia, who was smiling slightly as she listened to the conversation with her gaze lowered. Engrasi recalled all the knowledge she had acquired during her years in the Psychology Department, which she had mentally reviewed hundreds of times, hoping that this day would never arrive.

"Post-traumatic stress is a sleeping assassin. Sometimes it stays in a latent state for months, or even years after the traumatic situation from which it originated. A real situation in which the individual was in real danger. The stress acts like a defense mechanism that identifies signs of danger with the aim of protecting the individual and preventing her from putting herself in danger again. For example, if a woman is raped in a car on a dark road, it's logical that in the future similar situations—nighttime, the open countryside, the inside of a dark vehicle—will cause her to feel uncomfortable, which she will identify as a sign of danger and try to protect herself."

"That makes sense," commented Ros.

"It does up to a point, but post-traumatic stress is like an allergic reaction, completely disproportionate to the threat. It's as if this woman were to pull out a can of pepper spray whenever she smells leather or pine air freshener or hears an owl hooting in the night."

"Pepper spray or a pistol," said James, looking at Amaia.

"This stress," Aunt Engrasi continued, "produces an extraordinary level of alertness in those who suffer from it, which manifests as light sleep, nightmares, irritability, and an irrational terror of being attacked again. This shows itself as an out-of-control defensive rage that causes her to become violent with the sole aim of defending herself from the attack she believes she is suffering, because she's reliving it—not the attack itself but all the pain and fear suffered at that moment, like the soldiers who've spent time on the front line."

"When we went into the workshop, it was as if she were acting out a stage performance . . ."

"She was reliving a moment of great danger. And she was doing so with the same intensity as if it were occurring at that instant," she said, looking at Amaia. "My poor, brave little girl. Suffering and feeling like she did that night."

"But . . ." James looked back at Amaia, who was holding a steaming cup of untouched tea in her other hand. "Do you mean to say that what happened in the workshop tonight was caused by an episode of post-traumatic stress, a defensive reaction to what Amaia believed to be warnings of mortal danger? Or rather, that Amaia thought she was going to be killed . . ."

Engrasi nodded, raising her trembling hands to her mouth.

"And what triggered this? Because it's never happened before," he said, looking tenderly at his wife.

"It can be anything, an episode can be triggered by anything, but I suppose that being here in Elizondo was a contributing factor . . . The workshop, those crimes involving young girls . . . And the truth is that it has happened to her before. It happened to her a long time ago, when she was nine years old."

James looked at Amaia, who seemed about to faint.

"You had episodes of post-traumatic stress when you were nine years old?" His voice was barely audible.

"I don't remember them," she replied. "In fact, I haven't remembered what happened that night for the past twenty-five years. I suppose that by repeating it enough times I came to think that it didn't really happen."

James took the untouched cup from Amaia's hand and put it on the table, took both her hands in his, and looked into her eyes.

Amaia smiled, but she had to lower her gaze in order to say, "When I was nine years old, my mother followed me to the workshop one night and hit me on the head with a steel rolling pin. She hit me again when I was lying unconscious on the floor, then she buried me in the kneading trough and tipped two fifty-kilo bags of flour on top of my body. She only told my father because she thought I was already dead. Because of this, I lived with my aunt for the rest of my childhood." Her voice had become impersonal and devoid of all affect, as if it were generated by a computer.

Ros was weeping silently and looking at her sister.

"For the love of God, Amaia! Why haven't you told me about this?" exclaimed James in horror.

"I don't know. I swear that I've barely thought about this in recent years. I had it buried somewhere in my subconscious. In addition to what really happened, there was always an official version, which I repeated so many times that I came to believe it. I thought I had forgotten. And, furthermore, it's so . . . embarrassing . . . I'm not like that, I didn't want you to think—"

"You have nothing to be embarrassed about. You were a little girl, and the person who was supposed to care for you harmed you. It's the cruelest thing I've heard in my life, and I'm so sorry, sweetheart, so sorry that something so horrible happened to you, but nobody can harm you anymore."

Amaia looked at him and smiled.

"You can't imagine how good I feel, I feel like a great weight's been lifted off me. The blockage," she said, suddenly thinking of Dupree's words. "I was probably already stressed because of that. And coming back here brought all those memories back too, and keeping them from you has made things even harder for me."

James moved away from her a little so he could look at her.

"And what's going to happen now?"

"What do you want to happen?"

"I understand that you feel good now, like a great weight's been taken off your shoulders, but what happened yesterday, Amaia, when you drew your weapon on your sister, and in the workshop tonight, is no joke."

"I know."

"You lost control, Amaia."

"Nothing happened."

"But it could have. How can we be sure you won't suffer another episode like that?"

Amaia didn't answer. She pulled free of James's hands and stood up.

James looked at Engrasi. "You're the expert, what do we need to do?"

"What we're doing now, talk about it. Retell what happened, get her to explain how she feels, to share it with those who love her. There's no other treatment."

"And why didn't you give her this treatment when she was nine?" he said without hiding his reproach.

Engrasi stood up and walked toward Amaia, who was leaning against the fireplace.

"I suppose that deep down I hoped that she would have forgotten it. I showered her with love. I tried to help her forget it, not to think about it. But how could a little girl stop thinking about the harm

39

VÍCTOR STILL shaved the traditional way, with a bar of La Toja soap, a shaving brush, and a razor. In an ideal world he would have used a cutthroat razor like his father and grandfather had, but he had tried it once and it wasn't for him. In any case, he achieved a smooth shave with the razor blade, and Flora loved the fragrance the soap left on his skin. He looked at himself in the mirror and smiled at the rather ridiculous figure looking back at him, his face covered in foam. Flora. If she liked him like that, that was how he would be. His life had changed the moment he had admitted to himself that he didn't want to give her up, that Flora, with her strong character and desire to control everything, was the woman who had his exact measure, and the things that he had come to hate about her, her exhaustive domination, her authoritarian nature, and how she dictated everything he did, were now things he knew how to value in her.

He had lost the best years of his life in a haze under what he now accepted was the malign influence of alcohol, which was the only way out then, the only escape route via which he could flee the instincts that rang warning bells against Flora's perpetual tyranny. He had been unable to realize that Flora was the only woman who could love him, the only woman he could love, and the only one he wanted to please. When he thought about it, he realized that he had begun to drink like that to take revenge on her, to both escape and appease Flora, because the alcohol allowed him to adapt to her iron discipline her own mother wanted to do her? How could she stop missing the kisses she would never give her, the bedtime stories she would never tell her?" Engrasi lowered her voice until it was a whisper, as if the terrible, harsh words she was speaking would hurt less that way. "I tried to play that role, I put her to bed each night, I cared for her and loved her more than anything else in the world. God knows, if I'd had a daughter of my own I wouldn't have loved her more. And I prayed, begging that she would forget about it, that she wouldn't have to drag that horror around with her for her whole childhood. We talked about it sometimes, we would always refer to it as "what happened," then she stopped mentioning it and I hoped with all my heart that she wouldn't remember it again." Two fat tears ran down her cheeks. "I was wrong," she said in a broken voice.

Amaia hugged Engrasi tightly and rested her face against her gray hair which, as usual, smelled of honeysuckle.

"It won't happen again, James," she asserted.

"You can't be entirely certain."

"I am."

"But I'm not, and I'm not going to let you go around with a weapon if you might suffer another one of those panic attacks."

Amaia let go of Engrasi and crossed the room in long strides.

"James, I'm a police inspector, I can't work without my weapon."

"Don't work, then," James declared.

"I can't abandon the case now. It would be a disaster for my career, nobody would ever have confidence in me again."

"That's secondary compared to your health."

"I'm not going to abandon it, James, I can't, and I wouldn't even if I could." Her tone of voice showed the decisiveness and strength that were normally typical of her. She wasn't Amaia, she was Inspector Salazar.

James got up and stood in front of her. "Okay, but unarmed."

He expected her to protest, but she stared at him and then looked at her sister, who was still crying.

"All right," she agreed, "unarmed."

by dulling his senses and making him into the husband she wanted him to be.

Until he lost control of the means, this has been the exact formula that could make life under Flora's domination tolerable. What an irony that the same thing that had kept their marriage going for years was the reason Flora gave for leaving him. During the first year following their separation, he had fought a fierce battle against the addiction, a battle that had caused him to hit rock bottom in the first few months, a state he could barely recall, since his memories were blurry and unsteady like an old black-and-white movie burned away by the nitrate on the film. Early one morning, after several days locked up in the house, having succumbed to drinking and self-pity, he woke up on the floor, half drowned in his own vomit, and felt a sense of emptiness and coldness like never before.

Only then, when he realized he was going to lose the one important thing in his life, did he start to make a change.

Flora had not wanted to get a divorce, although they had separated in every other sense, as distant as strangers and as far from one another, not that he wanted things to be that way. Flora made the decision and applied new rules to their relationship without asking his opinion. To be fair, he recognized that he had been unable to make any decision that didn't involve drinking at that stage, but never, even in the worst of his many alcohol-induced abysses, had he wanted to separate from her.

Now things seemed to be changing between them. His efforts, the number of dry days, his neat appearance, and the little things he did to please her seemed, finally, to be bearing fruit. He had been visiting Flora at the workshop every day for months, and every day he had asked her to come and eat a meal with him, to go for a walk, to go to Mass together, to accompany him on his business trips. And she had refused until that very week, when she had appeared to soften and accept his company again after he had taken her the bunch of roses to celebrate their anniversary.

He would have given anything, he would have done anything, he felt capable of meeting any condition necessary to return to her side once more. Giving up alcohol had been the most important decision of his life. At first he thought that each day he spent without drinking would consist of a horribly torturous reality hanging over him, but in recent months he had discovered that there was extraordinary strength hidden within the act of deciding to give it up. He encouraged himself with this each day, finding freedom and indomitable resolution that he had known only in his youth, in the self-control he exercised over himself when he had still been what he wanted to be. He went to the closet and chose the shirt she liked so much and, after inspecting it, decided that it was a bit rumpled from the way it had been hanging and needed to be ironed. He whistled to himself as he went down the stairs.

~

The clock on the Church of Santiago showed that it was almost eleven, but it seemed more like twilight than morning. It was one of those days when dawn got stuck at first light and the sun never really rose fully. These dismal mornings were part of her childhood memories, in which she remembered the many days when she dreamed of the warm, affectionate presence of the sun. One of her classmates had once given her a travel agency's huge full-color brochure, and she had spent months poring over its pages, stopping at the photos depicting sunny coasts and impossibly blue skies while wisps of fog from the river drifted up nearby streets. Amaia cursed that place where the sun sometimes failed to rise for several days, as if a criminal mastermind had come in the night and stolen it away to an Icelandic island, leaving them deprived of its joy, like the people at the Poles with their long sunless nights.

Night in the Baztán Valley was dark and sinister. The walls of the houses continued to mark the outer edges of safety just as they had done in yesteryear, while beyond them everything was uncertain. It was hardly surprising that barely one hundred years ago ninety percent of the population had believed in witches, the presence of evil roaming abroad at night, and the use of magic charms to keep them at bay. Life in the valley had been hard for her ancestors—men and women as brave as they were stubborn, determined to establish themselves in that damp, green land in the face of all logic, despite the fact that it had shown them its most hostile and inhospitable face, swooping down on them, rotting their crops, making their children ill, and decimating the few families who stood their ground.

Landslides, whooping cough and tuberculosis, flash floods and deluges, crops that rotted where they were planted, without even making it aboveground . . . But the Elizondarras had stood firm next to their church, fighting back in that bend of the River Baztán, which had given them everything and then taken everything away as it pleased, as if warning them that this was not a place for men, that this land in the middle of a valley belonged to the spirits of the mountains, the demons of the springs, to the *lamias* and the *basajaun*. However, nothing had managed to break the will of those men and women who had surely also looked at that gray sky, just as she did, dreaming of another clearer, friendlier one. That valley was known as the land of the wealthy hidalgos and the voyagers who left for the Indies but who always returned from overseas, bringing with them the great wealth that was sung about in "Maitetxu mía." They invested in remodeling the town, showing off to their neighbors the gold that they had earned, and filling it with luxurious palaces and mansions with huge balconies, monasteries dedicated to giving thanks for their luck, and bridges over rivers that had previously been impassable.

True to her word, Aunt Engrasi declined their invitation to join them on the walk, preferring to stay and cook and using the deplorable state of her knees as an excuse, but Ros and James insisted on going on the expedition in spite of Amaia's many protestations and attempts to convince them that it would rain before midday. They drove along the edge of the river and then upward until they came out in a huge meadow that stretched as far as the beech wood that grew at the edge of the river and the foot of the mountain. As they drove through the open meadows, she understood why people came from far away to visit Elizondo, and she sighed, overwhelmed by the outstanding beauty of that idyllic world hidden among low mountains interspersed with valleys and impossibly lovely meadows, punctuated only by woods of oak and chestnut trees and small rural hamlets. Its damp climate made for long autumns, so that the meadows were still green even in the middle of February, in spite of the fact it had snowed. Only the sound of the Baztán broke the silence of the countryside.

This was the most mysterious and magical forest ever. The huge oak, beech, and chestnut trees covered the slopes of the mountains and mixed with other species to adorn them with different shades, shapes, and contrasts.

The forest that offered such a multitude of sensations: the ancient interaction with nature, the wild sound of water among the beech trees and the firs, the freshness of the River Baztán, the occasional sound of the animals and the leaves that had fallen in autumn and still blanketed the floor like a silky carpet that the wind rearranged at will to form mounds like fairy dens and paths along which the *lamias* walked, the aroma of forest fruits and the smooth cloth of grass that covered the meadows, glowing like a magnificent emerald that a *jentil* giant had buried in the woods. They walked between the trees until the sound of the river showed them the way to the fabled place. Ros led the way and turned around from time to time to make sure her fellow walkers were not too tired. She needn't have feared for James, who didn't stop talking, enchanted with the beauty of the winter woods. They crossed an area thick with ferns before starting to move upward.

"It's not far now," announced Ros, pointing to a clearly visible crack in the rock. "It's just there."

The path was quite a bit narrower than they had expected. Angular rocks formed a natural and irregular staircase that they ascended as the path turned again and again, going back on itself like a snake as it went up the mountain. At each turn, the brambles and scrub made the path even narrower, making their progress more difficult. One more turn and they arrived at a flat platform covered in sparse grass and completely carpeted in yellow lichen.

Ros sat down on a rock and frowned.

"The cave is twenty-five meters farther up," she said, pointing toward a path almost completely hidden by gorse bushes, "but I'm afraid this is as far as I can go. I twisted my ankle on the way up."

James squatted down at her side.

"It's not serious," she said, smiling. "My boot saved me, but it would be best if we go back soon, before it starts swelling and I can't walk on it."

"Let's go, then," said Amaia.

"Don't even think of it. You can't go without seeing the rock after coming this far. Off you go."

"No, let's go. Your ankle will start swelling and you won't be able to walk, you said it yourself."

"Just as soon as you come back, Amaia. I'm not moving from this spot unless you go and see it."

"I'll stay with her and wait for you here," James encouraged her.

Amaia pushed her way among the gorse bushes, cursing their spines, which made a noise like nails scratching against fabric when they brushed her anorak. The path stopped abruptly in front of a cave with a low but very wide mouth that looked like a grim smile on the face of the mountain. There were two large rocks to the right of the entrance, which were also very strange. The first, standing on end, resembled a female figure with large breasts and pronounced thighs looking out over the valley; the second was magnificent in both size and shape, perfectly rectangular, like an altar for sacrifices, its huge surface cleaned by the rain and the wind. On its surface were a dozen small stones of different colors and types arranged like the pieces on an incomplete chessboard. A beautiful woman in her thirties was holding one of the stones in her hand and looking toward the valley, admiring the view. She smiled as she saw Amaia coming and gave a friendly greeting as she placed the stone next to the others.

"Hello."

Amaia suddenly felt like an intruder in a private place.

"Hello."

The woman smiled again, as if she were reading her mind and could see her discomfort.

"Get a stone," she said, pointing toward the path.

"What?"

"A stone," insisted the woman, pointing at the ones on the table. "Women ought to bring a stone with them."

"Ah, yes, my sister told me, but I thought they were supposed to bring one from their home."

"That's true, but if you've forgotten, you can take one from the path. When all is said and done, it's a stone from the path to your home."

Amaia leaned down and picked up a pebble from the path, went over to the table, and put it next to the others, surprised by how many there were.

"Wow, were all these stones brought by women who've come up here?"

"It looks like it," replied the woman.

"It's incredible."

"We're living through uncertain times in the valley, and when the new solutions fail, people fall back on the old ones."

Amaia was left openmouthed at hearing the woman repeat almost the same words her aunt had spoken a few nights earlier.

"Are you from around here?" she asked, studying the woman's appearance. She was wearing a moss green shawl over what looked like a silk dress in shades of green and brown, and her mane of golden hair, which was as long as Amaia's, was held back from her face by a golden diadem.

"Oh, not exactly, but I've been coming here for many years because I have a house here. I never stay long, though. I'm always moving from place to place."

"My name's Amaia," she said, holding out her hand.

"I'm Maya," said the woman, taking it in her smooth hand, covered in rings and bracelets that jingled like bells. "You're from around here, though, aren't you?"

"I live in Pamplona, I'm here for work," she answered evasively.

Maya looked at her, giving her a strange, almost seductive smile.

"I think you are from here."

"Is it that obvious?"

The woman looked at the valley again. "This is one of my favorite places, one of the places I most like to visit, but things haven't been going well here recently."

"Do you mean the murders?"

The woman continued without directly replying, and she was no longer smiling. "I often pass through this area and I've seen strange things."

Amaia's interest suddenly increased dramatically. "What sort of things?"

"Well, while I was here yesterday, I saw a man going into one of those small caves down on the riverbank and come out again a while later." She pointed toward the thick undergrowth. "He was carrying a bundle when he arrived, but he didn't have it when he came out."

"Did his behavior strike you as suspicious?"

"He seemed satisfied."

A curious adjective, thought Amaia.

"What did he look like?"

"I couldn't tell from up here."

"But did he look like a young man to you? Could you see his face?"

"He moved like a young man, but he was wearing a hood that completely covered his head. When he came out, he looked back, but I could only see one of his eyes."

Amaia looked at her perplexed. "You saw part of his face?"

Maya remained silent and smiled again. "Afterward, he went down the path and left in a car."

"You couldn't have seen the car from here."

"No, but I clearly heard the motor start and move away."

Amaia went over to the path.

"Can you get to the cave from here?"

"Oh, no, it's quite well hidden, to be honest. You have to go up from the road, first through the trees, up to there, see," she said, pointing, "and then you have to walk through the undergrowth, because the old path is hidden . . . The cave is about four hundred meters farther on, behind some rocks."

"You seem to know this area very well."

"Of course. As I said, I come here a lot."

"To leave offerings?"

"No," she said, smiling again.

The wind blew in strong gusts that caught the woman's hair, revealing some long earrings that looked like they were made of gold. Amaia thought it was an unusual choice of outfit for coming up onto the mountain, and even more so when she spotted the woman's feet poking from under the bottom of her silk dress, encased in Roman-style sandals. The woman seemed so absorbed in studying the pebbles on the rock they could have been precious stones, her expression remaining enigmatic.

Amaia suddenly felt uncomfortable, as if somehow aware that her time was up and she should no longer be there.

"Well, I'm going to go down . . . are you coming?"

"No," the woman replied without looking at Amaia. "I'll stay a bit longer."

Amaia turned toward the path and took a few steps before turning to say goodbye, but the woman was no longer there. She stopped, looking at the spot where the woman had been standing just a second earlier.

"Hello?" she called.

It was impossible for the woman to have gone in any direction. She couldn't have gone to the mouth of the cave or passed Amaia without her seeing her, even without the jingling of her bracelets.

"Maya?" she called again. She took a step toward the cave, determined to find her, but stopped short as the gusts of wind became stronger and a vague fear stirred within her. She turned back to the path and almost ran down to the platform where Ros and James were waiting for her.

"Wow, you're really pale . . . Have you seen a ghost?" joked Ros.

"Come with me, James," she demanded, ignoring her sister's teasing.

He got up, alarmed. "What's up?"

"There was a woman, but she disappeared."

She pushed back into the bushes on the path without explaining further or answering James's questions, scratching herself on the undergrowth and thinking that it was impossible that Maya could have come down here.

When they arrived, Amaia went over to the huge lumps of stone to check that the woman had not thrown herself over the edge. There was a sloping path at her feet, thickly overgrown with gorse and covered in sharp rocks. It was obvious that she had not fallen down there. She went to the entrance of the cave and bent down to look inside. It smelled strongly of earth and something that made her think of metal. There was no sign that anybody had been in there in years.

"There's nobody here, Amaia."

"Well, there was a woman. I spoke to her for a while and suddenly I turned around and she'd disappeared."

"There aren't any other paths," said James, looking around. "If she's gone down, she'll have had to go down this one."

The stones that had been on the rock table, including the one she had put there, had disappeared.

They went back to the path and down to where Ros was waiting.

"Amaia, Ros and I would have seen her if she had come down this way."

"What did she look like?" her sister wanted to know.

"Blond, pretty, about thirty, she was wearing a green wool scarf over a long dress, and she was wearing lots of gold jewelry."

"All you need to tell me now is that she was barefoot."

"Almost. She was wearing Roman sandals."

James looked at her in surprise. "But it's about forty-five degrees. How could anybody wear sandals."

"I know. Her whole appearance was strange, but elegant at the same time."

"Was she wearing green?" inquired Ros.

"Yes."

"And she was wearing gold jewelry. Did she tell you her name?"

"She said she was called Maya and that she came here often because she had a house nearby."

Ros covered her mouth with her hand and stared at her sister.

"What?" Amaia urged her.

"The cave in those cracks is one of the places where, according to legend, Mari used to live, and she would move around by flying through the air from Aia to Elizondo, from Elizondo to Amboto in the middle of a storm."

Amaia turned toward the path down with an expression of contempt.

"I've already heard enough nonsense . . . Or have I really been speaking with the goddess Mari on her doorstep?"

"Maya is the other name for Mari, smarty-pants."

A flash of lightning split the sky, which had continued to darken until it was the color of old tin. There was a crash of thunder nearby, and then it started to rain.

40

DENSE CURTAINS of rain doused the street from one end to the other, as if someone were randomly wielding a gigantic watering can in the hope of washing away evil, or memory. The surface of the river was choppy, as if thousands of small fish had all decided to come to the surface at once. And the stones of both the bridge and the façades of the houses were soaked, with water bouncing off them and forming small pools that emptied themselves back into the river, pouring down the artificial walls along its edge.

Flora's Mercedes was parked opposite their aunt's house.

"Your sister's already arrived," announced James, parking behind it.

"So has Víctor," added Ros, looking toward the archway at the entrance to the house where her brother-in-law was busy drying a gray-and-silver motorbike with a yellow chamois towel.

"I don't believe it," murmured Amaia. Ros looked at her in surprise but said nothing.

They got out of the car and ran through the rain to the porch where Víctor had parked his motorbike and exchanged hugs and kisses.

"What a surprise, Víctor. Our aunt didn't tell us you were coming," explained Amaia.

"That's because she didn't know. Your sister called me this morning to invite me and, as you'll have guessed, I was delighted to come."

"And we're delighted you've come, Víctor," said Ros, giving him a hug while she looked at Amaia, still confused by the comment she'd made in the car.

"It's beautiful," said James, admiring the motorbike. "I haven't seen one of these before."

"It's a Lube, an LBM, named using its creator's initials, with a two-stroke ninety-nine-cc engine and three speeds," explained Víctor, only too happy to talk about his motorbike. "I've just finished it. It took me a long time to restore it because some of the parts were missing and finding them has been a bit of an odyssey."

"Lube motorbikes are made in Biscay, aren't they?"

"Yes, the factory opened in Lutxana in Barakaldo in the forties and closed in sixty-seven. It's a shame because they were really lovely bikes."

"It is lovely," agreed Amaia. "It reminds me a bit of the German motorbikes from the Second World War."

"Well, I suppose they were all influenced by that design during that period, but it was in fact the other way around. The creator of the Lube already had prototypes designed years earlier, and he's known to have had contacts with German factories before the war . . ."

"Wow, Víctor, you're a real expert. You could give classes or write about this."

"That would be a possibility if anyone was actually interested."

"I'm sure there would be . . ."

"Shall we go in?" said Ros, unlocking the door.

"That's probably a good idea. Your sister will be getting impatient already. You know she thinks all this motorbike stuff is nonsense."

"That's her problem, Víctor. You shouldn't let Flora's opinion influence you so much," said Amaia.

"Yeah," he said, pulling a face, "as if it were that easy."

The rain, which had only started recently, kept thundering down outside, but this made the warmth of the house more welcoming. The aroma of the roast drifted from the kitchen and whetted everyone's appetites as soon as they came in. Flora emerged from the kitchen carrying a glass of amber liquid in her hand.

"Well, it's about time. We were beginning to think we'd have to start without you," she said by way of a greeting. Her aunt bustled out after her, drying her hands on a small maroon towel. She kissed them one at a time. Amaia noticed the expression on Flora's face as she took a couple of steps back, as if escaping from Engrasi's affectionate influence. Yes, she thought, heaven forbid you should kiss anyone by mistake. Ros sat down in the chair nearest the door, doing her utmost to avoid going near Flora.

"Did you have a good time? Did you get as far as the cave?" asked Engrasi.

"Yes, it was a really nice walk, although only Amaia made it to the cave. I stayed behind. I twisted my ankle, but it's nothing serious," said Ros, as her aunt bent over to look at it. "Amaia went all the way up; she made an offering and saw Mari."

Their aunt turned toward Amaia with a smile. "Tell me what happened."

Amaia caught sight of the scornful expression on Flora's face and sighed, feeling uncomfortable.

"Well, I went up as far as the entrance to the cave, and there was a woman," she began, looking at Ros, intentionally leaving the word "woman" to the end. "I chatted with her for a while. Nothing more."

"She was dressed in green and told Amaia that she had a house nearby, and when Amaia turned toward the path, she disappeared."

Her aunt looked at her, smiling openly. "There you go, then."

"Aunt Engrasi . . ." protested Amaia.

"Well, if you've finished with the folklore, perhaps we can think about eating before the roast is spoiled," said Flora, passing around glasses of wine, which she poured at the table and then handed to each of them. She left Ros to get her own and left Víctor out on purpose.

"Go into the kitchen. Víctor," Aunt Engrasi said, turning to him, "there's all kinds of things in the fridge, help yourself to whatever you'd like."

"I'm sorry not to offer you anything, Víctor," Flora excused herself, "but unlike everyone else, this isn't my home."

"Don't talk such nonsense, Flora. My home is my nieces' home. *All* my nieces," she emphasized, "yours too."

"Thank you, Aunt," she replied, "but I wasn't sure how welcome I am here."

Her aunt sighed before speaking.

"As long as I'm alive, you will all be welcome in my home, since, when all is said and done, this is my house and I'm the one who decides who is welcome and who is not. I don't think you've ever experienced any hostility on my part. Sometimes, Flora, rejection stems not from the hostess but the one who feels out of place."

Flora took a large gulp from her glass and didn't reply.

They sat down at the table, full of praise for their aunt's amazing cooking and the roast lamb with roast potatoes and peppers in sauce that she'd prepared. For most of the meal, it was James and Víctor who kept the conversation going, which, to Amaia's delight and Flora's evident disgust, continued to focus on her brother-in-law's motorbikes.

"Spending all your time restoring motorbikes seems almost like an artistic endeavor."

"Well," said Víctor, flattered, "I'm afraid that with all that muck and filth, it's more a case of mechanics than doing a delicate restoration job, especially at first when you've only just bought the bike. I bought the Lube that I rode here today from a smallholder over at Bermeo who'd kept it in a shed for over thirty years, and it was covered in shit from at least a hundred different animals."

"Víctor," Flora reproved him.

The others laughed, and James encouraged him to continue.

"But once you've got it home, I imagine you dismantle it and clean it. That part must be a real joy."

"Yes, that's true, but that's almost the easiest part. What really takes time is finding replacements for the parts that are missing or beyond repair and, most of all, restoring the parts that are no longer available, which I've sometimes had to make myself by hand."

"What normally takes the most work?" Amaia asked, to encourage her brother-in-law further.

Víctor seemed to think about it for a moment. Meanwhile, Flora was sighing with a boredom that didn't seem to be affecting anybody else at the table.

"There's no doubt about it: one of the things that takes most work is restoring the fuel tanks. It wasn't at all unusual for some gas to be left in them in those days, and with the passing of the years, the insides of the tanks oxidized because they used to use tinplate instead of stainless steel like they do now. As a consequence, the plate would disappear over time, and as the metal oxidized, it would flake off and settle in the fuel tank. That sort of tank doesn't exist anymore, so you have to use every trick in the book to clean them and repair the insides."

Flora stood up and started to clear the plates.

"Don't worry, Aunt," she said, putting a hand on Engrasi's shoulder, "I'm not at all interested in the conversation, to be honest, and I'll bring the dessert back in with me."

"Your sister's made us one of her amazing desserts," said Aunt Engrasi while Flora went to the kitchen, gesturing to Ros, who had got up, to sit down again.

Víctor had suddenly fallen silent, looking into his empty glass as if it held the answer to all the questions in the world. Flora came back in carrying a tray wrapped in tissue paper. She handed out plates and cutlery and unveiled the dessert with great ceremony. The sweet, greasy aroma of a dozen sticky little cakes wafted among the diners. There was a wave of admiring exclamations among those present while Amaia covered her mouth with her hand and looked in amazement at her sister, who smiled back at her in satisfaction.

"*Txantxigorris*, I love these," exclaimed James, taking one.

Indignation and disbelief bubbled up inside Amaia while she fought the desire to grab her sister by the hair and make her eat every single cake. She looked down, keeping silent, trying to contain the rage she felt inside. As Flora chattered on obliviously, presumptuously, she could almost feel her cruel, calculating gaze observing her, entertained in a way that sometimes made Amaia afraid. The same gaze with which her mother used to look at her.

"Aren't you eating, Amaia?" Flora asked sweetly.

"No, I'm not hungry."

"Not even for these?" she joked. "Don't disappoint me, eat a little bit." She put one of the *txantxigorris* on Amaia's plate.

Amaia looked at it, unable to prevent herself from thinking of the girls' bodies giving off that greasy smell.

"You'll have to excuse me, Flora. Certain things have been making my stomach turn recently," she said, staring at her fixedly.

"Who knows, maybe you're pregnant," Flora pushed her still farther. "Aunt Engrasi said you were trying for a baby."

"For the love of God, Flora," complained her aunt. "I'm sorry, Amaia. It was just a passing comment." She put her hand over Amaia's.

"It doesn't matter, Aunt Engrasi," she said.

"Don't be so insensitive, Flora. Amaia's had to deal with a lot of unpleasant things over the last few days," Víctor intervened. "Her job's really tough; I'm not surprised she can barely eat."

Amaia noticed how Flora was looking at him. Surprised, perhaps, that for once he had dared to disagree with her in public.

"I read that you've arrested Johana's father," said Víctor smoothly. "I hope these crimes will stop at last."

"That would be great," Amaia agreed. "But unfortunately, although we have evidence that he killed his stepdaughter, we're also certain that he didn't carry out the other murders."

"Well, I'm happy you've caught that bastard in any case. I know his wife and I knew the girl by sight, and you'd have to be a monster to harm a girl that sweet. That guy is a bastard, and I hope he gets what's coming to him in prison," said Víctor, displaying a passion rarely seen in him.

"A bastard, you say?" Flora jumped in. "And what about the girls? Because the truth is they go looking for it."

"What are you trying to say?" Ros interrupted Flora indignantly, addressing her directly for the first time in the whole meal.

"What am I trying to say? I'm saying that those girls are just common sluts. I'm fed up with how they dress, how they talk, and how they behave. They're like whores, it's embarrassing to see how they carry on with boys. I swear that sometimes, when I walk through the square and see them almost sitting on their laps like tarts, it doesn't surprise me that they end up like this."

"Flora, what you're saying is barbarous. Are you really justifying someone killing these young girls?" her aunt snapped.

"I'm not justifying it. But if they were the sort of well-behaved girls who are at home by ten, then none of this would have happened, and if they go around provoking men like this I'm not saying that they deserve it, but they do go looking for it."

"I don't know how you can talk like that, Flora," said Amaia incredulously.

"It's what I think; they're not saints just because they're dead. I'm entitled to my opinion, aren't I?"

"That man who killed his daughter is a bastard," declared Víctor, "and there is no justification for what he did."

They all looked at him, surprised by the unusual forcefulness with which he spoke, but Flora was truly astonished.

Amaia took advantage of the opportunity.

"Flora, Johana was murdered and raped by her father, her stepfather. She was a good girl who got good grades, dressed suitably, and was at home by ten. She was harmed by someone who should have been protecting her. Perhaps that only makes it more incomprehensible, more horrible. Because it's terrifying that someone who ought to care for you can harm you."

"Ha!" exclaimed Flora, forcing a laugh. "Here we go! Why not?! Let's dig up traumatic events that wouldn't be out of place in a trashy melodrama. The person who was supposed to care for me hurt me," she said in a childish voice. "What? Poor little Amaia, the traumatized child. Well, let me tell you something, little sister, you didn't protect her when you should have either."

"Who are you talking about?" asked James, taking his wife's hands.

"I'm talking about our mother."

Ros shook her head, aware of the tension building around her.

"Yes, our weak and elderly mother, a very ill woman who once lost her temper. Just once, and that was enough for the whole family to condemn her," said Flora, full of disdain.

Amaia looked at her carefully before answering.

"That's not true, Flora. *Ama's* life continued as normal; it was mine that changed."

"Because you had to come and live here with Aunt Engrasi? That suited you. It was what you'd always wanted, to go your own way and not have to work in the workshop. It turned out well for you, and what *Ama* did was just a mistake, a one off, an accident . . ."

Amaia pulled her hands free from James's hold and brought them up to her face, covering it completely. She breathed through her fingers and said very quietly, "It wasn't an accident, Flora. She tried to kill me."

"You've always exaggerated. She told me. She slapped you and you fell against the kneading table."

"She hit me with the steel rolling pin," said Amaia, without uncovering her face. The pain of her words was evident in her voice, which trembled as if it was about to disappear completely. "She hit me on the head until she broke the fingers of the hand I was using to defend myself, and she kept on hitting me when I was lying on the floor."

"Liar!" shouted Flora, standing up. "You're a liar."

"Sit down, Flora," ordered Engrasi in a firm voice.

Flora sat down without taking her eyes off Amaia, whose face was still hidden behind her hands.

"Now listen to me," said their aunt. "Your sister isn't lying. The doctor who attended Amaia that night was Dr. Manuel Martínez, the same one who was treating your mother for her illness. He recommended that Amaia should not return home. It's true that she only hit Amaia on that one occasion, but she almost killed her. Amaia spent the following months shut up here without going out until her wounds healed or were hidden by her hair."

"I don't believe it, she only slapped her. Amaia was small and she fell, her injuries are from when she fell. She gave her a slap like any mother would give her daughter, and it was more common in those days. But you . . ." She looked at Amaia as she pursed her lips in disdain. "You stayed bitter forever, and you didn't care for her, either, when you had the chance. You were like that father: you took advantage of the situation to be abusive."

"What are you trying to say?" shouted Amaia, uncovering her tearstained face.

"I'm saying that you could have helped her when that thing happened in the hospital."

Amaia's voice became so low it was almost inaudible as she made an effort to contain the fury that, once again, was boiling up inside her. "No, I couldn't help her, nobody could, least of all me."

"You could have gone to see her," Flora reproached her.

"She wants to kill me, Flora," shouted Amaia.

James intervened, standing up and embracing Amaia from behind.

"Flora, it would be best if you dropped this. Amaia is finding this subject very difficult, and I don't know why you keep going on about it. I know what happened, and I can assure you that your mother was lucky not to end up in prison or in a psychiatric institution. It would definitely have been the best thing for her, and it would certainly have been the best thing for Amaia, a little girl who had to grow up with the weight of an attempted murder. She had to hide it by lying about it and she had to leave her own home, as if she were the one responsible for the horror she had had to go through. What happened to your mother is sad. I'm sorry that she couldn't go home when she was ill, but you're wrong to blame Amaia for the fact that she died in the hospital."

Flora looked at him, stunned.

"That she died? That's what she told you had happened?" she said, turning to Amaia in a rage. "You dared to tell him that our mother is dead?"

James looked at Amaia, visibly confused.

"Well, I guessed that was the case, the truth is that she didn't tell me she was dead, I assumed it. It was only yesterday that I heard what happened at the hospital, and when you said that she got worse, I inferred that . . ."

Calmer now, Amaia resumed her explanation.

"After my last visit, my mother fell into a catatonic state, in which she remained for several days. But one morning, while a nurse was leaning over her to take her temperature, she sat up, grabbed her by the hair, and bit her on the neck so hard that she pulled off some skin, which she chewed and swallowed. When the other nurses arrived, the nurse was already on the floor and my mother was on top of her, hitting her again and again while the blood poured out of her neck and my mother's mouth. The nurse suffered serious injuries. They took her down to the operating room and they gave her several blood transfusions, and her life was saved because she happened to be in a hospital. She was lucky, although she'll have a scar on her neck for the rest of her life."

Flora looked at her, fixing her with her eyes full of scorn, while her mouth pursed in such a tight, harsh line it could have been chipped onto her face with an axe.

"We were lucky," Amaia continued. "Our mother entered a psychiatric institution by order of the judge, and the hospital was found civilly responsible for not anticipating such danger in a patient who had already been diagnosed."

She looked Flora in the eyes. "I couldn't have done anything, and there was nothing we could have done at that stage. It was the judge who made the decision."

"And you agreed," spat Flora.

"Flora," said Amaia, gathering her patience, "it's taken me a lot of time and pain to be able to say this out loud, but *Ama* wants to kill me."

"Oh, you're crazy! And not just that, you're evil."

"*Ama* wants to kill me," she repeated, as if doing so could free her of that evil.

James put a hand on her shoulder. "Darling, you shouldn't talk like that. This all happened a long time ago, but you're safe now."

"She hates me," murmured Amaia, as if she had not heard him.

"It was just an accident," Flora repeated stubbornly.

"No, Flora, it wasn't an accident. She tried to kill me. She only stopped because she thought she had succeeded, and when she thought I was dead she buried me in the kneading trough."

Flora stood up, banging the table with her fist and making the glasses ring.

"Curse you, Amaia. Curse you for the rest of your life."

"I don't think the rest of my life will be any different from my past," answered Amaia in a tired voice.

Flora picked up her bag, which was hanging on the back of the chair, and left, slamming the door behind her. Víctor murmured his apologies and went out behind her, visibly concerned. The others remained silent, not daring to say anything to break the tension of the storm that seemed to have engulfed them.

In the end it was James again who tried to bring things back to normal. He embraced his wife.

"I ought to be very angry with you for not having told me everything sooner. You know that I love you, Amaia, there's nothing that could change that, which is why I find it hard to understand why you didn't confide in me. I know that everything has been very painful for all of you, and especially for you, Amaia, but you have to understand that I've learned more about your family in the last few days than I had in the last five years."

Folding her napkin carefully, Engrasi said, "James, there are times when the pain is so great and buried so deep that one hopes and believes that it will stay like that forever, hidden and silenced. We're unwilling to face the fact that pain that hasn't been wept for and dealt with at the time comes back into our life time and again. Pain such as this arrives on the beach of our reality like the debris of a shipwreck, reminding us that there is an entire sunken ship beneath the waves that will always keep coming back, bit by bit. Don't reproach your wife for what she hasn't told you. I don't think even she has thought about it this clearly one single time since the night it happened."

Amaia looked up, but all she said was, "I'm very tired."

"We need to put an end to this, Amaia," James begged, "and now is the time. I know that it's very painful, but, perhaps because I see it from the outside, I think you ought to look at it from a different point of view. What happened is horrible, but in the end you have to accept that your mother is just a poor, unbalanced woman. But I don't believe she hates you. Very often the mentally ill turn on those they love the most. It's true that she hit you, like she hit that nurse, as the result of an attack of insanity that unbalanced her, but there was nothing personal in it."

"No, James. The nurse she attacked had long blond hair, was about my age, and had a similar complexion. When the other nurses found her, my mother was laughing and shouting my name as she hit her. She attacked her because she mistook her for me."

41

T HE TELEPHONE was whining with its annoying buzz.

"Good evening, Inspector."

"Ah, hello, Dr. Takchenko," she answered, recognizing the scientist's voice. "I didn't expect you to call so soon . . . Have you looked at the footage?"

"Yes, we've looked at it," the woman answered evasively.

"And?"

"Inspector, we're at the Hotel Baztán. We've just arrived from Huesca, and I think you ought to come over here as soon as you can."

"You're here?" She was surprised.

"Yes, and I need to speak to you in person."

"Is it about the footage?"

"Yes, but not just that. We're in room 202." She hung up.

The hotel parking area was unusually quiet for a Sunday evening, although there were several cars parked at the far end by the entrance to the restaurant. Only half the lights in the café where they had met last time were on. The chairs were upside down on the tables and a couple of women were cleaning the floor. The teenage girl at the reception desk had been replaced by a boy of about eighteen with a face covered in acne. Amaia wondered where they found their receptionists. Like his predecessor, he was absorbed in a noisy online game. She headed to the stairs without stopping, went up to the second floor, and found herself in front of room 202 as soon as she entered the corridor. She knocked and Dr. Takchenko let her in immediately, as if she had been waiting behind the door. The room was pleasant and well lit. On the bed were a laptop and two folders with brown cardboard covers.

"I was surprised to receive your call. I wasn't expecting to see you here," said Amaia by way of a greeting.

Dr. González greeted her as he unwound some cables, placed a computer on the small desk, and switched it on.

He turned to Amaia. "This is the recording made last Friday in observation zone seven. It corresponds with the place where we spoke on the day we arrived in Elizondo and where you said you'd seen a bear. The images are a bit out of focus since we always position the cameras in high places so they can cover more ground and focus them on the natural paths through the wood. These are the routes that animals take out of instinct, which, as a rule, are not the same as those taken by humans."

He started the recording. Amaia could see a portion of the majestic beech wood. For a few seconds the image appeared motionless, but suddenly a shadow burst into view, occupying the bottom part of the screen. Amaia recognized her blue jacket.

"I think that's you," commented Dr. Takchenko.

"Yes."

The figure moved from one part of the screen to another and then disappeared.

"All right, now there are ten minutes when nothing happens. Raúl has skipped over them so you can see the bit that interests us."

Amaia looked toward the screen again and when she saw it she felt her heart miss a beat. She had not dreamed it, it had not been a hallucination brought on by stress. There it was on the screen, and there was no room for doubt. The anthropomorphic figure was more than eight feet tall, and its powerful musculature was visible under the dark mane of hair that hung from its head, covering a strong, defined back. The lower part of its body was so hairy that it looked like it was wearing animal-skin trousers. It was busy picking bits of lichen from a tree, burrowing with long, capable fingers. It stopped to do that for more than a minute, then it turned slowly and lifted its majestic head. Amaia was amazed. Its features reminded her of a big cat, perhaps a lion. The lines of its face were rounded and well-defined, and the absence of a muzzle gave it an intelligent and peaceful air. The hair that covered the face was dark and grew longer beneath the chin, forming a rough beard that hung halfway down its stomach in two locks.

The creature looked up very slowly and gazed at the camera lens for a moment. Its eyes, with their various shades of amber, were frozen on the screen when Raúl stopped the recording.

"Tell me, is this your bear?"

Amaia looked at it, without knowing what reaction to expect. She answered evasively.

"Yes, I suppose so, I'm not sure."

"Well, let me tell you, this is not a bear."

"Are you completely sure?"

"We are completely sure," said Dr. Takchenko, looking at her husband. "There is no breed of bear with those features."

"It might be a different kind of animal," suggested Amaia.

"Yes, a mythological one," he replied. "I know what I think it is, and so does Dr. Takchenko. Now, you tell me, what do you think it is?"

Amaia hesitated, weighing the response that was on the tip of her tongue. They seemed two genuine people, but what effect might something like this have on them?

"I don't think it's a bear," she answered ambiguously.

"I see you're still reluctant to take a risk. I'll say it for you. It's a *basajaun*."

Amaia sighed again as the tension spread to her legs, causing a slight tremor, which she hoped the scientists hadn't noticed.

"Okay," she conceded, "regardless of what this creature we've seen might be, the question is, what's going to happen now?"

Dr. Takchenko went over to her husband and looked at Amaia.

"Inspector, Rául and I have dedicated our lives to science. We have an important role and a research grant, and the principal objective of our work has been and will continue to be the protection of the natural world, in particular large plantigrades. The thing that appears in this recording is not a bear. I don't think it's an animal of any type; I think, as does my husband, that it's a *basajaun.* And I think the fact that the cameras recorded it isn't the result of chance, or the creature, as you call it, being careless, but a fulfillment of the creature's desire to show itself to you and to us in order to be accepted. You needn't worry, neither Raúl nor I have any intention of making this discovery public. It would definitely destroy our careers. Its authenticity would be questioned, because I'm sure that we wouldn't manage to record any further images of this creature even if we put a camera in every tree in the forest. And, what's worse, the mountains would be assailed by a plague of obsessives searching for the *basajaun.*"

"We've erased the original and we only have this copy," said Dr. González, opening the CD drive and handing Amaia the DVD.

She took it carefully. "Thank you," she said, "thank you very much."

She remained seated on the end of the bed with the DVD throwing rainbows in her hands, unsure what to do.

"There's another question," said Dr. Takchenko, interrupting her thoughts and jerking her out of her reverie.

Amaia stood up and took one of the brown-covered folders that the scientist was holding out to her. She opened the cover and saw that there was a copy of the flour analysis inside."

"Do you remember I told you I'd do a further analysis of the samples you gave me?"

Amaia nodded.

"Well, I did a mass spectrometry test on each of the samples. We didn't use that test to begin with because we wanted to compare the samples to establish matches, for which we use the DNA amplifier. But since we didn't get any matches, I decided on this test, which provides a complete rundown of the minerals present, establishing even the slightest trace presence and listing each and every one of the minerals that comprise each sample. Are you following me?" Amaia nodded expectantly. "As I've explained, such a detailed analysis wouldn't have helped us much at the start when we were trying to establish a simple match."

Amaia was growing impatient, but she waited in silence.

"I analyzed all the samples again, and in one of them there's a partial match with a lot of elements."

"What does that mean?"

"It means that the elements in that particular sample were present in one of the flours, but together with others that weren't in the cake."

"And what might be the explanation for that?"

"A very simple one: the sample you brought me had a mixture of two types of flour, the one used in the cake and another one."

"And why might that be?"

"It's possible that the container holding the flour used to make the cake had been used to hold a different type of flour previously and they hadn't bothered to empty it entirely of what was left, so that although the overall flour sample doesn't match and the quantities in which the other flour appears are very dilute and almost unnoticeable, they're still there. The chromatograph misses nothing."

Amaia started to leaf through the pages with the graphs, the colored columns mingling to form random patterns.

"Which one is it?" she asked urgently.

Dr. Takchenko came to her side, took the report, and looked carefully through the pages.

"It's that one, S11."

Amaia looked at her in disbelief. She slumped down onto the bed, looking at the perfectly drawn graph. Sample number 11, S for Salazar.

It was raining again when she left the hotel. She considered running to the car, but her low spirits and the speed at which her brain was processing thoughts left her steps slow as she walked through the parking lot, letting the rain soak her hair and clothes, an act of pure baptism that she hoped would wash away the confusion and bewilderment that were bubbling inside her. When she reached her car, a figure standing out in the rain caught her attention. The leather jacket and the light glinting off the Lube were unmistakable.

"Víctor? What are you doing here?" she asked.

Her brother-in-law looked at her. He was distraught with pain. In spite of the rain, Amaia could see the tears pouring down his cheeks.

"Víctor," she repeated, "what . . . ?"

"Why's she doing this to me, Amaia? Why is your sister doing this to me?"

She looked toward the interior of the restaurant and saw her sister. Flora was laughing at something Fermín Montes was telling her. He leaned in toward her and kissed her on the lips. Flora smiled.

"Why?" repeated Víctor, completely dejected.

"Because she's a bloody fool," said Amaia, her eyes still fixed on the window. "And a total bitch."

Víctor started to moan, as if his sister-in-law's words had opened a bottomless abyss in front of him.

"We spent yesterday evening together, and this morning she called me to invite me to dinner with you all. I thought things were better between us, and now she does this. I do everything for her. Everything. So that she's happy with me. Why, Amaia? What does she want?"

"To do harm, Víctor, to do harm because she's a bad person. Like *Ama*. A manipulative witch with no heart."

His weeping grew louder, and he doubled over, as if he were about to collapse to the ground. Amaia felt immense sadness at the sight of him like that. Víctor had not been a good husband. Or a bad one. Just a drunkard left to rot under the weight of her sister's tyranny. She took a step toward him and hugged him, inhaling the aroma of his aftershave mixed with the smell of his damp leather jacket.

They remained like that for a few minutes, hugging in the rain, and Amaia listened to Víctor's hoarse weeping as she watched her sister smiling with Fermín and tried to marshal her thoughts. Her mind was churning at full throttle as it worked through all the information the scientists from Huesca had brought, which was going around and around in her head and starting to give her a severe migraine.

"Let's get out of here, Víctor," she suggested, sure that he would put up some form of resistance. But he agreed meekly. "Do you want a ride?" she asked, gesturing toward the car.

"No, thank you. I can't leave the motorbike here, but I'm okay," he murmured, wiping his eyes. "Don't worry."

Amaia looked at him, concerned. With the state he was in, he seemed capable of doing all kinds of stupid things.

"How about we go somewhere and chat for a bit, then?"

"Thanks, Amaia, but I think I'll go home, have a hot shower, and go to bed. You ought to do the same," he added, trying to smile. "I don't want to be responsible for you catching a cold."

He put on his helmet and gloves and leaned down to kiss his sister-in-law, squeezing her hand gently. He started the motorbike and drove off, heading toward Elizondo.

Amaia stayed where she was a few seconds more, thinking about Víctor and watching her sister dining with Montes beneath the warm golden light of the restaurant. She took off her soaked anorak and tossed it into the car, got into the driver's seat, and made a call.

"Ros . . . Rosaura."

"Amaia, what's up?"

"Listen, Ros, this is important."

"I'm listening."

"Do you still keep up the tradition of taking flour home from the workshop for personal use?"

"Of course, just like we always have."

"Right, think carefully. When was the last time you took flour from the workshop home?"

"Well, it must have been at least a month ago, before I stopped working there."

"Okay, I need you to do me a favor. I'm going to send Jonan Etxaide to Aunt Engrasi's. He'll take you to your house and take a sample of the flour in your kitchen. You can wait outside if you don't want to go in. You can trust Jonan."

"Okay," she answered, very seriously.

"One other thing. Who else can take flour from the workshop?"

"Who? Well, I imagine any of the workers could, but . . . What's going on, Amaia? Are you investigating a flour theft?" she asked, trying to make a joke.

"I can't talk to you about it, Ros. Just do as I've asked, please."

She hung up and dialed again.

The woman who answered delayed Amaia for a couple of minutes with her incessant chatter before Amaia could bring up the reason for her call.

"Josune, I'm going to send one of my colleagues to you with some samples for analysis and comparison. It's really important, I wouldn't ask you if it weren't, Josune. I need it done as soon as possible . . . And you need to be discreet, so don't discuss it with anybody or send the results to the police station. Just give them to the person who brings you the samples for me."

"Okay, Amaia, don't worry."

"How long will it take you?"

"It depends how soon I have the samples."

"They'll be with you in two hours."

"Amaia, it's Sunday today, and I won't be back in the lab until eight o'clock on Monday morning . . . But I'll make an exception and go in at six to process your samples . . . You'll have them tomorrow, but not until the end of the day."

"Heaven be praised. I owe you one," said Amaia before hanging up and dialing again.

"Jonan, take the S11 flour sample and the one from the *txantx-igorri* and go to my aunt's house. Take my sister to her house, get a sample of the flour she has there, and then go to San Sebastián. Josune Urkiza from the Ertzaintza is expecting you at the Institute of Forensic Medicine. You'll need to stay with her until she's got the results. When they're ready, I want you to call me, nobody else, and don't say anything about this at the station. If Iriarte or Zabalza calls you, say you're in San Sebastián to deal with a family issue and that I said you could go."

"Okay, chief," he stammered. "Chief, is there something I should know?"

Jonan was the most trustworthy police officer she knew, definitely one of the best people she had ever met, and her dealings with him had really made her appreciate him.

"You ought to know everything, Deputy Inspector Etxaide, and I'll tell you as soon as you get back. For now, I'll only say that I suspect that someone is taking information out of the station."

"Ah, I understand."

"I trust you, Jonan." She could almost see his smile before she hung up.

Iriarte finished putting his children to bed at about nine. It was the time of day he liked most, when he no longer had to stick to a timetable, and he could relax and look at his two boys, surprised almost daily by how fast they were growing, hug them, respond again to their pleas that he shouldn't turn out the light yet, and tell them again the same story they knew by heart. When he'd finally managed to say good night, he went to the bedroom where his wife was in bed watching the news. Going to bed early had become a habit since they had had the children, and although they usually stayed awake chatting or watching TV, they were normally in bed by nine. He undressed and lay down next to his wife.

"Are they asleep?" she asked.

"I think so," he said, closing his eyes in one of his expressions that she knew well and that had nothing to do with sleeping.

"Are you worried?" she asked, running a finger across his forehead.

"Yes." There was no point in lying to her, she knew him well.

"Tell me about it."

"I don't know what it is, that's what's worrying me. There's something that's not right and I don't know what it is."

"Does it have to do with that pretty inspector?" she asked sarcastically.

"Well, I guess she might have something to do with it, but I'm not sure. She's got a slightly different way of doing things, but I don't think that's so bad."

"Do you think she's good at her job?"

"Yes, I think she's very good, but . . . I don't know how to explain it, she's got a kind of dark side, a part that I can't quite see, and I suppose that's what worries me."

"Everyone has a hidden side, and you haven't known her long. It's a bit early to pass judgment, don't you think?"

"It's not that, it's a sort of feeling, like an instinct. You know I don't normally make judgments based on first impressions, but perceptions are very important in my work. I think we ignore the signs of things that worry us about other people a lot of the time just because we don't have a sound basis for them. But sometimes the feeling we've decided to ignore comes back after a while, and this time there are reasons to back it up. Then we regret having failed to pay attention to what some call perception, instinct, or first impressions which, deep down, have a firm scientific basis, since they're based on body language, facial expressions, and little white lies."

"So you think she's a liar, then?"

"I think she's hiding something."

"And yet you say you have confidence in her judgment."

"That's about right."

"Perhaps what you're noticing is emotional imbalance, someone who doesn't love or isn't loved. People who have problems at home can give you that feeling."

"I don't think that's the case. Her husband is a famous American sculptor, and he's come to Elizondo with her for the duration of the investigation. I've heard her speaking to him on the phone, and there's no tension there. Furthermore, she's staying at her aunt's house with one of her sisters. It seems like everything's normal on the family front."

"Do they have children?"

"No."

"Well, there you go," she said, lying back on the pillow and switching off her bedside lamp. "I think that no woman of child-bearing age can be complete if she doesn't have children, and I assure you that that can be a huge, dark, and secret burden. I love you, but I'd feel incomplete if I didn't have children," she said, closing her eyes. "Even though they leave me exhausted."

He looked at her with a smile, thinking about her simple and direct way of looking at the world and how often she was right.

42

AMAIA FELT much better after a long hot shower, although no more relaxed. Her muscles were as tense as an athlete's before a competition. She still didn't understand how instinct, that complicated machinery in an investigator's head, worked, but in a very subtle way she could almost hear the cogs of the case turning, interlocking, their slow movement dragging together hundreds of little pieces that meshed in with hundreds more in turn, so that everything made sense, as if their advance were clearing away the fog that had been clouding her vision. She heard Agent Dupree's voice in her head again: the blockage.

That man's instinct had hit the bull's-eye as usual, even with an ocean between them.

Whatever was causing the blockage had not diminished in the slightest. She was certain deep down in her soul that what came to her in the night had only taken a step back to hide itself in the shadows, like an old vampire intimidated by the sunlight flooding in through the crack she had opened up the night before. She had been afraid of the crack, torn between a desire to free herself and fierce panic at the sight of the light. It was a small gap in the prison of fear, silence, and heavy secrecy that she had built to contain the monster, but she was sure that something more dazzling would break through it in the coming months, unless she allowed it to close and the vampire to lean over her bed once more. But, for today, she could imagine a world where the ghosts of the past let her sleep in peace, where she could be as honest with James as she ought to be, and where the capricious spirits of nature would align the stars to reveal her destiny.

But there was something else Dupree had said that was going around and around in her head like one of those jingles you can't stop singing, even if you don't remember all the words. Where did the killer come from? It was an intelligent question she had already asked herself and to which she didn't have the answer, but that didn't mean it lost its importance. A murderer like that didn't just appear out of nowhere overnight, but their search for delinquents who fit the profile had not shone any light on the case. Reset. Switch off and then on again. Sometimes the answer is not the solution to the enigma. Everything depends on knowing the right question and how to ask it. The question. The formula. What is it I need to know? I need to know what the question is. She looked at her reflection in the mirror and was struck by a certainty. She hurriedly tossed her bathrobe aside and dressed again in the same clothes she'd been wearing before. When she arrived at the police station, only Zabalza was still there.

"Hello, Inspector, I was just leaving," he said, as if apologizing for still being there.

"Well, I need to ask you to stay a little longer."

He nodded. "Of course, whatever you want."

"I need you to access all the records concerning murders of young women in the valley in the last twenty-five years."

His eyes bulged. "That could take us hours, and I'm not sure we'll even have all the information. It will be in the general records, but the Policía Foral weren't responsible for murder investigations back then."

"You're right," she said, without disguising her annoyance. "How far back can we go?"

"Ten years or so, but Inspector Iriarte and I already did that, and we didn't find anything."

"Okay, you can go."

"Are you sure?" he asked.

"Yes, I just thought of something . . . Don't worry, we'll talk to-morrow."

She took out her phone and looked up a number.

"Padua, you remember that favor you owe me?"

Fifteen minutes later she was at the Guardia Civil barracks.

"Twenty-five years is a long time, and some of those cases aren't even in the system. If you want to access the paper copies, you'll have to go to Pamplona. The homicide team was part of the Policía Nacional at that time, and we were more concerned with policing roads, the mountains, and the borders and with counterterrorism duties . . . But I'll do what I can. What exactly do you want?"

"Crimes committed against young women anywhere in the valley. We've gone back ten years, but I need almost everything from before then."

He nodded as he worked out what she was asking for and started to look up records on the computer.

"From eighty-seven onward . . . If you could be more specific . . . What sort of murders are you looking for?"

"Ones where the victims were found by the river, in the forest, strangled, naked . . ."

"Aha!" he said, as if he had remembered something. "There was a case, my father used to talk about it, a girl who was raped and strangled in Elizondo. It was a long time ago, I was only a little boy. She was called Kraus, she was Russian or something similar . . . Let me look it up." He began typing again. He put in a few dates until he found it. "Here it is: Klas, not Kraus. Teresa Klas. She was found raped and strangled in the fields of the estate where she worked as a companion to the old mistress. They arrested the woman's younger son, but he was released without charge. They questioned various workers, but it came to nothing in the end."

"Who carried out the investigation?"

"The Policía Nacional."

"Does it say who exactly?"

"No, but I remember that when I started at the Academy," he said as he searched, "the head of homicide was a captain in the Policía Nacional in Irun. I don't remember his name, but I can call my father, he used to be a *guardia* too, and he's bound to know," he went on, dialing the phone number. He spoke for a few minutes and hung up. "Alfonso Álvarez de Toledo. Does that ring any bells?"

"Isn't he a writer or something?"

"Yes, he retired to focus on his writing. He still lives in Irun, my father gave me his phone number."

In contrast with Elizondo, Irun was unusually busy given that it was one o'clock in the morning. The bars on Calle Luis Mariano were overflowing with drinkers who spilled over and out of the nightspots, accompanied by the sound of music. In a stroke of luck, Amaia managed to park in a space vacated by two noisy couples who had just got into their car.

Alfonso Álvarez de Toledo had a real beach tan, which was surprising at that time of year, and seemed unconcerned by the thousands of tiny lines that crisscrossed his face, due as much to his excessive taste for the sun as to his age.

"Inspector Salazar, it's a pleasure. I've heard a lot of very good things about you."

She was taken aback, especially bearing in mind the fact that the former head of homicide had retired early after achieving considerable fame with a series of detective novels that had been a great success some years earlier. He led her down a wide hallway into a living room, where a woman in her sixties was watching television.

"We can talk here. And don't worry about my wife, she's been a policeman's wife her entire life, and I've always discussed my cases with her . . . I can assure you that the police lost a great detective in that woman."

"I don't doubt it," said Amaia, smiling at the woman, who shook her hand and then turned away to concentrate on a talk show that looked like it would continue for some time.

"I hear you want to talk about the Teresa Klas case."

"I'm definitely interested in any cases in which the victims were young women. In Teresa's case, it seems that she was raped, and the profile that I'm looking for doesn't include rapes. In fact, there's no sex of any type involved."

"Oh, don't let yourself be fooled, sweetheart. The fact that the report says that the girl was raped doesn't necessarily mean that she was raped."

"Why not? Raped is . . ."

"Look, I was once head of the homicide team, and things were very different then . . . To give you an idea, there were no women on the force and the detectives had little more than basic training. We didn't have the benefits of the scientific advances you do now. If the semen was visible, there was semen; if it wasn't, there wasn't any . . . It wasn't much use for anything because we didn't carry out DNA analyses back then. It was the eighties, and you have to realize that the attitude of the police then tended to be sanctimonious and proper, not to say prudish. If they arrived at a crime scene and there was a girl with her underwear around her ankles, they took it as given that there had been sexual violence. Consensual sex was almost never considered unless the case involved a prostitute."

"So was Teresa raped or not?"

"There was something very sexual about the way the corpse was laid out: she was completely naked with her eyes open and some cord around her neck, which had come from that very farm. You can imagine the scene."

Amaia could imagine it.

"Did she have her hands arranged in any special way?"

"Not that I remember. Her clothes were scattered around nearby, as if tossed carelessly next to the contents of her handbag, a few coins and candies . . . There were even some on the body."

Amaia felt something like a powerful nausea contract her stomach.

"There were candies on her?"

"Yes, a few, they were thrown all over the place. Her parents told us she had a real sweet tooth."

"Do you remember how they were arranged on her body?"

Alfonso inhaled and held his breath for a couple of seconds before exhaling, giving the impression that it took a great effort to remember.

"Most of them were scattered around her and between her legs, but there was one on her lower stomach, more or less on her pubic mound. Does that mean something to you? We assumed that they'd fallen out of her bag when her attacker grabbed it looking for money. It was the start of the month and perhaps he thought she was carrying her salary with her. Everything was paid in cash back then."

She was struck by a sudden certainty. "What month was it?"

"It was around this time of year, February. I remember it because my daughter Sofía was born a few days later."

"Can you tell me anything about this crime, anything that caught your attention?"

"I can tell you something that caught my attention years later in other crimes, which happened to involve young women and made me remember Teresa, although it was just a detail, something slightly strange. Do you remember, Matilde?" he said, addressing his wife. "The dead girls whose hair had been brushed?"

She nodded without taking her eyes off the screen.

"The body of a German camper was found 'raped' and strangled near a campsite in Bera six months or so later. In spite of the similarities, it was a different type of crime. He tried to rape the girl, there were signs she had fought back, and the animal cut off her hand and took it with him. She was also strangled with a cord from her own tent, and he cut her clothes to see her naked after she was dead. He was a pervert, a caretaker on the campsite, a disgusting fifty-something-year-old who already had a record of spying on female campers while they showered. The strange thing is that in spite of all the signs of violence evident on the body, her hair was parted down the center and brushed as if she were posing for a photo. The guy denied everything—killing her, brushing her hair—but there were witnesses who had seen them arguing several days earlier when the girl caught him sniffing around her tent while she was changing. They put him away for twenty years.

"A year later we had another case of a dead girl whose hair had been brushed. A girl became separated from her hiking group on the mountain. At first they thought she'd got lost, and they organized search parties; we found her almost ten days later. She was under a tree, as if she were napping, and her body presented with an unusual kind of dehydration that a forensics expert could explain better than I can. The fact is that the body seemed mummified; her clothes weren't there, and her bun had been undone and her hair arranged perfectly to either side of the body, as if somebody had combed it."

Amaia could barely control the tremor in her legs.

"Was there anything on the body?"

"No, nothing, nothing at all, although she did have her hands palm upward. There was something very strange about it, but there was nothing on the body. He'd taken everything off her: clothes, underwear, shoes . . . Although now that I think about it, her shoes did turn up. In fact, it was thanks to that that she was found: they were at the edge of the path that led into the forest."

"Arranged side by side, like when someone goes to bed or for a swim in the river," Amaia recited.

"Yes," he admitted, looking at her in surprise. "How do you know that?"

"Did they catch the attacker?"

"No. There were no clues, there were no suspects . . . Her friends and family were questioned, just routine. The same as with Teresa, the same as with the others. Young women, some of them almost still children, only just waking up to life. And someone cut their wings off . . ."

"Do you think there's any chance I could have access to those reports?" she asked, almost begging.

"I suppose you know what I do for a living nowadays . . . When I left the police, I made myself a copy of all the cases I'd worked on."

Amaia drove to Elizondo with the information Álvarez de Toledo had just given her bubbling in her head. The reports contained common factors, suspicious dates, the same type of victim, a modus operandi that had been perfected, that had been fine-tuned . . . She had found his origins, his trail of death that had extended across the whole valley to Bera and possibly beyond. Now she was sure that the killer lived in Elizondo, and she knew that Teresa had been the first victim, an opportunistic crime that had led him to distance himself as far from his home as possible in the following ones. Teresa, who was prettier than she was clever, a *freska* as her *amatxi* Juanita would have called her, sassy and sure of her charms, a girl who enjoyed flaunting her assets. The killer had been unable to resist the temptation of her daily presence, the provocation of seeing her every day and thinking of her as dirty and evil, playing at being a woman when she should have been doing little more than playing with dolls. Her existence seemed unbearable, and he killed her like the others, without raping her but exposing her little girl's body that had crossed the boundary of what he considered decent. Afterward, he had focused on perfecting his technique, the cut clothing, the hands in an offertory pose, the hair neatly brushed to either side of the head . . . And suddenly there was nothing, years of silence, years when he might have been serving his time for a minor crime or had moved away to another area, but he had come back, mature and cold, in February, perhaps as a macabre homage to Teresa, with a more refined technique, replacing the candy, the detail that symbolized childhood, with a sweet handmade cake, which, in Amaia's opinion, represented his true signature.

43

AMAIA HAD slept beside James after slipping silently into the bed like a stowaway at almost four o'clock in the morning, knowing that she ought to sleep but afraid she would not manage to due to the uneasiness ruling her mind. However, she had gone out like a light, straight away and it had had the distancing and reparative effect that her body and, most of all, her mind needed. She woke before dawn, feeling calm and focused for the first time in a long time. She went down to the living room and paused to light the fire in the hearth, following the ritual she used to carry out every morning when she was a little girl, which she had not performed for so many years. She sat down opposite the fire, which was catching tentatively, and she managed to do it. Reset. That was good advice, analytical Agent Dupree, she thought. And it gave immediate results.

Fermín Montes woke up in the room at the Hotel Baztán, where he had spent the night with Flora. There was a note on the other pillow that said, "You're wonderful. I'll call you later. Flora." He picked it up and kissed it noisily. He smiled, stretched until he touched the padded headboard, and got into the shower singing a little tune, unable to stop thinking for a moment about what a miracle meeting that woman had been. Life meant something to him for the first time in more than a year. He had been like the walking dead in the last few months, and now he was more aware of it than ever. He had been like a zombie trying to pull off the illusion of appearing alive, an illusion that couldn't seem more false to him now. Flora was the miracle that had brought him back to life, resuscitating a heart that had ceased to beat. Like a human defibrillator, she had got it working again, unexpectedly and with a big shock. Flora had arrived imposing herself, steamrollering him, and had installed herself in his life without asking permission, making him recover his senses and his direction. He had been surprised by her strength as soon as he met her, the indomitable character of a woman who had made herself what she was, who had built up her business and watched over her family. He smiled again as he thought of her, of her warm body between the sheets.

His fear of that moment had been almost as strong as his desire for it, because the shot of poison his wife had delivered when she left him had been releasing itself slowly during the last few months, acting like a chemical castration that had prevented him from having sex with any women since she left. His face clouded as he recalled her parting words . . . The pathetic nature of his pleas almost made him blush. He had begged her on his knees, wanting to make ten years of marriage worth something. He had groveled, he had wept as he pleaded with her not to go and, in a final act of desperation, he had asked her for explanations, he had asked her for a reason, as if a rationale or a motive could justify the way she had wrecked his life. But the absolute bitch had replied with a parting shot, a final salvo with its sights set exactly on the waterline.

"Why? Do you really want to know? Because he fucks me like a stud, and when he's finished he fucks me all over again."

Then she went out, slamming the door behind her, and he didn't see her again except in court.

He knew that it was satisfaction, spite, scorn, and weariness mixed in equal measure, provoked to a certain degree by himself in the death throes of love, but even so, her words had festered inside him and echoed in his head like unwelcome tinnitus. Until he met Flora. The smile returned to his lips while he shaved, looking at himself in the mirror at the hotel where she had preferred to stay so as not to cause talk in the town. A discreet, confident woman, so beautiful it made him catch his breath. She had surrendered herself passionately in his arms, and he had responded.

"Like a macho man," he said to himself as he looked in the mirror again and thought that he hadn't felt this good for a long time, and that perhaps, when this case was closed, he might apply for a position in Elizondo.

Amaia wrapped up warm and went out into the street. It wasn't raining that morning, but the damp fog covered the streets with a sheen of ancient sadness that made the people walk hunched over as if they were carrying a heavy burden and seek refuge in the warm cafés. She had rung San Sebastián first thing to find how the analyses were going.

"I've already got them under way," Josune had replied. "Listen, you could've told me that Deputy Inspector Etxaide was that good-looking so I could shave my legs."

It was a running joke from their university days, although she was aware that Josune's interest was more than feigned. She was about to tell her that she was wasting her time but decided not to. Her smile lasted for some time after she hung up.

She dawdled for as long as she could before going to the police station. She walked up to the Church of Santiago first, but she found the building closed. Instead she walked through the gardens and the children's playground, deserted on a Monday morning. Then she admired the plumpness of the gang of cats who seemed to live under the church and could barely squeeze themselves through the external vents. She walked around the church following the line of its wall and remembering the not-so-old belief described by Barandiarán that said that if a woman walked three times around the perimeter of the church, she would become a witch. She went back to the entrance and looked at the slender trees that were competing with the clock tower to see which could be tallest. She considered going to the town hall, but the strong gusts of wind that were starting to buffet the low clouds brought discouraging drops of freezing water. She changed direction and set off up Calle Santiago as far as the patisseries, where various women were eating breakfast in little groups of friends. She went into Malkorra and felt the curious looks as she went over to the bar. She ordered a cup of milky coffee, the best she had tasted in ages, and bought a couple of bars of the café's famous *urrakin egiña*, Elizondo's traditional local handmade chocolate with whole hazelnuts.

Amaia tried to keep out of the rain, walking briskly beneath the balconies. She bought the *Diario de Navarra* and the *Diario de Noticias* and went to her car, which she had parked on the premises of the old police station about halfway along the street. She waited for a woman driving a small car to pass and thought she recognized her from the photos that Iriarte had on his desk. She drove through the streets at delivery rush hour, and finally, when it was almost midday, she arrived at the police station.

The same photos were on her desk, along with a report that she had already received on her smartphone that told her what Dr. Takchenko had already said two days ago: that there were no matches among the flour samples. DNA amplification. And something new. The oily mark on the goatskin found on the cord with which the girls had been strangled was an oxide with traces of hydrocarbons and wine vinegar. All very enlightening.

Iriarte and Zabalza had gone out. One of the duty officers explained that they were reinterviewing the last people to see the girls alive. The Hospital of Navarra phoned to tell her that Freddy was making good progress and his condition was now less serious.

Padua called just before one o'clock. "Inspector, some of the results from Johana's case have arrived, and I think this might interest you: either an electric knife or a jigsaw was used to cut her arm off, although they think the former is more likely due to the direction of the cut. We're assuming it must have been battery powered since there's no electricity there. And the apparent erosion present higher up on the wound is a bite. You remember they took a mold during the autopsy . . ."

"Yes."

"Well, it turns out that they are undoubtedly human tooth marks."

"Fuck!" she exclaimed.

"I know what you're about to say, but we've already compared it with her father's dental imprint and it doesn't match."

"Fuck!" said Amaia again.

"Yes, that's what I thought," he replied. "Johana's funeral and burial will take place tomorrow. Her mother asked me to let you know."

"Thanks," she said as if she were thinking about something else. "Lieutenant, an informant told me that they noticed suspicious activity on the right bank of the river in the Arri Zahar area. It looks like there are some caves the other side of the beech wood, about four hundred or so meters up the slope. I'm sure it's nothing, but . . ."

"I'll let the Nature Protection Service know."

"Yes, do, thanks."

"Thank you, Inspector." He stammered a bit and lowered his voice so that nobody could hear what he was about to say next. "Thank you for everything. I owe you, you've proved to me how good an investigator you are. And a good person too. If you ever need anything . . ."

"You don't owe me anything, we're in the same boat, Lieutenant. But I'll keep it in mind."

She hung up and stayed very still, as if any movement might upset the flow of her thoughts, then she looked up an Internet forum and sent a question to the administrators. She made herself a cup of milky coffee and drank it in small sips while looking out the window. She called James around one.

"Do you fancy having lunch with your little woman?"

"Always. Are you coming home?"

"I was thinking of eating out."

"Okay. I'm sure you've thought of where as well."

"You know me too well! I'll see you at two at Kortarixar, it's one of Aunt Engrasi's favorites. It's very near the house, next to where the road from Irurita comes into town, and I've already made a reservation. Order the wine if you get there before me."

She left the police station but saw that there was still three-quarters of an hour before they were due to eat. She went up the

Camino de los Alduides and drove to the cemetery. There was another car parked at the entrance, but she couldn't see anyone inside. She walked unhurriedly among the graves, getting her shoes wet in the overlong grass that grew between the tombs, until she found what she was looking for. It was marked with a small iron cross. She was saddened to see that one of the arms had fallen off. The plaque in the center read FAMILIA ALDUBE SALAZAR. She had been seven when her grandmother Juanita died, and she didn't remember her face, although she did remember the smell of her house, sweet and slightly spicy, like nutmeg. The mothball smell of her closet, the smell of her freshly ironed clothes. She remembered her white hair, tied back in a bun secured with hairpins, silver pins decorated with flowers embellished with tiny pearls, which had been the only jewelry she wore apart from the slim wedding ring on her finger that Amaia had never seen her take off. Amaia remembered the way she used to swing her legs rhythmically when she sat on her lap, like a little horse trotting, and the songs her grandmother sang in Basque in her sweet voice, so sad they sometimes made Amaia cry.

"*Amatxi*," she murmured. And a smile spread across her face.

She went to the top of the graveyard and mentally drew the lines, starting from the cross that established the subterranean pathways of that underworld Jonan had been talking about. She heard a hoarse murmur, but although she looked around she didn't see anybody. The rain drumming on the fabric of her umbrella hid the sound completely, but when she turned around she thought she heard it again. She closed the umbrella and listened carefully. Although the sound was muffled by the rain splashing on the tombs, it was perfectly audible this time. She opened her umbrella and walked in the direction from which it was coming.

Then she saw the umbrella. It was red with maroon and orange flowers around the edge. Its color was incongruous in that place, where even the indestructible plastic and silk flowers were washed out by the rain. But, even more incongruous, it was a man who was holding it. He was resting it on his shoulder at an angle, almost entirely covering his upper body. He was motionless, and although the position of the umbrella projected almost all of the sound of his voice in the opposite direction, she could hear his ceaseless weeping while he murmured something she couldn't catch.

She went back to the cross and turned toward the upper path, from where she would have a better view of the Elizasu family tomb. The wreaths and bunches of flowers from the funeral were piled on the marble, forming a kind of pyre. The flowers had become waterlogged and the bouquets wrapped in cellophane were white and misted by the drops of condensation from the flowers rotting inside them. As she drew near, she recognized the black-and-white sneakers belonging to Ainhoa's brother, who was sobbing like a little child, unable to control himself, his eyes fixed on his sister's tomb, and repeating the same words over and over again: "I'm sorry, I'm sorry, I'm sorry."

Amaia took a few steps back, deciding to leave without his seeing her, but the boy seemed to sense her presence and started to turn around. She just had time to cover herself with the umbrella. She pretended to be praying in front of the tomb before her until she no longer felt the boy's penetrating gaze. She turned back the way she had come, making a detour to the gate and keeping her face covered to avoid his recognizing her.

~

James and her aunt had already ordered a bottle of Remelluri red wine and were chatting animatedly when she arrived at the restaurant. She had always liked the atmosphere of Kortarixar, the dark beams that held up the ceiling and the fire that was always lit, combined with a familiar aroma a bit like roast corn, which made her feel hungry as soon as she walked through the door. She was happy to join them in ordering fried cod and T-bone steak, but she refused the wine and ordered a glass of water.

"Are you really not going to try this wine?" James was surprised.

"I expect I'll have a hectic afternoon and I don't want that drowsy feeling I get if I drink wine."

"Does that mean you're making progress?"

"I'm still not sure, but I think that I'll get a few answers at least." Sometimes the answers are not the solution to the enigma. Step by step, she thought.

They ate hungrily, chatted about the improvements in Freddy's condition, which they were all pleased about, and enjoyed James's anecdotes about his first steps in the art world. Amaia's telephone began to ring as they were bringing the coffee. She got up and went outside before answering.

"Jonan, what have you got to tell me?"

"The flour from Ros's house and the flour used to make the *tx-antxigorri* are a complete match, and the S11 flour and the flour from the little cake are a thirty-five percent match."

"Thank Josune for me, and find a fax machine and wait for me to call you."

She hung up and went back inside to say goodbye, in spite of James's protests and the untouched coffee, waiting until she was back outside before dialing Inspector Iriarte.

"Good afternoon," he greeted her. "I was just about to call you."

"Any news?"

"There might be. One of Ainhoa's friends remembered that she walked past her on the opposite side of the street on her way to meet her sister, who was waiting for her farther down the road, while Ainhoa was waiting for the bus. She says a car stopped at the bus stop, and it looked like the driver was talking to Ainhoa from inside the car, but then it drove on without Ainhoa getting in. She says she hadn't remembered it because she didn't think it was important, she's not even sure whether the driver was a man or a woman, but she says that the girl didn't get into the car either way."

"It might be someone who stopped to ask her something, or to offer her a ride."

"It could also be the killer. Perhaps he offered her a ride and she refused because she was still hoping the bus would arrive, but as the minutes passed and she saw that it wasn't coming, she started to get nervous and he didn't have to do anything other than wait patiently until she was impatient enough to agree to get into the car. The second time he offered, it didn't seem like such a bad option, her salvation, even . . .."

"Does she remember anything about the car?"

"She said it was light colored, beige, gray, or white, with two doors, like a small delivery van, and she thinks that it had some writing on the side. I showed her photos of the eight most common van models and she couldn't tell the difference. We can look for owners of vans fitting that description in the valley, but I should warn you that there are heaps of them: almost all the shops, supermarkets, and estates have at least one, and they're normally white by default. It's a work vehicle, so most of them are registered as belonging to men between twenty-five and forty-five."

She thought for a moment.

"We'll go through them anyway; we don't have much else to go on. We'll check first whether any relative or friend of the victims had a similar one, or if anyone remembers somebody who has one, and we'll start with Ainhoa Elizasu's family. Her brother was in the cemetery this morning, asking for forgiveness in front of his sister's tomb."

"Perhaps he feels guilty for not telling their parents sooner. They blame him. I was at their house after the funeral and he was a pitiful sight. I wouldn't be surprised if they have to bury another child if they keep putting all this pressure on him."

"Sometimes this sort of act hides more than is visible at first glance. Perhaps they're a pair of savages, or perhaps they suspect something and this rejection is their way of channeling their suspicions. Are you at the station?"

"I'm just heading down there now."

"I saw your wife this morning, I recognized her from your photos . . ."

"Oh, did you?"

"Do you think you could persuade her to lend us her car this afternoon?"

"You want to borrow my wife's car?"

"Yes, I'll explain later."

"Well, I don't think it'll be a problem if I leave her mine."

"Good. Bring it with you, but don't park it at the police station."

"All right," he agreed.

Amaia went up to the meeting room and read the statements made by Anne's and Carla's friends and the information about the families' vehicles while she waited for Iriarte to arrive.

"I see you've started without me," said Iriarte.

"I'm afraid we'll have to stop soon. I've got something else planned for this afternoon."

He looked at her in surprise but said nothing and sat down and got to work. Amaia picked up the phone and called Jonan.

"Have you found a fax machine?"

"I've got one here now."

"Good, send the results to me at the police station in Elizondo."

"But . . ."

"Just do as I say and come back as soon as you can."

Five minutes later, Deputy Inspector Zabalza appeared at the door.

"This has just arrived by fax from the Forensic Anatomy Department at San Sebastián."

Amaia stayed where she was and let Iriarte be the first to read it. When he had finished, he looked at her very seriously.

"Did you request this analysis?"

"Yes. The scientists who did the analyses in Huesca carried out a second analysis of the samples and found what appeared to be a partial match. They suggested that there might have been a change of flour somewhere, which would explain why it appeared mixed in, in very small quantities. Last night, Deputy Inspector Etxaide took a sample of the flour that was used at the Salazar workshop until a month ago, and I sent it to San Sebastián and called in a favor from a colleague in the Ertzaintza. And these are the results. The twenty employees of Mantecadas Salazar have access to the flour, and it's customary that they can help themselves to as much as they need for use at home. They may also have shared it with relatives and friends. It's something we now need to look into."

Zabalza left the room and returned to his office. Iriarte was unusually silent as he read and reread the report on the analysis. Amaia closed the door.

"Have you realized the implications this has for the case, Inspector? It's the most reliable clue we've had so far."

She nodded firmly.

"And it's connected to your family."

"Yes, I know. The commissioner put you in charge of the case alongside me in case something like this happened, which is why I called you," she said, going over to the window and looking out. "Now I need you to come here and look at this."

He went to stand beside her. She looked at her watch.

"It's barely a quarter of an hour since the fax arrived, and he's here already." She pointed to a car that had just parked below the window. Inspector Montes climbed out and looked up toward where they stood before making for the entrance. They stepped back instinctively.

"He can't see us, they're mirrored windows," said Iriarte.

Amaia went over to the door in time to see Fermín Montes go into Zabalza's office and come out again a few minutes later carrying a rolled-up envelope.

They watched from the window as he looked around carefully, got into his car, and left the parking area.

"It's obvious that relations between Inspector Montes and whoever's in charge, you, in this case, leave a lot to be desired. He shouldn't take information out of the station, and neither should Zabalza let him. But he is part of the team working on the investigation, so it's not strange that he should want to keep up to date."

"And don't you think he should attend the meetings, which are held for exactly that purpose?" asked Amaia, fed up with the macho solidarity that men always tried to use to justify behavior that would be criticized in a woman.

"I thought he was ill, that's what Zabalza told me."

"Yes, and now you can see with your own eyes just how serious the illness ailing Inspector Montes is," she said, visibly angry. "Did you manage to get your wife to lend us her car?"

"It's parked behind the building," he replied, offended. "Just as you requested," he added, as if to make clear that he was not the enemy.

She felt a bit mean for being so hard on him, the one person who had given her his full support right from the start. Softening her expression, she picked up her bag from the back of the chair.

"Let's go."

Iriarte's wife's car was an old maroon four-door Micra with child seats in the back. Iriarte handed her the keys, and she took a few seconds to adjust the seat and the mirrors. By the time they left the parking area there was no sign of Montes's car. But that didn't matter. She knew exactly where he was going. She drove slowly, to give him time to arrive, and when Inspector Iriarte started to get impatient, she left Elizondo in the direction of Pamplona. After five kilometers she pulled up at the Hotel Baztán. Iriarte was about to ask what was happening when he recognized Montes's car parked by the entrance to the restaurant. Amaia parked opposite and remained silent until she saw Flora's Mercedes arrive and Flora look around several times before going inside.

"Now I understand why you needed this car," said Iriarte.

Amaia signaled to him without saying a word, and they both got out of the car. It was now completely dark, and although there were not as many cars about as there had been the previous day due to the early hour, they were able to get close enough to see the dining room quite well through the window. Montes was sitting closest to the window, and they couldn't see his face. Flora sat down opposite him and kissed him on the lips. He gave her the rolled-up envelope, which she opened.

The change in the expression on her face was obvious even from a distance. She tried to smile, but she managed only a kind of grimace. She said something as she stood up. Montes got up too, but she put a hand on his chest and made him sit down. She leaned over to kiss him again and quickly left the restaurant.

Flora came down the three steps leading to the exit with the envelope in one hand and her car keys in the other. She went over to her Mercedes and unlocked it.

Amaia approached her, appearing from behind the car.

"Do you know that acquiring evidence relating to an investigation is a crime?"

Her sister stopped short, putting a hand to her chest and looking upset.

"What a fright you gave me!"

"Aren't you going to answer me, Flora?"

"What? This?" she said, holding up the envelope. "I just found it on the floor, I haven't even looked inside, I don't know what it is. I was going to hand it in to the local police station. You say this is evidence? Inspector Montes must have dropped it. I'm sure he'll tell you the same."

"Flora, you've opened it and read it, your fingerprints are on every page, and I've just watched Montes giving it to you."

Flora smiled, playing down the importance of the situation, and opened the car door.

"Where are you going, Flora?" asked Amaia, pushing the door shut. "You already know there's a match. We need to talk and you'll have to come with me."

"Just what I needed to hear," Flora screamed. "Are you so desperate that you're going to arrest your whole family? Freddy, Ros, and now me . . . Are you going to lock me up like *Ama*?"

Some people going into the restaurant turned to look at them. Amaia felt her rage toward Montes growing. Had that gullible shit given her sister an account of every step of the investigation?

"I'm not arresting you, but you know from Montes that the flour came from the workshop."

"Any of the employees could have taken some home."

"You're right, which is why I need your help. That and an explanation of why you didn't tell me you'd changed flour."

"It happened months ago. I didn't think it was important. I'd almost forgotten about it."

"Not months ago. The flour Ros has at home is a month old and it matches."

Flora ran her hand nervously across her face, but she quickly recovered her control.

"This conversation is over. Either arrest me or don't, but do not expect me to stay and talk to you."

"No, Flora, the conversation will finish when I say so. Don't make me call you in to the police station, because I will."

"You're so wicked!" spat her older sister.

Amaia was not expecting that.

"I'm wicked . . . ? No, Flora, I'm just doing my job, but you really are wicked. Your existence has no purpose except to do harm, to spread poison, to make people feel guilty, and to blame everyone around you. I couldn't care less about you, because I've had it up to here with dealing with scum, but there are others whom you harm intentionally until you destroy them, undermining their confidence, like you did to Ros, or breaking their hearts like you did to poor Víctor when he saw you with Montes yesterday."

The cynical smile Flora had kept on her face while she listened to Amaia became a look of surprise at her last words. Amaia knew she had hit the bull's-eye.

"He saw you yesterday," she repeated.

"I need to talk to him."

Flora opened her car door again, determined to go.

"There's no need, Flora. Everything was very clear to him when he saw you kissing."

"That's why he's not answering my calls," Flora said to herself.

"How do you expect him to react if one day you're saying he's your husband and the next day he sees you kissing someone else?"

"Don't be stupid," she said, recovering her composure. "Montes means nothing."

"What do you mean?"

"Víctor is the man I married. He is and will always be the only man for me."

Amaia shook her head, incredulous.

"Flora, I was here with Víctor. I saw you kiss Montes."

Flora smiled, full of herself. "You don't understand anything . . ."

Suddenly Amaia saw things clearly. Too clearly.

"You've just been using him. You've been using him to get the information he's been giving you, like he did just now," said Amaia, looking at the envelope.

"A necessary evil," replied Flora. There was a hoarse moan from behind her.

His face contorted and haggard, Inspector Montes stopped two meters away and started trembling as the tears poured down his face. His expression was one of absolute desolation, and Amaia understood that he had heard if not everything, at least Flora's last few words. Flora turned toward him with the same look of disgust she might wear when faced with a broken heel or a scratch on her Mercedes.

"Fermín," called Amaia, worried at how Montes seemed to be breaking down.

But he didn't listen to her, turning instead to meet Flora's eyes. Amaia saw that he was holding his gun loosely in his hand. Amaia started to shout when he lifted his arm, very slowly, without taking his eyes off Flora, pointed it at her chest for a couple of seconds, then turned it, held it to his own head, and squeezed the trigger. His eyes were as empty as a dead man's.

"Fermín! No!" shouted Amaia as loudly as she could.

Iriarte grabbed him under his arms, dragging him backward and snatching his gun, which fell to the ground. Amaia ran over to help Iriarte subdue their colleague. Montes didn't resist. He fell like a tree struck by lightning and stayed there among the puddles, his face against the ground and crying like a little boy, with Amaia kneeling at his side. When he felt strong enough to look up, he saw Iriarte's eyes, which made clear without the need for words that he would have done anything not to have witnessed Montes's breakdown, and he could see that Flora's Mercedes was no longer there.

"Damn our fucking bitch of a mother," Amaia said, getting to her feet. "Stay with him, please. Don't leave him alone."

Iriarte nodded and put a hand on Fermín's head.

"Get out of here. And don't worry, I'll take care of him," he told her.

Amaia bent down to pick up Montes's gun and tucked it into her belt. She drove to Elizondo like a madwoman, making the wheels of the little Micra squeal, crossing Calle Muniartea and setting off down Calle Braulio Iriarte until she was right outside the workshop door. Just as she was about to get out of the car, her phone rang. It was Zabalza.

"I've got news, Inspector Salazar. Ainhoa Elizasu's brother worked at a plant nursery, Viveros Celayeta, last summer, and he still usually goes there on the weekends. I checked the vehicle registration, and they have white Renault Kangoo vans. I called them and they told me that since the boy got his license last year, he's often driven them. And, brace yourself: Ainhoa's family have been doing some work in the garden at home during the last few weeks. The girl who answered the phone let slip that they sometimes lend the vans to trusted clients, and Ainhoa's father recently bought thirty saplings that he took home himself in a van along with some other purchases. She couldn't say for certain, but she's sure that he's taken a vehicle at least twice."

Her brain dredged up a distant memory as she listened to Zabalza. White vans. She suddenly remembered something that had been going around and around in her head.

"Zabalza, I'm going to hang up and call you back in a minute."

He heard him sigh in disappointment. She dialed Ros's number.

"Hi, Amaia."

"Ros, you used to have a white van at the workshop. What happened to it?"

"Um, that was quite a while ago. I suppose that Flora would have taken it back to the dealer when we bought the new van."

Amaia hung up and phoned the police station.

"Zabalza, check the vehicle registrations for all the vehicles listed in the name of Flora Salazar Iturzaeta." She waited. She looked at the workshop's small window, which was always open just below the edge of the roof, while she listened to Zabalza typing at his computer. There didn't seem to be any lights on inside, although Flora's office was at the back of the building and she wouldn't have been able to see those lights even if they were on.

"Inspector," Zabalza's voice betrayed his discomfort, "there are three vehicles in the name of Flora Salazar Iturzaeta: a silver Mercedes from last year, a red 2009 Citroën Berlingo, and a white 1996 Renault Terra. What do you want me to do, chief?"

"Call Inspector Iriarte and Deputy Inspector Etxaide. I need a warrant for the Terra, for Flora's house, and for the Salazar workshop." She ran her hands across her face in the same gesture that Flora had used earlier, which she recognized as expressing deep shame. "And all three of you meet me at the workshop. I'm already here." When Zabalza had hung up, she murmured, "At home."

She got out of the car, went over to the door, and listened. Nothing. She took out the key she wore around her neck and instinctively checked for her pistol before opening the door. As she touched it, she realized she was carrying Montes's gun.

"Shit . . ."

She remembered the ridiculous promise she had made James not to carry her weapon. Grimacing, she decided that when all was said and done, she wasn't breaking her word. She opened the door and turned on the light. She looked inside, which seemed to be perfectly clean and well ordered, and went in, ignoring the ghosts who called to her from dark corners. She walked past the old kneading trough and the kneading table and made for Flora's office. She wasn't there, but the whole place seemed as ordered and correct as Flora herself. Amaia could feel the traces of rage Flora had left behind her. She looked around, searching for the discordant note, and found it in the form of a solid wooden wardrobe whose doors had been left ajar. She opened them and was surprised to find that there was actually an armory hidden in there. Two large hunting rifles rested in their places, but an obvious gap made it clear that another weapon was missing. At the bottom of the wardrobe were half a dozen overturned boxes of ammunition, which suggested that some of the contents were gone.

How typical of Flora. She never would let anyone do anything for her, not even this. She looked around, trying to extract the missing information from the air. Where would Flora go to finish the job? Certainly not her house; she would have chosen the workshop or a place that was more connected to her old life. Perhaps the river. She went to the door and noticed the proofs of her sister's new book as she walked past the desk. The color photograph, evidently taken in a studio by an expert photographer, showed a tray decorated with summer fruits on which rested a dozen cakes with a dusting of glinting sugar. The title written above it in capitals said TXANTXIGORRIS (JOSEFA TOLOSA'S RECIPE).

She picked up the telephone and dialed a number.

"Aunt Engrasi, do you know of anyone by the name of Josefa Tolosa?"

"Yes, although she's dead now. Josefa Uribe, more commonly known as La Tolosa, is your sister's late mother-in-law, Víctor's mother. She was a real character . . . Truth be told, poor Víctor used to be quite downtrodden, and then he went and married another strong woman on top of that. He jumped out of the frying pan and into the fire. Poor boy. Víctor's second surname is Uribe, but that family have always been known as the Tolosas because the grandfather was from there. I didn't have much to do with her, but my friend Ana María was also friends with her, so I can ask her more about her if you like."

"No, Aunt Engrasi, don't bother, there's no need," she said as she rushed out of the workshop and checked her email on her phone in search of the response to the question she had asked on the forum, which she knew had been answered. The inside of sheet metal fuel deposits on old motorbikes used to be cleaned with baking soda or vinegar, which cleared out the inside and removed all the oxide particles from the outside. Particles of oxide mixed with hydrocarbons and vinegar, which in turn had soaked into the fine goatskin leather. The fine leather of a motorcyclist's clothes. She could still feel the smoothness and smell the aroma of Víctor's gloves and jacket when she had hugged him in the rain.

She remembered visiting Víctor's family's farm a couple of times when she was little and her sister Flora was recently married. It was a typical farm back then, dedicated to livestock, and Josefina Uribe was still alive and ruling over the running of the house. She didn't remember much more than that. An elderly woman had offered her a snack, and the front of the house had been covered in yellow flowerpots full of colorful geraniums. Her relationship with Flora was cold and distant even then, and she had never gone back to visit her there again.

She drove the small Micra along the road toward the cemetery at top speed. She began counting the farms, remembering that it was the third one on the left past the cemetery. Although it wasn't visible from the road, there was a stone marker to indicate the entrance. She was slowing down to make sure she didn't miss the marker when she saw Flora's Mercedes parked at the side of the road by a path that led into a small copse which, now that night had fully fallen, seemed impenetrable. She left the Micra behind the Mercedes, checked there was no one in it, and cursed again at her brilliant idea of changing cars since she had left all her equipment in her own one. She checked the trunk and was pleased to discover that Iriarte's wife was sufficiently well prepared to keep a small flashlight there, although the batteries were running low.

She dialed Jonan's number before she went into the wood and was stunned to realize that she had no coverage; she tried the police station and Iriarte's phone. Nothing. It was a pine wood with low branches and lots of needles that carpeted the floor, making progress slow and dangerous even though there was an obvious path between the trees. She guessed the local residents had been using that shortcut since forever, and her sister must have learned about it during the time when she lived on her parents-in-law's farm as a newlywed. The fact that Flora had decided to approach the house through the woods instead of using the access road gave Amaia an idea of her plans. Despotic and domineering Flora had put two and two together before she herself had, manipulating the information she received punctually from the unsuspecting Fermín, who had been captivated by her hypnotic litany of suffering. Amaia thought of the shameless way she had behaved during dinner on Sunday, the offensive comments about the young girls, her ideas about decency, and the *txantxigorris* placed on the table, trying to distract Amaia's attention from the real perpetrator, the man she had never loved but whom she considered one of her responsibilities, like looking after their *ama*, running the family business, or taking out the trash each night.

Flora dominated her world using discipline, order, and rigid control. She was one of those women forged by force in the valley, one of those *etxeko andreak* who assumed leadership of their family and their lands while their menfolk traveled far away in search of opportunities, the women of Elizondo who had buried their children after epidemics and gone out into the fields to work with tears in their eyes. One of those women who were well aware of the dark and dirty part of existence, who simply washed its face, combed its hair, and sent it off to Mass on Sundays with shining shoes.

For the first time, she began to understand the way her sister had led her life, mixed with an overwhelming repugnance at her heartlessness and the way she gloried in it. She thought of Fermín Montes collapsed on the ground, and of herself, awkwardly defending against her sister's carefully calculated attacks.

And she thought of Víctor. Dear Víctor, crying like a little boy as he watched his wife kissing someone else on the other side of the window. Víctor restoring old motorbikes, reclaiming a longed-for past, Víctor living in the house that used to belong to his mother, Josefa "La Tolosa," who was a true master when it came to making *txantxigorris*. Víctor who had gone from a domineering mother to a tyrannical wife. Víctor the alcoholic, Víctor with enough strength of will to remain sober for the last two years. Víctor, a man between twenty-five and forty-five. Víctor outraged at the upstart imitator of his mise-en-scène. Víctor obsessed with the ideal of purity and integrity that Flora had taught him as a way of life, a man driven by his passions to take utmost control, a killer who had made the jump by taking the reins of a master plan to control his passion and desire, his tendency to see young girls in a sexual light, and the dirty thoughts that those same girls provoked in him with their shamelessness and constant exhibitionism. Perhaps he had tried to stop his fantasies with alcohol, but a moment arrived when the desire was so urgent that one glass was followed by another, and another, in order to silence the voices that clamored inside him, begging him to unleash his desires. His eternally repressed desires.

But the alcohol had only made Flora leave his side, and that had been like being born and dying in the same moment, since at the very time that he was liberated from the tyrannical presence that had subjugated him and made him control his impulses, the umbilical cord that had connected him to the only relationship with a woman he considered clean and the only person who had been able to control him had been cut. Amaia was sure that Flora had noticed something. Flora, the despotic queen who missed nothing . . . It was impossible that she hadn't realized that Víctor was harboring a demon in the deepest depths of his soul, which he fought to control and sometimes succeeded. And she knew, of course. There was no doubt she knew that morning when Amaia took her the *txantxigorri* found on Anne's body. The way she had held it in her hands, smelling it and even tasting it, knowing that that cake represented the clearest and most unmistakable proof, an homage to tradition, to order, and to Flora herself.

Amaia wondered how long Flora had waited to change flour supplier after she had walked out the door, at what point Flora had put in motion her plan to seduce Montes and had been sure of everything. Had she really needed the confirmation from the laboratory, or did she already know when she tried the *txantxigorri*, when Anne was found dead, when she sat at her aunt's table and justified the crimes? Or was it only a ploy to gauge Víctor's reaction?

The hill sloped away from the road, and the dense smell of resin irritated her nasal passages, making her eyes itch, while the weak light of the flashlight faded away, leaving her in absolute darkness. She stood still for a few seconds while her eyes adjusted to the lack of light, and she could just about make out a glimmer of light between the trees. Then she saw the unmistakable dancing glint of the flashlight Flora was carrying jumping between one tree and the next, like lightning bolts in the undergrowth. Amaia set off toward the area that seemed lightest to her, stretching her hands out in front of her and using the screen of her cell phone, which barely lit her feet and switched off every fifteen seconds, to help. Placing one foot in front of the other, she tried to hurry so as not to lose the trace of Flora's light. She heard a noise behind her, and she was hit in the face by a rough branch as she turned around, resulting in a deep cut on her forehead that left her stunned and that immediately started bleeding. She felt two trickles running down her cheeks like thick tears, and the phone came to rest somewhere near her feet. She probed the wound with her fingers and discovered that, although deep, it wasn't big. She pulled off the scarf she was wearing around her neck and knotted it tightly around her head, pressed on the cut, and managed to make it stop bleeding.

Confused and disoriented, she turned slowly, trying to locate the cloudy light she had spotted between the trees, but now she saw nothing. She rubbed her eyes, noticing the sticky blood that was starting to dry and thought about what she must look like as a feeling similar to panic started to take hold of her and her growing paranoia made her listen carefully, trying not to breathe, certain there was someone else there. She gave a startled shriek when she heard a powerful whistle, but she knew immediately that it wouldn't harm her, that it was somehow there to help her, and if she had any chance of getting out of that wood before she bled to death, it would be with him. Another whistle sounded clearly to her right. She stood up straight, forcing her head up, and went toward the sound. Another short whistle came from in front of her, and suddenly, as if someone had opened a curtain, there she was at the edge of the copse where it met the lawn that stretched up to the Uribe house.

The recently cut grass made the cross-country run easier for Amaia, who had not remembered the lawn being so vast. The house was lit by various lamps positioned around the manicured lawn, interspersed with old farming implements intended as works of art arranged around outside. She spotted Flora's armed outline under the gentle light of one of the lamps, advancing from the back of the house with a determined step and turning toward the main entrance. Amaia felt an impulse to shout Flora's name, but she repressed it as she realized that she was still on open ground and it would also warn Víctor. She ran as fast as she could until she reached the protective wall of the house and, pressing herself against it, drew Montes's Glock and listened. Nothing. She walked with her back against the wall, looking behind her from time to time, aware that she was as visible there as Flora had been before. She advanced cautiously toward the main door, which appeared to be ajar and from which a faint light was shining. She pushed it and watched it open heavily inward.

Except for the fact that the lights were on, nothing suggested that there was anybody in the house. She checked the rooms on the ground floor and discovered that they had hardly changed since La Tolosa was mistress of the place. She looked around in search of a telephone but couldn't see one anywhere. Carefully, with her back against the wall, she embarked slowly up the stairs. There were four rooms with closed doors that opened off the landing and one more at the top of an additional short flight of stairs. One by one she opened the doors of solid bedrooms full of hand-polished wood and heavy floral bedspreads. She crept up the last flight of stairs, certain that there was no one in the house but holding the gun in both hands and ready to fire nevertheless. By the time she reached the door, her heartbeat was pounding in her ears like a series of thunderclaps, leaving her almost deafened. She swallowed and took a deep breath, trying to calm herself. She moved to one side, turned the door handle, and switched on the light.

In all the years she had been an Inspector with the Policía Foral, she had never found herself in front of an altar. She had seen photographs and videos during her time at Quantico, but, as her instructor had told her, nothing could prepare you for the sensation of finding one. "It might be a little space, inside a wardrobe or a trunk, it might occupy an entire room or fit inside a drawer, it doesn't matter. When you come across an altar, you'll never forget it, because this bizarre museum where the killer hoards his trophies is the greatest demonstration of sordidness, perversion, and human depravity you can find. However many studies, profiles, and behavioral analyses you may have studied, you won't know what it's like to look inside a devil's head until you find an altar."

She gasped in terror when she found blown-up versions of the photos they had at the police station. The girls were looking at her from the mirror of a large antique dressing table on whose glass Víctor had arranged reports from the paper, articles about the *basajaun*, the girls' obituaries that had been published in the paper, and even some orders of service from the funerals. There were photos that had appeared in a local gazette, showing the families at the cemetery, the tombs covered with flowers, and the groups of students from the school and, below these, a collection of shots undoubtedly taken at the scenes of the crimes showing the different stages he had worked through in preparing his scene step by step, like a guide to death. A documented and graphic explanation of the horror and history of the milestones in the killer's macabre career. Amaia observed the number of reports incredulously, some of them yellowed by the passage of time, curling up at the edges due to dampness, some of them dated twenty years earlier and so short that they barely took up a couple of lines about the disappearance of female campers or day-trippers in places far from the valley and even on the other side of the border.

They were arranged in a sort of staircase, at the top of which was the name of Teresa Klas, declaring that she was the queen of that particular circle of hell. She had been the first, the girl for whom Víctor lost his head so badly that he even ran the risk of killing her barely a few meters from his home. But far from filling him with fear, her death excited him so much that he killed at least three more women during the following two years, propitiatory victims, young women with a clear profile of provocative teenage girls, whom he attacked on the mountain in an amateurish way compared with the sophistication of his recent crimes.

The altar narrated the evolution of an implacable killer who had dedicated himself to his work for two years and then had stopped for almost twenty. The same twenty years he was with Flora, while he knocked himself out each day with prodigious amounts of alcohol, which served as a self-imposed yoke, one he accepted and considered to be the only way he could live side by side with Flora without giving in to his instincts. A destructive vice he had kept at bay, right up until the moment he stopped drinking, free from Flora's iron control and liberated from the calming stupor of the alcohol. He had tried again. He had gone back to her to show her his progress, to show her what he had been able to do again for her, and instead of the open arms he had dreamed of, he found Flora's cold, stony gaze.

Her scorn had been the fuse, the detonator, the starting gun in a race toward an ideal of perfection and purity that he demanded of all other women, and all those who tried to be women with their young and provocative bodies. Amaia found her own eyes among the photos on the altar, and for a moment she thought she saw her reflection in the mirror. Occupying pride of place in the center of the altar was a picture of Amaia herself, printed on photo paper and cut out from the original in which she appeared with her sisters. She reached out a hand to touch the image, almost sure that she was mistaken, brushed the smooth, dry paper and almost pulled it out of place when she jumped on hearing the unmistakable thunder of a shot being fired. She hurled herself downstairs, certain that it had come from somewhere outside the house.

Flora positioned herself in the entrance to the stables and aimed the rifle at Víctor without saying a word. He turned, surprised, although not startled, as if he found her visit pleasant and desirable.

"Flora, I didn't hear you arrive. If you'd called me beforehand, I would've made myself more presentable," he said, looking at his greasy gloves as he slowly took them off and advanced toward the doorway. "I could even have cooked something."

"I haven't come for dinner, Víctor." Flora's voice was so icy and lacking in emotion that Víctor started talking again, never losing his smile or his conciliatory tone.

"In that case, let me show you what I was doing," he said, gesturing behind him. "I was working on restoring an old motorbike."

"It's not baking day today, then?" asked Flora, maintaining her stance and pointing toward a small cast iron door that gave access to the stone oven built into the wall of the house.

He smiled at his wife. "I was thinking of baking tomorrow, but we can do it together if you want."

Flora blew out a breath of air in a habitual gesture of fatigue as she shook her head to show her irritation.

"What have you been doing, Víctor, and why?"

"You already know what I've done, and you know why. You know because you think the same as me."

"No," she said.

"Yes, Flora," he said in a conciliatory tone. "You said so, you always said so. Those girls, those girls were looking for it, dressed like prostitutes, provoking men as if they were whores, and someone had to show them what happens to bad girls."

"Did you kill them?" she asked, as if, in spite of the fact she was pointing a gun at him, she wanted to believe that everything was just a ridiculous mistake and he would deny it, that it was all just a terrible misunderstanding after all.

"Flora, I don't expect anyone else to understand, only you. Because you're like me. Everyone can see it. Lots of people think like you and me, that the young people are ruining our valley with their drugs, their clothes, their music, and their sex. The girls are the worst, they don't think about anything except sex; there's sex in what they say, what they do, the way they dress. Little sluts. Someone needed to do something, to show them the traditional way and respect for their roots."

Flora looked at him in disgust without trying to hide her astonishment. "Like Teresa?"

He smiled tenderly and tilted his head to one side as if remembering. "Teresa, I still think of her every day. Teresa with her short skirts and those necklines, as shameless as the whore of Babylon. I've only seen one better."

"I thought it was an accident. Back then you were young and confused, and they . . . they were all loose women."

"You knew, Flora? You knew and you still agreed to marry me?"

"I thought you'd left all that behind."

His face darkened and he grimaced in pain.

"I did leave it behind, Flora. For twenty years I stood firm, making the biggest effort a man can make; I had to drink to control it, Flora. You can't imagine what it's like fighting against something like that. But you held me in lower esteem for my very sacrifice, you sent me away from your side, you left me alone and you made me promise to stop drinking. And I did it; I did it for you, Flora, as I have done all my life, as I've done everything."

"But you've killed young girls, you murdered them," she said, amazed. "Young girls."

He started to feel irritated.

"No, Flora, you didn't see them making advances like whores . . . They even agreed to get into the car, in spite of the fact they only knew me by sight. They weren't young girls, Flora, they were sluts. Or they would have become sluts shortly. That Anne, she was the worst of all of them. You're more than aware that she was sleeping with your brother-in-law, that she attacked my family, that she destroyed the sacred bond of Ros's marriage, our darling, stupid Ros. Do you think Anne was a young girl? Well, that young girl offered herself to me like a whore, and when I was finishing her off she looked me in the eyes like a demon, she almost smiled and she cursed me. 'You're cursed,' that's what she said to me, and not even death could wipe that smile off her face."

Flora's face suddenly contracted into a grimace, and she started to cry.

"You killed Anne, you're a murderer," she said as if finally convincing herself.

"As you're always saying, Flora, someone had to make the right decision. It was a question of responsibility, and somebody had to do it."

"You could have spoken to me about it. If what you wanted was to preserve the valley, there are other ways of doing it, but killing young girls . . . Víctor, you're ill, you must be crazy, otherwise this is impossible."

"Don't talk to me like that, Flora." He smiled meekly, like a little boy who is sorry for some mischief. "Flora, I love you."

The tears poured down her face.

"I love you too, Víctor, but why didn't you ask me for help?" she whispered, lowering the gun.

He took two steps toward her and stopped, still smiling.

"I'll ask you now. What do you say? Will you help me bake?"

"No," she said, raising the gun, her face serene again. "I've never mentioned it to you before, but I hate *txantxigorris*." And she fired.

Víctor looked at her, his eyes wide, slightly surprised by her action and by the intense wave of heat that spread through his chest, clearing his vision and making him aware of the other woman who was present to witness his end. Wrapped in a white cape that partially covered her head, Anne Arbizu was looking at him from the doorway with a grimace of something between disgust and pleasure. He heard her *belagile*'s laugh before the second shot hit him.

Amaia left the house and made her way quickly to the corner, holding Montes's Glock firmly while she listened carefully for any sound of movement. She heard the second shot and broke into a run. On arriving at the end of the wall, she cautiously followed the north side of the house, where the stables had stood a long time ago. A powerful light was shining from beyond the enormous green door, turning the lawn the color of an emerald and looking out of place coming from what used to be an animal shed. Flora was standing in the doorway, holding the rifle at chest height and aiming inside with no hesitation.

"Drop the rifle, Flora," shouted Amaia, pointing her gun at her.

Flora didn't reply. She took a step inside the stables and disappeared from Amaia's view. Amaia followed her but saw only a shapeless shadow lying on the floor like a heap of old clothes.

Flora was sitting next to Víctor's body. Her hands were stained with the blood pouring from his abdomen, and she was stroking his face, streaking his forehead with red. Amaia went over and bent down beside her to take away the gun that was resting at her feet. Then she put the Glock in her shoulder holster, leaned over Víctor, and put two fingers to his neck, trying to find his pulse while she searched through his clothes for a phone, which she used to call Iriarte.

"I need an ambulance at Camino de los Alduides, it's the third farm after the cemetery. Shots have been fired. I'll wait for you here."

"It's no use, Amaia," said Flora, almost whispering, as if she were afraid of waking Víctor. "He's dead."

"Oh, Flora." She sighed and put a hand on Flora's head, her heart breaking at the sight of her sister stroking Víctor's inert body. "How could you?"

Flora looked up as if struck by lightning. She sat up as dignified as a medieval saint in a niche. Her voice was strong and contained a clear note of annoyance.

"You still don't understand anything. Somebody had to stop him, and if I'd waited for you to do it, I'd have the whole valley covered in dead girls."

Amaia removed the hand that was resting on Flora's head as if she'd received an electric shock.

Two hours later

Dr. San Martín was leaving Víctor's stable after confirming his death, and Inspector Iriarte was coming over to Amaia with a frown on his face.

"What did my sister tell you?" she wanted to know.

"She said that she found the report about the source of the flour lying on the ground in the parking area of the Hotel Baztán. She put two and two together, and she took the rifle with her because she was scared. She wasn't entirely sure, but she decided to take it with her in case Víctor was the killer. She asked him about it, and he not only admitted it but also became very violent. He advanced on her in a threatening manner and, believing herself to be in danger, she fired without thinking. But he didn't fall and he kept advancing on her, so she fired again. She says she wasn't very aware of what was happening, that she did it instinctively because she was terrified. The white van is inside, under a tarpaulin. Flora said he was using it to go and collect the motorbikes he was restoring. There were bags of flour from Mantecadas Salazar inside the oven and in the kitchen, in addition to the collection of horrors in the loft."

Amaia sighed deeply and closed her eyes.

Ten hours later

Amaia attended the funeral of Johana Márquez. Blending into the crowd, she prayed for the eternal repose of her soul.

Forty-eight hours later

Amaia received a call from Lieutenant Padua.

"I'm afraid you'll have to make a statement about your informant. The *guardias* from the Nature Protection Service found human bones of a distinctive size and origin in the cave you mentioned to us. Based on the number they found, they've calculated that they comprise the remains of a dozen or so bodies that have been thrown into the cave haphazardly. According to the forensic scientist, some of them have been there for more than ten years, and they all display human tooth marks. I know what you're going to ask me, and the answer is yes, they match the bite on Johana's body, and no, they don't match Víctor Oyarzábal's dental imprint."

Two weeks later

On the day of the national launch of her book *Con mucho gusto*, the judge released Flora without charge, and she decided to take a long holiday on the Costa del Sol while Rosaura took charge of the management of Mantecadas Salazar. Not only were the sales unaffected, but in a few weeks Flora became a kind of local heroine. Ultimately, the valley always respected women who did what had to be done.

Eighteen days later

She received a phone call from Dr. Takchenko.

"Inspector, it turns out that you were right in the end. The French observation service's GPS picked up the presence of a female bear age about seven and quite confused, which had descended as far as the valley. You needn't worry. Linnete is already back in the Pyrenees."

A month later

Her period didn't arrive. Nor the next month, nor the next . . .

GLOSSARY

aita. Father.

aizkolari. A woodcutter who cuts up the tree trunks. Nowadays, a specialist in wood chopping in rural Basque sports competitions.

ama. Mother.

amatxi. Grandmother.

basajaun. Literally, the "gentleman of the woods"; a mythical big, hairy monster.

belagile. A dark, powerful woman; witch; sorceress.

belena. Passageway.

botil-harri. A stone pot or bottle used in the game of *laxoa*, a variation of *pelota*.

Día de los Reyes Magos. In Spain, Epiphany is a national public holiday. According to Spanish tradition, it is the Three Kings rather than Father Christmas who bring presents for good children, and many towns hold colorful parades to celebrate the occasion.

eguzkilore. A symbol representing the dried flower of the silver thistle that is hung at the entrance to a house to ward off evil spirits. In Elizondo, the literal meaning is "beside the church."

Ertzaintza. Basque police force.

esparto. Sandal with a sole woven from dried esparto grass.

etxeko andreak. housewives.

freska. A girl who is sassy, who flaunts her assets.

gorape. Portico.

Guardia Civil. Spanish national police force.

hilherria. Cemetery.

ikastola. A school where lessons are taught in Basque.

jentil. A mythical Basque giant.

lamia. A beautiful forest-dwelling, blond-haired seductress with ducks' feet.

mairu. Spirits who guard a house and protect it from evil.

Olentzero. A Navarran folk character who is a traditional part of Basque Christmas celebrations. He is a mythical coal miner who brings the presents on Christmas day.

pelota. A traditional Basque ball game that is played against a wall.

Policía Foral. Police force of Navarra.

serora. Sister who cares for the church, rectory, cemeteries, and the like.

sorgiña or sorgin. Witch.

tartalo. One-eyed giant.

trinquete. Pelota court.

txikitos. Glasses of wine.

urrakin egiña. Chocolate with hazelnuts.

verbena. Outdoor summer festival.

ACKNOWLEDGMENTS

I would like to express my thanks to everyone who was so generous with their knowledge and time and who helped this novel become a reality.

To Señor Leo Seguín of the Universidad Nacional de San Luis for his assistance regarding molecular biology.

To Juan Carlos Cano for his advice on the restoration of classic motorbikes. He helped me understand how fascinating that world is.

To the spokesperson for the Policía Foral de Navarra, Deputy Inspector Mikel Santamaría, for his patience in answering my questions.

To the Jorge Oteiza Baztán Ethnography Museum, which provided me with the material I needed to get started.

To my agent, Anna Soler-Pont, for making this happen.

Thank you, Mari, for coming out of retirement and doing me the honor of manifesting yourself in this storm, which has had me at its mercy since I started writing the Baztán trilogy.